THE DEATH BRINGER

THE DEATH BRINGER

THAUMORIAN LEGENDS
BOOK ONE

A M ENO

ISBN
979-8-9910605-0-9 - Paperback
979-8-9910605-1-6 - Hardcover
979-8-9910605-2-3 - Ebook

CONTENT WARNING

Graphic, on-page violence, torture, decapitation, death, loss of a parent(s), allusion to genocide

ALSO BY A.M. ENO

THAUMORIAN LEGENDS

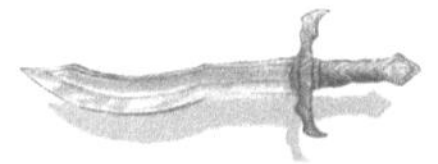

Novellas

Origins of a Guild Master

Secrets of a Sagacious Witch

Dawn of a Ruinous Love

Creation of a Fated Thief

Heart of an Outcast Mistress

Books

The Death Bringer

PROLOGUE

Shadows tugged at the edge of Malaina's mind, begging for her attention. But she knew that acknowledging them would bring nothing but trouble. Though tempting, the shadows and darkness, curling and crawling in every corner of the city, would only draw the attention of every city guard with nothing better to do than sniff out a Dark Magic child.

Desperate to block a little bit more of the harsh winter wind, she pulled her ragged jacket tighter. Her once silky hair, now matted and dirt-streaked, flew into her face, sticking to her chapped lips. One almost couldn't tell it used to be shining silver. Not the silver of the old, like that of the grandmother she'd once met. More like that of the locket her mother had worn, kept in her father's vest pocket after her death.

Fingers tingling on the verge of freezing, she didn't dare reach up and brush the strands away. Uncurling them from the folds of her jacket might be what pushed them to full-on frostbite.

She only hoped for a better tomorrow.

Tomorrow, she would earn enough money to buy food for herself. Three days had passed since she had eaten anything, but Malaina had grown used to the unceasing hunger gnawing against her ribs in the six months they'd been living on the streets. Tonight, she would use the few coins in her pocket to feed Lybbi.

A sudden, twisting wrench in her gut stopped her in the middle of the sidewalk. She didn't look at the people who brushed past her, bumping her, trying to push her out of the way.

The crippling hunger sucked the breath from her aching lungs. Her stomach clenched so hard that her entire body threatened to cave in on itself. She wanted to cry. Let the tears fall right there, curled up against the stone beneath her feet. If only she could find a dark corner to sit in. Somewhere where the silky comfort of her shadows would shield her from the world.

But she couldn't, not yet.

She didn't have the water in her veins to spare for tears, nor did she have the time. The baker would run out of two-day-old rolls if she didn't get there soon. They weren't any good or sought after by anyone with more than five coppers to their name. But they were cheap, and he didn't have very many.

For two copper coins, she might be able to buy a small one. Hard around the edges, turning from stale to inedible. But, it would be enough to get Lybbi through the night.

The ration might even fill her belly enough to lull her into sleep.

Malaina risked a deep breath, the cold threatening to freeze her lungs if she took in too much. As she tried forcing herself to her feet, another body knocked against her.

Something on the edge of her mind tugged, and she reached for her coat. Someone touched her shadows, the ones deep in her pocket. The one that held....

The coins. The two pathetic little copper coins that were going to buy bread for Lybbi.

Reaching deep, she searched for something that wasn't there. Anger flared up in her, strangling the hunger and cold. The city had taken too much from her already. She wouldn't lose those, too. Not after she spent all day on the street corner, begging. She had endured being spit on, scorned, mocked, and ignored for those two coins.

Pushing herself to stand, she searched through the crowd until she spotted him. The boy weaved around shoppers, ducking and dodging, an expert at slipping through the cracks. Something about the way the shadows moved about him called her forward. No one else would notice the way they shifted through the air. The way the darker ones wiggled, insisting she notice them. They screamed at her, "This one! Right here!"

She bolted after him, squeezing between the adults around her. Lack of food had reduced her to almost nothing, shrinking her already small frame until she hardly existed at all.

Veering between bodies, she aimed for the young boy.

Glancing over his shoulder, his ashy brown eyes spotted her chasing him through the crowd. He had the look of someone who'd never been, and had never expected to be, caught in his thieving ways.

Aiming for a dark alley, he darted for the edge of the street.

Malaina smirked. If he was planning to hide in the dark, he pickpocketed the wrong girl. No one hid from her shadows.

Flying on deft feet, he avoided the boxes and garbage that tripped her up. She didn't stop, determined to take back her coins or make him buy the bread she deserved.

A wooden wall blocked the other half of the alley. There was nowhere for him to go, and she paused to catch her ragged breath. She nearly cried out when the boy didn't hesitate, heading straight for the wall as if he would pass right through.

He seemed willing to drive himself headfirst into the barricade, all to avoid returning her two copper coins, when he leaped. Flying through the air, he smacked against the wood. A violent force that shook the wall so hard she thought it might come crashing to the ground, but he didn't fall. Instead, he clung to it, seeming to know exactly where to hold and how to hoist himself over.

Straddling the top, he looked back at her still crouched over, hands on her knees, sucking in one agonizing breath after another. The mocking smirk he gave her as he tipped his hat made her blood boil. The promise of revenge painted her features as she narrowed her eyes at him and scowled.

The boy wasn't fazed. Instead, he barked out a laugh and disappeared over the other side.

Malaina screeched, utterly defeated. She considered turning around and weighed her chances of still finding something salvageable in the baker's trash. But by then, the other homeless and hungry would have already stripped it of anything worth eating.

Before she could talk herself out of it, she bolted for the wall. Launching herself at it, she tried to mimic how the boy had clung to it. Missing the footholds, she hung on by her fingertips, finding the handhold he'd used. Her feet scrambled to find a grip on the slick surface.

Balancing on the edge of her battered shoes, the weight of her body crushing her toes, she refused to let go. The tips of her dirt-encrusted fingers fought to grip the next handhold as they edged ever closer to frostbite.

Nothing but the overwhelming rage of a scorned child held her up as she leaped for the top. Her elbows hooked onto the top of the wall, the worn-out soles of her boots slipping against the wood. Too focused on keeping herself from plummeting back to the ground, she almost missed the boy slipping through a high window.

She gritted her teeth and used her little remaining strength to pull herself until she straddled the top of the wall. Confident the thief wouldn't be going anywhere, she took her time finding her way down the other side. Adrenaline leached from her veins, and her fingers were not only cold but shaking from fear of falling. The wall hadn't appeared nearly as high when she was safely on the ground.

Slowly, she picked her way down, and when her feet

met stone, she silently thanked the only Goddess she knew, Elosyn, the Goddess of Fire.

Standing beneath the window the thief slipped through, her fists resting on her hips, she contemplated her options. At her height, reaching the ledge was hopeless, but she tried anyway, reaching from atop her tiptoes.

She hopped and jumped, wishing she would grow a little taller and jump a lot higher. Her fingers didn't even skim the ledge once—still inches from brushing it, even on her best attempt.

Stepping back, she evaluated everything abandoned there, trying to find the tallest items. A crate with a few broken slates lay discarded nearby, so she dragged it over and flipped it upside down beneath the window. One foot tested it first and then the other; it moaned but didn't break under her. Even with the added height of the crate, her fingers only skimmed the underside of the window.

Jumping was an option, but if she couldn't grab the sill, the crate might break beneath her ever-dwindling weight on the way back down. Upon further inspection, she spotted a wooden palette that looked to her like a short, flat ladder. Three of the five planks were broken, but the other two were still intact.

Fingers turning an alarming shade of blue under her broken nails, she shivered in the cold wind as she found a grip on the wooden planks. Little slivers dug into her hands, but she hardly noticed, too determined to retrieve her coins. The thunderous grinding of wood against stone was painfully conspicuous. Anyone nearby would hear it, but she hoped no one would come to investigate.

Every starving muscle in her body strained to lift the makeshift ladder and prop it against the stone wall. It wasn't perfectly level, tilting slightly when she poked it, but it was good enough. With painstaking care, she climbed, using both hands and feet to keep steady. She flinched with each crack and creak of the wood under her weight, the precarious palette tipping with every shift of her feet.

From the ground, the tipping seemed small and inconsequential. From the top plank, though, the whole world seemed to be wobbling beneath her.

She steadied herself against the wall, one hand letting go, gripping the brick before her. When her fingers wrapped around the window ledge, she let out a satisfied squeal. The clearing of a throat from nearby distracted her as she reached up with the other.

A man in a gray suit, hands clasped behind his back, stood at the opening of the alley. He observed her clinging to the window ledge, head falling to the side in a purely inquisitive tilt.

Startled, Malaina gasped, losing her balance and slipping against the wood.

Dangling in the air for a moment before her fingers gave out, she fell. Scraping first against the side of the building, then down her makeshift ladder, and finally landing in a heap on the stone floor. Rolling onto her side, she clutched her bleeding hand to her chest.

The man's feet, clad in shiny black leather shoes, came into view. Slow, deliberate steps that sent staccato clicks through the alley until he stood right in front of her.

Touching her chin to her chest, she curled in on herself, hoping the man would let her be if she were small enough.

Maybe he wouldn't call the city guards and get her in trouble if she appeared as pathetic as she felt. Maybe if she didn't look, he would just go away.

All around her, shadows slunk to her side, uncalled. They were responding to her desire to hide, but she wished they wouldn't. They would only cause trouble. If she didn't stop them and he noticed how they responded to her fear, he'd surely call the city guards. They would take Malaina to Lord Kevah, if they let her live that long, and Lybbi would be left alone. There would be no one to take care of her or ensure Lybbi ate every day.

No matter how much she tried to stop them, though, the shadows kept coming. Her growing panic made them swirl closer and denser.

They stayed like that for, what she felt, an eternity. The man, her, and her shadows. He appraised her as the blanket of darkness thickened and settled around her.

Crouching down, balancing on his toes, he reached forward with a hand, waving fingers through the murky curtain as if trying to disperse smoke. But the shadows held; they'd only ever responded to her.

Then he reached out, holding his palm open to her. An invitation. A gesture of kindness. One she'd never experienced before.

Skeptical, she looked up at him at last, taking in his kind gray-green eyes and graying hair. Trusting him would've been so easy, to take his hand and accept his help. There were so many stories, though. Stories of girls who were on the brink of starving to death when someone offered them shelter if only they were willing to do certain things. If only they sold themselves in exchange for food and a bed.

That wasn't an option. Swore she'd never consider it, not for her own sake, but for Lybbi's. She couldn't take Lybbi unless her younger sister did those things as well, and Malaina would never let her do that. She was too young. Too innocent. It was Malaina's job to protect her younger sister, so while her own pride meant nothing to her, Lybbi's was everything.

When Malaina didn't move, the man took his hand back, retracting his offer. They sat there a moment more.

Eventually, he asked her a question. "Why were you trying to break into my home?"

His home? She inspected him more closely. His suit wasn't only clean and well-tailored but expensive. The type of suit her father used to wear so everyone would know he wasn't just anyone.

The contradiction didn't make sense to her. No one who dressed like that should be living in such a poor part of the city. She liked the city's poorest neighborhood because the nobles were meaner to her when she begged in the nicer areas. They kicked and cursed and threatened. The poor simply ignored her.

"A boy stole my coins." Her admittance came out quieter than she intended, barely a whisper, making her sound even younger than her ten years.

He rubbed his chin. "A boy stole your coins and then climbed through that window?" He wagged an accusing finger up at the glass in question.

She nodded. Looking up together, they saw the boy peering out at them through the still-open window, his ashy brown eyes now wide. The man's gaze grew dark as he and the boy exchanged a loaded look. With a sharp dip of the man's chin, the window snapped shut. The boy jumped behind the glass and darted out of view.

He was in trouble, and she hoped he wouldn't be allowed to keep her coins.

"I'm sorry. He knows better."

The man held out his hand again, crossing the barrier of her shadows, his fingers growing dark. "Would you like some help?"

Malaina sat up, still clutching her hand to her chest, and scooted away, trying to create as much space as possible. Her shadows followed her, keeping her shielded. "I'm not alone; someone is expecting me."

"Is that so?" He looked her up and down, taking in her tattered, dirty clothing. "Do they need help too?"

CHAPTER
ONE

NINE YEARS LATER…

A shadowed figure crouched on the rooftop across from an open bedroom window. Sitting as still as the worn stones beneath her, she watched. Waited.

The breeze coming in from the coast had long since blown away the heat of an unnaturally warm spring day, playing with the loose strands of silver hair that had slipped free from her braid. Even though it was the far side of the city, away from the docks and closer to the inland of Thaumoria, a hint of salt still hung in the air.

Long past midnight, the sliver of the moon high above provided plenty of light for her to see. At that time of night, the entire city lay asleep. Those still awake were quiet, skulking down the streets, keeping to themselves and trying to go unnoticed.

This time of day – the night – was her favorite. The shadows were thick and eager to swallow. Keen to respond to even her slightest suggestion, even though she didn't call on them. Rather, she made them stay right where they were, keeping them waiting. She'd learned to resist their pull long ago. Calling on her magic when she was bored or allowing the shadows to come to her when she was emotional were gateways to calling on them by accident. Instead, she kept her magic locked away behind steel bars, a constant cage in the back of her mind bolted tight until she intentionally turned the key and let her magic out to play.

Pulling her hood further over her face, she tucked away every stray strand until not a single one showed. She would be unmistakable if anyone caught a glimpse from the street or one of the nearby windows, making her too easy to spot in a crowd.

After significant contemplation, she allowed a single shadow to darken her face beneath the hood even further to give herself an extra layer of protection. That minuscule use of her magic made every muscle in her body uncoil, like finally releasing a breath she'd been holding until her lungs screamed. Closing her eyes for a moment, she reveled in the relief.

The only small solace she would allow herself.

When she opened her eyes again, she went back to watching the man who slept on the other side of that bedroom window. He continued to dream, not even bothering to toss and turn, unaware of being stalked just as he had been every night for the past three weeks.

The way he slept, undisturbed and at peace, sickened her. After tonight, though, he would never sleep again. That little piece of knowledge gave her a small bit of satisfaction, knowing tonight would be his last.

A bird's call caught her attention. Her eyes tracked a large black shape soaring overhead, blocking out Elosyn's constellation.

She waited.

One breath.

Two.

Then, a third cry as the bird flew closer. She recognized the raven, twice the size of a normal bird, distinguishable from the sea birds that often flew in from the ship ports.

The corner of her mouth pulled up into a slow predator's smile.

It was time.

Pulling her cover up from where it bunched around her neck, she covered her nose and cheeks, leaving only her eyes exposed. Still noticeable. Still obvious. But the one shadow she allowed herself made the silver of her eyes more of a dull gray. More Kinetic and less unique.

Effortlessly, she rose from her crouched position. The hours since she'd last moved stiffened her muscles, but her control outweighed their objections.

Taking intentional steps backward, she made her way to the opposite side of the roof on silent feet.

She flexed her fingers, bounced on her toes, and double-checked that her knives were secure and her pockets closed tight.

Then she ran in eerie silence on the balls of her feet,

her boots barely making a sound. When she reached the point where the roof met open air, she pushed off one foot and leaped. For a moment, she floated, gliding through the air like an Air Wielder in the Games. No matter how many times she leaped like this, it still sent a shot of adrenaline through her throat.

Then, the wall of the opposite building was in front of her. Practiced fingers grabbed the ledge, and the soft soles of her boots rested against the stone without a sound.

Hanging, she ensured her hold on the stone was secure before descending. Carefully finding her hand and footholds, she remembered a time when heights bothered her—so many years ago. Now, she scaled buildings without thought, unfazed by the distance between her and the ground.

She perched outside the window. Slipping her thinnest knife from its sheath on her wrist, she slid the blade into the crack between the bottom of the window and the sill. A quick flick of her wrist, a quiet click, and the lock unlatched. Using the pads of her fingers to lift the window, she slipped inside. Silent feet landed on the wooden floor.

Hiding her colorless skin in the moonlight, she pulled her sleeves lower over her hands. If he woke, she wanted him to see nothing but a dark figure, if he noticed her at all.

Stalking to his bedside, she loomed over the man in the bed, watching him sleep. Tilting her head, she looked every bit like the predator lurking within her. Her fingers twitched at her sides, eager to reach out and run through his Air

Wielder's dirty blonde hair. It looked so soft, and his features so peaceful, she almost forgot what he'd done.

Almost.

Because, in reality, she would never forget. She'd make sure of that.

The sound of wings fluttered through the window behind her. Between one beat of its wings and his first silent step in the room, the bird shifted from raven to man.

Sterling's massive form commanded the room, as if the walls were closing in around him. He came to her side, standing a whole head taller than her. His fingers brushed against the back of her hand, assuring her he had her back.

She wanted to lean into the comfort he offered, but she had a job to do first.

Reaching into one of the pouches on her belt, she pulled out a syringe and vial. Her experienced, scarred hands gripped the syringe, and the needle pierced the wax seal. Thin, shimmering orange liquid filled the belly of the syringe as she pulled back the plunger. Tapping out any air bubbles after she pulled the needle from the vial wouldn't make any difference now.

Slipping the empty vial back into its pouch, she knelt beside the bed. Carefully, she lifted the blanket from the man's side, revealing his bare arm. He would never feel the way her fingers skimmed up the inside of his forearm, even if he woke. Pressing her fingers into the crook of his elbow, her fingertips found a rolling vein. Without hesitation, the needle pierced the vein, and she forced the contents of the syringe into his bloodstream. Once empty, she hid the needle and syringe in its pocket.

The man's eyes flew open. Instinctually, he slapped at his arm, like someone swatting at a particularly obnoxious bug. But he was too slow.

He gasped. A ragged, desperate intake of breath, filling the otherwise silent room with the sound of death.

She drank in the satisfying sound. The first gasp of a target who utterly deserved their death always sent a shiver across her skin.

His pupils widened, irises so thin they almost disappeared, as his organs quickly started to give up. One by one, they would shut down, giving him the sensation of having life drained from his body. He would feel every excruciating second of it, just as she wanted him to.

Silently, she thanked Jade for giving her this moment.

Fleetingly, his eyes found hers, and she held his gaze, savoring the way the light of life flickered before completely snuffing out. His brown eyes glazed over, becoming unseeing and distant.

A flicker of respect stirred in her chest. He hadn't tried to scream, but it wouldn't have mattered either way. He'd sent the woman away when he was ready for bed, the way he always did. He died alone in his large bed, with no one by his side but the people who took his life.

Isn't that what he wanted? To be alone?

Reaching down, she placed her fingers on his throat. Waiting for a pulse to thrum through his veins, she held her breath, but there was nothing. Nothing but warm skin turning cold and muscles becoming stiff.

Only then did she allow herself to run her fingers through his hair. It was, indeed, as soft as it looked. Her tender touch turned to a tight grasp as her fingers tangled in his hair, and she yanked his head back, exposing his throat. Leaning in close enough to brush her lips against his, her breath brushed his cheek.

Mere inches from his permanently pain-laden face, wishing he could hear her, she whispered, "We're going to take this now."

The hiss of metal drawing against leather tugged at her side. Sterling removed a long, partially serrated blade from its sheath on her hip. He held the handle out to her, but she shook her head. Tonight was his honor.

Taking her place when she backed away from the bed, he loomed over the body. He flipped the long blade in his hand, watching the metal shine in the moonlight.

"This will be my pleasure," he growled.

Then he began sawing.

SHARP THUDS ECHOED each time the heel of her boots struck the marbled floor of the lavish hallway. Deliberately, she took her time, letting the drip of blood seeping through the bulging sack hanging by her side punctuate the air.

Entering through a window closer to the study, creating a shorter pathway between her and her client, would have been easier. Picking a thicker bag wouldn't have soaked through so fast. Walking faster would have gotten every-thing over with quicker.

But that wasn't her job. Not what she needed.

Savoring the moment, she made the whole thing a performance. The show she put on bore the same impor-tance as the meeting itself. They meticulously thought through, organized, and orchestrated each heartbeat and step as though she were the main character in a gruesome play. They cast the characters, set the scene, and picked each detail down to the material of the sack she held.

Sterling stood guard beside the study doors. He had entered the house first to clear her path and make sure that everything was in place, that no traps had been set. It wouldn't be the first time one of her clients regretted his contract and tried working with the city guards in exchange for not being charged with the murder himself.

That client hadn't gotten far.

The massive Shifter couldn't see the smirk behind her face covering, still pulled high, but he could read the twinkle in her eye—the same way she read the dark, mustard-seed yellow of his cold anxiety. His own face covering pulled high over his nose concealed everything but those ever-changing eyes.

He didn't want to be here, but the spectacle was all part of the show. The key to preserving her reputation.

Sterling opened the double doors with a flourish, presenting her to those inside. Seated at the imposing wooden desk was a man who looked like he had never smiled a day in his life. Behind his left shoulder stood a young woman, his same red-brown hair curled around her shoulders. The same burning eyes. But where his features were sharp, hers were soft. Like her mother's.

Malaina had observed them as intensely as she'd monitored her target, getting to know both her client and her kill.

Stopping her steady, slow stride to stand before the desk, Sterling closed the doors behind them. Blood dripping, she lifted the sack above the desk and let it hang in the air for one drawn-out breath before it fell to the desk with a squelching *thud*.

The man behind the desk didn't flinch, his eyes following the falling sack, but the girl jumped. Failing to fight a look of disgust, she held a hand to her nose. The metallic scent of blood and early stages of decay began to fill the warm room, made worse by the dancing flames in the fireplace on the wall behind her clients.

"What is that?" The Fire Wielder asked quietly, punctuating each word. The fire flicked with each syllable, tutting like a tongue.

"You wanted proof," Malaina purred, begging him to try and scold her.

Her client placed his hands flat on the desk and stood, never breaking eye contact. His cushioned chair creaked when he stood, emphasizing the movement and fueling the tension in the room. He reached for the sack and opened the top, peering inside. His daughter leaned over his shoulder to get a look. His throat bobbed with a heavy swallow; his only reaction to what he saw was trying not to gag. But the flames revealed what he tried to hide, draping the room in darkness for the span of a heartbeat as they, too, tried to escape the sight.

From over his shoulder, his daughter gasped, moving back as far as she could get. Hand at her throat, she retreated to the safety of the fire. Not only her father's element but hers as well.

"That's…Is that…You…Why would you…" his daughter cried, starting one sentence after another, unable to find the words to finish any of them. Each one became more and more of a sob. Turning away before completing any of her thoughts, she covered her mouth and gagged.

"You brought me his head," the man stated matter-of-factly, his eyes burning with disgust as they met Malaina's once again.

The assassin smiled behind her face cover, letting amusement dance in her eyes.

"You wanted proof," she repeated.

"You brought me his head," the man said again, more to himself than to her. Venom laced his words, no longer hiding his raging temper. "You could have brought his family ring or something else off his person. But you brought me his head." He grew louder, his daughter starting to wretch in the corner.

Malaina smiled wider. "You wanted—"

The man cut her off sharply. "Don't say it again!" The fire in the hearth raged, licking up the chimney and turning the office from warm to stifling.

Trying to settle himself, a deep breath shuddered through his chest. The look on his face revealed instant regret when he got a nose full of the awful stench, made worse by his own raging fire. "What am I supposed to do with a head?"

She shrugged, indifferent. "That's not my problem."

"I am not paying for this!" His fist pounded against the wooden desk, emphasizing his point.

Malaina didn't flinch at the man's anger. Truly deadly people didn't concern themselves with the petty outrage of those beneath them. Sterling stepped forward protectively from where he had been standing. His massive form filled the space, a wall of muscle by her side.

At least the Fire Wielder had the sense to look away, to look afraid, though he tried not to let his shoulders cave beneath Sterling's stare.

"This isn't what I wanted. This isn't what I ordered." This time, he didn't have nearly the same conviction and volume as before, sounding more like a whining child than a governor.

Claiming the desk for herself, she rested her fingertips on the surface and leaned in to invade her client's space. At this, the man had the good sense to step back, putting space between himself and her.

"If I remember correctly," she dragged out the words, "You ordered the murder of one sleazy asshole by the only Death Bringer." She bowed her head, gesturing to herself. *Death Bringer*. A person who brought death with a single touch, or at least that's what the stories said. Despite how wrong and inaccurate it was, the title rolled off her tongue easily. "And proof of his death."

Reaching forward, she grabbed the bottom of the blood-soaked bag and upended it. The head rolled onto the desk, the unseeing brown eyes bulging out of the blood-smeared face staring at the ceiling. "Is this not the asshole who left bruises on your daughter?"

The governor's stare hardened, his fingers curling until his knuckles went white. His daughter shrieked at the sight, answering Malaina's question without words.

The Death Bringer pushed the severed head forward until the unseeing eyes were staring right through the man.

"Is this not proof?" It was her turn to punctuate each word, drawing out the question.

The Fire Wielder's jaw tensed and flexed. The sound of his teeth grinding together was the only sign of discomfort he would allow, even going so far as to tame his flames. After a moment of internal debate, he opened a drawer on his desk and tossed a bulging pouch at her. Keeping her eyes locked on him, she caught it without looking.

Gold coins clanging together was like music to her ears.

Counting was unnecessary. The sack was plenty heavy enough, and besides…she'd overcharged him.

"Thank you for your business," she purred again.

Rubbing it in the man's face a little more, she tossed the pouch in the air and caught it again. Sterling by her side, she turned and left.

The doors started to close behind them. Before they shut completely, she heard something heavy being thrown into the blazing fireplace. An intense heat wave, hotter than it should be, pushed against her back but was abruptly cut off when the door slammed shut. But they couldn't hold back the scent of burning hair and flesh filling the hallway.

They exited the townhouse and stepped out onto the lowly lit street. In this part of the city, street lamps were set at regular intervals, lit by actual electricity rather than flames. The night was quiet, and they walked straight to a waiting carriage pulled by a sleek black horse. The driver sitting up front tipped his hat at them. He wasn't dressed extravagantly. Like the carriage itself, he was average. Able to blend into any crowd and go completely unnoticed. Graying hair and kind, creased eyes put him somewhere in his fifties.

But something about him looked...off. Different from the last time the assassin saw him. Not a big difference. So subtle she couldn't quite put her finger on what it was, but enough that he would seem like a different person to a stranger.

Malachi always hired Shifters, specifically those who could alter their own appearance, to drive the carriages.

They stepped inside, plopping onto the cushioned seats, and Malaina wished, not for the first time, that Malachi would allow them to have one of the personal motor cars many of the wealthier residents had. They looked far more comfortable and would allow Sterling and her to move around the city without relying on someone else. Driving would also be far faster than roof hopping or walking. But they couldn't afford to draw that kind of attention.

They were headed to a part of the city where a motor car would stand out like a Kinetic in a temple. The invention would cost more than anyone living in that part of the city should be able to afford. A run-down open carriage would draw an equal amount of attention in the wealthier areas, the sight inevitably becoming the source of gossip for anyone who might look out their window and see it parked in front of one of the expensive townhouses.

So instead, they had something in between – a plain carriage, well-built but not ostentatious, able to pass unnoticed down any street, the same way the guilders themselves did.

When they settled, the door closed tight behind them, Sterling pulled his face cover down, blowing out a long breath and enjoying the unobstructed, clean air. The side of his fist knocked against the wall of the carriage, letting the driver know they were ready. The coach started with a lurch and both of them sank into their seats, settling in for the ride home.

"Do Fire Wielders always have to keep things a million degrees? I swear I was going to start melting when the fire flared up." Sterling pulled his hood off and yanked his black long-sleeve shirt over his head to reveal a sleeveless shirt underneath. The top hugged his massive frame, tailored to fit him like a second skin.

"Seriously though. I don't know how that desk doesn't just burst into flames with those doors shut," Malaina muttered, pulling her hood and face cover off.

Sterling waved a finger at her. "That shirt is covered in blood." He reached under his seat for a stashed bag, pulling it out. He rifled through it, pulling out a clean shirt, and nodded at her. "Strip."

Grabbing the hem of her blood-soaked top, she raised a teasing eyebrow. Her voice low and seductive, she gave him a playful look. "Oh, I love it when you flirt."

He rolled his eyes. "Just shut up and strip."

Dropping the facade she laughed lightly, pulling the shirt over her head, leaving her in nothing but her favorite bra for training and jobs, her midsection and arms exposed to the cool night air. After the Fire Wielder house, the breeze felt glorious on her bare skin.

Sterling didn't bother glancing at her when they exchanged the shirts. A content sigh slipped from her lips as she shimmied into the clean, loose fabric draping around her. Watching him, she sank back into her seat while he continued examining the remaining clothes.

His nose wrinkled. "Is there anything in here for me?"

"I don't think so, you're running out of usable stuff."

He grumbled something under his breath before shoving everything back into the bag and deciding to remain in the sleeveless shirt. Thick muscles bulged beneath the fabric. Years of training had given him the girth of the predators he often took the shape of. "I'll have to make a trip to Syn's for more."

"What are you grumbling for? You like Syn."

Sterling crammed the bag back under the seat, his eyes shifting to an obstinate gray-brown. "Of course I do. He's a genius and a lifesaver. But that doesn't mean I want to spend one of our few days off shopping."

Hardly listening to his grumbling, she stretched out in the small space, made smaller by the Shifter across from her. Kicking her feet up, she could barely straighten her legs if she splayed them across his lap, sitting diagonally across the seats.

He raised an eyebrow at her. "Seriously?"

"The ride back takes forever, and we haven't been home in three weeks. Can't I just stretch out and relax?"

"Your boots are gross." He scowled, pushing her feet off his legs.

Her bottom lip pushed out in an exaggerated pout. "What if I take them off?"

"I've smelled your feet after a long job, there's no chance you're putting *those* things on me either."

Rolling her eyes, she sat up straighter. Then Sterling stretched out, nestling into one corner and pushing his feet to the opposite corner. If he sat up straight, back pushed right up into the crease, he could almost straighten out his knees. If he didn't mind the top of his head brushing the ceiling.

"Oh, so you're allowed to stretch out, but I'm not?" She scoffed.

The wiggle he gave reminded her of a happy puppy,

getting himself comfortable in an overly fluffy bed. He lifted his arms, lacing his fingers together like a pillow behind his head. Closing his eyes he already looked half asleep. "Grow a foot, and we can talk."

Ready to quip back, she set her jaw but decided against it. He had a point. Malaina stood taller than about half the other women in the guild, and yet, even with boots on, her height couldn't hold a candle to his. Standing at least a foot taller, Sterling had well over a hundred pounds on her.

Where her training left her lean and toned, it had bulked him up into a mountain of a man. Sometimes Malaina wondered how much of his size was natural and how much was Shifter manipulated. But Sterling was consistent in everything he did. From his size to his tanned brown skin and long black hair, to his undying loyalty, nothing ever changed. Even his ever-shifting eyes were a constant in her life. So, she assumed it was genetics.

Instead of arguing further, she crossed her ankles across his shins. Surely he couldn't complain about that. Despite closing her eyes and finding the cushiest part of her seat to nestle her head, sleep stayed out of reach. Memories from the last three weeks haunted her.

Some parts of her job never got easier.

The killing didn't get to her anymore, not really. She'd long since grown used to the way she walked side by side with death.

The watching was what ripped her apart from the inside. People could be truly heinous when they thought no one was looking.

For the last three weeks, she watched *that man* hit

woman after woman, forcing them into his bed and then sending them off covered in bruises when he'd gotten his way. That's why picking a night when his bed was empty had been so easy.

He never spent a night alone but always slept peacefully with no one by his side. Finding satisfaction in his death, in the way he'd experienced a speck of the fear and pain he loved to inflict on others almost every night, was easy.

Determined to remember each woman, she replayed each night again in her mind. Watching yet again while he whispered cruel words. Relived the way skin struck skin, leaving bruises where he thought no one would see. Every gut-wrenching sob and cry sent pain through her chest when he pushed them to the bed and lifted their skirts.

Her job forced her to watch and observe, but that didn't mean the role was easy. Those moments would haunt her dreams. But even when she woke up in a panicked sweat, she wouldn't let herself forget. Because if she, the only observer of their pain, forgot and everyone else moved on like it never happened…who would suffer with them? They would be left to remember those nights by themselves. Alone. She was determined to share their pain, even if they didn't know it.

Sometimes, she liked to think only so much pain existed in the world at once, and everyone had to take turns with their share. So if she hurt alongside them, then perhaps they wouldn't hurt so much.

Recalling each woman, she brought back the scene from earlier that same night. Of the woman he'd sent away before he died. From hours before the pain, when the two of them had been smiling, because she'd thought he was a good person. Because she didn't know the horror he would soon become.

They all deserved to be remembered that way: smiling and happy, a blush creeping up their cheeks as he flattered them.

"Stop that." Opening her eyes, she found Sterling watching her, his eyes a warm dark orange. Comfort. Understanding. Empathy.

"I don't know what you're talking about," she lied.

"We agreed you wouldn't do that anymore. It's not good for you."

Yes, they'd had the conversation. He talked, and she'd ignored him. That didn't mean she agreed. She wasn't any less a monster than some of the people she killed. But the ones her targets hurt? They were innocent. They didn't deserve to bear their burdens on their own. Why not put some of the pain on her shoulders? Someone who deserved to bear it.

"We should have stepped in sooner," she mused, watching out the window at the passing buildings.

"Yes," he agreed, quiet and distant, lost in the same memories that haunted her. "We should have."

They fell into a heavy silence as they rode, having long since passed the point where they needed to talk to understand each other.

Familiar townhomes passed outside the carriage, streaks of color dulled by the night.

The two of them often worked in that part of the city. Their fees were so high that only those living in the richest districts could afford them. These districts were surrounded by solid walls draped in tapestries, sheltered by ceilings painted with stories of the gods, and unshattered windows gilded in gold.

Recognizing many of the houses, she already knew who lived within, but she liked to pretend she didn't.

With each one, she took in the beauty of the architecture. Admired the way the wealthier residents cared for their homes and decorated them for each season. Sometimes she would even create her own stories for those who lived inside.

The fantasies played in her head, of happy couples sitting on cushy couches. Not the decorative kind of couch so many of them had, the ones that were too old and valuable to sit on even if you wanted to, because it may have once been owned by the cousin of an advisor who once worked for a long-dead Elemental Lady. Even if you did sit on it, it would be so uncomfortable the hardwood floor would be preferable.

No, you would sink into this kind of couch. Soft, cozy fabric you couldn't help but run your hands over, wrapping around you like a hug. A fire would be crackling in the fireplace, making the space warm, but not too hot, and a fluffy, well-fed dog curled up on one of their feet. Dozing, never once having worried about being struck, or where its next meal would come from.

Behind at least one of those doors, a family like that existed somewhere in the city. At least, that's what she hoped.

Happiness wasn't a part of the city she would ever see.

Slowly, the street changed from a well-maintained stone, laid in curving patterns that turned even the street into art, to a worn cobblestone that made the carriage bounce and rattle.

The buildings were no longer immaculately maintained townhomes. They passed through a business district, where the buildings were still kept up, but not to the same level as the townhomes. Front doors disappeared, replaced by colorful awnings decorating windowed business fronts. From bakeries to tailors, goods from all over Thaumoria were brought in, and sale signs advertised something for everyone.

The bakers would start to wake in a couple of hours, always the first to rise. If they were well enough off they may have had a few electric lamps in their apartments above their stores, but most would have to light candles or oil lamps, reserving the electricity for their shops below. In the crippling hours of night turning to morning, when Malaina and Sterling were just getting to bed, the bakers would start their day. Heading down to their kitchens to start kneading dough. Some of them may be Fire Wielders, who would use their magic to light and maintain the perfect wood-fired stove to bake their bread and pastries.

When the bakers opened their doors, the first goods would be sold to the Witches across the street, readying to open their apothecaries. Muffin in hand, they would mix concoctions of all kinds for customers. From tea to reduce anxiety to medications that relieve pain and accelerate heal- ing. The more powerful and traditionally trained Witches may have clinics, where they tended to patients, offering spells and charms to ensure pregnancies were healthy and the sick were properly diagnosed. Sending their magic deep into the bones and muscles of their patients, searching for illnesses the person may not even have known they had.

Watching the businesses pass, the Death Bringer softened. The business district was her favorite place in the entire city. It's where magic classes of every kind went to mingle and trade. One of the only places where she passed unnoticed, pretending to lead a normal life. She could buy a beautiful new gown from one of the most talented Shifters she'd ever met, then walk to the Kinetic next door and make a deal, bargaining over the latest inventions from the City of Kinetics.

While they were home she would have to make a point of taking Lybbi shopping. Perhaps buy her a new pair of gloves or a chocolate-filled pastry. Or both.

Both would be better.

Eventually, the road turned to dirt, pockmarked and rough as they rolled into the part of the city Malaina knew best. There, when the city slept, slumbering was done outside next to buildings or hidden down alleys, hunched over in corners to conserve body heat.

The Witches didn't sell cures. They sold things far darker and addictive, knowing people would have to come back for more or go crazy. Many clinics ran out of living rooms, and patients paid whatever coppers they had to their name.

Kinetics at the corners were just as likely to snatch an untethered purse as they were to sell a fake gadget. Fire Wielders charged five coppers to start a fire, more if the night was below freezing or snow was falling. Water Wielders might clean a glass of water, removing salt and dirt from whatever flowed in from the coast, but it would be at a price.

No matter how average their carriage appeared, it always drew attention in that part of town. Not because people hadn't seen one before, but because they were trying to decide if it was worth robbing.

The dark stares they pulled didn't bother Malaina. Rather, they made her feel at home. Those were the streets she grew up on. The part of the Elemental City she'd memorized first. She knew where all the alleys were, which ones were blocked, and which ones would let her pass through to another street. Where each drain pipe was and which ones were the best for climbing. Which buildings were best for sleeping, because the windows were broken and easy to slip through, but high enough most people wouldn't bother.

These were her people.

This was home.

The carriage took a sharp turn down a familiar dark alley. One hid a window she tried to break into when she was ten.

THREE

When the carriage came to a stop, Malaina and Sterling stepped out into the dark.

Sterling made a point of walking to the front and placing his hand on the edge of the driver's seat.

"Thank you."

Unsaid words of understanding weighed down the thanks, making it heavy. All the jobs in the guild were dangerous, but usually, the risk was obvious. Something you'd expect.

A thief couldn't break into a noble's home to steal a priceless family heirloom or be the drug dealer to an influential businessman who couldn't afford to sleep and not expect they may not come home one day.

The carriage drivers had a risky job that only seemed safe. Malachi saved those positions for Shifters in need of help. Those who didn't want to engage in the guild's illicit dealings but were willing to help where they could in exchange for a safe place to sleep and a warm meal on a cold night.

They'd been through many carriage drivers. Each time one of the Shifter drivers got arrested, never to return, Sterling took it personally. He felt responsible for every Shifter that joined the guild.

The driver tipped his hat, his voice gravelly with age. "Of course."

Walking further into the shadows, Malaina ran a hand over the old window sill that now sat at shoulder height. Each time she passed it she touched it like a thank you to the building itself. Greeting an old friend every time she came back from a contract.

Her fingers skimmed the shadows, and a moan rose in her throat at the silky feel of them brushing against her fingertips. But she ignored them, savoring the feeling in private silence.

They came to a stop in front of a part of the wall that was indistinguishable from the rest and blended seamlessly into the surrounding stones. Malaina ran her fingers over the pattern, counting in her head, though by now, she didn't need to. After so many years, she instinctually found the right spot.

When she brushed over the correct groove between stones she pressed, the coarse grout scratching against her calloused fingertips. The grout gave way where she pushed, her finger sliding between the stones. They scraped her skin, the groove just big enough for her slim fingers and far too small for Sterling's.

On the rare occasions he went out without her, he had to use one of the other entrances.

Pushing deeper, a hole opened up beneath her fingertips, revealing a hollowed-out stone in the wall. Hooking her fingers into the hole, she used the stone like a handle and pulled. A hidden door slid forward without a sound, opening to reveal a dark hallway.

Once inside Sterling grabbed the large handle spanning the width of the inside of the door and pulled it shut, plunging them into complete darkness.

While the hallway had been designed for two people to enter at a time, Sterling's size made it feel smaller. His chest brushed against the back of Malaina's head as they waited, trying to fit comfortably in the confined space.

For a moment, a heartbeat, Malaina closed her eyes and drank in the presence of the shadows.

Through them, she *felt* every nook and crevice of the room, every corner, and every ridge along the wall. They occupied every inch of space in the sealed-off room. Each breath out brushed the shadows with air, and she felt it like someone breathing trails along her bare skin.

That simple moment of embracing her shadows allowed something in her chest to loosen, letting her breathe a little easier, and she savored it every time.

"What's the password?" A muffled voice came from the other side of the door in front of her. The pitch was off, like someone trying to sound deeper than they actually talked.

Her exaggerated sigh filled the small space and she hoped the person on the other side of the wall heard it.

Opening her eyes once again, she glared into the darkness before her. "Ra, open the damn door."

"That's not the password," he answered, maintaining his comically fake deep voice.

"There is no password, you dork." Her hands moved to her hips in impatience.

"Man, why do you have to be so mean?" Ra whined, dropping the fake tone and opting for his true, higher pitch. If she didn't know him so well, she'd think he was hurt, but there was a bit too much whine for it to be genuine. Her arms crossed, fingertips tapping against her bicep.

"I'm sorry, Ra. Please open the door." Her words were coated in a sickly sweet syrup he would be rolling his eyes at on the other side of the wall. They continued to stand in the dark, and when it became clear he still wasn't going to let them through, Sterling laughed, trying and failing to hold it in.

"You know what he wants to hear," Sterling prodded.

Malaina rolled her eyes so hard that her head tipped back against Sterling's sternum. She stared at the ceiling above her, which was there but she couldn't see. Lips pursed to the side, she tried to decide if the smug look she'd find on the other side was worth gaining entrance.

Finally, her impatience won out, and she forced the words through her teeth: "Ra is the greatest thief in the city."

"We were looking for, 'in the world,' but I guess that's good enough," Ra proclaimed, sounding only a little disappointed. The door before them slid open, casting them in light, momentarily blinding her. The shadows skittered away, and she had to keep herself from hissing in response.

Blocking the doorway stood a boy two years younger than herself. His ashy brown hair stood on end, as though he'd been running his fingers through it far too many times out of boredom. His hair matched his always glittering eyes. Gangly, he had a good three to four inches on her and resembled a deceptively strong twig. His recent ability to overtake her while grappling in the training room made her woefully aware of that. She made a mental note to check their one-on-one scores later and make sure to kick his ass.

He held out a hand, palm up, expectantly. "Tip for your doorman?"

Malaina gaped at him, a look that would have any number of others squirming, but Ra didn't bother to wipe the smug look from his face. He continued to stand in the way, hand out, until she unzipped a secure pocket on her pants where she kept the two copper coins and threw them in the air.

They paused for a heartbeat, mid-air, before changing directions and finding themselves in Ra's waiting palm. His critical eye inspected them, holding them up to the light.

His lips pursed, twisting to one side and then the other while he inspected the coins. "These look old."

The copper coins shone in the light. They'd become so worn from being passed between them that the Elemental seal had been worn until the ridges were round and shining.

"Let us in quicker, and you'll get a better tip," she quipped.

"Where's the fun in that?" Ra whined, large round eyes looking down at her.

"Ok, children, some of us have things to do," Sterling scolded, waving her forward.

"Fine," Ra breathed, stepping aside. The coins bounced across his knuckles, disappearing into the palm of his hand and reappearing in the other so quick the sleight of hand was almost imperceptible. The movements, though flawless, were lazy, almost absent of thought. Something he did out of habit.

Once the two of them were through the door, Ra flicked his hand, and it slid shut. Heading back to his hiding hole next to the entrance, he flipped the coins in the air and let them hang for a second too long before swishing in unnatural swoops and falling right back into his palm.

Over the course of her career, Malaina had visited—perhaps more accurately, broken into—some of the city's most beautiful buildings, but the grand room of the guild always took her breath away.

Gold, silver, and purple swirled in intricately carved designs around each of the pillars in the four corners of the room and along the tops of the walls. The domed ceiling had been painted to mimic the night sky, stars, and galaxies gleaming above them. Meant to not only be beautiful but a reminder of their way home. Most of those in the guild worked at night, taught how to find their way home using the stars. Studying the ceiling for hours, she'd learned her constellations by lying in the middle of the floor. Lengths of gem-studded midnight fabric wrapped from pillar to pillar.

But the people brought the stunning room to life. The

grand room acted as the common area, the place where everyone gathered when they wanted to mingle and relax outside their living spaces. A large fireplace, always roaring in the colder months, warming the space ran along one wall. An array of wonderfully cushioned chairs and couches surrounded it, flanked by wooden end tables, perfect for cuddling into and chatting. The lounge area was her favorite place to read.

Currently, three guilders occupied the area, chatting about who knew what. In another corner of the room, two more guilders were playing chess, both looking equally over-invested in the game.

None of this drew Malaina's attention tonight. Instead, she and Sterling headed for the large double doors against the opposite wall.

"You're home!" A young girl with brassy brown hair braided in a rope down her back, flying behind her, came barreling from halfway across the room. Clothing covered her from the neck down, with long sleeves, elbow-length gloves, and pants tucked into boots. Bouncing, she hung on Sterling's arm. "How'd it go?"

At the sight of her, Sterling's eyes swirled periwinkle purple and sunshine yellow. Grabbing his wrist, she lifted his arm over her head so it hung around her clothing-covered shoulders.

Malaina waved a hand before the girl. "Excuse me! I'm here too."

Lybbi gave the assassin a look that portrayed a level of sass only a thirteen-year-old could pull off. "Yeah, and? You don't tell the stories right."

Malaina stuck her tongue out at her younger sister, who made an identical face in return.

"Okay, you two," Sterling chided. "We need to meet with Malachi first, and then I can tell you all about it. Why don't you head upstairs and we'll be up in a bit." It was a voice he saved exclusively for Lybbi. One that couldn't hide the brotherly love he had for her and only her.

Lybbi bounced again. "Promise?"

"Promise."

She ran off toward the elevator, jabbing the button impatiently, waiting for the doors to open to take her to the top-floor apartment the three of them shared. Malaina was grateful for the odd contraption, otherwise, the trek up those stairs would be a nightmare.

When she'd first moved into the guild, she made Malachi explain again and again how he'd had it built by a popular inventor in the City of Kinetics. Apparently, it was a common contraption around the City of Witches, but she'd never seen one before in the City of Elementals. A true appreciation for the thing hadn't come until the three of them moved higher in the guild.

"So what story are you going to make up this time?" Malaina asked under her breath, making sure no one heard, and headed for the double doors to Malachi's office.

Sterling shrugged, indifferently. "I'll figure something out." They paused before the doors. "Who knows, maybe I'll tell her the truth."

Malaina narrowed her eyes at him. "That's not funny."

His lips pressed into a thin line. "You have to tell her what we actually do for a living someday."

"Yeah," she sighed, "but not today."

Malaina rapped her knuckles against the large doors twice, so lightly she wasn't sure anyone inside would hear the knocks through the thick wood.

Groaning, the doors opened. No one stood on the other side, but then again, they didn't expect there to be. Instead, a single figure occupied the office before them, sitting in one of two plush chairs flanking a cozy loveseat that faced a low-burning fireplace.

The office had no windows. Instead, tomes ranging in genre from children's fairy tales to anthologies about the political relations between the cities filled the bookshelves that covered the walls from floor to ceiling. A scarcely used leather chair sat behind a desk in the center of the room. Malachi preferred to sit anywhere but behind that desk.

The doors closed behind them with little more than a wave of Malachi's hand. He didn't bother to look up from the book laid open in his lap. The Kinetic had one ankle propped on a knee, his head held up by a finger so he could rub his graying temple as needed.

Normally put together at all times, this late in the evening, the cuffs of his white button-down shirt were rolled up to the elbow, and his gray suit jacket was hanging on the back of his chair.

Malaina and Sterling didn't wait to be invited over, and instead headed straight for the sitting area.

Malachi didn't look up from his book. "You are back."

Sterling rounded the corner of the loveseat and grunted

when he sat, stretched out his long legs under the coffee table, and laid an arm across the back. Opting for a less traditional approach, Malaina sat on the back of the seat and fell, her head landing in Sterling's lap.

Malachi gave her a scolding glance from beneath his brows. "Must you do that every time?"

"Must you always have your nose in a book?" She mocked, mimicking his tone and giving the ceiling a mischievous smile.

Sterling let out a snort, while Malachi sighed heavily and snapped his book closed. Malaina hung her legs over the arm of the loveseat and swung them back and forth, knowing it would drive Malachi crazy.

"Why are you here?" He breathed, already exasperated by them.

"I just thought you might want to get paid, is all." Malaina pulled the pouch she'd gotten from her client and tossed it in the air. The coins made an unnatural arc before smoothly making their way to Malachi's palm. He opened it, counted the coins inside, and pocketed his commission.

"You overcharged." The statement was less an accusation and more a fact. He'd reprimanded her for it in the past, but that had never stopped her.

Waving, she shooed away the comment the way she would shoo away a fly. "He could afford it."

"Young lady, I am trying to run a business here, and you cannot charge all the Fire Wielders rate and a half more than everyone else."

Throwing her hands into the air, she waved them

around dramatically. "I thought that was one of the perks of being the only Death Bringer in Thaumoria. We can charge whatever we want."

"Not exactly." Amusement coated his words, though he tried to sound annoyed. "You are simply supposed to fulfill the contract requested, not set your own rates."

Malaina chuckled. "We *did* fulfill the contract requested."

Lifting her head enough to peek at Malachi, the guild master raised an eyebrow and turned his attention to Sterling. "What did she do?"

Malaina scoffed, feigning offense. "She? You assume that *I* did something?" She placed her hand over her heart. "I'm insulted."

Malachi didn't budge, continuing to watch the Shifter, raising his eyebrow even higher, deepening the lines on his forehead.

Sterling averted his gaze, picking at an invisible thread on the arm of the loveseat. "He wanted proof of death, so we presented him with proof of death."

Malachi narrowed his eyes. "How?"

There was a beat of tense silence when Sterling looked at Malaina, and Malaina suddenly found the titles on the bookshelves utterly fascinating.

"We gave him the head," Sterling finally admitted.

Malachi rubbed his eyes and pinched the bridge of his nose between thumb and forefinger. "Why in the world would you do such a thing?"

Malaina laid her head back on Sterling's leg again and studied the ceiling. Shadows swirled above her, growing and shrinking in the dancing firelight. Quietly, she answered, "That guy was disgusting."

"Even so, that does not mean it is appropriate to —" Malachi started, going into lecture mode, but Malaina cut him off.

"He got off on their pain," she whispered, hypnotized by the shadows above them.

They sat in heavy silence while Malachi contemplated her words, waiting for one of them to explain.

"Three weeks," Sterling started, absentmindedly running a hand through Malaina's silver hair. "Three weeks of watching him bring home new girls, terrify and beat them and when he could tell they were truly submissive, giving him all the control, that's when he would take them to bed."

Malaina closed her eyes, picturing it all again. Brought the images of each woman's face to the front of her mind yet again, vivid and horrible. Sterling tugged on a strand of her hair, forcing her back to the present. His reprimanding eyes were full of exasperated muddy orange. She stuck her tongue out at him and he did the same, a comical sight on such a hard face.

With indignation, Malachi shook his head.

"I will take care of any complaints," he promised them softly before sticking out a finger and waving it between them. "But in the future, if you could avoid traumatizing the clients, it would be greatly appreciated. We could use the repeat business."

"Fine," Malaina and Sterling muttered in unison.

"Thank you." Just like that, the serious conversation

concluded, already taking on a more casual tone. He tossed the pouch of remaining coins at Sterling, who caught it before it hit his chest.

"You know, you can trust me with the money sometimes," Malaina complained.

Sterling held the pouch over her, dangling it like a prize just out of reach. A rare, small smile played at Malachi's lips, giving the assassin a pointed look. "Sterling is far more responsible with the money, and while money is not everything I do enjoy having rent and such things paid on time and in full."

Just because he had a point didn't make it fair. "You need to stop holding the past against me."

"You took Lybbi on a shopping spree so extensive you could not afford your rent," Malachi reminded her.

Malaina sank into Sterling, letting herself fade into the memory. Her first contract paid more than she ever could have imagined. In her months of begging on the streets, she hadn't received a fraction of what that job paid. The work had been awful, and almost immediately, she'd forced herself to forget every single detail. Opting, instead, to focus solely on the money that appeared in her hand at the end of it. At thirteen years old, the concept of rent and savings had been beyond her.

After having only their barest expenses covered during three years of training, the idea of spending money had been too tempting to pass up. Instead, she'd taken Lybbi to buy new clothes and stuffed themselves full of as much delicious expensive food as they could afford. At least they had still been in the group living quarters and the rent hadn't been much, so she'd been able to make it up by taking an extra contract that month.

Of course, that was long before Sterling came along.

Malachi opened his book again, turning his attention back to it in a dismissal. "You two should head upstairs. Lybbi has been eager for you to get back. She talks my ear off about it every day during lessons."

Malaina sat up, stretching her arms in front of her, rounding her back like a cat. "How are those going?"

Malachi flicked his fingers in thought. "She is… distracted. Antsy. I think it is time we revisit the idea of…"

Malaina shook her head. "No."

His voice turned stern, jaw tightening at her defiance. "It will need to be dealt with sooner or later."

"We've talked about this."

He stared at her, debating if the argument was worth continuing. He turned back to his book. Another dismissal. "And we will talk about it again. Goodnight."

Sterling stood from the couch, ready to end this regular debate and head upstairs. He held out a hand to Malaina and helped her stand, leading her to the doors of the office.

They exited without looking back, Malaina's back rigid. Tilting her head from side to side, stretching her neck, she tried to shake off her irritation as the doors closed behind them.

Per usual, the pair drew the attention of everyone in the grand room. Her skin itched beneath when their scrutinizing eyes tracked her, analyzing every twitch of her fingers. They were always wary when she was in a bad mood, and most around the guild learned to spot her tells from a safe distance and give her a wide berth.

They made their way to the elevators, and Malaina jammed her thumb into the button. She stared at the doors in front of her intensely, willing them to open faster.

Sterling brushed the space between her shoulder blades in an attempt to calm her and leaned in.

"He's right, you know," he said under his breath, keeping his tone neutral.

Crossing her arms, she drummed her fingers against her arm, refusing to tear her eyes from the doors.

"I know," she admitted, and the doors opened

FOUR

"Do you think dragons are real?" Lybbi mused, sending the question into the room for no one in particular. Her favorite book, about a girl who rode dragons, laid open on her bent knees. She leaned back against a giant black wolf, splayed out on the rug in their living room. Reading allowed, she gave each character crazy voices and waved her hands through the air.

"Don't you think if there were actual dragons in Thaumoria we would know about them by now?" Malaina countered from where she lay stretched out on their couch.

Earlier, when Lybbi's prodding had become unending, Sterling conjured a story about the last three weeks out of thin air about fantastical nights full of espionage and spying, which had satisfied her curiosity. Where Malaina danced in the arms of a governor's son, drawing information out of him to sell to the highest bidder. No mention of death and severed heads, the way Malaina preferred it.

Now, Lybbi sat forward, sandwiching the book between her chest and thighs. Her brassy eyes wandered around the room in thought. "I don't know. Thaumoria is massive, they could be hiding somewhere."

"Where could hoards of giant flying lizards be hiding?"

Lybbi wiggled back into Sterling's fur-covered side, her face scrunched in thought. "Maybe in those humid jungles where the City of Witches is. Jade has been teaching us about it, and said they are always finding new stuff over there."

Malaina raised a brow. "New stuff? What does that mean?"

Lybbi pinched her lips together into a hard line as she thought. "Like, new plants and animals and stuff. She says that's where most of their herbs and plants come from and that it's more diverse than anywhere else."

Malaina mimicked her sister's expression, skeptical. "But isn't it pretty dense? Seems like there wouldn't be space for dragons."

"Yeah, probably," Lybbi admitted. After contemplating it for a few moments, her gloved hand reached out without thought, disappearing into the thick fur of one of the wolf's soft, massive ears. On all fours, his shoulder was equal to hers, standing bigger than any wild wolf would be—a fierce guardian no one would dare cross.

"What about the mountains up north?" Malaina offered.

Lybbi thought for a moment. "Isn't that where the Shifters are?"

Sterling let out an indignant huff. If Malaina didn't

know any better, she'd think the insinuation insulted him. But the powder blue of his irises, ringed in happy daisy yellow, gave him away.

Lybbi giggled. "Ok, I guess not. Who is up there then?"

"The Kinetics."

"Oh, duh." Lybbi crossed her arms, throwing her head back into the pillow of Sterling's thick fur. "Well, I don't think the dragons are hiding there. I can't imagine they like the cold."

Malaina stared up at the painted ceiling, trying to come up with the best answer she could. "You never know. With their fire and everything, they might not care."

An abstract version of the constellations in the grand room swirled across their ceiling. Golden molding framed flourishes of dark blues and purples splattered with white specks.

"But the Kinetics are so…what's the word?"

Malaina smirked, a wisp of shadow dancing between the swirls of the galaxy painted above her. "Stuck up?"

Lybbi rolled her brassy brown eyes. "Analytical. They would definitely notice dragons." The tip of her boots ran through the shaggy rug, making patterns in the fabric.

"I don't know, they spend an awful lot of time underground in those mines."

Her head tilted to the side, eyebrows creased. "They have mines?"

Sterling grimaced, shooting Malaina a disbelieving glance out of the corner of his canine eye.

"What?" Lybbi asked.

"Isn't Malachi teaching you anything in those lessons of

yours, or has he gone soft?" Malaina teased, remembering attending Malachi's lessons herself when they had first arrived.

"Yeah, right," Lybbi scoffed, "I bet he's even worse now than when you were my age."

Malaina laughed to herself, knowing that definitely wasn't true. Malachi had a clear soft spot for Lybbi, just like anyone else who met her.

"Where does the book say dragons live?" Malaina asked.

Lybbi held the book up and shook it at her older sister. "This book is make-believe about another planet that doesn't exist. I don't think it's going to be very helpful in finding the dragons in this world. Have you even been listening?"

"Yes, yes, I'm listening. Keep going."

Lybbi shimmied her shoulders, readjusting herself until she once again rested against Sterling's side. "Fine, but pay attention this time."

Lybbi continued to read until they all nodded off. So much time apart had them all exhausted. Now that they were able to relax, sleep became a heavy cozy blanket that had consciousness slipping through their fingers.

They'd only been asleep a couple of hours before Malaina woke again, her magic stirring. Immediately, she knew that if she threw open the thick window curtains, she would find a wall of black. It was the darkest hour, moments before the sun rose. The shadows called to her, tugging at her heart, drawing her into the night.

The fire in the hearth had died down to nothing but

coals. She rolled onto her back, her head resting on the arm of the couch. Staring up at the painted ceiling, she almost convinced herself that she was studying a moonless sky, stars popping through the dark. Breathing it in, she savored the way her shadows clung to her, heavy in the lightless room. Rejoicing in the blackness.

On silent feet, she slipped off the couch and tiptoed to her room, shutting the door until just before the lock engaged. Lybbi and Sterling deserved to sleep, and she didn't want the sound to wake them.

She headed to the on-suite bathroom of her master bedroom that Sterling had insisted she take. This time, she shut the door completely. In no time, the sun would start to rise, and the world would start to shift from the blackest blues to hints of gray. Her shadows would start to hide, and that ever-persistent sunlight would force its way into her room no matter how thick the curtains.

The door snuggly closed behind her, and the bathroom was plunged into total darkness. Soaking in every inky drop of shadow, her knees started to buckle. For the first time in three weeks, she allowed her magic to run free. She couldn't see it, but she felt the shadows come alive. Exploring every inch of the room, they danced through the air, celebrating their freedom.

A moan slipped through her lips when they found her, her back still pressed against the door. They wrapped around her, caressing every inch of her exposed arms. If she gave in more often, embracing her shadows wouldn't be so overwhelming. Sooner or later, her magic would level itself out. Like clothing brushing against her skin, the magic would be mundane. Common. But that would never be an option for her.

So instead, she stole moments when she could. But relenting to it in stolen private moments would never be enough. After so many years of suppressing it, she wasn't sure she would ever be able to get enough.

Once she had drank enough to regain her composure and relieve some of the pressure in her chest, she pushed away from the door and moved toward the bathtub. Allowing her shadows to guide her she used them to feel her way through the darkness. The only space they couldn't occupy was where they brushed against something solid. So, that's where she headed.

Her fingers found the cool metal of the handle, and she twisted, calling forth a stream of steaming hot water. As the tub filled she stripped off her clothing, taking her time and letting herself adjust. Little shadows always hid beneath her clothes, but exposing herself to so many at once forced her to pace herself. The thicker shadows were easier to feel, almost corporeal. In such a dark room, the shadows could have been physical beings. Hands and fingers brushing against every inch of her skin, intensifying each touch. Begging for her attention.

When the last of her clothes hit the tiled floor she leaned down to grip the edge of the tub. The cold of it centered her, bringing her back to reality.

The darkness skimmed every inch of her, never sitting still. Whenever she gave into her magic they constantly moved, feasting on her attention, using it to fuel their ardor.

Always moving. They didn't sit against her skin in times like this, instead, they caressed.

The tub was finally full, she turned off the water and reached for a vial nearby. A concoction she got from the Witches in medical before she and Sterling left to fulfill the last contract. Jade told her it would help her relax, and promote the healing of both physical and emotional aches. An overwhelming scent filled the air as she poured it into the tub, the heavy aroma mixing with the thick shadows. The fragrance reminded her of eating fresh cookies on a spring night: sweet and floral.

Stepping in, she slowly sank into the heat, letting the tension release as each muscle hit the hot water. When she was fully submerged, she let her head fall back, a sigh escaping her lips.

For a long time, she let magic continue to pour out of her as she soaked, becoming top heavy bucket tipping over and flooding the space until there was nothing left. When it seemed satiated, and the weight of her unused magic no longer beat against the cage she kept it locked inside, she sank below the surface.

Floating beneath the surface her fingers pressed against the tub to keep her from floating back up. She imagined floating in a sea of nothing but an endless expanse of black. The way she imagined it would feel to jump from a ship in the middle of open water and sink into the deepest depths of the sea, wearing her shadows like a protective cloak.

Surrounded, she almost heard a hum. A song emanating from the dark around her, lulling her into submission. Keeping her from reliving all the horrible things she'd seen and shielding her thoughts.

Her lungs screamed in protest, reminding her she couldn't stay under forever.

Comfort like this didn't last. Bliss wasn't real.

In the end, her mind started to go fuzzy at the edges, and she couldn't stay under another heartbeat.

She broke the surface gasping, her lungs desperately gulping air, fingers digging into the cool ledge of the tub. When her body was completely out of her control, fighting for breath, that's when the tears came. Her resolve crumbled, and alone, comforted by nothing but the dark, she sobbed.

She learned to sob silently years ago so Lybbi wouldn't hear her cry. After so many years, she wasn't sure how else a person cried anymore. She preferred to cry in the tub anyway. It saved time with clean-up, letting the tears fall directly into the water instead of onto whatever she wore at the time. The practice was efficient, and if Malachi taught her anything, it was how to do multiple things at once.

For the first time in weeks, she allowed herself to feel the effects of her life. Of watching those women get abused night after night. Forced to clench her jaw and look past the reality. Like staring through a foggy window. Looking with a clinical mind, she'd observed his movements, memorized his patterns, and analyzed his weaknesses.

But she couldn't stop herself from flinching when skin hit the skin.

She felt the effects of taking yet another life. The actual killing didn't bother her anymore, but each one left her feeling dirty. She was no better than a shovel being pushed into the dirt, a tool to be used by those who wouldn't dare bloody their own hands. To most, she was something to be bought and discarded when her usefulness expired.

She went through life pretending everything was fine—like she was fine. But alone, in the dark, she didn't have to pretend. She could let go. She could let herself feel the hate, disgust, and anger, not only at her clients but towards herself.

In the safety of her shadows, she let herself cry.

Long after the water turned cold and her tears dried, Malaina stepped out of the tub and drained the water. Wrapping herself in a silky soft ice-blue robe that almost brushed the ground, she took one last deep breath of solid darkness before cracking open the door.

Upon seeing the sight on her bed, she stopped in the doorway and leaned against the frame, watching.

Light streamed in from a crack in her curtains, a clear sign of the morning sun starting to rise. In the center of her room sat an oversized bed, easily big enough to fit four of herself...or one of herself, one massive shifter, and one teenage girl. Lybbi clutched one of Malaina's many pillows to her chest, curled up in a ball under Malaina's fuzzy down-filled comforter. Sterling splayed across the foot of the bed, taking up at least half of it, laying on top of the covers. Always several degrees warmer than everyone else, he was probably too hot to use a blanket.

Sterling started snoring, loud enough to make the bed shake. Lybbi's face scrunched, and she stretched her legs under the covers to kick him in the side until he rolled over.

The familiarity of it all warmed Malaina from the inside out. Pressing a fist to her lips, she bit her knuckles to hold back a laugh.

Of course, she would complain when they all woke up. Tell them how she bought the bed so she would be able to stretch out by herself. They saw enough of each other as it was, and they paid an exorbitant amount to stay in the oversized apartment on the top floor, so they should be using their own rooms. Sleep in their own beds.

But the objections would be a lie, and they knew it.

This had been the reason she'd insisted on an oversized bed.

There was a time, back when she and Sterling were still establishing their partnership, working on their reputation, and building their client base, when they rented one of the single-bedroom apartments instead. Sterling took the couch, legs hanging off the end every night, while she and Lybbi had twin beds in the single bedroom. And yet, they had still made a habit of sleeping in the living room together. Malaina and Lybbi curled up on the floor, every blanket and pillow they'd been able to afford at the time cocooned around them. Becoming a family hadn't taken the three of them long, and they soon realized they preferred to be together while they slept the day away.

The habit kept the nightmares away.

Most of the time.

Some days, they came no matter who was nearby. But the company made them easier to forget.

On the empty side of the bed, she slid in beneath the covers. Without fully waking, Lybbi rolled over to face her, reaching out a still-gloved hand to rest on Malaina's arm. The assassin's heart sighed, feeling at home shoving her cold toes beneath Sterling.

When sleep came, so did the nightmares. But she'd been expecting them. They were always the worst the first night home.

They started as they always did: on the night Lybbi was born. In her dreams, Malaina was six years old once again. Finally tall enough to see over the counters in the kitchen and steal snacks while the cooks had their backs turned.

A single doorway illuminated the dark hallway she crept down. A baby's wailing cries emanated from that room, echoing through the hallway. Her newborn sister. Malaina hadn't seen her yet but was eager to get a glimpse of the new baby.

Her parents had kept Malaina separate from the other children, and she was so lonely. Finally, at six years old, she was going to have a friend to explore the attic with and teach to swipe sweets. Her parents couldn't keep her hidden from her own sister. She couldn't wait to show the new baby her shadows, and the way they followed at her heels.

Malaina inched along the wall until her fingers found the edge of the doorway. Peaking her head in, just enough to peer inside the room, the sound of the crying baby got louder. A wailing lump rested in her mother's lap, swaddled tightly, but something wasn't right. From that distance, she couldn't tell if her mother was sleeping or simply sitting very still. Disturbing her mother and the new baby had been strictly prohibited. Father warned her she would be in a lot of trouble if she did, but she couldn't help herself.

Bare feet tip-toeing across the wooden floor, she crept to where her mother sat. As she got closer her mother's skin started to look wrong, the color off. Her mother had always had a pink complexion, contrasting her fiery hair, but now it looked…ghostly. No touch of blush colored her cheeks or lips.

The baby's wails grew louder the closer Malaina crept, and in her dreams, the crying was almost unbearable. The screaming surrounded her, beating against her ears, drowning out her own thoughts.

In real life, her father interrupted the moment and explained what happened to the best of his abilities.

But in her dreams, Malaina reached out to touch her mother's hand, if only to wake her so she'd make the new baby quiet. Touching her mother's hand was like touching the icicles that hung off the tree in the backyard in the depths of winter, the skin too thin and frail. So different from the usual warmth that radiated off her. As though it had been pulled taught against her mother's bones. In her dreams, her mother decayed beneath her fingers, crumbling away and fading into nothing.

Then the flames came.

Suddenly, she was ten and crouching in the corner of Lybbi's room. Lybbi continued to cry, now four years old, no longer the swaddled baby she had been. Smoke filled the room, and the flames licked under the locked door. The door her father locked from the outside before he set fire to the house.

He had never intended for any of them to live. He

wanted to burn their home to the ground until they had all joined her mother in the afterlife.

In her dreams, the walls closed in around them and Malaina couldn't see a way out. Her shadows darted around the room, trying to find sanctuary from the coming flames. Their manic energy fed off her fear, her heart pounding, desperately trying to think of a way out.

Smoke hung lower and lower in the ever-shrinking room. Fumes forced their way into the girls' lungs, choking them until there was no more air, and they started to cough.

When Malaina woke with a start, sweat dripped from every inch of her body. Throwing off the comforter, she swallowed down gulps of cool air. For a moment, her panic continued to rise. The air around her was warmer than it had been when she'd fallen asleep, and immediately, she pictured her apartment going up in flames.

It's daytime, she reminded herself, *of course, it's warmer.*

Remembering reality was painful, but she forced herself to do it. Forced herself to go back to her dreams and remind herself what had actually happened.

The flames did come, her home did burn, set ablaze by their own father. But she and Lybbi didn't burn alongside him. In her panic, she'd searched through her shadows and followed the flow of the smoke to where it pushed itself through an open window in the bathroom her father had forgotten about. It had only been open a crack, but that small space was enough. Malaina got her fingers between the window and the sill, forcing it open, and pushed Lybbi through it before climbing through herself.

They ran. Hid on the streets.

Malaina held her head in scarred hands, taking deep breaths, trying to stop her shaking.

Something hit the bed in front of her, and when she opened her eyes Sterling's hand was stretched out to her. His bleary, half-open eyes were a hazy lilac, his fingers curling lazily. Sighing, she grabbed her pillow and propped it against his side. Laying down, her head rested against his stomach. He wrapped an arm around her waist before falling back into a deep sleep.

The weight of his arm was comforting, reminding her she wasn't alone. Eventually, her heart slowed, and sleep came once again, despite how hard she fought it.

This time, the nightmares didn't come. She was safe next to the family she'd chosen. Sterling would never let the flames touch her, the same way she'd kept them from burning Lybbi.

FIVE

Too soon, Malaina awoke to the hollow ringing of metal crashing to the ground. She shooed away the shadows that settled around her in her sleep as Sterling groaned beneath her head, reaching up to rub his face.

"Please tell me that's someone breaking into the apartment to kill us." He yawned, using the heels of his hands to rub the sleep from his eyes.

Malaina rolled over to find the spot previously occupied by Lybbi empty. Pulling her knees to her chest, she buried her face in her pillow. "I don't think so."

The Shifter sighed heavily. "Is the sun even set yet?"

Malaina reached out with her magic. Just a trickle. Like brushing the tip of a finger against her reserves, which were already full and waiting again. Her magic searched for darkness behind the thick curtains and found nothing but light.

"No," she moaned. "There's at least another hour or two."

They waited a minute, then another, listening to the quiet. A silent agreement between them to lay motionless because maybe if they didn't make any noise, Lybbi wouldn't realize they were awake.

"Maybe she changed her mind and went to her room," he whispered. "Maybe, if we sit really *really* still…"

Another crash.

Malaina couldn't help herself; she half sobbed, half laughed while trying to bury herself further into Sterling's side. She wasn't ready to be awake yet.

Sterling poked her side. "Are you going to see *her* today?"

Malaina's heart skipped a beat at the thought. It made her a little more eager to get out of bed, but she needed to be responsible…at least for a few hours.

"After we see Syn. Chores first, fun later."

He nodded. "Then I guess we better get started."

Neither of them moved.

Malaina let out a nonsensical laugh, muffled by her pillow. Her partner's belly shook beneath her head as he quietly chuckled along with her.

"You're a terrible parent," he laughed, running a hand over her hair.

An accusing finger wiggled against his side. "You're one to talk. On the count of three, ok?"

"Deal." He took a deep, readying breath. "One, two…"

Crash.

"Three," she groaned.

They both sat up, moaning with the lethargy of people twice their age. Malaina's muscles ached, and from the way Sterling winced when he stretched, he clearly felt the same. Couldn't Lybbi have waited another hour…or three?

Malaina stumbled to her closet to get dressed while Sterling made his way to the living area of the apartment.

Excited talking trickled from the kitchen, Sterling sounding far more awake than he had a few moments before.

"So, what do we have this morning?" He asked.

"Pancakes!"

Malaina pressed her head to the door frame, suppressing the desire to crawl right back into bed and pull a pillow over her head. She adored her sister, loved her with every fiber of her being. And the fact Lybbi insisted on cooking their first breakfast back after each contract? The sweetest thing in the world. But for the love of the Gods… she needed to be less of a day person.

Taking one more steadying breath, she wiped the sleep from her eyes and plastered a smile on her face before heading for the kitchen. Holding back a cringe took all her self-control when she saw the state of things. Flour dusted nearly every surface. At least three times the necessary bowls and utensils to make pancakes were scattered across the counters, all of them somehow covered in batter. But Lybbi bounced on her toes in front of the stove, flipping another pancake.

Some oddly shaped but delicious-smelling, berry-filled pancakes were already piled high on three plates. Malaina slid into one of the stools at the breakfast bar, giving her a full view of the disastrous kitchen. Using a fist to prop up her head, she could hardly keep her eyes open.

Sterling slid a cup of Witch magic-laden coffee in front of her. So strong just the smell of chocolate-laced roasted beans made her perk up. *Thank you*, she mouthed.

Sipping from his own cup, his raised eyebrow told her she was going to need it.

"So," Malaina started, wondering how in the world she would eat all those pancakes, "Who taught you this recipe?"

Lybbi turned, smiling from ear to ear, a smear of batter on her nose. "Serena! She came to stay with me for a few days."

Sterling snorted his coffee, turning away to hide his reaction. Malaina pressed her lips together to keep from laughing when Lybbi glanced between them, confused.

"What?" Lybbi asked, concerned.

"Nothing," Sterling coughed, unruly strands of black hair falling into his eyes as he shook his head.

"She's just not usually one of the people who stays with you while we're gone, that's all," Malaina said, trying to cover.

"But..." Lybbi hesitated, "Isn't she one of your friends?"

Malaina nodded, staring into her coffee, trying to hide her blush. "Yes, yes she is."

"What did you guys do together?" Sterling quickly recovered his composure, reaching over to tear a piece of pancake from his plate.

Lybbi studied them warily, still not convinced every-thing was fine. "We just read books and played games. She made pancakes one time for dinner, and I asked her to teach me so I could make them for you."

"You…you didn't go to her apartment, did you?" Malaina scratched at the back of her neck, watching a particularly fascinating spot on the counter. While they were gone, it wasn't unusual for Lybbi to get lonely in their big apartment, and would crash on the couches of others. Usually, though, she slept amid the younger guilders down in the group living areas. If Ra and Layshan were home, she would spend nights with them before coming home for the day. Serena had never been on the list before.

Lybbi shook her head, spinning the spatula back and forth between her fingers. "No, she came here."

Malaina let out the tense breath she'd been holding.

Raising his coffee cup, Sterling gestured to where smoke started to rise from the pan on the stove. "Your pancake is going to burn."

Lybbi jumped into action, their questioning already forgotten.

Malaina crossed her arms on the counter before her and laid her head down on her forearms.

Sterling chuckled. "It's too early for this," he whispered.

Syn held a measuring tape up to Sterling's outstretched arm, measuring the width around his shoulder and bicep.

Despite his age, Syn maintained a full head of hair.

Once a dark brown, his mane was now a beautiful shade of gray that nearly matched Malaina's own silver. Lush and immaculately styled, it was shorter on the sides and longer on top. His beard was always kept neat and brushed, matching the rest of his flawlessly composed aesthetic, the clean lines cut to compliment his strong cheekbones.

He wore a thin pair of glasses which always laid at the end of his nose, so precarious they should fall off but never did. He'd perfected the ability to look over them critically many years ago.

He was a colorful man, and Malaina always looked forward to seeing what he wore. Today, his outfit was a royal purple vest stitched using lilac thread, pressed white pants, and a light gray button-down shirt. A series of chains hung on his vest, and Malaina wondered if they served a purpose or were exclusively for style.

Malaina loved Syn's shop. Shelves and shelves of fabric samples covered one wall, making the sales floor feel intimate and cozy. Every color and texture imaginable was available. Syn's magic revolved around fabric, and if one could imagine it, then he made it happen. He was the only tailor in the Elemental City who could imbue his magic into fabric, and the main reason Sterling exclusively shopped from him.

Malaina sat on a deep purple velvet-clad settee near the front window that matched Syn's outfit, lounging while Syn fussed over Sterling. Fingering the skirt of a corseted dress on display, the shimmering material slipped through her fingers. The gown had a sweetheart neckline that started white at the top and faded into a deep blue-green color at the hem. The material sparkled in the sunlight from the metallic thread that had been woven into the fabric itself. The full skirt had layer after layer of sheer fabric, growing deeper the closer it got to the wearer.

"You really don't have to measure me every time I come in, do you?" Sterling whined.

"Shush," Syn scolded him, "I swear you grow every time you visit, and I'll be cursed by Aais if I let you walk out of this shop wearing something that doesn't fit properly."

Sterling rolled his eyes but raised his other arm at Syn's request.

Malaina smirked when Syn made him spin, only wanting to giggle more when he sneered at her. Lybbi skipped and twirled around the shop, looking at every new outfit on display, holding the fabrics up to the light and letting them run over her covered arms.

"Can I get a new shirt?" Lybbi leaned into one of the sample shirts on display, taking in all the little details.

"We'll have to see what Sterling's clothes cost first," Malaina replied absently, but they'd brought more than enough.

Out on the street, two kids Lybbi's age ran down the bustling street, rolled-up papers bulging against their satchels. They weaved between patrons, who threw dirty looks over their shoulders before going back to their shopping, stopping at every blank wall along the main street of the business district and hanging posters. They were too far away for Malaina to read what the poster said when one of them took a turn and started down the side street that Syn's shop sat on.

The kid stopped at a blank wall across from Syn's front window and plastered two posters before taking off again.

A few patrons stopped to examine the posters, and those who did became excited at the sight. Malaina tilted her head back and forth, trying to read the announcement. Once the street cleared enough, she could discern the colors slashed across the page, a familiar illustration drawn across the bottom.

"Opening night of the Games!" Malaina cried, ready to run outside to check the date on the poster.

"It's here already?" Lybbi squealed, running to the window.

Syn looked over his glasses at Sterling, who still stood on the pedestal, in the way only the tailor could. "Don't tell me…"

Sterling nodded. "Oh yeah. Every year."

Syn sighed. "I don't understand the Elementals and their fascination with watching people attack each other." He waved a hand, dismissing Malaina and Lybbi's excitement.

Lybbi's mouth went slack. "You don't watch the Games?"

Syn shook his head. "No, child. I don't."

Malaina wasn't surprised. The only people who seemed to truly appreciate the Games were those born and raised in the Elemental City.

"These two are obsessed. They make me go just so they can fawn over the players," Sterling teased, knowing full well he equally enjoyed the Games. Betting on the plays, eating junk Malachi would never approve of, passing coppers back and forth with every play.

"Only Valis," Malaina reminded him

Lybbi's eyes went wide. "Is he going to be playing on opening night?"

Malaina leaned back on the settee, fanning blushing cheeks. "Gods I hope so."

"Enlighten me," Syn said, "What is so special about this Valis?"

"They think he's hot." Sterling wagged his eyebrows at them. A gesture from Syn had him stepping off the pedestal and putting on his over-shirt once again.

"He's married," Malaina pointed out, using her eyes to attempt and fail at boring a hole through him.

"To a Shifter," Lybbi gushed.

Syn stepped back, giving them a small smile while he wrote numbers on a pad. "So he has good taste."

Her partner laughed, pulling down the cuffs of his shirt. "Careful, Syn. What would your husband say?"

"I think he would agree." Syn winked at Lybbi, who giggled conspiratorially. Syn's husband was the sweetest Elemental Malaina had ever met. He wasn't the most powerful Air Wielder in the city, but when the couple was together, he practically walked on air.

Syn made his way behind the front counter and started writing out their bill.

Lybbi bounded up to the other side, resting her elbows on the wood and leaning forward. "Valis is a bi-wielder. One of the best in the city."

Syn raised an eyebrow, glancing up from his

notepad. "A bi-wielder, eh? I'm starting to see why you're so impressed by him."

"He's only one of two bi-wielders in the whole city." Lybbi drew out the words as if to say, *duh, it's more than impressive.* "Both of them are in leagues, but he's the best. It's practically cheating, having him in a league. Everyone knows he's going to win, it's just a question of by how much."

Syn grunted in uninterested acknowledgment. Of all the classes, the Shifters always seemed to be the least interested in the Games, but he was clearly trying to please Lybbi.

"How many will you be needing this time?" His brows furrowed at the math on his pad, tension carving deep lines on his forehead.

Sterling walked over, steely blue eyes studying the tailor. "Preferably five, though if that's too many…"

"No, no," Syn cut him off, studying the bill. "Five is doable. Would you still like that shirt?" he asked, looking first at Lybbi and then at Malaina.

The assassin stood fluidly from her lounge on the settee and made her way over to the counter. "What's wrong?"

Syn rubbed a manicured thumb against his forehead. "Nothing, nothing at all. It's just…well, the total is going to be a bit higher than usual."

He spun the bill around to show them the total. It was almost an entire gold coin more than usual.

"Whoa," Lybbi whispered, brassy eyes going wide.

Malaina's mouth fell open, at a loss for words. They'd been buying all of Sterling's clothes from Syn for years. The only Shifter in the entire city who created a fabric that shifted when Sterling did. The only reason Sterling didn't need to strip every time he wanted to fully shift was Syn's ability to permanently infuse Shifter magic into the very being of his clothing. Otherwise, he would risk them tearing at the seams or falling off altogether.

And in all those years, their total had never been so high for a few shirts.

"Syn, what's going on?" she asked, sure it must be a mistake.

Syn stared down at the bill, his throat bobbing. "Well, the thing is…" He shifted from foot to foot. "You know what. Forget it. For my loyal customers, I'll waive the new tax." He went to snatch the bill off the counter, but Malaina grabbed it first, holding it in place.

"What new tax?" Sterling asked carefully, leaning in, protective onyx streaking his steely eyes.

Syn ran a thumb across his forehead again, a ringed finger shining in the setting sunlight. Then he sighed, relenting to their stares. "Lord Kevah instituted a new tax. As of yesterday, all artistic goods are subject to triple the usual."

"That's insane." Malaina's eyebrows rose so high she thought they might disappear into her silver hairline.

"I'm so sorry, but please, don't worry about it. I will take care of the extra tax and charge you the normal price. You three almost single-handedly fund this shop." He forced a small smile, but the amusement didn't meet his eyes. "I don't know what you lot do, but with the way this one goes through clothing, I hope you never stop."

Sterling reached for the sack of coins they brought. "We'll pay the full price, Syn."

Syn pulled on the bill again, hands shaking. "No, no, I told you not to worry…"

Syn almost looked…scared, and the expression was an unsettling sight. One of the most confident people she had ever met, aside from herself, the tailor always held himself in a way that said he knew who he was and was proud of it. He was the best of the best in the city, and even at his already higher-than-usual prices, he always had a steady stream of nobles to his shop requesting whatever his genius created this time.

Now, his shoulders were…hunched, his tongue tripping over words.

"We're paying the full price, Syn," Sterling repeated, almost growling the assertion.

Syn bowed his head, shoulders sagging. "Thank you."

Malaina placed a hand on Lybbi's shoulder. "I'm sorry, but I don't think that shirt's going to happen this time. Next time we'll be better prepared."

Lybbi's chin dipped, her lips twisting into a pout. "Ok."

As Sterling counted out the coins Syn considered Lybbi, sharing in her disappointment. He tapped his fingers on the counter, then leaned down and pulled out a slim box.

"I've been holding onto these, unsure what to do with them. I think they may be just your size, though." He pushed the box across the counter to Lybbi, who lit up at the sight. She nearly lunged for the box, then stopped, looking up at Malaina for permission.

Malaina opened her mouth, ready to protest, but Syn

held up a ringed hand to silence whatever she was about to say. "Why don't you try them first?"

The young girl didn't wait this time, tearing into the box. Inside, a pair of beautifully crafted gloves rested on tissue paper. Malaina held her breath when Lybbi pulled off her well-worn gloves, revealing smooth, pale skin untouched by sunlight—or anything else, for that matter— always protected. The assassin didn't breathe again until the new gloves went on.

They didn't look like they were going to fit, practically falling off Lybbi's skinny wrists. When she tugged them up, though, they perfectly formed to her fingers. They laid halfway up her forearms, overlapping with the sleeve of her linen shirt. Fine perfect stitches closed the seams, Syn's seal emblazoned on the underside of each one. Lybbi flexed her fingers, testing the seams, but there wasn't a stiff spot to be seen.

"They're so pretty," Lybbi said in wonder at her flexing fingers.

"Syn, we really can't…" Malaina started, but a sharp look cut her off again.

Syn held up an engraved button between two fingers and held it out to the young girl. Lybbi looked warily between Syn and the button, not sure what she was supposed to do. The tailor nodded encouragement and held it out further. Lybbi took it gingerly, running a thumb over the design.

When her fingers ran over the ridges, shock froze her for a heartbeat. She repeated the gesture, pressing harder and exploring the topography of the button.

"They're amazing!" Lybbi shrieked, clutching the button close to her chest.

"Why? What's so special about them?" Malaina asked.

"I can *feel* the design!" Lybbi squealed, bouncing as she reached out and touched everything in sight.

Malaina threw a questioning glance at Syn, his warm eyes following Lybbi as she pranced about the shop. "Scraps, I assure you. A governor's daughter wanted riding gloves that would fit perfectly every time and wouldn't impede her ability to feel the tackle. This was test fabric, so it's not perfect, but it would be a shame for them to go to waste."

"How much are they?" Malaina bit her lip. If five shirts of magic-infused cloth were that expensive, she couldn't imagine what a pair of magic-infused gloves fit for a governor's daughter was.

Syn shrugged, taking the coins from Sterling's outstretched hands. "A gift."

Sterling shook his head. "Come on, we have to give you something."

"I've lost several well-paying customers to the new tax, and many more have been…upset, to say the least. As I said, they were scraps I wouldn't want to waste. I was paid to throw the fabric away, so thank the governor who bought the final pair." He gave Lybbi a soft smile as she ran around the shop before looking back to Sterling. "I'll send word when the shirts are ready."

Malaina sighed at Lybbi, grinning from ear to ear. "Thank you, Syn."

SIX

Excited chatter echoed around the dining hall.

The guild's massive dining hall took up an entire underground floor. The elevators and stairs stood at one end of the hall. Long tables stretched the length of it until they met the other side, where the cooks laid out two meals a day: breakfast and dinner. Except on Fridays, when they laid out a third at midnight.

Lybbi wiggled in her seat on the bench across from Malaina, sitting on her heels so she could reach everything on the table. Sterling plopped down next to Lybbi, dropping a plate piled high with roasted chicken, vegetables, and a mountain of mashed potatoes overflowing with gravy—a much larger version of what Malaina picked for herself.

Malachi ensured the guilders ate well. They were rarely permitted treats they didn't buy for themselves, but the cooks always did an amazing job of making the food tasty, no matter how healthy.

Normally, Sterling's half-meat plate would warrant a disgusted sneer from Lybbi. Tonight, though, touching things with her new gloves was far too distracting.

The young girl tore yet another piece of bread and rolled it between her fingers, adding the bread ball to the line already on the table next to her bowl of potato and bean stew.

Using a fork to gesture at Lybbi's untouched bowl of food, Sterling prodded, "You should try eating some of that."

Lybbi giggled. "Sorry. I'm just too excited." She smiled down at her waggling fingers. "Can I go show Layshan my new gloves? He's going to be totally jealous."

Malaina hesitated. She wasn't a fan of Lybbi's unrelenting crush on the Air-Wielding thief. An arrogant, perpetually self-absorbed criminal wasn't her first choice for her sister's affection, but he was also Ra's partner and ultimately unavoidable.

Sterling gave Malaina a knowing look, waiting for her response, always eager to hear what she had to say about Layshan.

Malaina ran her fork through her mashed potatoes, pulling her lip between her teeth. "Yeah, go ahead. He's probably around here somewhere. You know he wouldn't miss story night."

Lybbi's words came out rushed. "I saw him come in. He's with Ra near the front." Already half out of her seat, her head whipped around, her long braid flying through the air as she searched for Layshan's bright blonde head.

"Are you going to come back after, or are you going to

hang with them near the front?" Malaina asked, studying Lybbi's mostly untouched stew.

Lybbi bit her lip. "I was thinking that maybe…I'd head upstairs to the apartment after."

"Seriously? You love story night." To her knowledge, Lybbi hadn't missed a story night since the guild master instated them a year ago.

"I know, but…" She wiggled her fingers in the air, her eyes sparkling.

Sterling laughed, shoveling a bite of mashed potatoes.

Malaina grumbled, "Fine, go ahead."

"Thanks!" Lybbi called, barely looking back before darting for the front of the room.

Sterling didn't hesitate before reaching over and claiming Lybbi's bowl for himself, sliding it over to join his feast. He took a bite, and his lip curled, almost exposing one of those unnaturally sharp canines. He poured half his shredded chicken into the stew before taking another bite.

"I don't know how she eats this without the meat," he said around a mouth full of food, nose wrinkling.

"Not all of us play part-time carnivore."

"Touché," he grunted, shoveling another spoonful into his mouth.

Two people walked up to the platform at the front of the dining hall, which was acting as the guild's makeshift stage. They were a pair of thieves, one Kinetic and one Anima. Apparently, the stories were about to begin.

Before, Malachi had discouraged them from sharing stories about their latest contracts in any detail, for fear of sensitive information getting around. About a year ago, he allowed a single night of storytelling to improve morale. The guilders saw that inch and took a mile until it became a weekly event.

Sterling turned, bowl in hand, ready to listen.

The thieves waved their hands, hushing the room so they could start their story.

"So, as you all know, we can't share the name of the contract. Let's just call him Mr. D, shall we?" That earned a round of laughs from the crowd, mainly because there wasn't a thief out there capable of keeping their mouth shut about their conquests. Everyone already knew Mr. D. was the head of the Desroc household. "We conducted surveillance for just three days before we decided on our plan. We made it to the forest that runs along the road to the farm he was scheduled to visit. We decided on a large tree in the middle of nowhere, right next to the road. No one was around for miles. No one heard Mr. D call for help." The Kinetic continued, waving his hands dramatically, lowering his voice to try and give the story extra *umph*. "We climbed the tree, and I was able to push us up in half the time. Capel here nearly fell, but I held her to the tree, keeping her on the branch."

The Anima, Capel, rolled her dark eyes so hard her whole head lolled around, and everyone in the hall laughed.

"You all laugh, but catching someone like that isn't an easy feat for some Kinetics. I just happen to be very good." The Kinetic crossed his arms, narrowing his eyes at all of them.

Capel rolled her eyes again, then stepped forward.

"When we got to our hiding spot above the leaves, Grif here *graciously* kept us tethered to the tree and we set in for the long haul. It took hours of waiting for Mr. D, but we knew we had just the right spot.

"Then I felt it—the edges of emotion from the dogs. I grabbed hold of them long before they came into sight and found what I was looking for." Capel paused for effect. "Excitement! I tugged until every one of those dogs was off on a rabbit's trail. Then I sensed the horses' emotions. Six of them!" The thief paused again; this time, the entire dining hall was truly impressed. The ability to discern and manipulate six creatures' emotions, especially ones as intelligent as horses, simultaneously was pretty impressive for any Anima. It wasn't the most Malaina had ever heard, but it was still impressive. "I grabbed onto four of them, the guards' horses. I had to be subtle, or the guards would have figured out what was going on. All at once I tugged, just a bit, at the fear the horses were feeling about the dogs' excitement. That little bit of well-placed fear got the horses rearing and bolting. Leaving Mr. D's carriage unguarded." Capel gave a conspiratorial grin.

Grif stepped forward, taking over the story. "Now that the carriage was clear and unguarded, I had to act fast. When the carriage passed under the biggest branch of our tree, I jumped down on the roof, softening my landing so neither Mr. D. nor the carriage driver heard me coming. I used my magic to reach inside the carriage and grab on all the gold I could find." Now it was clear why the two were paired. Capel was definitely a talented Anima if her story was true, and for a Kinetic to be able to discern between metals he couldn't see and pull on it alone was equally impressive. "I got every single cent from the guy. And some jewelry for good measure."

Grif winked, wrapping up their story. Everyone in the dining hall clapped and shouted. Another good haul was another contract earned. If they weren't the best at their jobs, then they wouldn't live the lives they did.

Grif and Capel left the stage together, making way for another pair to head up and tell their story. A lower-level pair of forgers went up, heads tilted together, talking quietly between themselves, getting their story straight. On story night, things didn't need to be true, only entertaining.

Sterling turned around, bowl empty, trading it for his still mostly full plate. "Maybe we should try something like that. It would be nice to take a trip to farm country."

The thought of playing in the bug-infested dirt and whatever else one did when they visited farm country had her skin crawling, making her vegetables seem much less appealing. "I don't know if I'm really the country type."

Sterling's eye caught on something behind her, and he reached across the table, nudging her arm.

Peering over her shoulder, the assassin saw what caught his attention. Behind her stood the most beautiful woman Malaina had ever seen. Golden undertones glowed beneath dark skin, with long legs and black hair that hung around her in thin, tight braids. The woman's bright green eyes tilted up in a subtle smile, meeting Malaina's from where she leaned against the back wall.

Malaina turned back to the table, heat creeping up her

neck. Taking another bite of her chicken, she tried to hide her burning face, but Sterling wasn't fooled.

The Shifter smirked, eyes already a playfully pastel pink. "I'm just going to go back to watching the stories. Lybbi's not here, so you're completely unsupervised." Grabbing his plate, he turned around, pointedly ignoring her.

Her lips pressed together while she debated whether or not to take him up on the offer. Another peek over her shoulder and her heart pounded when she locked eyes with the woman again. Pushing her plate across the table, knowing Sterling would be happy to take her leftovers, the assassin stood.

Casual, Malaina instructed herself, *just another stroll down a dark alley.* Malaina pressed the *up* button and waited for the doors of the elevator to open.

The woman sidled up next to her, gliding across the room, her loose white shirt flowing around her. Leaning in, her low words brushed against Malaina's skin. "Mind if I join you?"

Despite the crowded room, the words felt intimate. Shivers ran over Malaina's skin. Voice stuck in her throat, she nodded instead.

An eternity passed before the elevator arrived, and the doors slid open. Malaina practically jumped into the small room, but Serena's movements stayed languid. Unbothered by their proximity. Malaina jammed her thumb into the button for the floor below her own.

The doors finally closed, cutting them off from the rest of the guild. Malaina let out a long-held breath, a weight lifting off her chest. She threw her arms around Serena's neck and pulled her close. Serena stumbled for a step before steadying herself and returning Malaina's embrace.

"My Gods, I missed you," Malaina moaned, nuzzling her face into Serena's neck.

The mistress ran a hand over Malaina's hair, smoothing it with each stroke. "You've been gone far too long this time, my beautiful Shadow Singer."

Malaina gave one last squeeze before pulling back, cupping Serena's face between her hands. When she pressed her forehead to Serena's, the elevator melted away, her sweet and spicy scent filling the small space. "I can't believe you came down. You hate story nights."

Serena played with the silky silver ends of Malaina's hair. "I don't *hate* story nights, I just opt to avoid them."

Malaina grinned, wider than she had in a long time. "Seems like a difference without a distinction, if you ask me."

"I guess you're worth it, then."

Malaina's smile grew, stretching from ear to ear. Serena reached up and ran a thumb along the assassin's jaw, and she had to hold back a moan when the mistress's Anima magic seeped into her. Serenity sent a fog over Malaina's chaotic mind, soothing her emotions, dulling the bad, and enhancing the good. Each of her muscles uncoiled, liberating every last bit of tension in her body. The release was so overwhelming tears sprang to her eyes. Her brows furrowed with the strain of holding them back, at least for now.

The door to the cell she kept her magic imprisoned within deep inside her cracked open as her body relaxed. It wasn't until she let go and let herself indulge that she realized how much the effort of suppressing it exhausted her. With her mind clouded, shadows started seeping from the corners of the elevator, from the creases of their fingers, from the gaps between their hair and their necks.

Serena watched them with playful eyes, pleased at the way the darkness twirled along her arms. The swirls fed off Malaina's emotions, drawn to Serena like a Water Wielder to the sea, a familiar to an Anima, a Shifter to color. They wrapped themselves gently around the mistress's arms, caressing her neck and playing between her red tipped braids.

"I love when they do this." She ran her free hand through the playful shadows, encouraging them.

Clutching Serena's hand, Malaina turned into it and kissed her palm. "They only do it for you," she whispered.

They kept their embrace until the doors opened on Serena's floor. Malaina scattered her shadows, sending them back to the corners and crevices where they belonged, for fear of someone seeing them who shouldn't. It wasn't uncommon for Kai, Serena's partner, to be entertaining the occasional guilder, and Malachi would lose his mind if one of them caught sight of her true magic.

Several wisps darted for Serena's door, gliding beneath it, as eager to get inside as the woman who so rarely commanded them.

Walking into Serena's apartment was like walking into a warm embrace. Deep reds and golds swathed the entire living room, and the lights were kept dim. It was an intimate space that seduced a person from the moment they entered. The decor reflected Serena's job as the Mistress of the Seductors, but to Malaina, the entire flat felt like the essence of the Anima herself: warm, inviting, nurturing, and passionate.

It felt like home.

Being there felt right. In the dusky light, shadows hung heavy in the air. Ever since Serena took over as Mistress, Malaina had never had to hide her shadows in that apartment. Her magic ran free there, fluttering around the rooms, twirling in the corners.

More than the alluring atmosphere, though, it was the smell that drew Malaina deeper into the apartment. She sniffed, nose twitching like a dog on a rabbits trail. Inhaling deeply, she filled her lungs with the cloyingly sweet scent of sugar, yeast, and apples. It mixed with the slightly spicy smell of cinnamon and the earthy aroma of nuts.

"Apple cinnamon nut rolls," Malaina moaned, saliva filling her mouth at the thought of them.

Serena nodded. "I just pulled them out of the oven when I came down to find you."

Grabbing Malaina by the hand, Serena lead her to the kitchen and motioned for her to sit on a stool at the small island. Within moments, she was sliding a plate across the counter, filled with a roll overflowing with cinnamon butter, apple compote, and icing. Starting at the end, Malaina unrolled the pastry, pulling off a chunk and popping it into her mouth. Flavor danced across her tongue, and she closed her eyes, savoring every moment.

"I could feel your tension from across the dining hall,"

Serena said gently, tearing off a piece of the roll for herself without ever taking her eyes from Malaina.

The Shadow Spinner sighed, shoulders slumping as she picked a nut from the gooey confection. Serena reached out, running her fingertips over the back of her hand, sending a heavy wave of vulnerability over Malaina that made her muscles heavy, ready to give out completely.

"It's been a long few weeks," she whispered, unable to stop herself. It wasn't uncommon for words to fall out of her mouth when Serena used her magic on her, and the assassin found that she didn't mind. It was nice to have someone to confide in. Someone who didn't need her to always been so strong. "This contract was awful."

Malaina found herself telling Serena every detail, from beginning to end. Though there was nothing she wanted to talk about less than her job, she needed to let the words out. After she finished her relaying every gory detail, the two fell into a heavy silence, picking at the roll until there was nothing but the soft center and globs of filling left on the plate.

She found herself mesmerized as Serena ran a finger through a bit of frosting and ran her tongue over the tip. Goosebumps rose along Malaina's skin, wishing she could be that finger.

"I'm guessing you got a starling today?" She asked, trying to keep her thoughts from going down a dirty path. Serena always made her mother's apple cinnamon nut rolls when one of her starlings dropped by.

Serena's emerald eyes flittered to hers, glittering in a

way that told Malaina she could already feel the assassin's shift in emotion.

The mistress nodded slowly, taking extra care to suck her fingertip clean of icing. "I did, Shadow Singer."

The corner of Malaina's lip quirked at the familiar nickname, and heat started to creep up her neck.

"You don't have to call me that," she murmured.

Serena came around the end of the island and ran a hand across Malaina's shoulders, sending a daze over her mind. She leaned back against the mistress, closing her eyes and letting herself get lost in her magic. Dark ribbons flowed from every corner, floating through the air in lazy swirls as Malaina gave in to the seemingly depthless pit of magic within her.

"Of course I do," Serena cooed. "You need to be reminded of who you are."

Malaina's heart ached at Serena's words. Knowing someone saw her for who she was, for the Shadow Spinner she was born to be, would have been enough. Serena, though, took it one step further. She saw Malaina's shadows and didn't flinch. Rather, she loved her for it and called it beautiful.

"But it's supposed to be Shadow Spinner, not 'singer'."

That was it, the truth Malachi had so thoroughly trained her to forget.

Malaina wasn't a Death Bringer in anything more than profession and title. Everything about her life was a lie. Down to her very core, she was a Shadow Spinner, and that would never change, no matter how much the guild master or the world tried to beat it out of her. She hadn't been born to kill; rather, she'd been molded into an assassin.

When she was born, it wasn't death, but the shadows who welcomed her into the world.

"I think you forget," Serena started, her liquid words floating in the air, rolling around them like steam from a hot shower. "I feel what you feel. I see the way they respond to your emotions and thoughts. I know how your heart calls to them, and I can see how eager they are to be with you." A surge of joy shot through Malaina from Serena's fingers, and the shadows jumped in excited twists, responding to the emotions the Anima pulled from her.

"You, my dear, are a *singer*." Purring the last word like a secret, Serena made it sound more beautiful than Malaina could imagine.

Sighing, Malaina turned on her stool and nuzzled into the mistress's neck, succumbing to the daze weighing her down and listened.

There it was, the humming of her shadows.

For a moment, she wondered if it wasn't the shadows whispering, but her heart. Perhaps she did sing to her shadows and didn't even realize it. And just maybe, they sang back.

The swirls clung to Serena, gliding over her arms and neck, creating patterns against her dark skin.

"What's the difference?" Malaina mumbled, her words like smudges on her tongue as she looked up at the beautiful woman before her.

Serena tilted her head to the side thoughtfully. "Singers

create art. How can you look around you and see anything else?"

She waved an elegant hand through the air, and thin little shadows laced around her fingers, mimicking the way Malaina longed to trace the lines of the mistress's palms. Reaching out, she pulled Serena into her lap until her long legs wrapped around the Shadow Spinner's waist.

Pushing Serena's long, thin braids behind her shoulders, the silver assassin studied those glittering green eyes. "Has anyone told you how beautiful you are?"

Serena gave a wicked smirk, her arms encircling Malaina's neck, her nails running over the back of her scalp. "All the time."

Malaina bit her lip to hide her embarrassment. Of course, people told her how beautiful she was.

Two years ago, Malachi recruited Serena to start a new sect of the guild and train their most successful spies to pose as courtesans for hire. Now, Serena acted as the guild's mistress, choosing her team of seductors with discernment so that only the best worked beneath her. They charmed their way into the beds of the city's most influential citizens and sold their secrets to the highest bidders.

Serena met with each client herself, using her magic to vet each one to ensure the safety of every spy and some of the highest wages in the guild, second only to Malaina and Sterling's. She was a mother bear through and through, ready to inflict dark emotions with a brush of her fingers upon any client who even thought of bringing harm to those beneath her.

Almost single-handedly, the mistress in Malaina's arms

had turned the title of courtesan from one of fear to one of esteem. Once, guilders spoke of the trade as a last resort; now, the line of those waiting to join could wrap around the block.

She was the most amazing woman Malaina had ever met, and considered every stolen moment together to be an honor.

She wrapped her arms around Serena's waist and pulled the mistress in for a kiss. Soft at first, then hungry. Desperate. She needed this. Needed to feel Serena against her. To hold the Anima close and lose herself to the fog of her presence.

Sometimes Malaina wondered how the Anima passed her over for the next Anima Mother until she remembered what brought Serena to the City of Elementals in the first place.

Then, Malaina remembered something.

Trying to catch her breath, she pulled back. "You taught my sister to make pancakes," she said, the words rushing out of her before she'd fully decided to say them.

Serena chuckled, pressing her forehead to Malaina's. "Yes, yes I did. She was lonely."

"Sterling snorted his coffee when he found out."

Serena smirked. "Were they good?"

Malaina stole another kiss. "They were delicious."

"Then I don't see the problem." Serena dug her fingers into the back of Malaina's neck, pulling her in again. When her tongue brushed against Malaina's lips, the Shadow Spinner couldn't suppress her moan.

That's enough talking, she thought, tightening her hold on

Serena's waist, and standing from the stool. Serena may have been a little taller than Malaina, but Malaina had been training hard for half her life. Her muscles were strong, and she had no problem carrying Serena to the bedroom, her shadows following at her heels.

SEVEN

Sterling scanned the paperwork laid out in his lap. "We're working for Desroc? Didn't those thieves, Capel and Grif, just hit him?"

"You are not supposed to know that," Malachi reminded them.

"Oh, come on. Everyone knows," Malaina muttered, taking the paperwork from Sterling's outstretched hand. Skimming through the information, she took in the important bits, leaving the rest for later. "Is this, like, a revenge thing?"

Malachi crossed an ankle over his knee from his usual chair near the fireplace in his office. "While that was the implication, I do not know for sure."

"Are we even targeting the right person?" Sterling leaned his head against his hand, using a finger to rub at his temple.

Malachi waved a hand in the air. "It is the right household."

Sterling shook his head, leaning back in his chair and stretching out his legs. His jaw clenched. "Close enough, I guess."

Malachi pointedly ignored the hint of sarcasm.

Another contract, another day. This time, though, something didn't sit right.

The timing of the contract felt off. They'd done revenge contracts in the past. One household places a contract against another, then vice versa, and so on. They never realized they were paying the same people all along. She and Sterling had two households they visited every year because of a feud started over a business deal gone wrong that had escalated into a full-on war.

It usually took time, though. A target identifying who hit them and buying a contract of their own didn't happen so quickly. The thieves completed their contract barely a week ago. Desroc figuring out who targeted him should have taken at least that long. Yet the evidence of his findings sat in her hands, written plainly in black and white.

Something was...off.

Her magic stirred uneasily, a slow, persistent itch beneath her skin. She clenched her fists, willing the tension away, knowing better than to indulge in Malachi's presence. If she did, no doubt a lecture would follow that she didn't want to hear. Nor did she have any desire to participate in the training session that would follow the said lecture. Instead, she pushed the anxiety down, ignoring the itch and focusing on the situation before her.

"Alman house…that's a new one for us," Malaina prodded, hoping to draw more information from Malachi.

Malachi flicked his fingers, spinning three metal balls the size of marbles in the air. His hands needed something to do, a clear sign of boredom. "New to you, but not to the guild. As I said before, it is the right household."

"But not the right person," Malaina added, more to herself than to anyone else. The name tugged at a memory, from a time when she was still attending lessons on political affiliations. Lessons that she had promptly ignored and immediately forgotten. Rolling the paperwork in her hand, she pointed it at Sterling from where she sprawled across the loveseat. "Aren't they…" She started, hoping he would finish her thought for her.

Sterling dryly finished for her, "The Water Wielders who own the dams that provide a third of the farms with water."

"Yes! Thank you."

"They're a pretty influential family. Dresoc owns, what? Four farms? He's well off, but he should hardly be on Alman's radar. Why would they want to rob him?" Sterling mused, looking curiously from her to Malachi, eyes burning orange.

Malachi's shoulders lifted in an indifferent half-shrug, the metal balls never faltering above his twirling finger. "I considered the discrepancy, but the Almans paid amply for their contract, and I was in no place to question the desire."

This caught Malaina's attention. "They didn't give a reason for the contract?"

"They did, but the excuse had clearly been contrived.

Again, they paid well enough. The circumstances were slightly suspicious. However, it was a simple thieving contract. No harm, no foul."

Sterling cocked his head to the side. "They've gone from thieving to assassination pretty damn quick for it to be no harm if you ask me."

Malaina unrolled the contract, looking it over again.

Name: Nyda Alman

Age: 15

"She's awfully young," Malaina realized, speaking to no one in particular. Maybe if she kept talking she'd figure out what about the whole thing was bugging her so much.

"Second born in the family, youngest child," Malachi informed them. The drone of his voice was that of someone reading data from an incredibly dull book.

"That seems…odd." An almost black blue crept from the edges of Sterling's curiously vivid orange eyes. Finally, he was getting the same nagging itch.

"I imagine they want to send a message without causing too much of a disturbance." Something about Malachi's casual tone grated on Malaina's nerves, but she brushed the annoyance aside. He never seemed to be much affected by the contracts that came in, no matter the details. The industry he practically ran single-handedly didn't seem to bother him until he sensed that a contract was dangerous for his guilders.

They weren't the only guild in the city, but they were by far the most influential and powerful. Malachi ran it with help from Serena to run the seductors and Jade to look after the guilders' daily lives. Malaina supposed that if he let every single contract eat away at him he wouldn't survive.

She understood. Too well, some days.

Reading over the paperwork again, she tried to pinpoint what felt so odd about the contract. A feeling in her chest nagged at her, like her magic was stretching out from within that cell it was securely locked within, its fingers brushing against her in a bid for attention. For a fleeting moment, she thought she might figure it out. Like a voice whispering from the back of that cell, telling her exactly what was off, but she couldn't understand the words.

The connection broke when a commotion came from the grand room, beyond the closed doors of Malachi's office. The ruckus sounded like a dozen people were talking at once. The three of them looked between themselves, listening.

"What could that possibly be about?" Malachi asked before he grabbed the metal balls and flicked his wrist at the office doors. They opened to reveal a raised fist hanging in the air, ready to knock.

"Malachi?" A young Witch asked, her eyes wide.

"Yes, Violet." Malachi stood from his chair, adjusting his suit jacket. "What can I do for you?"

Fidgeting, she twisted the end of her jet-black ponytail. "It's Aneyra and Bren. They just got back, and something happened to Len."

Malachi's eyes became downcast, shoulders slumping slightly as he sighed.

Sterling jumped to his feet, out the door in only a few

strides, easing around Violet. Malaina followed Malachi through the door at a calmer pace.

"Len. That's the…" She whispered, trying to place the name.

"The carriage driver," Malachi finished under his breath.

Internally, Malaina sighed as well. That explained why Sterling had practically run through the door.

This was going to get ugly.

The guild master and assassin went straight for the crowd of guilders amassed near the entry door, the same one she and Sterling had come through just days before. A path opened where Sterling pushed through to the center, and Malachi calmly walked straight for it.

"Everyone, the show is over. Head for the training room or dining hall or even to your sleeping quarters, but please make yourself scarce." Malachi's voice echoed through the room, heard from every corner.

The crowd dispersed, partners huddling together and bumping into each other on their way to the stairs and elevator. They didn't grumble about their dismissal; no one was willing to disagree with a direct order from Malachi. But they all threw dirty glances over their shoulders at Malaina as they gave her a wide berth, as if she wouldn't see so long as they didn't meet her gaze.

No one wanted to risk brushing a Death Bringer.

Malachi's dismissal had clearly been directed at her, too, but she wasn't leaving without her partner, and he wouldn't leave before knowing what happened to Len. Sterling and Bren knelt next to Aneyra where she panted on her hands and knees, trying to catch her breath. Inky black hair hung around her like a curtain, hiding her honey face and deep brown eyes that looked purple in the right light.

Malachi joined them on the ground, squatting on the balls of his feet.

Bren looked up. "It was a clean drop. We should've been fine."

Bren's bulky frame wrapped around Aneyra, protectively huddling over her small form. Though he kept his hair sheared short, it matched the fiery blaze in his eyes. Bren was one of the few Fire Wielders Malaina not only tolerated but liked. Cute and sweet, he always fawned over Aneyra, a Witch who would work herself to death if it weren't for Bren's carefree attitude keeping her grounded.

Malachi reached out and gingerly placed a finger beneath Aneyra's chin, lifting it to look into her purple-brown eyes. "Aneyra? Are you hurt?"

Shiver racked her body, despite shaking her head no. Leaning into Bren's side she used him to prop herself up.

"What happened?" Malachi asked Bren.

"The city guards jumped the carriage on our way back. They pulled us out and searched us, but we had already made the drop, so we had nothing on us. Honestly, they didn't even seem to care what we were doing, they only wanted Len."

"Why?" Sterling cut in, his eyes already edging towards a charcoal gray.

Malachi shot him a warning look that told him to hold his tongue and not overstep.

There weren't many Shifters in the guild, but Sterling

always felt a personal responsibility for each and every one of them. As though being one-half of the highest-paid team put him in a position of authority that no one had ever granted him.

Many of the Shifters regarded him with a mixed awe, for a variety of reasons. Some had never seen a Shifter like him before. Even legends were hard-pressed to find a Shifter like Sterling. Someone with magic that dug so deep that he could shift his entire body into something completely different. Magic clung to every inch of him, from the outermost shell of his body to the innermost core of his soul.

Most Shifters, though, swung between reverence and disgust at Sterling's position. Pacifism was admired in Shifter culture. They simply couldn't understand how he killed for a living. That didn't stop him from charging himself with their wellbeing. Checking in on them regularly to make sure they were adjusting to the lifestyle. Even if they were only working as carriage drivers, in the kitchens, or helping temporarily shift guilders' appearances to keep them from being recognized.

Bren gave a small shake of his head. "I don't know. They didn't say. They just drug him away 'under the Lord's orders'."

Thought creased Malachi's brows. "They simply allowed you two to walk away?"

"Not…exactly." Bren bit the inside of his cheek, looking guiltily down at Aneyra. A shudder went through her body again, and she turned her face into his chest.

"What the hell does that mean? Under the Lord's

orders?" Sterling asked. "Why would Lord Kevah care about Len?"

Malachi shot Sterling another hard look, but Sterling didn't look away. The challenge was one he wouldn't win, but he was ready to fight it anyway.

"Bren, take Aneyra down to medical. Have Jade look her over and get something to help her calm. You and I will talk later," Malachi ordered, the hard edges of his tone targeted at the Shifter, rather than the Fire Wielder.

Bren nodded, but Sterling continued to glare at the guild master. He opened his mouth to argue, but Malachi didn't give him the chance. "Bren and I will talk later. Alone."

A tense moment passed between the two forces of nature before Sterling helped Bren get Aneyra to her feet. He stared Malachi down, protectiveness blackening his eyes, but Malachi didn't flinch in the face of the wolf that was surfacing. Malaina wasn't sure the Kinetic was capable of flinching.

Without breaking eye contact, Malachi ordered, "Malaina, take Sterling down to the training room. He could use a workout." The guild master turned and walked straight back into his office, closing the doors without even a wave of his hand.

Bren led Aneyra away to the elevator, a protective arm wrapped around her hunched shoulders. Sterling stood unnervingly still, clenching his hands into tight fists by his side, staring at Malachi's closed office doors.

Malaina approached him slowly. "Sterling, don't."

His eyes blazed again. "I told him. I told him there

needs to be better protection for the Shifter drivers. I told him, and he did nothing. Too many have been arrested, and all they do is drive the damn carriage."

Malaina took a deep breath, having heard this rant time and time again. "Len understood what he was signing up for when he took the carriage driver job. Remember? He said he was going to do it so the younger Shifters didn't have to."

"It doesn't matter," he snapped, turning his angry gaze on her. "We aren't raised like the rest of you. Elementals think power is everything, and grow up practicing for the Games. Shifters aren't like that. They grow up going to the temple and learning to love everyone. They won't fight back! If the city guards ask them to hand themselves over, they will, no questions asked."

"I know, but there's nothing you can do about it," she said, knowing she was talking to nothing but the air.

"He shouldn't be putting them in the field!" He started pacing, a hand running over his lips, goosebumps rising along his skin with the effort of staying in human form.

"You're in the field," she breathed without thinking, regretting it the moment the words left her tongue.

Sterling's nostrils flared, glaring at her. "It's not the same thing."

Nothing she said would make the situation better, so instead, she threw her hands into the air. All she wanted was to get him downstairs to the training room so she could work out some of his pent-up energy.

But maybe there was something they could do. A way to ensure that things like this happened less often. Even though she knew it was the wrong thing to suggest before she even said the words. "Maybe…maybe we should be training them. Teach them to fight back and defend themselves while they're out in the field."

He gave an almost hysterical laugh. "Yeah, right. Shifters training. What next? Lybbi training?"

Malaina stiffened. Crossing her arms she pinned him with a silver glare of her own. "That's not funny."

He opened his mouth to retort, then thought better of it, taking a deep breath to calm himself. It wasn't enough to bleed any of the pitch-black from his eyes, but enough to stop him from shaking. His hands ran through his wavy dark hair, fingers knotting behind his head, watching the ground while he rocked from foot to foot. "No. No, it's not."

"Come on." Malaina patted him on the shoulder a little harder than was necessary. "Time for me to kick your ass. Malachi's orders."

He gave a weak smile that didn't reach his black eyes. "We'll see about that, Shadow Girl."

Her finger hung in the air, pointing at him as she backed away, heading for the stairs that lead to the lower levels. "That's Death Bringer to you."

"Yeah, whatever."

Holding open the door for him, she waited. "Stairs today. Think of it as a warm-up."

He snorted. At first, he didn't move, instead staring down at his hands. Thinking. Malaina continued to wait, letting him gather himself.

When he was ready, he let out a long breath and pushed

his shoulders back. Playfully he ruffled her hair when he passed. "You're annoying, you know that?"

They raced down the stairs, crashing shoulders as they pushed each other into the walls until they reached the level that housed the training room. The floor was the same size and shape as the dining hall one level up, but the furnishings couldn't have been more different.

Weights, weapons, and training rings filled the room rather than tables, a stage, and a kitchen. One of the walls was covered with different textures that mimicked the various architecture of the city. Wooden slates, stone, and brick walls with gutters, pipes, and window sills poking out —all perfect for learning to climb.

Painted on the floor near where they entered were training rings. Three made up the width of the room, and the wall next to the elevators held double-decker benches for groups to watch and wait.

Weapons used during training covered the wall opposite the climbing area. There wasn't a weapon in Thaumoria that didn't hang on that wall, as if Malachi had stocked it using a weapons encyclopedia as a shopping list. There wasn't a single one she hadn't held at some point. That she wasn't deadly with.

The middle of the training floor had strength equipment of all kinds: a track for running and conditioning, weighted balls that started small and then grew to the size of boulders, tires for flipping, heavy ropes for hauling, and metal plates for lifting. On the far end of the room was the med unit, consisting of several offices and exam rooms for select Witches to work out of and tend to guilders' injuries.

One of the medical rooms was closed, and through the window, she saw Bren's vague form and bright red hair. They occupied the largest room and office combo, which Jade, the head Witch, claimed.

Most Witches in the guild were partnered and worked as substance dealers. They took the Witch's knack for medicine, healing, and herbs, and used it to provide custom substances to clients. The higher-level Witches would create elixirs to help a businessman stay awake for days straight without becoming too jittery. A pain medication for one of the Elementals who played in the Games, so they wouldn't have to drop out due to injuries that would otherwise be crippling.

One Witch had the ability to sense chronic illnesses in the body and create teas that mitigated the symptoms but were so strong they were illegal. Her magic wasn't strong enough to heal her clients, but they still paid well for her services. The lower-level Witches usually dealt directly to the streets outside the guild, until they became more skilled at their craft and were able to create more complicated concoctions for return clients.

Aneyra and Bren were somewhere in the middle. Aneyra wasn't very good at sensing the body like Jade was, but she was incredibly creative when it came to producing her tonics.

Malaina didn't know the Witch well, having spent more time around Bren than her. But Bren never stopped talking about her, so she felt like she knew Aneyra better than she did. Bren was paired with Aneyra not only for protection but also for aid. He couldn't concoct things the way she could, but he burned, melted, and fought better than most.

The whole of the training room was busier than usual for this time of the night. The buzz of whispered conversations filled the air, many people watching Jade's office for any sign of how Aneyra was holding up. Malaina recognized many of the guilders from upstairs, having opted for training over their sleeping quarters when they were dismissed.

When the assassin team entered the training room, they drew attention to the way Lord Kevah himself might walking down the streets. Half the whispers suddenly changed subject upon their entry, focusing on them instead.

Good, she thought, *watch us, and let them be.*

Only one of the training rings was occupied. Layshan and Ra faced each other in the far left ring, both dripping with sweat. She and Sterling skirted the ring, heading for the weapons wall. Out of the corner of her eye, she saw Layshan use his air to slash at Ra, missing when his hand jerked out of his control. Ra manipulated Layshan's body like a puppet, grabbing at limbs the way only some Kinetics could, and moving them the wrong way. Lucky for Layshan, he'd been sparring with Ra for years and had tricks of his own up his sleeve.

Sterling studied the weapons wall, pulling her attention. The sound of a body hitting the padded floor made her grimace. A string of curses flew from Ra's lips, followed by an arrogant laugh from Layshan.

Eager to start, Sterling grabbed a staff and weighed it in

his hands before handing it to Malaina. It was made of hard, heavy wood and would break bone when swung at full strength and speed. At least, when used against a normal person.

But Sterling wasn't normal. When he shifted and gave in to the animal within, something that heavy would be needed just for him to feel it. Tonight, he needed to feel it. A true sparring match, without holding back.

Malaina threw off the oversized shirt she wore over her tank top and threw it to the side of the ring they claimed, putting up her silver hair so it wouldn't be in her face. Her pants were loose and comfortable, ready to move. Opting to go barefoot, her bare soles would grip the mat better than her slippers.

The weight of the onlooker's attention made her skin itch as they analyzed to bet on their sparring match. After so many years pretending to be the resident Death Bringer, she'd grown used to the attention and ignored them.

Swinging the staff back and forth, the familiar practice sequence calmed the assassin, warming her muscles and loosening her wrists. She imagined an opponent on the other end of her blows, and she practically heard the cracking of bones already.

As she warmed up, Sterling started stalking the outskirts of the ring. She didn't dare take her eyes off him. They were both in sparring mode and like flipping a switch, they were no longer partners. No longer friends. They were opponents, and only one of them could win.

In the real world, outside the cushioned walls of the guild, they were all just criminals. And criminals weren't granted leniency. They had one chance to walk away. One chance to live. Going easy on each other, pulling their punches, and swinging at half-strength wasn't kindness. It was a death sentence. Better to break a rib in the guild, where Jade could fix it within moments than to get your throat slit on the other side of the city.

The familiar movements of the staff sent an ache through her shoulders.

She ignored that, too.

When she was fighting, she didn't care. Couldn't care. No matter what everyone thought, she was the one at a disadvantage in this fight, and if she had any chance of walking away without Jade's help, she could only focus on one thing.

Winning.

Sterling shifted, his already large form growing. In a fluid motion, between one step and the other, he slipped into the form of a large black mountain cat. At least two to three times the size of any normal lion in nature.

Their excited spectators let out muffled gasps as Sterling shifted, ready to watch the two go head to head. Legendary Shifter versus the one and only Death Bringer, assassin versus assassin.

Sterling continued to stalk her, staying low to the ground, his ears plastered back against his skull. His paws tipped in razor-sharp claws bit into the mat, leaving small punctures in the thin cushioning. They were longer than they had any right being. At least the length of her finger, if not bigger.

Those were going to hurt.

The opponents locked eyes, and Sterling's sleek body tensed, muscles coiling as he prepared to pounce. When those animal instincts kicked in, he was all too eager to attack first.

In everyday life, when Sterling was…well, *Sterling*, he was patient. Stoic, even. Kind and tender and playful.

In form, though, he became one with the animal that lived within him. Sometimes she feared that one day he would lose himself to that animal, giving too much of himself until the animal devoured him whole.

Malaina waited. An eerie moment of calm passed as he stilled, his feline eyes narrowing. In slow motion, his weight shifted from one paw to the other.

Tightening her grip on the staff she blocked out the attention they drew. Forgetting the stares and whispers.

Then Sterling attacked.

EIGHT

"Who brought the snacks?" Sterling dropped to the roof's edge next to Malaina.

"Oh! That's me," Ra answered through a mouth full of food. Reaching into his bag, he pulled out a bundle of fresh jerked meats from the butcher. A wave of his hand sent it flying for Sterling's waiting palm, who eagerly plucked it from the air.

They perched on the roof of a building overlooking the stadium where the Games were held. Malaina sat between Sterling and Ra, muscles aching from her sparring match. Lybbi wiggled excitedly from her spot between the thieves.

They'd been too late to buy seats inside the stadium, but anyone trained by Malachi could scale a building. Thanks to Ra's Kinetic help, they got Lybbi up too, guiding her hands so even her untrained fingers made it to the top.

Malaina wished Serena was beside her, reveling in the excitement, but the mistress couldn't stand crowds. She said she could taste the emotions in the air when too many people gathered at once and that it felt like drowning on solid ground.

Overhead, sea birds circled the bright sun beating down on the stadium. Skilled thieves that they were, they scanned the streets below, waiting for any opportunity to swoop down and steal anything they could get their beaks on. Whether that be a fried bun straight out of someone's hand or a chunk of cheese dropped in the street.

The afternoon sun seared Malaina's skin, more accommodated to moonlight than the light of day, but she pushed the discomfort to the back of her mind. Scattered patches of clouds provided enough shade for her to tolerate the heat. Either way, the Games were worth a few unpleasant hours.

Crowds gathered around the stadium, clogging the streets below. The buzz of excited conversation floated up to the roof, eager spectators pushing their way through the arches to find their seats. The oblong stadium was surrounded by tiered rows of benches and seats, enough to fit half the city. At one end of the stadium was a balcony reserved for the Lord or Lady of the City of Elementals. While Lord Kevah didn't attend every game, he never missed opening day. Traditionally, the current Lord made the opening move from the balcony, which kicked off the first round of the season.

"Have we made bets on what element Lord Kevah is going to use for the opening move yet?" Layshan dug through a pouch for a copper coin.

"Not yet." Lybbi held open her palm to show the

copper coins Malaina gave her to bet with. "I'm going with water."

"I'll take that bet." Layshan reached across Lybbi to pick a roasted nut from the bag Ra held and popped it into his mouth. "I'm going with fire. Far more dramatic."

"No way, he's going earth, all the way," Ra bet, adding a copper of his own to the growing pile on the lip of the roof.

"You bet earth every year, and you've been wrong every year," Malaina countered, digging out her own coin.

"Which means…" Ra leaned in dramatically. "It's time for him to switch it up."

Sterling snorted, using slightly elongated teeth to rip off a chunk of meat. "From what I've heard, he hasn't 'switched it up' since he became Lord. That's fifteen years of consistency. I think you're betting on a lost cause."

"What can I say? I like to hold out hope that maybe he'll surprise us." Ra shrugged.

"Well, I'm on Lybbi's side. I think it'll be water." Malaina held her copper up for emphasis before placing it on the ledge. Lybbi gave a victory pump of her fist and took a bite of a chocolate pastry, flakes sticking to her chin.

Layshan rolled his eyes. "Of course, you would side with your sister. Sterling? Come on, back me up."

Malaina gave Sterling a cheeky look, raising her eyebrow to challenge him to take Layshan's side. "Yeah, Sterling. Which element are you betting on?"

Sterling blew a breath through tight lips. "I might regret

this later, but I'm going with Layshan on this one. I'm putting my coin on fire."

Malaina let her jaw drop, bemused. "Traitor!"

Layshan reached a long around around them, and the boys high-fived behind Malaina's head.

The five of them continued their initial bets, passing snacks until the crowd in the stadium hushed, their shouts turning to reverent whispers. Lord Kevah and Lady Atana stepped through the doorway to their balcony. They sat in the two high-backed chairs, holding hands and talking between themselves. From the rooftop, they were hard to see, but the group had sat close enough before for Malaina to catch a glimpse of the Lord and Lady.

They both appeared to be in their mid-thirties and while many stories rumored how the two met, she wasn't sure which version was true. What the assassin did know is that she'd never seen a man look at a woman the way Lord Kevah gazed at Lady Atana. He always appeared utterly entranced by every plane of her face, enamored by every word she said. Nothing else mattered but her.

Kevah himself radiated power, the physical manifestation of the elements he wielded. All Elementals seemed to show a physical sign of their elemental affinity, but the more powerful their magic, the more it showed in their appearance. Lord Kevah, especially.

He had dark, deep skin the color of freshly turned earth. His hair was long and fiery, the color of dancing flames. But it was his eyes that always caught Malaina's attention. They were deep blue, almost green, the color she imagined the deepest parts of the sea to be. Those eyes stood out even from across the stadium.

Lady Atana, on the other hand, was made of solid gold —from her hair to her eyes to her clothing. Between her golden blonde hair, golden-brown eyes, and sun-kissed skin, she was practically sculpted from the precious metal itself. She was beautiful in a way Malaina had never seen before —rare and the perfect complement to her God and Goddess-blessed husband

Nobody was sure what magic class the Lady belonged to. She was incredibly private, but of course, rumors spread. Many speculated she was a powerful Air Wielder, filling in the only element Lord Kevah couldn't seem to touch, and that theory was Malaina's favorite. Completing the idea of the perfect couple balancing each other.

Bodies filed into seats, packing themselves tightly when a horn sounded, sending the crowd into a tense silence. Lord Kevah lifted Lady Atana's hand to his lips and kissed her knuckles before standing to face the crowd.

"I am so honored to present to each of you the Elemental City's famous Games." Lord Kevah's voice carried through the stadium on Kinetic enhanced sound waves, reaching each citizen in attendance. The crowd cheered, shaking the air. The roar was so loud Malaina felt it in her chest, her heart pounding in response. The five of them cheered, too, wishing they were in the stands. When the cheering died down, Lord Kevah continued, "I know you are all thrilled to get to the Games, so I will not hold your attention longer than necessary. However, I do ask that once today's Games have concluded, you stay seated for an announcement concerning the city."

Whispered conversations erupted from the crowd, dulling to a buzz when Lord Kevah waved his hand.

Malaina's mind raced with the possibilities. In all the years she'd been attending the Games, she couldn't remember Lord Kevah ever making an announcement before or after the Games. Possibly the statement would be about a new law or policy, or maybe something concerning one of the other cities.

"Without any further delays, may I present this afternoon's playing leagues," Lord Kevah continued.

Immediately, the crowd roared again, loud enough to shake the ground. The shaking of the ground then became more powerful.

The stadium itself was long and round, like an extended oval. A wide strip of land lay in the middle of the arena, surrounded by a wide moat of water. At either end sat five posts of varying height, topped with round targets. Tremors shook the ground, growing in intensity until the water went from agitated ripples to swells of angry waves.

On either side of the strip of land, a tunnel of rock rose from the water. When they became level with the land, they stopped and out walked six players from each tunnel, one side dressed in blue and green and the other in yellow and red.

The crowd screamed and applauded when the players emerged, and the tunnels sank back beneath the water, waving flags of every color to show their love for their favorite team. The players waved to the crowd, smiling as they turned to meet each other in the center of the stadium and shake hands.

"Today, our leagues are," Lord Kevah announced over the crowd, gesturing to the team in red and yellow, "the Suns," then to the team in blue and green, "and the Serpents."

"There he is," Lybbi gasped, pointing to a flamboyant figure dressed in blue and green.

Valis.

Standing proud in his Serpents uniform, he addressed the crowd more than any other player. He was tall and lean, with bright yellow hair striking against his bronze skin. Based on the posters, he had dark brown eyes so warm they were almost red, framed by strong cheekbones and a square jaw.

As he shook the hands of the opposing team, their shoulders started to slump in his presence, already accepting their inevitable defeat.

When all the pleasantries were over, the teams took to their respective sides of the field.

An announcer's voice rang through the stadium, carried on enhanced sound waves, given strength by the scattered Kinetics around the stadium's rim.

"And now it's time for the traditional opening game ceremony!" Malaina wasn't sure where the announcer was but pictured someone over gesturing into a microphone somewhere in the stands.

Lord Kevah smiled broadly, his white teeth gleaming in the afternoon light. All of them on the roof held their breath. The tension thickening the air wasn't just from their bets, still laying on the edge of the roof from which their legs dangled, but the excitement of the show of power to come.

Lord Kevah raised his hands out before him, taking a solid stance from where he stood on the balcony. Hesitating for a breath, he turned his palms to the sky and curled his fingers into fists. Despite his distance from the ground, the earth trembled throughout the stadium, the players bracing themselves to keep their balance.

"No way!" Layshan yelled.

Ra jumped to his feet.

Two boulders rose from the earth, leaving divots the size of a carriage in the ground. The crowd erupted into incoherent hoots and hollers as they watched the first earth-based opening move in over fifteen years.

Smoothly, Lord Kevah brought the knuckles of his fists together, the boulders continuing to hover.

Lybbi looked around to confirm everyone was witnessing the same thing she was. "He's not even struggling."

"Those boulders must weigh a ton each," Sterling muttered, more apprehensive than admiring.

They all sat up straighter to get a better view. With a fierce pull, Lord Kevah tore his fists apart, as if splitting a log bare-handed. The boulders shattered, breaking into a dozen smaller rocks that flew in all directions.

The players dropped to their stomachs, sending out waves of Elemental Magic of all kinds to deflect the rocks. With deadly precision, the skull-sized stones shattered each target at either end of the stadium.

For a heartbeat, everything was still. The players looked between themselves, trying to figure out what to do next. The crowd erupted again, and the players slowly got to their feet.

"Uh…With that, the games will begin!" The announcer hesitated, their voice wavering, trying to match the energy of the crowd, though they were clearly thrown off balance. "After a short intermission to replace the targets," they rattled off.

Ra jumped up and down, doing a victory dance around the roof. "Oh! Look whose persistence paid off! Hand them coppers over!"

Lybbi and Layshan groaned in unison, throwing their heads back in frustration. Ra flicked his fingers, and the coppers zipped into his hand on invisible strings. Continuing his dance around the roof, his lanky limbs awkwardly attempted dance moves that had never been in style.

Layshan narrowed his eyes at Ra's victory dance. "You're an embarrassment to be partnered with."

Ra dramatically clutched at his chest. "Oh, how I've been hurt. My dear, four coppers richer, heart!" A foot kicked into the air. Layshan flicked his wrist and sent a gust of wind at the Kinetic, sending him wheeling off balance and falling on his butt.

Malaina laughed, turning back to Sterling, who'd been unnervingly quiet. Dull blue uncertainty clouded his eyes, mimicking the thoughts running through his head. She bumped his shoulder with hers to draw him out of thought, but he barely blinked. "You ok?"

Sterling shook his head, eyes distant and unsettled. "I've

never seen anything like that," he murmured, almost as if to himself.

Confused for a moment, she remembered Sterling didn't live in the City of Elementals when Lord Kevah came to power. Hadn't been there to see Kevah's challenge against the previous Lady, having still lived in the City of Shifters with his moms.

Malaina had only been four when it happened, but the match was one of the few events her father allowed her to attend, permitting her to leave the house and be around other people. A historic moment, he'd told her, and she shouldn't miss it, even if she was a disgrace to father. She'd had to promise to keep her shadows under control, and it had taken every drop of her four-year-old's concentration to keep that promise.

What she remembered most, though, was being in absolute awe of what Lord Kevah was capable of. Lady Aladonna hadn't even stood a chance. Lord Kevah's three elements effortlessly overwhelmed the previous Lady's two, ending the whole thing quickly.

Sterling had attended all the games with her and Lybbi since he'd joined the guild and they'd been partnered, but normally Lord Kevah's displays weren't so grand. Simple displays of water or fire that were dramatic, but not quite so deadly.

Eventually, the new targets were erected, ready for the actual Games to begin. The process took some time since no one anticipated all the targets being destroyed during Lord Kevah's display and they'd had to search for extras.

Eager to start, the players took their standard positions,

placing three close to the midline, two in the middle, and one guarding the targets.

Tension filled the stadium, everyone eagerly waiting for the Games to start.

The players faced each other. Taught springs waiting to be set free.

The horn sounded.

In the blink of an eye, the Serpents' side of the field was being flooded, water came in on waves taller than any player on the field. A Water Wielder dressed in red and yellow raised her hands in concentration from where she stood halfway to her goals, going on the offensive.

Valis raised his hands in response, erecting a protective wall of rock around his team and his goals.

One of his teammates jumped into the air, aided by Valis's air to clear the wall, and a slide of ice appeared atop the water. The player skated on the ice, using the upsurge of water to direct himself toward the Suns' targets. Pushed by another Air Wielder, he flew at an incomprehensible speed. Halfway across the field a wall of fire broke through his ice slide, blocking his pursuit.

The defensive Fire Wielder created a cage around the Water Wielder from the Serpents, blocking his attack.

The battle continued, players attacking not only each other but the targets opposite them, in grand displays of magic. Players in the Games were specially chosen for their power, usually trained from a young age to be able to compete in little leagues for the chance to move on to one of the professional leagues. The tournament was a display of magic unlike anywhere else in Thaumoria. No other city glorified pure power the way the Elementals did, and the Games reflected it.

Eventually, Valis got a chance to make his move. Aiding wherever needed, playing part-time defense and part-time offense, he waited until he found his opening. Sending a blast, he shot himself into the air far above anyone else. Using the air to keep himself balanced, he flew towards the Suns' targets.

The Suns' guard was an Earth Wielder, who erected pedestals from the ground for her to hop between, guarding against any attack with shields of stone.

Until Valis, mid-air, reached out a hand, using his Earth Wielding to grab onto the center pillar, and pulled. The pillar shattered, leaving the target unprotected. When he got closer to the target, he lifted one of the rock shards from the shattered pillar into the air. A kick, combining both his Earth and Air Wielding, sent the rock shard flying at a deadly speed right through the center target.

The target splintered into a million pieces. Malaina and Ra cheered, having won the first round of bets, as Layshan and Lybbi sighed with defeat. A horn sounded, and the round ended.

THE SUNS' final target fell, sliced at the base of the pole, and was sent flying into the moat. With three targets still standing on the Serpents' end of the field, the Game came to an end. The horn blasted, and the players fell to the ground, boulders, waves, and pillars of fire falling away alongside them. A calm came to the field while the players fought to catch their breath, but in the stands, the crowd went wild.

On the roof, the five of them divided up their wins. Lybbi came out the richest, having predicted how many targets would be left standing and who would be the one to break the last one standing. Layshan came in second, accurately guessing the final element used and how. Ra came out neatly in the middle despite his lead, and Malaina came out second to last, thanks to Sterling being the only one not to guess anything correctly.

Watching him out of the corner of her eye, she tried to figure out what he was thinking. This was the worst he'd ever done betting on a Game, and he had been distracted ever since Lord Kevah's opening move.

Elbowing him, she took one last bite of leftover pastry. "I guess I'll be paying for dinner, huh?" Eager to get off the roof and out of the sun, she started picking up her things and readying to leave.

Sterling shook himself from his thoughts and slung an arm over her shoulder. Joining in on the fun, he smiled too wide, and his eyes remained a worried cloudy blue. "I think Lybbi will be paying for dinner."

"No way!" Lybbi shrieked, "I'm keeping every coin for myself."

"Ya know, sharing is caring and all that crap," Layshan teased, stealing one of Lybbi's roasted nuts. "Maybe you should hand one of those coins over since you so cheated."

A flush started to creep up Lybbi's neck, her ears

turning pink. "I did not! The only one who cheated here is Ra, with that opening move bet."

"Woah, woah, woah. Hold up." Ra held up his hands defensively. "You all are just jealous you can't have my mad guessing skills."

Another argument ensued, the three of them bickered over who should have won which bet and if one of the targets should have counted at all because of how much had been left on the post.

Malaina leaned into Sterling and lowered her voice so the others wouldn't hear. "Seriously, what's wrong?"

"I just have a bad feeling about this announcement," he murmured, using pointed teeth to chew on his lip.

Malaina had forgotten about the after-game announcement, and from the looks of it, so did a lot of other people. A third of the crowd was on their feet, readying themselves to head home, when Lord Kevah stood again. Clapping his hands twice, the sound carried through the air louder than a clap had any right to be.

"Please, just one more moment of your time," Lord Kevah called out. The crowd stilled, watching him. Lady Atana sat up straighter, preparing herself for whatever was coming next. "As of tomorrow, any non-Elemental will be required to register with the City Guard regarding their residency within the City of Elementals."

A rumble of murmurs erupted through the crowd, and Malaina straightened. "What the hell? Why?" she whispered to Sterling, but he didn't seem to hear her. His jaw clenched so hard that she worried his teeth might crack.

"Those who do not classify as Elemental, Witch,

Anima, or Kinetic will no longer be welcome in the City of Elementals and will not be eligible for residency," Lord Kevah continued.

Malaina's heart stopped beating in her chest, the world around her began to blur at the edges. All she could see was Lord Kevah standing proudly on his balcony, Lady Atana grinning.

The five of them froze on the rooftop, the air dense around them, the tension so thick it was palpable. Everyone was waiting for Lord Kevah to take it back, for it all to be a joke.

"That only leaves…" Ra ran a hand through his brown hair, mouth hanging open with unsaid words.

"The Dark Magics," Lybbi's voice trembled, finishing Ra's sentence. Her brassy eyes became downcast, watching her gloved hands.

"And Shifters," Sterling snarled, onyx streaking wine-red eyes.

"He…he can't do that," Ra said with little conviction. His shoulders slumped as he looked at Layshan. "Can he?"

Layshan rested a hand on Ra's shoulder in comfort. "Don't worry. You're a Kinetic, so we're fine."

"Yeah, but…" Ra glanced from Lybbi to Malaina and then to Sterling.

Suddenly, their little group of friends was split into two, like a curtain had come down, separating them. The screen was foggy, making them feel distant—part of another world even though they were living in the same city. Ra and Layshan's lives hadn't changed, but a single proclamation had cast Lybbi, Sterling, and Malaina out.

The guild believed Malaina to be the Death Bringer, and everyone knew Dark Magic should be killed off at birth. They believed Lybbi to be a Shifter in the most basic sense, with little to no magic to speak of.

And Sterling…

He couldn't hide who he was. His eyes gave him away to anyone who glanced his way. It was the one part of his shifting he couldn't control. Yet another thing that made him truly unique. Malaina had never met another Shifter who had bits of their shifting so connected to their soul, changing with their emotions. It had always seemed like a manifestation of his power, something to be proud of, but now…

"We hope," Lord Kevah continued after a moment of letting his words sink in, "That this will help create a better functioning and more unified city. Thank you." Facing his Lady, he turned away from the crowd. The spectators gawked at the couple in silence. Malaina had never seen so many people at a loss for words at once. Every single person watched Lord Kevah take Lady Atana's hand and guide her by the arm, leading her through the back door of the balcony, out of sight.

Then, the crowd burst into chaos.

NINE

When the five of them got back, the guild was in an uproar. Guilders of every profession packed the grand room. During the Games, the city guards had hung posters announcing Lord Kevah's news. Nothing so far specified what would happen to Shifters who couldn't register but she imagined it wasn't good.

"What does this mean for us?" One person yelled to Malachi, who stood before his office doors, facing down the mob looking to him for answers.

"Are we required to register?" Another shouted.

Malachi listened to the questions without saying a word. Leaning back against the doors in his usual gray suit, his hands were pushed far into his pants pockets as he considered the guilders.

Malaina stood at the back of the crowd, her arms wrapped around Lybbi's cloth-covered shoulders, Sterling by her side. Pulling Lybbi close, she kept her little sister away from the crowd, feeling suddenly protective among the criminals she knew so well. Ra and Layshan melted into the mass of guilders, talking to friends about what they'd seen and heard. Searching the crowd, her eyes landed on Serena, standing at the front with Malachi and Jade.

Patiently, the mistress listened to what Malaina assumed were concerns from the courtesans in her care. Occasionally, she would reach out and place a hand on someone's arm or trace her fingers along theirs, spreading calm with every touch.

Finally, Malachi held up a hand, commanding attention and calling for silence. Everyone turned, looking to the guild master for guidance. The pressure he must be under was unimaginable. Most days, Malaina felt like she was going to crumble under the pressure of being responsible for just her little family. She couldn't imagine having to lead an entire guild.

For a few breaths, Malachi said nothing, rubbing his forehead. The number of people throwing question after question at him was overwhelming. Every hour of his age creased his face, but he handled it all with ease. Clearing his throat, he straightened, adjusting the sleeves of his coat.

"Everyone," his voice boomed, silencing the room, "I understand your concern. However, for now, we do not know what this means for us. This change in city policy was as much a surprise for me as it was for you, I promise you. I will ask around to gain a better understanding of what exactly will be required for this registration." Digging his hands deep into his pockets, he looked around, making eye contact with each guilder. His normally stoic face was now turned down, sad and concerned. As if he were seeing all of them for the first and last time. As though he were uncertain of their futures.

The Kinetic was never uncertain about anything.

He let out a long breath. "If it is safe, I will ask all Elementals, Kinetics, Witches, and Anima to participate in this registration. I know your jobs generally require you to go largely unnoticed. However, should you be approached by the city guard, I want to be sure you are safe. For the rest of you..." Malachi's eyes skimmed the crowd, briefly landing on Malaina and Sterling in the back. "I will be... reconsidering arrangements."

Sterling pushed forward, gently placing a hand on the guilders' shoulders to move them out of his path. "What does that mean, Malachi?"

Malachi and Sterling locked eyes, a silent argument brewing. Malachi broke eye contact first, looking down at the ground to gather himself. When he looked back up, he was prepared to face them with renewed confidence—or at least the facade of it. "It means Shifters and... others." Heads turned to look at Malaina. "May be taken off the streets and given new assignments within the guild."

Malaina's scarred fingers tightened, gripping Lybbi's shoulders hard.

No, her mind screamed, *No, he can't do that.*

All she knew was her job. Since she was ten years old, she'd trained to do one thing: kill. Working for hours in the training room, she destroyed herself to become what he asked of her. All so she could sell herself under the title of

Death Bringer. So she was capable of doing the job that kept Lybbi safe.

If she couldn't kill...what would she do? If Malachi took her and Sterling off the streets...they had nothing else to offer. What else was there for a Death Bringer?

"Why wouldn't it be safe?" Someone shouted from the middle of the mob.

Jade stepped forward from where she'd been leaning against the wall, arms crossed. Piercing narrow eyes scanned the guilders, meeting as many stares as possible. Everywhere her gaze fell, shoulders slumped, and heads dipped.

"Excuse me?" She asked, her voice a blade cutting through the tension, ready to stand as a unified front by Malachi's side. Her fingers weaved while she talked, mimicking her words.

Someone cleared their throat, as if deciding whether or not to answer the question. "He said, 'if it is safe.' Why wouldn't it be safe for those in permitted classes to register?"

The head Witch stared down at whoever had dared question her, sucking on her cheek the only sign of uncertainty she would show. Then she looked around the room again, unflinching in the face of those she cared for.

"Are you all aware of what you do for a living?" No one answered the clearly rhetorical question. "While this guild may be run like any other business, you are still breaking the law. What will you do if they ask for an address or occupation?" She held her fingers down by her stomach, rather than up by her face like most fresh from the City of

Witches. The constant movement was far less noticeable than most, but still, they talked with her. A habit from being born and raised in the City of Witches. A tight bun of jet-black hair emphasized her sharp features and kept her hair out of her face. When her hands finished their question, she crossed her arms again, her dark hooded eyes staring down the room.

After a quiet shock went through the crowd frenzied questions burst from every corner of the room. Sterling pushed between bodies, making his way back over to Malaina and Lybbi.

"I think we should head upstairs," Sterling said under his breath. His entire body was rigid, ocean blue-green eyes rapidly scanning the guilders who were watching them. He met every glare head-on, daring them to step forward and voice their thoughts.

Suddenly uncomfortable in the crowd, she nodded in agreement and let him herd her and Lybbi toward the elevator.

Drawing attention was a norm for her. Especially back when she had joined and Malachi introduced her, for the first time, as the Death Bringer they had all heard about. But this was different. She didn't like the way they were looking at her. As though she, Sterling, and Lybbi were outsiders. As though they were personally responsible for the registration.

Her head spun, trying to come to terms with what was happening. She didn't remember much of what Malachi taught her about politics and the history of Thaumoria, mostly because she'd never taken much of an interest in it, but one thing she did remember was the cities were created to unify Thaumoria. Everyone in Thaumoria was a citizen of Thaumoria, not the city they lived in. The cities were meant to be a common place for people of each magic class to go and be represented, not a way for those in charge to own those who lived in their city.

The assassin searched for any possibility that this registration wasn't as malignant as it seemed. Possibly, the registration wasn't meant to keep people in or out. Maybe it was for accounting purposes. A way to track how many people were currently residing in the city to better help Lord Kevah, Lady Atana, and their council to better provide for those who lived within its limits.

But then why wouldn't they let everyone register? Why had he said the rest of them were unwelcome? Obviously, Dark Magics wouldn't be allowed to register. Usually, they weren't even allowed to live, but Lord Kevah had always seemed lenient towards the Dark Magics. Neither hunting them down, nor publicly acknowledging them. Simply letting them be. But Shifters? Since when did that become a crime?

When the small family of three were safe in their apartment they all stood quietly in the entryway. None of them could decide what to do now. Nothing felt right. How could they go about their normal day-to-day life when it may not be a possibility anymore?

When it could all be taken away…

"What'll happen to us if we can't register?" Lybbi's voice was quiet, shuffling around the room with no particular destination.

Malaina and Sterling exchanged a loaded look, neither of them knowing how to answer. No one did. Never in the history of their forming had a city required citizenship, let alone denied it to anyone.

Sterling took a deep breath and centered himself, forcing himself to appear calm despite the telling color of his eyes, and went to the kitchen. The Shifter rummaged through the cabinets, probably looking for something that didn't truly exist, his hands needing something to do. "I guess…we'll just have to see what happens. It's possible nothing will come of it."

Lybbi blanched, eyes glistening. "But what if something bad does happen? What if we aren't allowed to stay?"

Malaina's stomach soured at the thought and she pressed her lips together to hold back a grimace. She hadn't let herself consider it yet. She didn't want to consider it at all. "We'll just have to find a home in another city then."

Lybbi's shoulders slumped, slouching on one of the living room chairs. "I wish we had a city."

Lybbi folded in on herself and a lump formed in Malaina's throat, her heart aching.

Her entire life, the Shadow Spinner had been hiding who she was. As a child, their parents kept her hidden from the world, hiring private tutors and monitoring every moment she spent playing with a colleague's child. They hadn't wanted anyone to know they birthed a cursed child, and she didn't blame them.

The shame of her existence was why they'd had Lybbi. They wanted a second chance at the perfect child.

When Malaina joined the guild, she'd never even

considered using her own magic to work, because what use was a Shadow Spinner? The decision to take on the guise of Death Bringer was an easy one. Trade her safety for Lybbi's? A no-brainer decision. But that had never stopped her from wishing for a day when she stopped pretending and could be herself.

Growing up, she'd learned about the cities and their forming the way all children did, and she had always secretly hoped there was a hidden city just for her. For those with Dark Magic. A group of people who would all understand, who would teach her about who she was and what her magic was capable of becoming. A place where she wouldn't be alone in the world.

Crouching on her toes beside Lybbi, looking up into her wet eyes, she said, "I think that might get a little lonely, don't you? With only three people for the whole city."

It was meant to be a joke, a bit of a twisted one. But Lybbi's shoulders only slumped more.

She nodded. "Yeah. Sometimes I forget."

A pained expression creased Malaina's face. She closed her eyes, trying to come up with something helpful to say.

She never forgot.

There was only ever one Shadow Spinner. *She* was the only Shadow Spinner.

Just like Death Bringers and Mind Benders. Because there was only ever one of each class of Dark Magic, and she was alone, like every Shadow Spinner who came before her.

Life wouldn't let her forget. It forced her to get used to the stares posing as the Death Bringer brought. The way those who didn't know her feared her. The way those who were new to the guild would watch her. Waiting for her to accidentally brush against someone and have them fall dead and lifeless at her feet.

Being a Shadow Spinner meant she was alone, but pretending she wasn't one was even lonelier. She didn't have a God or Goddess like the Wielders. She didn't have a Mother like the Anima. No Deity watched over her like the Shifters.

The one thing the Dark Magics had in common was they would always be completely and utterly alone.

Hoping to change the subject she forced her lips into a small smile. "How about we make some dinner? Are you hungry?"

Lybbi shook her head. "No. I just want to go to my room." Avoiding Malaina, she pushed to her feet and headed for her room, slamming the door behind her.

Shocked, the Shadow Spinner watched her go. Lybbi rarely used her own room when they were all home. If she was choosing to block them out…

Malaina bee-lined for the front door.

"Where are you going?" Sterling tore apart a chunk of bread with thick fingers.

"I'm going to see if Serena's home yet."

"She needs you." His voice was low and quiet, stopping her in her tracks, her hand hovering over the door knob. He wasn't talking about Serena.

Hands extended to her sides she turned to face him, to show him she had nothing. Nothing to offer. Nothing to give. "What can I do? What could I possibly say to make her feel better?"

"You're her sister and one of the only people in all of Thaumoria who could possibly understand how she's feeling. You can't just walk away."

"Nothing I say is going to change the facts." Clutching at her chest, she tried to keep her heart from ripping in two. "You think I want this? That I wanted to be like this? That I asked for this? I was born a Shadow Spinner, just like you were born a Shifter, and nothing anyone says or does will ever change that." Not Malachi training her as a Death Bringer. Not Serena calling her a Shadow Singer. Nothing.

"So was she," he snapped, whisper-yelling so Lybbi wouldn't hear them. He threw out an arm, gesturing to Lybbi's closed door.

"It's not the same!" She hissed. "You don't get it, because every Shifter is like family to you. No matter how different your magic is, it all stems from the same place. You have people who understand. You had parents who taught you about a Deity who loves you, and neighbors who invited you over to play with their kids. You have people who are like you." Tears filled her eyes, making him appear blurry at the edges, but she refused to cry. Wouldn't let those tears spill over. "Lybbi and I will never have that. We'll never have somewhere to go to learn about where we came from or why we were put here. Why we're like this."

Without looking back, she yanked open the door and walked out.

When she got to Serena's apartment she didn't bother

to knock. The door slammed behind her as she stalked into the empty rooms.

It would be a while before the mistress returned to her apartment, given everything that was happening downstairs. She'd be easing worries and helping Malachi develop a plan to move through this unprecedented situation smoothly. Because she was needed. Important. Respected.

But without her, the apartment felt empty—lifeless. The walls were the same deep red and gold they always were, but the color was dull in Serena's absence. The Anima's signature scent was faded but still lingered in the dark living room. Malaina took a deep breath taking in as much of the apple sweet and cinnamon spice scent as she could, hoping the smell would relax her.

It didn't.

Instead, it fed the gnawing loneliness clawing at her heart. A monster lurking deep inside, prowling, ready to pounce at the smallest signs of weakness within her. A feeling she often experienced as a child but had since learned to stomp down, far beneath the surface. This ferocity of loneliness hadn't grabbed hold of her in a long time, and she ached.

One Shadow Spinner.

One Death Bringer.

One Mind Bender.

She didn't know why it was like that. No one did, and it didn't seem like anyone cared. Possibly, there could be more. If more parents accepted their Dark Magic children, rather than handing them over to the city guard to be killed, maybe there *would* be more.

But that's not what the legends said. Not what the history of Thaumoria revealed. The stories said there has only ever been one of each.

Perhaps, at one point, she would have been considered special. Sacred. But if that time ever existed it was missing from every book she'd ever read, from every lesson she'd ever pretended not to hear.

Seeing the reality of her life written across a page somehow made it so much worse. The pain of it was why she never paid attention to the history books or legends of Thaumoria. To read tales of parents waiting to see what amazing magic their baby would possess, only for the shadows to gather around the child when it started to cry. They would be so distraught by the revelation they would dispose of the tainted child, claiming a stillbirth so their family wouldn't be marked as cursed.

Because a dead baby was better than one like her.

The legends said when one died another was born, continuing the line of magic by some act of a cruel God, or possibly just angry ones. Cursing the children of unworthy families.

Long before the cities formed there was a time when families who produced a Dark Magic child wouldn't be allowed to have another, for fear of them having another. The parents were sterilized. Sometimes forcibly. Sometimes voluntarily.

Shivers ran across the Shadow Spinner's skin at the thought.

Why her Mother loved her enough to let her live, Malaina didn't know. But on days like this, she wasn't sure she was grateful. What kind of parent would willingly allow their child to be this alone in the world? It wasn't her Father's doing that kept her and Lybbi alive following the discovery of their magic. From the day he realized he had been cursed with not one but two Dark Magic children, he became angry. He would yell to Elosyn, the Goddess of Fire Wielders, while drunk on anything he had on hand. Asking what he had done to deserve the fate he had been given.

Two Dark Magic daughters, how could fate be so cruel?

He'd loved their Mother and blamed the two of them every day for her death. Until the day he set the house ablaze and joined their Mother wherever the soul went after death.

After a long time of standing alone in the empty apartment, the door creaked open, and Malaina realized she hadn't moved the entire time. She'd just…lost herself. Stood there, unflinching, staring at the walls. The Shadow Spinner hadn't even noticed the way her magic had been leaking out of her without her stopping it, the shadows of the room swimming, vying for her attention.

The two watched the way the dark naturally responded to the assassin when she didn't keep it locked up tight in the dungeon that was her soul.

Serena didn't seem surprised to see her. Simply locked the door behind her and studied Malaina standing in the middle of the living room. They considered each other for a long minute, tears still floating in Malaina's eyes but refusing to fall.

Serena didn't say a word as she turned to the kitchen

and grabbed a bottle of wine and two glasses. Popping open the bottle she poured them each a glass. Shivering fingers took the glass Serena offered, and together, they tipped them back. She drank the entire thing in one long swallow before setting the glass down on the table.

Serena grimaced a little, finishing her glass, then poured them each another. "It's just the cheap stuff. Definitely too sweet for my preference, but it does the trick." Malaina hadn't even noticed the flavor. "Talk about a crappy day, huh?"

The assassin threw her arms around the mistress's neck, pulling her close, and let the tears fall. Serena wrapped her arms around Malaina and ran a hand over her hair, letting her cry. Letting her feel everything, The Anima didn't use her magic to calm Malaina or ease her hurt. Instead, she let her sob and shake until she ran out of tears.

When the tears finally stopped, Malaina pulled back, using the heels of her palm to wipe her eyes. "I'm sorry. I just cried all over you."

Serena cupped Malaina's cheeks, her thumbs swiping at the tear tracks that ran down the assassin's face. "You can cry on me anytime you need, Singer."

A trickle of Serena's familiar magic brushed against Malaina's heart, easing her emotions, but it was nothing compared to the usual waves of calm. Serena had clearly been draining herself, using her magic constantly downstairs, giving more than she had to give. Down to her last drops of magic, she was still giving it away, still working to make everyone else feel better.

Gently, she grabbed Serena's wrists and pulled them

away from her face. "Stop that," her voice cracked. "You must be exhausted."

Searching Serena's captivating green eyes for any sign she had been pushing herself too far, and found none. Her eyes were still bright, her posture still perfectly poised.

Serena gave a sad smile. "I have a lot more stamina than you do, remember."

Sighing, Malaina closed her eyes. "Right."

Magic was like a muscle, Malachi said to others during training, *the more you train it, the better you can use it. The longer it will last.*

Those words had never been directed at her.

Pressing their foreheads together, she breathed in the mistress's presence. "What are we going to do?"

Serena shrugged. "It'll be alright. Once word of this reaches the other cities they'll do something about it. The Anima Mother and Shifter High Sage won't let this fly. No one wants a repeat of Alvar Andelit."

That was a name Malaina hadn't heard in a long time. Not since Malachi's lessons.

The last Elemental to exist who wielded all four elements tried to use his power to gain control of all of Thaumoria. He claimed that the right to rule had been blessed upon him by the Gods themselves, proof of his rightful place as emperor of all of Thaumoria.

It was because of him the cities existed.

The people realized they needed people to lead them, to prevent the tyranny Andelit had tried to reign. Each magic class individually decided how they wished to be represented and created their own governments and cities.

The chosen representatives of each class signed the City Establishment Treaty, which was still held to that day.

The Elementals chose power to be their deciding factor. One powerful Elemental to rule them all the way Andelit had wanted it.

Eyes widening, Malaina pulled back. "You…you really think that's what this is? A power trip?"

Serena broke eye contact, pushing a strand of silver hair behind Malaina's ear. "Thaumoria hasn't seen such a powerful Elemental since the death of Alvar and the rest of the Andelit line."

Absentmindedly, the distraught assassin pulled away and paced around the coffee table. "What if the other leaders don't do anything, though? Shifters are pacifists. What if the high sage chooses to do nothing?"

Serena lounged back on the couch, swirling her glass of wine. "I don't foresee that happening."

"You don't know, though." Malaina couldn't mask the pleading tone in her voice. She wanted to sit beside Serena, take in her presence, and let her very being calm her heart. But she couldn't, she needed to move. "What if those of us who aren't granted citizenship are forced out of the city?"

Serena's feline eyes darkened as she stared into a memory she rarely visited. She stared down into the purple-red depths of her glass, losing herself in the way the wine splashed up the sides, twirling the stem between her fingers. "I don't think that's the worst thing that can happen to a person."

Frozen in her tracks, Malaina realized what she just said. "I didn't mean it like that…"

Serena pressed her lips together in thought before downing her glass and standing. Without looking back she headed for her room. "It doesn't matter. It happened a long time ago."

Malaina reached for Serena's arm, stopping her. "I'm sorry. Please, listen…"

Serena's gaze snapped to her, green eyes blazing, and Malaina shrank in on herself. "I know what you meant." Serena paused, breathing hard. "I remember feeling the same way." She gestured to the door linking her apartment to her partner's. "Kai remembers what it was like. People are constantly forced out of their cities, being sent out on their own to find a way to survive. Imagine being forced out of your city, away from your family, because people simply think you *could* have Dark Magic when you don't. At least…" Trying to sift through her thoughts, she looked Malaina up and down, deciding what words to use. "At least you won't be alone."

Serena pulled out of Malaina's grip, walked into her bedroom, and slammed the door behind her, leaving the Shadow Spinner surrounded by nothing but her shadows.

TEN

Perched on the sill of her bedroom window, knees pulled tight to her chest, Malaina watched the day turn from dusk to night. The reds, golds, and oranges that had been burning the city faded to grays, blues, and blacks as the sun set. Occasionally, a stray seabird flew past, casting a shadow over the bricks and concrete.

Leaning her temple against her knee, Malaina blanketed the world before her with magic. Not enough to call on the shadows or bring them to life, just enough to *feel*. At this time of day, the shadows were lazy, stretching and bending like an old cat waking up from a nap. They unfurled behind people, following on their heels.

Sometimes, the shadows felt so alive to her that she imagined they were filled with secrets. That each person had a shadow always close, always watching, collecting their secrets like pennies in a jar. And that if she just reached out, let herself tap into her magic enough, she could access those secrets. That the shadows would whisper them into her ear as gently as a lover.

"You ready for tomorrow?"

Malaina jumped at the sound of Sterling's deep voice. Lost in her own world, she hadn't even noticed him standing in the doorway to her bedroom.

She ran a hand through her still-damp silver hair, her nails skimming across her scalp in an attempt to ease her worries.

"No," she answered honestly.

Sterling perched on the sill beside her, leaning against the glass to look out over the darkening city below.

"Feels like we're gone more than we're home anymore," he mused absently.

Malaina sighed, letting her head fall back. "Should be an easy job this time. Quick."

Sterling side-eyed her, watching her closely. She didn't sound convincing even to her own ears.

"This one feels different," she answered his unspoken question.

The Shifter pondered her words, eyes swirling with color as he mulled over the details of the upcoming contract. They had gone over every little detail they had access to, memorizing every piece of information in Malachi's provided file until they could recite it back to each other. Their usual ritual. But each time Malaina parroted the details back to him, the words felt wrong on her tongue, like the slimy texture of an over-ripe fruit.

"We could say no. Tell Malachi we need more time home."

Malaina had considered it. Every day, she'd debated marching down there and telling the guild master to cancel the whole thing. But then she'd think about their coming rent and their already precarious position in the guild in the wake of this new registration. She remembered how everyone had stared, judged, and ridiculed her with sharp looks and whispered insults she hadn't been meant to hear.

They needed to take this job to remind everyone who she was.

What she could do.

She shook her head again.

"No. After this one, I'll talk to him."

Sterling nodded slowly, hearing the unsaid words as easily as if she'd said them aloud.

They sat in silence for several more moments before the apartment's front door slammed open, and a chorus of voices poured into the previously quiet room.

Forehead creasing, she shot the Shifter a questioning look.

The corner of his mouth lifted in a mischievous grin.

"Our going away dinner," he answered cryptically.

"What?" Malaina laughed, smiling and jumping to her feet as someone clanged a wooden spoon on a pan in a makeshift dinner bell.

"Calling all big sisters and brooding Shifters to the living room!" She heard Ra bellow loud enough to wake the dead. "Come greet your guests before I rob you blind!"

Malaina covered her ears, cringing at the deafening racket he was making.

"Would you stop that!" She cried, thinking of poor Serena and Kai in the apartment below. "We have neighbors, you know."

Ra paused as he bounded up to her in the doorway of her bedroom, his face wide-eyed and mockingly innocent "I know. They're here too." Then he rattled the spoon inside the pot again, inches from her face.

Pursing her lips, her hand darted out, grabbing his wrist and pulling him into a headlock until his arms were flailing at his sides, and he squealed. She grabbed the spoon with her free hand, leading him by the neck towards the kitchen, where she found Lybbi and Serena setting up an array of ingredients along the counters.

"I see you invited some people over," Malaina pointed out.

Lybbi turned from her station in the kitchen, lifting her chin. "Yes. You guys are leaving tomorrow, so I'm having a dinner party, and you need guests."

"But we just woke up. The sun has barely set. Shouldn't we be having a breakfast party or something?"

Lybbi scoffed. "Breakfast parties aren't a thing. So we're having a dinner party at night like normal people. The fact that we just woke up has nothing to do with it."

Serena glanced back over her shoulder, lifting an eyebrow at the now limp Ra in the crook of Malaina's arm. "Have you ever considered that *this* is why you have no friends?"

"You're my friend."

The Anima lifted her brows in a scolding expression, and Malaina sighed dramatically, releasing the gangly boy.

He scrambled to his feet and chopped at the air next to her with the blades of his hands in the most unimpressive faux attack she'd ever seen.

"Evil woman," he spat.

Malaina gasped, offended, and prepared to pounce on him again when Lybbi whipped around and pointed a threatening finger. "No! I need him."

Narrowing her eyes, she stuck her tongue out at him. "You got lucky this time, thief."

The Kinetic straightened, brushing non-existent dirt from his sleeve and flashing her an obscene gesture.

"Don't make me turn the Shifter on you."

"Ha!" Ra barked, "I'm not afraid of no Shifter."

Sterling appeared behind Ra's shoulder, a feral smile revealing elongated canine teeth as he leaned against the wall, arms crossed. "Oh, really?"

The thief jumped, then backed into the kitchen, face red and flushed with guilt. "Heh, I'm just gonna…" he pointed over his shoulder at the in-progress meal before darting to the far end of the kitchen.

Chuckling, Malaina and Sterling high-fived as she slid into the kitchen, stepping up beside Serena.

The Anima cut her a glance out of the corner of her eye before turning her attention back to the tomato she was chopping with fierce concentration.

"I'm sorry," Malaina whispered. "I'm not very good at thinking before I rant sometimes."

Serena's shoulders sagged a hair as she sighed. Her gaze

faltered, going distant for a moment before she started chopping again.

"I just miss them. It's hard knowing they're so close, and yet I may never see them again."

Malaina didn't need to ask who she was talking about. In every spare moment amidst her duties as the mistress of the guild, Serena was thinking of her family back in the City of Anima. Her mother worked as the head of the communication department for the Anima Mother, and every now and then, one of her starlings would find its way to Serena's window, detouring from whatever mission her mother had sent it on in the Elemental City.

Anima magic was as much a mystery to Malaina as Kinetic or Shifter, but Serena had told her that the starling was checking in. She could tell it she was fine, and it would take the message back to her mother in the City of Anima. Serena couldn't glean anything from the birds herself, but it was her only remaining connection to her family, and she treasured the little visits all the same.

As much as she missed her parents, though, she talked of her twin, Seth, most often. Of how proud she'd been seeing him sworn in as a city guard after so many years of preparing. Malaina couldn't fathom personally knowing a city guard, let alone being *proud* to be related to one, but Serena beamed every time it came up.

It had been a long time since Serena had learned to contain her emotions and prevent them from overflowing and affecting others when she didn't want them to. But her fondness for her family seemed to be the one exception.

Feelings of grief, pride, love, and loss surrounding the thought of them often tinged the air around her.

Even now, as she sighed, one of her red-tipped braids falling forward, heartache started to leak from her, weighing down the air around her.

"You're not alone," Malaina whispered, as much to herself as to Serena.

The mistress gave her a sad smile, then reached out and squeezed her fingers. "I know."

"Would you get!" Lybbi screeched, waving Malaina out of the kitchen.

"What did I do this time?"

Lybbi rolled her eyes to the ceiling. "You're distracting."

Throwing up her hands, Malaina backed out of the small kitchen. "Fine, I'm going."

She wandered over to the living area, where Layshan, Sterling, and Kai lounged.

"Move," she ordered Layshan, giving him just enough time to sit up before dropping onto the end of the couch.

"You're supposed to be courteous to guests. Hospitality and all that shit," he scowled at her.

"I haven't kicked you out or put *you* in a headlock, have I?"

"Children," Sterling warned from his chair, flipping a page in his book.

"I'll trade you," Layshan offered. "Information on the Desroc-Alman situation for a spot at the dinner table."

"You're not supposed to know about that," Sterling said, straightening is his chair as Malaina interjected, "Deal."

Kai snorted. "Oh, please. Everyone knows. Theft to assassination with a single contract? The whole guild's talking about it."

Kai stretched out his legs. A stunning Witch, his body seemingly sculpted as if carved from marble by the most talented Shifters. His purple eyes were piercing, mesmerizing in a way that made a person feel like the only important thing in the world.

Just his voice brought back memories, both good and bad. Thanks to his magic, he was not only one of the best-paid and most sought-after courtesans in the city but also one of Malachi's favorite training tools.

"Well, of course you know," Malaina said, words dripping with sarcasm. "Selling secrets is your job."

He chuckled. "While true, this rumor spread the old-fashioned way."

"Do you want the info or not?" Layshan asked.

"Fine, yes."

Layshan leaned forward and lowered his voice to keep Lybbi in the kitchen from overhearing.

"Capel said that the contract was suspicious but straightforward. Alman claimed Desroc owed him a debt that was never paid. So he hired them to get the payment… with some interest."

"Of course," Malaina muttered.

"Debt for what?" Sterling asked.

Layshan shrugged. "Never said, but they assumed it had something to do with Desroc's usage of Alman's waterways for his farm."

"Why wouldn't Alman just go to the farms and demand

payment? Malak Alman is one of the wealthiest men in the City of Elementals, and Desroc, while well-off, is nowhere near his level. It would be way easier and cheaper to go to one of Desroc's farms and use the intimidation factor. Or… turn off the water," Sterling offered. "Especially if Desroc was just riding around with all the money right there."

"That's what Grif said," Layshan hissed, nodding to Sterling's words. "He said the whole thing seemed too easy. Almost perfectly set up. They were out and back in less than a week. And that included the trip to and from farm country."

"So, let me get this straight…" Malaina started, trying to put the pieces together. "Malak is saying that Desroc owed him a vague unpaid debt. Instead of just demanding the money back, he hired two thieves to go and steal the debt back, which just so happened to be sitting perfectly in Desroc's carriage as he was riding around checking on the businesses everyone knows he owns. And in return, Desroc wants to…" she lowered her voice even more, "*Assassinate* one of Alman's daughters?"

Layshan nodded. "And what's even weirder, Grif said Mr. Desroc is super soft-hearted. He was upset when the family cat got out for the night and didn't show up until morning. You're telling me the guy who panicked over his daughter's pet wants to off a fifteen-year-old girl over a debt he owed?"

The uneasy feeling Malaina had about the contract began to grow, turning her stomach into knots. Exchanging a look with Sterling, she knew he felt it, too. Nothing about this contract was sitting right. People could shield their personalities to an extent, but it was in private that their true selves came out. People didn't get kinder and nicer in the privacy of their homes. If anything, fretting over a missed pet was something a malicious person did for show outside the home, only to close the door and never lose a moment of sleep.

"Do you have anything on the Desroc family?" She asked Kai, leaning around Layshan to make eye contact with the Witch at the end of the couch.

He shook his head. "I've asked around, and there isn't a single courtesan in the guild who has worked with them or even really heard of them. Not even a moderately scandalous rumor. They seem like a low-key family doing their best to run an honest business." He snorted, shaking his head as he remembered something. "Malak, on the other hand? That guy seems like a piece of work."

Malaina didn't know if it said more about her or her profession, but hearing that put her at ease. Learning that a client was a generally good person put her on edge. But finding out that her target had a bad reputation in the underground world was just another day at work.

She opened her mouth to ask what Kai knew when something came flying through the air, colliding with the back of Layshan's head.

"Ow!" The Air Wielder jumped up, turning as he ran a hand through his hair until it sat perfectly again.

They all looked up to find Ra watching them from the kitchen.

"Dinner's ready!" He beamed, a roll in hand.

CHAPTER

ELEVEN

Unaware shoppers brushed her shoulders as Malaina stepped between crowds in the street. Her simple but elegant updo kept her ears open and her appearance plain. One of the resident Shifters temporarily changed her hair from silver to a dull blonde for the outing to keep her from drawing too much attention.

As the seasons started to turn from spring to summer, the City of Elementals was starting to get what most would consider truly beautiful days. Unless you were a Shadow Spinner who couldn't stand the sun and delighted in overcast clouds. Dreadfully bright days and humid afternoons made the little hairs on the back of her neck stick to her skin was all summer meant to her.

The only true advantage she saw in the changing seasons was the clothes. An egg-blue dress hung off her

153

shoulders, and a light-layered skirt was like liquid rippling around her ankles under the command of a graceful Water Wielder. Her fingers brushed against the soft fabric, delighting in the way it swayed.

Dressing nice while working wasn't something she got to do often, so she took advantage of it whenever possible.

Sterling tracked her from where he leaned against the front of a Kinetic repair shop, arms crossed over his broad chest. His unchanging dark brown eyes rolled as she played with her skirts. But even from across the street, she saw the smile playing on his lips.

After all, he helped her pick it out.

The unchanging neutral brown of his eyes was unnerving, and Malaina couldn't look at them too long. Another trick from a Shifter back home at the guild.

Not being able to tell what he was thinking at a glance felt wrong, but it kept his Shifter identity a secret, which they truly needed right now.

In the two weeks since the announcement of mandatory registration, Shifters seemed to vanish from the city. Where once they had been plentiful, now they were scarce enough to draw attention just by existing. Rarer than the last blooming bud of a spring flower in fall. Rumors spread through the guild as to why, including a few outlandish theories, but the overall consensus was that Shifters no longer felt safe in the city, so nearly all had fled.

For those first few days, it had been common for city guards to stop Shifters and ask for their registration cards, taking down their names and addresses when they couldn't provide one. Nothing generally came of the instances otherwise. No one was hauled down the streets or thrown in the dungeons of the estate, but it kept everyone on edge.

And yet, their touch was already starting to disappear. Posters announcing the Games were dull, devoid of an artistic eye. Several businesses had switched out their signs and window decorations for something muted and less intricate. Whether the Shifters were hiding in their homes until the registration ended or had fled the city altogether, they had vanished from public view.

Trying to appear like a girl who'd been caught staring at a crush, Malaina glanced away. She raised her lips in a small, embarrassed smile, willing a blush into her cheeks. Really, though, she was scanning. Watching the people pass around her, ignoring the constant noise and chatter, keeping an eye out for one group in particular.

They had followed the Alman daughters from their house to the business district. Now, Malaina kept her distance so as not to draw the girls' attention. Or the attention of either of their personal guards.

They'd been watching Nyda every day for the last two weeks, learning everything possible about her and the Alman family as a whole. How many members were in the house at any given hour, the rooms they frequented the most, what time everyone went to bed, and even their favorite foods.

They'd learned not only which room Nyda slept in but that she organized her closet into night and day clothes, she always kept a book in the drawer of her nightstand for the nights when she couldn't sleep, and which guard her father had personally assigned to her twenty-four hours a day.

They'd observed the Desrocs a few times as well, making sure they understood their client and their target. But thanks to the report from Capel and Grif, they had more than enough information.

But the pair knew better than anyone that appearances were deceiving, and Desroc had purchased the contract nonetheless, so here they were.

This job should have been simple—in and out, no mess —over by now. But one thing had been holding the pair back. The thing they were hoping to find answers to today.

As Malaina navigated her way down the middle of the sidewalk, Sterling jerked his chin at the expanse of brightly lit windows to her right. Looking between passing heads, she realized what he was nodding at.

Nyda's personal guard stood out front, hands clasped behind his back, chin held high. Black eyes scanned the crowd, scrutinizing each face that passed. As a whole, he was stocky and wide. A wall of a man whose skin and hair matched his pitch eyes. On either side of him sat a large, fierce-looking dog. They were almost identical, with long snouts and pointed ears. The dogs surveyed the people in tandem with the guard, their heads and eyes moving in sync with his. Altogether, they made an intimidating team, a force to be reckoned with.

A single targeted thought from the guard was all it would take for his dogs to go into attack mode.

Shivers ran through her at the thought of teeth ripping through her flesh, and she averted her gaze.

Given their ability to sense the emotions and thoughts of various creatures, Anima tended to be peaceful and empathetic. Despite the City of Anima being the main exporter of meat, many opted for vegetarianism on principle. For some Anima, though, their empathy only extended as far as the animals they connected with, making them excellent security.

Malaina was never more nervous for a job than when a strong Anima was on guard. An animal's senses were far sharper than any human's, and their loyalties fiercer. A familiar didn't care about her feelings or whether they tore her to shreds. They only cared about what their Anima felt. If that guard felt she was a threat to him or Nyda, those dogs wouldn't hesitate to rip out her throat.

It was the guard's presence that ultimately made her pass by the shop, opting instead to study a display of books in the neighboring bookstore's window. She could feel the dogs' eyes pass over her, analyzing every inch of her body language for any threat. It made maintaining a relaxed facade while minding her periphery an effort of endurance.

The Alman girls exited the shop, gossiping between themselves, followed by Kaida's personal guard. The two guards followed the girls down the street, never falling more than a couple of steps behind.

Kaida's guard had a plain look about him. There was nothing striking about his appearance, similar to most Kinetics, though he matched the Anima muscle for muscle. On closer inspection, Malaina noted that he was a decent-looking fellow with a strong jaw, but he easily blended into the background. He was pale, but not too pale. His dull hair cut short, and his hard eyes had no discernible color. Unless she made an effort to look right at him, her eyes passed right over the Kinetic as if he were a transparent apparition floating down the street.

And yet, the small group of four drew attention from the passersby. It was the beauty of the sisters that caught everyone's eye, making it impossible not to stare.

They could have been twins if Kaida wasn't a few years older than Nyda. Both had their deep blue-black hair brushed up and off their shoulders, their sapphire blue eyes lined in a thick stroke of coal. They were daughters of the moon, placed on Thaumoria by Sarhea, Goddess of Water, in her own image—just like their Mother.

The group paid Malaina little attention as they passed, though when the Anima's dark eyes grazed over her it made goosebumps crawl across her skin.

They passed so close they nearly brushed against her back. Reaching out and bumping a guard's arm would have been so easy. Prick his skin with the underside of her spiked ring, tip dipped in a concentrate of Jade's Death Bringer poison. Taking the guard out would make her job that much easier…but the guards weren't her target, and the street was too busy, thrumming with people.

When all she could see were glimpses of the guards' heads between large brimmed hats and styled hairdos studded with spring-flower clips, she locked eyes with Sterling. Standing taller than everyone else on the street, he tried to weave between people without drawing attention, following their targets from a distance. His curly black hair was loose, flying about his face. His wide shoulders, clad in a white linen shirt, blended in as best he could among the day's shoppers.

Malaina started in the general direction the Alman group had gone until a whistle that mimicked the grating shriek of a circling seabird with unnerving accuracy cut through the noise of the crowd.

Sterling's signal made her ears twitch, and immediately, her head started to swivel, searching for what caught his attention.

Keeping her pace slow and casual, she meandered through the shoppers. It seemed that everyone in the city with more than a silver to spare had crammed themselves into the business district, eager to take advantage of the grossly beautiful day. Malaina overhead the occasional whine of a couple pressing their heads together, asking if any of these people had anything better to do (forgetting whatever circumstances allowed them to afford a day of shopping), but the shoulders pressing together made it all the easier for her to blend in.

Another whistled signal, and Malaina followed Sterling's gaze to a storefront just ahead.

She hesitated outside the store, studying the carved wooden sign above the door proclaiming it *The Witch's Doorway*. The assassin recognized the business, though she had never visited it herself. From where she stood, it appeared to be the average apothecary, but the whispered rumors around the guild told her of a very different side to the business.

Normally, if the girls were inside, at least one of their guards would stay out front, but neither of them was in sight. Glancing through the window, trying to see around her own reflection, Malaina caught sight of Kaida's guard disappearing behind the counter.

This was what she and Sterling had been hoping for.

Every night since they'd started their observations, Nyda's guard would wait outside her door for her to get ready for bed. At exactly ten o'clock, she would be waiting on the edge of her bed for him to enter. He would leave his dogs to guard her door and hand her an unlabeled vial full of a milky liquid. After she downed the vial in a single gulp, she would hand it back to her guard and he would leave to sit outside her closed door for the rest of the night.

She and Sterling had done everything they could think of to figure out what was in the vial, to no avail. The guard kept the vial in his jacket pocket at all times, and they had yet to figure out when it was getting filled or who was filling it. They couldn't go forward until they knew exactly what they were dealing with. Being present when the liquid was procured was the best solution they'd come up with.

When she entered the shop, a high and cheerful bell chimed. Immediately, she was met by the overwhelming aroma of incense and herbs—the earthy scent of dried peppermint, rosemary, and lemon balm mixed with something dusty, and she had to wiggle her nose to keep from sneezing at the abrupt change.

She beelined for one of the walls, inspecting the generic remedy-filled tins that lined the shelves, doing her best to appear like any other interested shopper who wandered on a whim. They were perfectly organized by whatever they promised to provide. Words like "calm," "sleep," and "focus" were written in perfect script across the labels, light streaming through the windows, dust dancing in the rays the way her shadows danced through the night.

Certain remedies worked the same for everyone—balm for the common flu, tea to ward off general morning sickness during pregnancy, and so on. The specialty stuff needed to be custom-made, like medications for those who suffered from rare diseases where their own cells attacked their organs. For maladies that were so specific and complicated, a Witch would need to make something uniquely tailored to that person.

Browsing the shelves, she listened for the slightest of sounds forcing her eyes to look anywhere but the desk she saw Kaida's Kinetic guard disappear behind.

A particularly dark corner of the shop called to her, and she lingered, pretending to study the display of selected oils. But really, she wanted to see the shadows. To most people, a shadow was a shadow, all the same, never changing. But to Malaina, each shadow was unique. The slightest change in color, a difference in the way one might swirl where another swayed. Some were more direct, their intentions clear, others more whimsical, floating without purpose.

She ran a finger through the shadow, its almost non-existent weight pressing against her skin. Calling to it, reaching a tendril of her magic out, and setting it free from its constraints wasn't an option. But she could acknowledge it, see it for what it was, and appreciate its beauty.

Her finger traced through one of the darker shadows, and her ears pricked at the sound of muffled voices.

The store was empty except for an employee sitting on a stool behind the counter. His mouth moved while deft fingers tied together a bunch of herbs, choosing each sprig carefully, but it wasn't his whispers that caught her attention.

No, what she heard was coming from somewhere else.

Crafting her face into a small, gentle smile, she approached the counter.

Dipping her chin, she glanced up from beneath her lashes, subtly batting them. "Excuse me?"

The Witch behind the counter smiled at her, setting aside the bunch of herbs he was working on.

"Yes, ma'am, how can I help you?" Nervous long fingers ran through his dark hair.

The muffled voices were louder and clearer now, though she still couldn't make out what they were saying, like hearing someone talk while wearing fluffy earmuffs. Various bowls and containers were displayed on the counter, and she let her finger trail through one of the shadows cast by the products on display. Just that contact settled her, clearing her mind, and the muffled voices started to take form as she concentrated.

The words were fuzzy, but the tones of the voices themselves were distinct.

One of them, she was sure, was Kaida's guard.

"I was hoping to find something for my sister," she drawled, trying to think of any lie that would keep her close to the voices.

"Oh? Are you looking for something in particular?"

"She needs something to help her sleep." Her shoulders lifted and fell, a tiny shrug. "Nightmares."

An open book behind the counter caught her attention. From where she stood, she could only glimpse the bottom of the page before meeting the Witch's hooded eyes again.

"Of course. We have plenty of options to help with that." Eager to help, he jumped to his feet. Ready to guide her back between the shelves and away from the counter, he reached out, letting his hand hover in the air next to her arm.

Ready to guide her away from the voices.

"Actually, could you just pull me everything you have?" That should keep him busy for a while.

He paused, looking around the shop at all the products they had lining the walls and shelving units. "Every…*every-thing* we have for sleep?"

Nodding, she stepped closer, looking up at him from beneath her lashes again. She made her eyes round without letting them bulge, urging him to simply comply and leave her be.

Doe, not deranged, Malachi used to scold her when her eyes would go too wide in training. The amount of time the resident Death Bringer had to spend learning to appear sweet was still joked about around the guild. "Yes, I would truly appreciate it."

"Everything we have for sleep would be a fortune. It would help if you could tell me a little more about why she can't sleep. You said nightmares, but are they from memories, or anxiety, or night terrors?"

Malaina resisted the urge to snarl and roll her eyes, eager to get him away from the counter and away from her. He was only trying to help, but it was truly getting on her nerves. "I don't know, she doesn't like to talk about it. Really, everything you have would be great."

Blowing a breath through tight lips, he ran a hand through his hair again. "Okay, well... give me a few minutes, and I'll see what I can do."

"Thank you," she gushed, "You're the best."

Starting at the nearest wall, he turned his back to her and scanned the shelves, picking up tin after tin. The moment he wasn't looking, Malaina leaned over the counter, scanning the book that lay open on the other side.

It was an appointment book split into two separate columns, one labeled 'Front' and the other 'Back', with a scatter of names written in a variety of ink colors in each. At least one thing she knew for certain was what the back column meant. More names were written in the back column than in the front one, which made sense given the shop she stood in. What the different colors meant, she couldn't guess, but one name stood out to her. 'Alman' was written in the back column in red ink. The time listed next to it was…now.

Suddenly, the floor behind the counter opened. A door swung up on up on invisible hinges, reveling a staircase beneath that lead down into pitch black. Out climbed an unfamiliar Witch, followed by none other than Kaida's Kinetic guard.

The Witch gave her a crooked smile full of mustard-yellow gapped teeth that made her want to gag, but she refused to look away. Holding her head high, she looked down her nose at them as the guard took notice of her.

Their eyes locked in a silent challenge. Confidence rolled off him, and a malicious glint in those colorless eyes told everyone around him to think twice before approaching. The way he looked her up and down told her he recognized her from the street, that he knew she was following him and the girls. Prickling, she waited for him to say something about it. To call her out and ask what she thought she was doing. But instead, he walked out of the store without a word.

"Are you looking for something, dear?" The Witch asked, flashing that skin-crawling smile. His words were slow and curious, his fingers twitching with suppressed movement. From the City of Witches, then, and trying to hide it.

Malaina smirked inwardly. This was going to be too easy. He was too curious about her. Too eager. Ready to corrupt an innocent shopper and offer her anything her heart desired. For a price, of course.

In her egg-blue dress, she was innocence at his fingertips, ready to be tainted.

The younger Witch from before returned, arms full of tins, jars, herb bundles, candles, and more.

"She's...she's not here for you." He refused to meet yellow-teeth's eyes, his voice trembling.

Yellow-teeth shrugged, uncaring, and turned back for the secret door behind the counter.

"Actually..." her voice cut through the air, and the two men froze.

Yellow-teeth looked up, another slow smile spreading across his lips as he looked her up and down. Hungry to hear what she had to say he placed his hands on the counter, leaning in closer.

Despite making things up as she went, practice kept her voice steady and sure. Years of role-playing are paying off. "I want something from the back."

"Do you have an appointment?" Yellow-teeth leaned in closer, studying her. She could smell decay on his breath and had to physically stop herself from flinching back.

"No," she stated matter-of-factly, hoping he would be too eager for her business to deny her. Disappointment flashed in his eyes, so before he turned her down, she added, "Malachi sent me."

A sharp intake of breath came from the young Witch beside her, arms still full of sleeping remedies, but she kept her gaze steady on yellow-teeth. He pulled back at the name, looking her up and down with new appreciation. His voice became low and threatening, hand movements turning sharp. "What could he possibly want?"

"He sent me to recruit. Interested?" Cocking an eyebrow at the man, she hoped the offer was too good to turn down.

Contemplating, he drummed his fingers on the counter before jerking his head to the side. A silent breath of relief escaped her, and she made her way around the counter to the secret door.

"Do you still want this stuff for your sister?" The younger Witch asked, eager to please.

Taking her first step down the staircase that would take

her far beneath the shop, she gave the young Witch a gentle smile. "Wrap it up for me, would you? This won't take long."

He nodded resolutely, dropping his gaze from hers, intimidated.

Good, she thought, *he should be.*

Descending the stone stairs, she walked confidently into the dank basement, followed by yellow-teeth, who closed the door behind her. When the hatch thudded closed the passage grew even darker, shrouded in dancing shadows cast by lanterns lining the walls. The air became cooler the further down they went, washing over her in refreshing waves.

The tactic was a clever touch, the darkness meant to intimidate customers, and she reveled in it. Goosebumps rose along her skin as she walked deeper into the shadows, breathing in the darkness.

Yellow-teeth followed her down the stairs until they reached a second door. He took the lead, using a key he'd kept hidden in his sleeve to open it. Beyond it was a room that seemed to stretch on forever, the walls spanning so far she couldn't see the other side through the labyrinth of stalls that filled the cavernous space.

They had descended into a darker version of the market they now walked below. Patched-together wooden stalls lined the aisles, selling goods that would be illegal just feet above their heads.

The people shopping there weren't eager to socialize like the patrons above them. Instead, everyone kept their heads down and eyes focused on the illicit commodities in front of them, whispering as they haggled for goods they couldn't find anywhere else in the city.

Holding her head high, she followed yellow-teeth down aisle after aisle of stalls, turning between seemingly random gaps. Some were wide enough that they could walk side-by-side, others so narrow she had to turn sideways just to fit.

Officially in enemy territory, she couldn't let her guard down for a moment. Few patrons realized the Dark Market was an entire guild of its own, all run by a single person she hoped to never cross paths with. Like a flame in the night, she drew the attention of vendors as she followed her guide through the stalls. She was a bright new toy in a world of dark-seedy dealings, and everyone was eager for their turn to play.

Eventually, yellow-teeth stopped at a stall, the inside obscured by a large piece of fabric hung across the front like a makeshift door. The stall looked like any other aside from the blanket covering the front, but now he was guiding her inside.

Every nerve in her body screamed, urging her not to enter, that she was doing something stupid.

Swallowing her gut instinct, the assassin stepped into the dark stall. She was willingly walking into a dark room, deep inside a rival guild run with no moral standards, cutting herself off from any possible witnesses. Malachi was going to kill her for doing something so impulsive without even giving Sterling the option of joining her for protection. But she'd come this far and had used Malachi's name. Turning back now wasn't an option.

A variety of things filled the jars crammed onto the crooked shelves lining the walls. Some she identified with a glance, others she couldn't even start to guess at the contents. Picking one at random and pulling down a jar, she inspected it from afar before putting it back and wiping the dust from her fingers.

Yellow-teeth secured the blanket back over the entrance and watched her every breath closely.

He crossed his arms, hands clamping into his armpits. "Dangerous game you play, girl. Throwing that name around here like that."

There was a sense of gratification at the way he danced around using Malachi's name now that they were deep in the Dark Market. Ears were everywhere.

"You seem like a smart man. You know what it is he can do for a person."

He tracked her every movement, holding back a sneer. "And what have I done to gain such a man's attention?"

Studying him out of the corner of her eye, she tried to determine how far she could take this ruse. "You're working for the Almans, no?"

Eyes growing dark, he bit the inside of his cheek. He couldn't deny it. Not after being seen with Kaida's guard, but it would be stupid of him to come right out and say it. "And if I am?"

"That's a formidable family. Quite wealthy. A lot of political influence. You have to be satisfactory at what you do for them to come to you instead of to us."

"From what I've heard, I ask fewer questions."

Standing in the center of the stall, she lowered her voice. "Is that your choice or theirs?" She didn't need to clarify who *they* were.

Names were as sacred as gold down in the dank depths beneath the city. Asking yellow-teeth's name hadn't been worth it because he wouldn't have given it to her anyway. But there was an overarching *they* everyone knew. Who everyone feared.

The person who ran the Dark Market.

Pulling his bottom lip between his teeth, his foot started to tap. Pride swelled in Malaina's chest. She'd hit a sore spot. He was eager to get out from beneath *their* thumb, even if he didn't want to show it.

Letting him stew on her question she wandered deeper into the stall. Further into the shadows. Yellow-teeth's eyes never left her as she did, but he didn't stop her, too eager to pass her inspection.

The shelves were dusty, but she noticed certain jars full of various herbs, flowers, and other things she couldn't even guess at, were more recently used than others. The dust beneath them recently disturbed.

Kaida's guard hadn't been down there long enough for yellow-teeth to have made whatever it was he sold on the spot, so he had probably made it shortly before. Fresh enough to be potent but ready for a quick hand-off.

Unfortunately, her knowledge of herbs wasn't extensive enough to identify all of them at a glance or know what they would do when combined. Even if she tried to guess what was made from the recently used jars, there were hundreds of ways a talented Witch could mix them for hundreds of different results. Depending on the amounts and what spells were cast as they were mixed, the concoction could be anything.

She took note of which jars had been used anyway so she could report back to Jade later.

Only another Witch could begin to guess what was made based on an ingredients list alone.

"What's he offering?" Yellow-teeth sneered, so quiet she almost didn't hear him.

"Not so fast. We have some questions first." She let her smile leak into her words, just to make them grate a little more. He grunted, and she continued her slow stride around the stall. "What are you making for the Almans?"

A disdainful smile curled his lips. "Confidential," he bit out.

She chuckled condescendingly. "Oh, please. You and I both know that's bullshit."

"And what would you know of this business? What do you do for him?" He was deflecting by turning the conversation around on her. Clever.

An offhanded flick of her fingers dismissed him as she approached the workbench in the corner. "That's unimportant."

The meticulously organized desk was surprising, given the state of the rest of the stall, but it wasn't unusual for Witches to be picky about their workspace. An old, well-worn book sat on the bench, with various things sticking out from the pages.

Reaching out, she lifted the pages, letting them cascade from her fingers. A folded corner marked a page, catching her attention. She paused on the page, scanning it, taking in the name, list of ingredients, and markings on the page, before yellow-teeth jumped up and snatched the book from her.

"I would think *his* recruiters would know better than to go through a Witch's personal tome." The Witch's lips curled further, practically bearing those rotted teeth of his. He clutched the book close to his chest. A single hand shot silent but scared signs at her. He was a cornered mouse, snapping in its best attempt at intimidation, and she was the cat.

Despite being the same height, she looked down her nose at him. Clutching that book, he looked small, his beady eyes wild. He was used to being in control, and her dominance of the interaction had him on edge. A man like this was used to being the one doing the intimidating, using his various little tricks to gain the upper hand, and she was getting to him.

Another amused smile pushed him further over the edge, and his entire demeanor darkened. She was laughing at his discomfort, jabbing at his pride, and he wasn't going to stand for it much longer. She half expected the Witch to start biting at her.

"I think I have everything I need." She brushed past him and towards the entrance of the stall. Her fingers wrapped around the blanket, ready to push it aside, when he gave her pause.

"Be careful on your way back, girl. Not everyone in the Dark Market is as accommodating as me." He gave her a sly smile, trying to gain leverage through fear, but a predatory grin of her own answered him.

"I appreciate your concern, but I'm not worried. I'm the scariest thing down here." Not bothering to grant him another moment of her attention, she walked out of his stall and started towards the exit.

TWELVE

Stepping back into the overbearing daylight of the street after the lantern-lit cavern of the Dark Market felt like walking into a completely other world, and the night-loving assassin had to shield her eyes from the blinding sun. The growing heat of the day shoved itself down Malaina's throat, choking out what remained of the cool underground air she'd just left. Swallowing down her discomfort and dread of the coming summer, she schooled her features into something relatively pleasant and headed down the street.

On her arm swung a bulging cloth bag, all the sleeping remedies a person could ever hope for filling it to the brim. The man behind the counter, who had gathered all the products for her, insisted on giving her the entire bag for free. Apparently, name-dropping the infamous guild master in the City of Elementals was a more effective intimidation tactic than she'd expected. She'd left him a tip the equivalent of the total, anyway. Walking out before he counted it and gave it back, she hoped it would be enough to keep his mouth shut about her mention of Malachi's name.

Malaina scanned the crowd for Sterling and wasn't surprised when she didn't find him. While she had been occupied, he had probably followed the girls and their guards. Eventually, she found the Shifter on a street corner, where a side street met the business district's main drag.

Sidling up next to him, she saw what he was watching when he wrinkled his nose at her bulging bag.

"What did you do? Rob the place?" Taking the bag from her, he weighed it in his hand before holding it down by his side.

Cocking her hip to the side with enough exaggeration her skirts ripped around her ankles, she crossed her arms. "Oh please, I'm not Ra and Layshan." He arched an eyebrow at her, and she rolled her eyes. "Fine, I name-dropped and got all this for free. But on the bright side, we can put the entire guild to sleep for the next month."

He snorted, shaking his head. "They're in the dress shop over there." He swung her bag at a storefront across the way. "From the looks of it, they'll be in there a while."

Standing on her tiptoes, she peered between people and found the guard dogs lying on either side of the door. They monitored the shoppers with heads pivoting in unison, but the guards themselves were inside.

Sterling leaned in close, whispering in her ear. "Did you learn anything?"

Trying to look like a woman in love rather than a conspirator, she stepped into his side. His arm wrapped around her waist, pulling her close without a lick of actual passion, used to this ruse.

She whispered back, "Yeah, I got it. Which is good because Kaida's guard is getting suspicious of me."

She told him what had happened, keeping her words vague so as to avoid any passersby catching on to what she was talking about.

"So? What is it?"

"It's a power suppressant," she hissed.

Power suppressants were illegal throughout Thaumoria because of their ability to dull or even eliminate a person's magic.

His unnervingly monotonous eyes narrowed, whipping his head around to look at her. "A power suppressant? Why?"

She shrugged. "I don't know. But it was weird. I'm no Witch, but the ingredients seemed off."

"Like they were rotten?"

She shook her head. "Like the recipe should have made something else entirely."

His head bobbed back, disbelieving. "Must be a different recipe than Jade taught us."

"Maybe," she muttered doubtfully.

They stayed on the street corner for a while longer, watching the dress shop. Sterling's eye color may have stayed consistent, but his pupils shifted subtly to something more animal-like, giving him far superior vision compared to hers.

Despite not having the vision of a cat, she still got an idea of what was happening.

Kaida twirled on a pedestal in front of a curved wall of mirrors, giving her a view of every possible angle of the gown she tried on. Sitting on a bench nearby, flanked by their guards, sat Nyda. Poised and demure, she regarded her sister intently. Ankles crossed, her hands rested in her lap, and a pleasant smile softened her face.

Malaina couldn't tell from so far away, but something seemed off about that smile. Like it didn't quite reach her eyes, a soft mask for the sake of everyone else. Not like Nyda didn't enjoy being out and about with her older sister, but like they were living in two separate worlds. Kaida's, whose world was easy and carefree, filled with decisions like dress colors, and Nyda's, surrounded by a wall built to keep her sister at arm's length.

Cooing over the stunning Water Wielder on the pedestal, a team of seamstresses nodded approvingly at every minor adjustment of the dress and sway of her hips. One of the seamstresses, in particular, stood out, occasionally reaching over and brushing a hand over the fabric. With each pass of her fingers, the color of the fabric would change from one shade of purple to another.

Malaina gasped at the sight, fingers finding her parted lips as her heart started to race.

A Shifter. Working in the open.

Her chest swelled seeing how relaxed the Shifter looked.

Changing the gown from one color to the next, she smiled wide, occasionally giggling at something Kaida said. The Shifter obviously loved her job, gushing over her latest client as she played with the fabric.

The Shifter giggled amid the other seamstresses, who all looked to her for direction. She knew what she was made to do, and she seemed to love every minute of it.

For a moment, something like jealousy hardened in Malaina's stomach, and she had to turn away. Every time she saw someone fitting into their life like a perfectly carved puzzle piece, a part of her resented them on principle. She couldn't hate the Shifter for loving her life and her job, for getting the chance to be wholly herself, but she could envy her for it.

Sterling prickled beneath her touch and lowered his voice to a near growl. "City guards."

Lost in her thoughts she hadn't noticed the three city guards who stopped outside the dress shop. They observed the group inside as they talked between themselves. Two of the guards broke off, turning down the alley next to the shop, and the third went inside.

Sterling straightened, his pupils becoming mere slits and more cat-like. They narrowed as the guard inside talked to the seamstresses, trying to read their lips and follow the conversation. Malaina couldn't see anyone in the shop clearly enough to read their lips, but from the way they all turned to watch the Shifter in unison, she had a pretty good idea of what was happening.

Sterling took a step forward, muscles tensing like a cat readying to pounce. Malaina put a hand on his arm, reminding him where they were and why they were there.

"Don't," she warned.

"He's asking them all for proof of registration, knowing

she doesn't have any." His jaw clenched and unclenched as he physically held himself in place.

The city guard waved a hand towards a door that led to the connecting alley. The Shifter's eyes widened, gaze darting from one co-worker to the next in the search for allies, but none of them would meet her eyes. They all watched their guiltily shifting feet and fidgeting fingers, anywhere but the Shifter who truly needed them. Frantically, she turned to the Alman sisters, desperate for support.

Kaida placed a hand on the Shifter's shoulder as if trying to calm her, and Nyda went to stand. For a heartbeat, Malaina thought the sisters might do it. Despite being young, they might actually use their status among the Elemental's elite to stand by the Shifter's side and lend her help.

But a gentle Anima hand landed on the young Water Wielder's shoulder, keeping her in her seat. Keeping her from interfering.

The elder of the sisters faced the city guard, looking for all the world like she was about to start negotiating a contract, when her Kinetic guard stepped forward, stopping her with a shake of his head.

The Shifter's face turned from desperate to terrified when Kaida's shoulders slouched, her resignation stripping away the seamstress's last hope for help.

The city guard held out a hand, ushering the Shifter out the door and towards the alley. The sisters watched the Shifter go, hands clutched to their chests in identical expressions of pity.

"They don't know there are more guards out in the alley," Sterling growled, "They're going ambush her."

Tearing from her grip, he barreled through the crowded street. People jumped back to keep from being crushed by his large frame.

Malaina jogged to keep up, only catching him when he was already across the street and turning the corner down the alley. Knowing he wouldn't plow her of all people over, she jumped in front of him. She tried to ignore the way people watched them, hoping they looked more like a couple in the middle of an argument than co-workers about to step in where they didn't belong.

"There's nothing we can do." She hissed, trying to make him look at her, ducking and weaving to catch his eye. "You make a scene now, and we'll draw the attention of everyone on the street. Look around," she snapped, "You've already got eyes on you."

He did, and instantly his shoulders started to sag, eyes softening back into human form. A debate warred behind those half-human eyes as he weighed his options, trying to decide if it would be worth blowing the entire job to step in on a fellow Shifter's behalf. His semi-feline eyes locked on hers, already more human than the beast in their melancholy.

Ready to lead him away from the dress shop, she thought she had him when a muffled scream came from the alley. Malaina's spine went ramrod straight, every hair on her body standing on end.

Sterling surged around the corner, his muscles already rippling, preparing for a full body shift.

Malaina followed him, grabbing his arm and trying to pull him back.

"Stop!" The plea came out louder than she meant it to, echoing off the stone walls of the businesses around them.

Sterling froze, the attention of all three city guards snapping at them. In-human growls vibrated his entire body, emanating from deep in his chest.

Fingers digging into the hardened muscles of his arm, Malaina swallowed hard as she took in the scene before them.

One city guard had the seamstress slung over his shoulder, unconsciousness causing her head to loll. A second guard shook his hand as though to release the tension as a drop of blood fell from the unconscious Shifter's nose.

For a long moment, the five of them stood in tense silence. One of the guards finally spoke up, in a voice accustomed to being obeyed, "This is official city business. Head back to your shopping, there's nothing to see here."

The other two guards turned, heading the opposite way down the open alley towards a metal box the size of a small room built onto the back of a large motor car. One opened the back, and the other tossed the Shifter inside, her limp limbs landing with a resounding *thunk* as she hit the metal floor.

Sterling surged forward, nearly ripping out of her grip. "What the hell are you doing?"

Malaina dug her fingers into his arm to keep her hold, yanking to get his attention, but she would never be strong enough to stop him.

"We need to go. Now!" she pled.

The remaining guard smirked at them, an evil-knowing glint in his eyes. "Proof of registration?"

Sterling froze, his muscles tensing so hard he became a living statue beside her.

Panic gripped Malaina's chest, making it hard to breathe as her heart raced. Neither of them was allowed to obtain real registration cards, and they hadn't had time to get fake ones from the guild forgers.

The guard took a threatening step forward, and this time, Sterling took a step back and used one massive arm to push Malaina behind his shoulder.

The guard's smirk grew darker at their fear. He planted his feet, raising his hands into the air. With a flick of his wrist, a wall of rock rose between them, blocking Malaina and Sterling from the rest of the alley.

The sound of the motor car coming to life echoed off the stone walls and started to fade.

Ready to bolt, Malaina turned and found a familiar dog standing guard where the alley met the street. A crowd was forming behind the dog, its hackles standing on end. The canine sank lower to the ground, growling, vicious eyes locked on her. It wasn't attacking, but she wasn't going to stick around long enough for that to change.

"Sterling," she whispered, the sour taste of fear coating her tongue. "We need to run. Now." Tugging on his sleeve, she pulled him towards the wall the guard had created.

With a predator's grace, Sterling turned and recognized the dog's long snout and pointed ears. Nyda's guard's dog.

The Shifter's muscles rippled instinctively, preparing to

shift into a form several times larger and scarier than the dog before them, but Malaina dug her nails into his arm.

He couldn't shift. Not now. Not in front of all those people watching as if their imminent attack were a street performance there for amusement.

"To the wall." He pushed her further down the alley, never putting his back to the dog and refusing to break eye contact with the snarling canine stalking closer.

When they came to the rock wall erected by the Earth Wielder guard, Sterling wrapped his large hands around her waist and tossed her straight into the air.

Using her elbows to catch herself at the top, Malaina pulled herself up and over the wall, the rough edge of broken concrete and brick scraped against her stomach.

When she started on her way down, Sterling jumped. His fingertips gripped the wall, and he hauled himself over to join her without a hint of strain. Together, they fell to the ground on the other side, landing on their feet.

Thankfully, the motor car was long gone, leaving behind a mostly empty street where no one noticed their escape. Or, if they did, they were smart enough to glance the other way immediately.

Malaina intertwined her long, scarred fingers between Sterling's, clutching his hand tight and pulling him towards the street.

Once she'd put a decent distance between them and the alley, they slowed to a casual walk, catching their breath.

"Have you completely lost your mind?" She seethed, whirling on him.

Sterling stopped. Still clutching her hand tight, she spun

them so that his back was to the street of passing people and hers was to the building, his looming form hiding her from view. "Did you not just witness the same thing I did? What they did to that Shifter?"

"Of course I did," she snapped back, "But there was nothing we could do. You nearly got us killed."

"They took her because she hadn't registered citizenship in a city where she isn't legally allowed to register. A registration that isn't even supposed to exist. And *I'm* the one who's lost my mind? *I'm* the one in the wrong?" He dropped her hand and started pacing back and forth before her, running large hands over his face until they entwined in his black hair.

Thankfully, this street was far emptier than the one they had fled. No one paid close attention to them, and the ones who did glance their way averted their gaze, refusing to get involved.

Watching the various shoppers, she let him pace it out, blowing off steam the best way he could in such a busy part of the city.

Lacing tanned fingers behind his head, his elbows spread like wings so that his broad chest could puff out. "Dear Aais, this is wrong. All of this is so fucked up. The cities aren't supposed to be like this."

"I know. But what are you going to do? Take on the entire city guard one by one?" By the Gods and Goddesses, she hoped he wasn't planning to do that.

"No. I don't know. I just…" He let out a frustrated bark, dropping his hands to his sides and letting them swing while he paced.

Having let out enough of his frustrations, the Shifter looked around them, noticing how people moved to the opposite side of the street to avoid the raging mountain of a man. He pressed his lips together into a tight line, turning his face to the ground, and stepped closer to her, letting out a long breath. "I'm sorry. I lost it."

"It's fine," she mumbled, running a hand over his shoulder, guiding him further down the empty side street and away from the busy business district. She hooked her arm through his and leaned her head against his bicep. "We got what we came for. Let's get back to our room and make a plan for tonight. Get this contract over with."

They walked in silence for a while until he shook his head for the dozenth time. "None of this is going to end with this contract. It won't change anything that's happening. Things are only going to get worse."

She hung her head resolutely, watching her feet poke out from beneath the swaying hem of her skirts. "I know, but it's something to focus on. Something we can control."

THE SILVER-EYED ASSASSIN lounged on the bed she and Sterling had been sharing for the past two weeks while they staked out the Alman house. The room was far more comfortable than their usual stake-out locations, and she was soaking in every moment of it, though she was itching to be back home. To Lybbi and Serena.

They owed this rare comfort to a horrible widow who

never had reason to enter her guest bedroom, which happened to have a window overlooking the Alman house. And more importantly, Nyda's bedroom.

Sterling sat in a rocking chair, feet kicked up on the nightstand. Behind him, the sun started to set over the city.

They had already changed into their work clothes, both dressed in black. Malaina's hair was tied back in a messy tail, ready to be tucked into her hood. The Shifter's magic had long since worn off, leaving it its usual silver.

Sterling picked at the hem of his shirt, a singular claw poking through a small hole in the fabric.

"Would you stop that?" She scolded him, sounding more like his mother than his partner, "You're going to make it worse."

"Hm," he grunted, "I was thinking. We haven't heard from Syn yet."

"We've been working. We'll probably hear something when we get home." Sliding a whetstone over the blade of her knife, she reveled in the sound of metal sharpening. The resonance made her skin shiver, and she rolled her shoulders, letting the familiar ritual relax her.

As the city grew darker, they sat in comfortable silence, waiting for ten o'clock to roll around. Malaina moved on to another knife, working her way through the set. The ritual of preparing put her mind at ease, even though she wouldn't need the blades for tonight.

"I've also been thinking about Lybbi," Sterling stated, seemingly out of nowhere, lost in thought.

"Oh, what about her?" she asked, continuing to stroke

her stone over the blade of her dagger, occasionally examining it in the light of dusk.

Sterling didn't look at her. "With everything going on, she needs to be trained. If not for the safety of others, then for hers."

Malaina's hand froze mid-stroke. Her eyes slid to his, her knuckles whitening as she gripped the stone tighter. Tension started to thicken the air when she didn't say anything.

"With the way things are, if she's going to be out in public she needs to be able to keep herself and others safe." He continued, unfazed by her deathly stare.

"No." It wasn't a question or up for debate. The Shadow Spinner wouldn't even consider the thought.

"If they are abducting people in broad daylight like that, she'll be at risk every time we take her out. Imagine what would have happened if she had been there. If she had seen that happening."

"We'll keep her safe," she snapped, her hands unnervingly still. "We'll get fake cards. She won't leave the guild unless one of us is with her. We can make it work."

"Just like we kept that Shifter safe?"

Malaina's jaw clenched so hard she wasn't sure she could have answered if she wanted to. Her teeth ground together as she refused to acknowledge his point. The accusation hit hard.

He let her stew in her own thoughts until her skin started to itch.

Jumping up from the bed, she started rocking back and forth on her feet, ripping her hair from its ponytail, shaking it out, and redoing it. She needed to move, do something to not think about the reality that was looming so close. Nearly unavoidable.

"You're pacing," he pointed out off-handedly.

She rolled her eyes, as if she hadn't noticed.

"You started this," she grumbled, "Why did you have to bring that up now?"

"Because you can't run away from me here."

"We spend every Gods and Goddesses forsaken moment together. I can't exactly get away from you any other time either."

"Yes," he said, "We live together in a giant guild where you can avoid the conversation by walking away and finding anywhere else to be. Because as long as there's another person around, you don't have to talk about it. Just because you use your secrets to your advantage doesn't mean they can't also be used against you." She wanted to hate him for how nonchalantly he threw those words at her, at the way he just stared out the window as he said them. As if the reality didn't shred her to pieces every day.

Out of spite, she debated throwing something at him and opted to stick her tongue out instead. It was quieter.

How well he knew her was truly obnoxious.

He ignored her. "You can't keep her locked up, and she needs to be able to protect herself in case she draws the attention of a guard. Not to mention the fact that she has no idea how to control her magic, and soon she won't be able to at all. You and I both know that unused magic builds up and eventually, it will force itself out at the worst possible moment. Like for example, when we are out on the street, and she sees the city guard abduct an innocent citizen."

He was right. Considering it hadn't had an outlet in almost nine years, it was a borderline miracle Lybbi's magic hadn't become a problem yet. But Malaina couldn't bring herself to accept the reality of what Lybbi's training meant.

Training would mean Lybbi's magic was real. If she trained, neither of them could pretend like it wasn't there anymore, and that was how they had gotten by for many years now. Some days, it felt like pretending was the only way Malaina could even breathe.

Once Lybbi started training and getting older, Malaina had to accept that she had to start working. Something Malaina wouldn't even consider. She knew what Malachi would want her to do…what it would take to prepare her to do it.

The Shadow Spinner wouldn't think about it. She couldn't. It would unlock every dark memory and painful thought she'd ever had.

Instead, she deflected.

"Seems awfully hypocritical for someone to care so much about an innocent citizen when they're about to go kill a fifteen-year-old girl for money." She spat the words.

When Sterling's entire body stiffened, his eyes growing darker by the second, she knew her words hit their mark.

He clenched and unclenched his jaw, turning her words over in his mind, carefully thinking through his reaction.

"Don't do that," he ground out. "Don't attack me just because you're scared."

She wasn't playing fair, and she knew it.

Sterling had never killed anyone for money, it was always her. When Malachi partnered them together, it had been Sterling's one stipulation. He would be an assassin's partner, but he would never be the one to take a life unless it was necessary to keep her safe. Sterling wasn't an assassin. Only Malaina was unfortunate enough to hold that title.

Not many people realized it, but the Shifter's actual job was to be the assassin's personal bodyguard. Not unlike Nyda and Kaida and their guards. He would kill to protect her, to protect Lybbi, but he would never, under any circumstances, be the one to push that plunger and kill for money.

Ripping at her hair again, Malaina bit her lip and redid it.

"Oh, come here," Sterling sighed, dropping his feet from the nightstand and waving a hand at her, eyes lightening in color as he calmed. Stomping like a moping child called to dinner, she sat between his legs, her back to him.

"You're going to tear out all of your hair if you keep doing that." Gently, he removed the strap that held her hair and used his fingers to brush it out. He worked out the knots caused by her repeated tearing, skimming his fingers against her scalp in a tender massage. He started to braid a section of her hair by her left temple, weaving it back from her face in a familiar rhythm.

Sighing, she let her own anger slip through her fingers in her lap.

"I'm sorry," she whispered.

"You're like a cornered dog, sometimes. Biting to keep

people from helping you, even when it's for your own good."

She snorted. "You're one to talk."

She'd asked him once where he had learned to braid hair, able to weave her silver locks into all sorts of complicated patterns she could never replicate. As though his fingers weren't thicker than two of hers combined, moving deftly while he worked.

"My Moms taught me when I was young. I've always had long unruly hair, and one of them had a gift for dealing with it. She'd told me that just because I was a boy didn't mean I could slack on personal hygiene," he'd told her.

Now, in the growing darkness, she thought about his past and the warmth that always filled his voice when he talked about home. Ever since she'd met him, she had envied it, and now more than ever, she wanted to live vicariously through his memories.

"Did you ever want siblings growing up?" She asked him.

He finished the braid he was working on and started on the other side. "Not really. The City of Shifters is very social, so I grew up close to all the kids on my street and at the temple. I was never a lonely only child."

"What was it like," she teased, "growing up as a temple boy?"

He chuckled. "That is not what it's called."

Her own smile spread across her face at her own bad joke.

Growing up in a Fire Wielder home she'd attended services at the Temple of Elosyn. Rarely, of course, because if she screwed up and let her fragile hold on her magic slip, people would know she was a Shadow Spinner.

Her parents were in good standing among the community, though, and needed to keep up appearances. So, a few times a year they all dressed up and attended the important holidays.

On the longest day of the year (her *least* favorite day of the year), every Fire Wielder would dress in their nicest clothes and pack into the Temple of Elosyn at midday, when the sun approached its highest point.

The temple was an open, outdoor half-circle amphitheater surrounded by connected pillars, giving the impression of an enclosed building despite its lack of ceiling or walls. All the seats faced a larger-than-life statue carved in the likeness of the Goddess.

They would all sing and pray, thanking her for the gifts she'd blessed them with.

Then came Malaina's least favorite part.

The priestess lit a candle using her own fire, and one by one, each of the Fire Wielders took a portion of the flame, holding it in their hands until it passed to all who were capable of taking their share.

The ritual sounded beautiful in theory, but all Malaina remembered was how bright it was—blindingly so. She would cry for hours leading up to it, dreading the way the flames would scare away her shadows, the way the sun would sit directly overhead, leaving her without a speck of darkness to lean on. Attending services with her parents left her with no positive memories; she couldn't fathom how people did it on a regular basis for the rest of their lives.

So when she'd met Sterling and learned Shifters were quite spiritual, visiting the temple for any number of reasons, even having a personal relationship with the High Sage who led their city, she had been skeptical. Malaina simply couldn't understand how someone found the practice not only enjoyable but soothing.

Only recently had she approached the subject openly, having avoided it for years.

"Well?" She prompted.

"I loved growing up as part of the temple. It was like growing up with a second family. Every morning and night, I would be home with my Moms, who spoiled me to no end, and then during the day, I had another family who would teach me about what it meant to be a Shifter. Learning how to use my magic and what Aais intended for me to do with it. The temple in the City of Shifters…it's nothing like the temples here. It's always open to everyone, and for many, it becomes a second home."

She had to admit, it sounded wonderful.

For a moment, jealousy burned in her chest, knowing how loved he was growing up. And how unloved she had been. But she pushed the feeling down far within her, burying it deep.

Instead, she closed her eyes and imagined she had grown up that way—in a house where she had been seen as someone to spoil rather than something to hide, in a community that believed she was a blessing and welcomed her with open arms.

The closest thing she'd ever felt to that was the guild. But even there, she spent nearly every moment pretending to be something she wasn't. Pretending to be the infamous Death Bringer instead of the Shadow Spinner she actually was. The citizens of the city feared her and told bedtime stories about her to scare children. The members of the guild who didn't know her revered her, looking at her like she was something separate from them.

Few saw who she really *was* and loved her for it anyway.

"Was it your Moms who got you involved at the temple?"

He finished her second braid and brought the two together, weaving all her hair into one thick rope down her back.

"No, actually. They attended casually, like most people. But I chose to become a member after what the High Sage did for me." He finished her braid, tying it off at the end. She glanced back over her shoulder and saw rose-pink swirling amid nostalgic heather in his eyes.

"What did the High Sage do for you?" Malaina thought she knew almost everything about Sterling's past, but in her avoidance of this particular subject, there must have been something he never told her.

He looked down at her thoughtfully. "They changed my life, they changed...*me.* They saw me for who I really was and helped me become the person I was meant to be."

Unsure what he meant by that, she was about to ask more when a movement from across the street caught her attention.

Nyda was sitting on the side of her bed, studying her

fidgeting hands in her lap, her sleeveless nightgown hanging down to her ankles.

The Anima guard entered, the dogs trailing at his heels, heads bowed low. One of them jumped up on the bed and lay by the young Water Wielder's side, and the other lay its head on her lap, waiting for attention. She petted both the dogs' heads, scratching between their ears, then leaned down to kiss one on its nose.

"Is…is she…crying?" Malaina asked, watching Nyda shower the two dogs with love. Her guard solemnly stood by the door, hands shoved deep in his pockets, pitch eyes glued to the ground.

Sterling's eyes shifted and watched Nyda's every movement with the attention of an alpha wolf watching the pack's pups. He nodded, brows furrowing.

Neither Nyda nor the guard said anything while she petted the dogs. With one last shaking breath, she whipped at her eyes and nodded to her guard.

He handed over the vial of milky elixir right on time.

She inspected it before downing it like a shot of liquor and handing it back the empty glass.

He considered her slumped form for a long time, and when she noticed him studying her with sad eyes, she straightened. She was trying to look strong, the facade was clearly for show, but he didn't seem convinced.

The Anima gave the young Water Wielder a sad smile and slipped the vial into a jacket pocket. He turned to leave the room, the dogs trailing at his heels, their heads and tails hung low. The guard lingered in the doorway a moment more before giving Nyda a slight bow and closing the door.

Tears continued to slide down Nyda's pink cheeks, but she didn't seem to notice them. She slipped beneath the covers of her bed and laid down on her back, hands clasped over her chest, blue-black hair spilling over her pillow like ink pooling around her head.

The young Alman sister could have been preparing for her own funeral, she laid so still.

Malaina and Sterling watched in silence until they were sure she had to be asleep.

Malaina shook her head, a rock settling in the pit of her knotted stomach. "This doesn't feel right. Something's wrong."

Sterling let out a frustrated sigh through his nose. "We have no reason to believe this won't go smoothly. Let's just get this over with."

THIRTEEN

They waited several more hours until the Anima guard began nodding off and Nyda had fallen into a deep sleep. They didn't worry about getting in and out of the room without notice since the Water Wielder left her window open despite the still crisp nights of lingering spring.

Her hood drawn up over her hair and her face covering pulled high, Malaina stood beside the bed studying Nyda's sleep.

Usually, Malaina wasn't bothered by her job. So many of her targets were truly terrible people who did truly horrible things. Usually, watching those terrible people do those horrible things was the hardest part of it all. Unable to interfere in any way until ready to kill, tore Malaina's soul to shreds. But every once in a while, she got contracts like this… Ones targeting wholly innocent people, unaware of what was about to happen to them, or why.

Nyda didn't seem aware of what was happening between the Alman and Desroc houses, yet she had been caught in the middle of it. She was a blameless bystander, no more than a sacrificial pawn over a few stolen coins, and her worth was decided by someone who didn't even know her.

Malaina saw so much of herself in Nyda. Whether younger or older, it never seemed to fail that one sister looked out for the other. Nyda had let her sister have the world while she sat back and faded into the background.

Sterling perched in bird form on the window sill, back to the room, standing watch. On jobs like this, he didn't like to be in the room; he didn't want to see what was about to happen.

The assassin didn't blame him.

For the first time, she studied Nyda's face up close, memorizing the curve of her cheek and the bow of her lips. The Alman girls had piercing blue eyes, but Malaina wondered what it would be like to see them up close, to watch them brighten when Nyda laughed surrounded by friends.

Malaina couldn't put it off any longer.

Resigning herself to reality, she pulled the syringe and vial from their hiding place. Her fingers hesitated at the half-full mark, and she looked over at Nyda again.

For fifteen, Nyda wasn't very big, and with the power suppressant flowing through her veins, she would be weaker than normal, especially after taking it so many nights in a row. One glance at Nyda's peacefully sleeping face was all it took for the assassin to pull the plunger all the way back and fill the syringe to the brim.

Sometimes, when she wanted the person to suffer a little longer, she wouldn't pull the full dose. The question was never if the poison would work. Made by Jade to recreate the effects of Death Bringer's magic, it always did the job. The question was how long it would take. How much it would hurt.

It was the only part of her job that Malaina could control: how much her targets suffered.

Tonight...she wanted it to be a quick hit that caused little to no suffering. She wanted this to be peaceful.

Kneeling, she gently took Nyda's arm and rolled it to the side, the inside of her elbow exposed. Her nearly transparent skin made it easy to find the vein Malaina was looking for. Piercing the skin, the assassin pushed the plunger to its max in the span of a breath. Squirreling away the syringe, she backed towards the window. Waiting, she had to make sure it took, but she wasn't worried.

Sterling chirped at her, telling her she needed to hurry. One foot propped up on the window sill, she readied herself to scale the building and flee into the night the moment Nyda took her last breath.

Then Nyda gasped.

Blue eyes flew open. Small hands frantically clutched at the Water Wielder's chest, then her throat.

"Shit." Malaina darted back to the bed.

Nyda scrambled to try and sit up, fighting for air as her organs started to shut down. Malaina held Nyda's down by the shoulders, keeping her small hands from scrambling about the sheets, clutching at everything within reach. Her wide, terrified blue eyes bore into Malaina's. A million questions passed through those ocean eyes, searching the assassin's face for answers as she fought to hold onto her young life.

Please die, Malaina silently begged her, *please just let go and die.*

Sterling appeared at Malaina's side, shifting back into human form and taking over holding Nyda down. A new wave of panic overtook Nyda's body at the sight of a colossal man pinning her to the mattress. Her wheezes grew louder, trying to force air into her lungs and use everything she had to cry out for help.

Once her hands were free, Malaina reached for another vial. She didn't bother to switch needles on her syringe as she pulled another double dose of Jade's poison. But her fingers were starting to shake, struggling to keep calm.

This wasn't supposed to happen.

It shouldn't be possible.

She'd already given Nyda twice the necessary amount. The overdose should have killed her instantly.

Sterling pinned one of Nyda's flailing arms to the bed, and Malaina jammed the needle into the crook of her elbow. Pushing the plunger quickly before tearing the needle back out.

The syringe slipped back into its pocket as the door to the bedroom flew open. The dogs flew into the room, leaping through the air, teeth bared in frothing snarls.

In the blink of an eye, Sterling pushed off the bed, shifting mid-air. He met the dogs in wolf form, double the size of either of them. His jaw clamped around the throat of one, and with a wicked whip of his head, he threw the dog against the wall. The sound of its bones cracking could barely be heard over the nightmare-inducing growls emanating from Sterling and the remaining dog.

Malaina stayed by Nyda's side, willing her to die like she was supposed to, but for the love of the Gods, the girl wouldn't. Seizing, the young girl's eyes rolled back in her head. Her body violently convulsed in response to the poison coursing through her veins, utilizing every fiber of her soul to hold on to life.

Malaina didn't know what to do. Her fingers itched to pull one of her knives and finish the job. With or without a weapon, there were a hundred ways for her to take a person's life in the blink of an eye. But she couldn't use a single one of them on a target. Her clients paid for a Death Bringer who could kill without a trace. If she slit Nyda's throat it would reveal her for the fraud she was.

No, Nyda needed to die from the poison. It needed to look like she died from her organs shutting down on their own.

Her death needed to look like magic.

But Malaina didn't have time to come up with a solution. Nyda's guard bolted through the door, dodging Sterling and the dogs, still in battle. The Anima missed a swipe of Sterling's giant paw by a hair's breadth, veering around it and barreling head-on for Malaina.

He lunged for her, but his movements were predictable. Malaina sidestepped at the last second, turning into him so he shot past her. Before he could react she stepped behind him, shoving the blade of her foot into the back of his knee and pulling on his shoulders. The joint gave a satisfying pop, dislocating itself around her foot. He fell to the ground, yelping in pain, and she hoped that would be the end of it.

She whistled two sharp, urgent notes, trying to get Sterling back to the window.

In the assassin's moment of distraction, the guard turned, tackling her at the waist and sending them both to the floor. He crawled on top of her, calves glued to either side of her waist, pulling back his arm to throw a punch. She registered the tell with a heartbeat to spare, turning her head in time for his fist to connect with the ground, sending all his weight forward. Anchoring a hand against his shoulder, she used her smaller size to her advantage, pushing her hips out from under him and freeing her legs. Fingers digging into her hood, he grabbed the back of her head, tearing at her hair to keep her pinned to the ground.

"Don't move," he commanded, as though she might actually comply. The Anima had been well trained, and if brute strength was all that mattered, he'd have the clear upper hand. Unfortunately for him, though, Malaina had been trained better.

She turned into him, wrapping her arms around his and pulling her body up. Throwing a leg over his shoulders, she hooked a knee behind his neck, interlocking her ankles. The guard's fingers started to loosen in her hair as she squeezed tighter, cutting off his oxygen and forcing him to the ground.

Trying to free his throat, he grabbed at her legs,

yanking to pry them apart to no avail. She continued to wrench on his arm, twisting it back until something popped and cracked.

The guard let more of his precious oxygen escape, trying to scream, and soon, he went limp in her grip.

Panting on her hands and knees, Malaina was tempted to leave him like that, unconscious but not dead. But all too soon, he'd wake up and ruin everything. If he started telling everyone that the legendary Death Bringer had choked him out instead of killing him with a simple touch, she would lose everything she'd worked so hard for.

The assassin didn't let herself think through what she was about to do. She moved on instinct and pure self-preservation.

A finger to the Anima's thick neck made it easy to find a vein, bulging from his recent exertion and lack of air. She pulled out a needle, clean or dirty, she didn't know or care. Instead of finding her last dose of poison, air filled the syringe when she pulled the plunger back. The needle pierced the vein, and she forced the air into his bloodstream. That would lead to an instant heart attack, and that was all she needed.

Malaina gathered herself, pocketing the empty syringe, and scrambled to her feet. She pushed the guard's body away and felt the lump in his jacket push into her hand.

The vial.

In her haste, she didn't stop to consider her next actions, but the vial felt important. Something whispered that it hadn't been filled with a power suppressant.

Opening the guard's jacket, she took the vial and slipped it into one of her many pockets.

Nyda lay mercifully still on the bed, empty blue eyes staring through the ceiling.

Behind her, Sterling whipped his canine head, breaking the neck of the remaining dog. He sprinted for her, but not before she saw who stood in the doorway.

Kaida's guard.

The Kinetic's colorless eyes surveyed Malaina closely, and she realized her face covering and hood had fallen during her struggle. Every instinct in her body fought to call her shadows to hide her, but it was too late now. The look on his face made it clear he recognized her, whether from the apothecary or the streets; it didn't matter. She readied herself to fight, but he didn't advance into the room. He simply stood there, taking in the chaos before him.

When Sterling passed her she reached out and grabbed his fur, swinging onto his back the way she had a thousand times before, moving on muscle memory alone.

As a wolf, the Shifter barely fit through the window, jumping head first. They fell from the third-story window, and Sterling shifted again midair.

Malaina hung on for dear life, arms wrapped around his neck as he became a massive ape-like creature whose thick fingers caught a ledge, using their momentum to swing and switch directions. Suddenly, they were no longer falling. Instead, they were climbing, scrambling for the roof.

Sterling threw them over the edge of the roof. On

impact with the hard surface, Malaina lost her grip and rolled until she hit the other side.

She stared up at the revolving stars, her eyes struggling to focus. Pushing herself to her stomach, she struggled to get control of her shaking legs, trying and failing to force them beneath her. Sterling fell to his knees by her side in human form, using his sweat-soaked shirt to wipe away the hair plastered to his face.

"Come on," he panted, grabbing her upper arm and dragging her to her feet. He puffed a couple more breaths, wrapping her arms around his neck again. "Hold on," he ground out, and they were off again.

She wrapped her legs around his waist, trying to keep her hold as he sprinted across the roof.

He shifted, taking the form of a midnight black mountain cat, and leaped from one room to the next. He didn't hesitate as he landed, just kept sprinting until he jumped again. With each new roof they crossed he picked up speed until the world blurred.

It wasn't until they were halfway back to the guild that he finally skidded to a stop.

Malaina let go, falling from his back and crumpling into a pile on whatever rooftop he'd stopped on.

Sterling, looking like himself once again, crawled his way to her side. He fell to his back, gulping air to catch his breath, reaching out his hand.

Malaina reached for him, too.

They lay on the roof, holding each other's forearms in a death grip to assure themselves the other was safe and alive.

Malaina didn't have the energy to reach out to her shadows, but she let herself get lost in their presence around her. Knowing they were close was a comfort enough.

Her torso felt like one big bruise from being tackled by the guard. The sharp pain when she breathed made it clear he had even cracked a couple of ribs. The bruises would fade, and Jade could fix her ribs. Training sessions had left her worse off than this.

Malaina was at a loss for words, trying to find something to say, a way to explain what had happened.

She had no idea what went wrong. Why didn't Nyda die after the first dose? Or even the second? Malaina had given her four times the amount she should have needed, and yet the youngest Alman girl had still been fighting for life.

It should have been instant. It should have been painless.

The image of Nyda convulsing beneath her grip, terror in her eyes, planted itself in Malaina's mind and it wouldn't leave. To her, Nyda would always be fighting for her life. She died in fear, and she would stay that way forever.

"She wouldn't die," Malaina mused breathlessly, still staring up at the stars. "Why wouldn't she die?"

She was asking the night around her more than Sterling. Asking the shadows for the answers they didn't hold.

One of them slid over her palm, and then she remembered...

Her free hand searched until she found the vial she had confiscated. She pulled it out, holding it up in the moonlight. It was made of crystal clear glass and about the length of her finger, stoppered by a cork. Drops of the power suppressant rolled over the glass, leftover from Nyda shooting it down earlier.

"You took the suppressant?" Sterling watched the vial spin between her fingers.

The Shadow Spinner tipped the vial from one side to the other, watching the leftover drops slide back and forth.

"I don't think it's a suppressant," she whispered.

FOURTEEN

Jade placed her palms over Malaina's ribs and closed her eyes to concentrate. The Witch's lips moved in a silent chant. Malaina couldn't hear the words she said but didn't care since she wouldn't be able to understand them anyway.

Malaina closed her eyes instead, concentrating on her breathing. Painful at first, her ribs protested every expansion of her lungs. They'd ached the entire way back, forcing the pair to cross the city far slower than they normally would. Now that they were back in the medical bay, the ache turned to stabbing pain, her adrenaline from the fight long since worn off.

Jade's palms warmed against her skin. Heat seeped deep into Malaina's bones, easing the pain, making it easier to breathe, and relaxing her muscles for the first time since the contract went wrong.

"Don't move," Jade ordered, her words sharp as she pulled away and turned to her workstation.

"No problem," Malaina assured her, content to stay where she lay on the table.

Usually, Witches needed some sort of potion or elixir to cure more than superficial wounds. Though Jade was one of the most powerful Witches Malaina had ever met, even she couldn't fix broken bones with just a touch.

"How bad is it?" Sterling asked from where he stood in the corner of Jade's office at the back of the training room.

All sorts of unidentifiable things filled shelf after shelf of jars lining the wall. Many of them were rare plants, dried and smuggled from the City of Witches all the way across Thaumoria to the City of Elementals. One of those small jars could cost more than Malaina and Sterling's rent for a year.

Jade automatically started pulling ingredients down, working from memory. "Fractures, but no breaks. Some bruises that I can heal easily. She'll live." The Witch paused every few words, her fingers making small movements to catch up with her words out of habit. Her eyes cut to Sterling, a piercing stare out of the corner of her eye, and pointed a single deft finger, "You're next."

"I'm fine," he grumbled.

Narrowing her hooded eyes at him, she cut him a hard look, her movements sharpening even more. "Wasn't a question. You're next."

His head fell back against the wall, eyes glued to the ceiling, but he didn't argue. Only those keen to lose challenged Jade.

"Yes, ma'am," he breathed. He held a rag to his neck where a bite mark still bled. The bites covered his arms, neck, and other places Malaina couldn't see.

Those dogs had done their best to tear into him. While they may not have stood a chance, they certainly left their mark.

The constant drone of noise from the training room beyond the office quieted. Yells became hushed, the crashing of metal against wood died, and weights dropped to the ground with a chorus of clattering.

"Brace yourselves," Malaina muttered, and Sterling grimaced, squeezing his eyes shut in anticipation.

The door to Jade's office flew open, slammed by invisible hands, and crashed against the wall. A moment later, Malachi stormed into the office. Malaina had seen that look before when he saw red, struggling to stay composed. The door slammed closed behind him, shaking the walls and sending the blinds over the windows flying.

Jade didn't flinch, or so much as glance up from her work, ignoring the fight that was about to go down.

"What. Happened?" Malachi barked.

"She wouldn't die," Malaina answered dryly.

"So you screwed up."

"I didn't screw up," Malaina spat back, sitting up out of irritation, then immediately falling back to the table, moaning in pain. *That was stupid.*

"I said don't move," Jade scolded her.

The Shadow Spinner ground her teeth together in frustration. If only everyone would shut up and let her breathe, but that wasn't about to happen.

"What's wrong with her?" Malachi asked Jade, as though Malaina wasn't in the room at all. He didn't raise his voice, but the words were aggressive. Anyone else would've crumpled beneath that grey-green stare.

Jade didn't flinch, simply repeating, "Fractures, but no breaks. Some bruises that I can heal easily. She'll live." She pointed at Sterling without looking up. "He's next."

The Shifter narrowed maroon eyes at her, and Malaina wondered if he was trying to see if he could use his Shifter magic to turn her into something unsavory, but it didn't seem to be working.

The guild master looked Sterling over, seeming to notice his injuries for the first time.

Jade turned back to Malaina, a bowl filled with an oil-like substance in her hands. She set it on the table next to Malaina.

"I still don't understand what happened," Malachi quipped.

Neither do I. "I told you, she wouldn't die. I gave her two full syringes, and she just started seizing."

Jade dipped her hands into the bowl, coating her palms in the oil and pressing them to Malaina's ribs. Having nearly her entire torso exposed in a room full of people she wasn't sleeping with should have embarrassed the assassin, but she couldn't bring herself to care. They'd all seen it before, anyway.

Bracing herself, Malaina closed her eyes, and the Witch began to chant again in the old Witch's language. The language of the Four Sisters, she called it. This wasn't the first time Jade had healed Malaina's broken bones, and the assassin knew what to expect. The Witch's magic started to seep beneath her skin, the oil aiding the intensity. It soaked into her muscles, then dove deeper. Working its way over her bones, it investigated her wounds, seeking out the spots that needed fixing. Finally, it settled, wrapping itself around the fractures.

"Was there something wrong with the poison? Maybe it was old or expired." Malachi crossed his arms, falling back against the door.

Then the agony came. Malaina clenched her teeth to keep from crying out as her bones pressed back together, knitting themselves over the fractures. Jade's magic forced the healing process to speed up, accelerating so what should have taken weeks took only moments. What should be a mild ache spread out over weeks, became a knife in the Shadow Spinner's side as she experienced all the misery of healing at once.

She cried out when the pain crested, clenching her teeth to muffle it. Sterling jerked forward on instinct, ready to protect and ease her discomfort. To be by her side and fight off what hurt her. But then the pain receded as quickly as it came.

"There is nothing wrong with my poison," Jade snapped at Malachi, then switched to a gentler (yet still authoritative) tone when she turned her attention back to the silver-haired girl on her table. "How do you feel?"

Malaina took a moment to catch her breath. Slowly, she tested her ribs, first reaching from side to side, then sitting up. What would have been excruciating moments ago was now a memory of pain. She sighed. "Better. Much better."

Jade gave her a curt nod. "Good."

Malaina took the damp cloth Jade held out to her, wiping the oil from her ribs and readjusting her shirt. "I'll never understand how you do that."

Jade already worked on cleaning up her workbench. "I learned from the best." For a moment her eyes became distant, lost in memory, but Malachi's insistence brought her back.

"If the poison was correctly administered and there was nothing wrong with it then. What. Happened?" He punctuated the words, trying to bring everyone's attention back to the problem at hand.

"We don't know," Malaina repeated. How could she make him understand? They'd done everything right. Things should have gone smoothly, an easy in and out, the same way they'd done it dozens of times.

"Was there *anything* odd about the night? Anything at all that could have caused things to go wrong?"

Malaina and Sterling exchanged a loaded look. Her thoughts went to the vial still sitting in her pocket. Her fingers explored its small, smooth shape through the fabric, contemplating.

"What?" Malachi asked, noticing their look. "What is it?"

Malaina pulled the vial from her pocket. She examined it rolling across her palm like a ship rolling at sea, cresting over waves. "She took something every night before bed. We looked into it, but it should've made things easier, not harder."

Jade's spine stiffened, her hands stilling on the bench in front of her.

Malaina handed the vial to Malachi, who examined it, holding it up to the light. Malaina recounted her journey to the Dark Market and the Witch she'd met.

"The book was folded on one page, so I put it all together. It had the name of the elixir, a list of ingredients, and a whole bunch of symbols. I didn't recognize the symbols, but the elixir listed was a power suppressant." The words felt off even as she said them like she missed something obvious that she couldn't put together.

Malachi's brows furrowed, his nose wrinkling when he uncorked the vial and sniffed it. "Why would such a powerful family want to suppress one of their children's magic?"

"It didn't seem important. Suppressing her magic even a little should've weakened her enough that it didn't matter." Sterling stepped in, reminding the room that it had been a team effort and that Malaina hadn't made the call all on her own.

"What were the ingredients listed?" Jade demanded, her hand movements slow and thoughtful, looking at Malaina over her shoulder.

Malaina closed her eyes, seeing the page in her mind, and listed the ingredients from memory, keeping them in order. Halfway through the list, Jade frantically opened one of her drawers, pulling out a pad of paper and a pencil. Before Malaina had finished her recitation, Jade shoved the paper and pencil into her hands.

"Recreate the page. Elixir name, ingredients, symbols,

everything," Jade ordered. Crossing her arms, she stepped back and watched Malaina expectantly.

The assassin's hands started to move over the paper, recreating what she'd seen down to every last detail. Seeing the page crisp and clear in her mind, she remembered every little curve, stroke, and symbol.

Back when she was still in training, preparing to start her work in the guild, Malachi had forced her through drill after drill just like this. He would show her something for a few seconds. Sometimes, a list of names. Sometimes, an incoherent line of letters and numbers. Followed by making her recreate whatever she'd seen precisely. No mistakes. Nothing missing. Every speck of ink or graphite accounted for. The drills were excruciating, but the skill came in handy more times than she could count over the years.

Not that she would *ever* admit such a thing to the guild master.

They all watched her work, the sound of pencil scratching on paper loud in the otherwise silent office.

When she'd drawn the unfamiliar symbols, including the string of them next to the name of the Elixir and each ingredient, she handed the pad of paper back to Jade. Scanning the page again and again, the Witch pressed her lips together, the only sign of what was going through her brilliant mind.

"Give me the vial," Jade ordered. Malachi handed it over without a word. Jade opened the vial, tipping it until the last drop fell into her palm. Setting the vial aside, she closed her hand, letting her fingers curl around the drops in her hand. Closing her eyes, deep in concentration, her lips moved. This time, though, it wasn't in the old Witch's language. Malaina watched Jade's lips, reading them as they moved. She was listing ingredients that weren't on the page. Malaina wasn't quite sure what she was doing.

Jade's eyes snapped open. "This isn't a power suppressant."

"What?" Malaina gasped.

Malachi held out his hand for the pad to scan it himself.

"What is it?" Sterling asked.

Malachi handed him the pad, barely contained rage on his normally stoic face.

Sterling looked it over, his eyes a dull orange, trying to understand what was off.

"It's an antidote," Jade stated matter-of-factly.

"There's an antidote to what you make me?" Malaina asked. "I thought that was impossible." The poison Jade made for her was unique, the formula guarded within Jade's office. The elixir was a creation of the Witch's own mind. A one-of-a-kind formula designed to mimic the magic of a Death Bringer. It was created for Malaina and Malaina alone; not even she knew the ingredients or how Jade made it.

"It is. It's not an exact antidote. It's more generalized. The blend would not have saved her. However, it would have prolonged her life. Whoever made it was quite talented and had a good idea of what they were counteracting." Jade tapped her fingers against her arms, a cross look in her eyes. Annoyed someone had the gull to try and counteract a creation of her own making, even if they had failed.

"How do you know for sure?" Malachi scanned the page again. "There is nothing here to indicate that."

Jade arched an eyebrow at him, unable to comprehend how anyone could question the conclusion she'd come to. "It's all written right there." She pointed to the pad of paper still in Malachi's hand.

He held the pad up, waving it in the air. "I am looking at the same thing you are, and there is nothing here to indicate that. Not even in the symbols."

"Writing their personal notebook in code is not uncommon for Witches who attend the University. No two are the same, but someone with enough experience can extrapolate a certain amount of information. With those last few drops, I was able to extract its exact formulaic makeup, and I was right." She raised her chin, meeting Malachi's critical gaze and challenging him to question her again.

All of them stared at her in disbelief.

Malaina dared to speak what they were all thinking. "You can do that?" Jade's jaw tensed as she stared at nothing in particular, the only confirmation she would give. The look on Malachi's face made it clear even he wasn't aware of this particular ability. "How?"

Jade sucked on her teeth, then stared down at her workbench, using the tip of her short thumbnail to scratch at nothing. "The ability is…not a common talent."

Malachi raised an eyebrow at her. "Did you learn that at the University?"

Malaina held back her gasp. Jade growing up in the City of Witches was common knowledge, but like many guilders, she didn't like to talk about her past.

The Witch's University was the most exclusive institute in all of Thaumoria. Only the most powerful and intelligent Witches were given the opportunity to apply, let alone attend. Graduates often went on to hold a position on the Witch's Council, the group that ran the city. Those who attended a single semester were sought after and compensated exceptionally. They were often private healers for the most influential families around Thaumoria.

Prior to that moment, Malaina hadn't imagined ever meeting a Witch talented enough to receive such an honor, and now she'd unknowingly met two.

Jade hesitated before answering, carefully considering her words. "No...I was born with the skill."

"Can you teach it to others?" Malachi asked.

Malaina stifled the urge to roll her eyes. Leave it to Malachi to try and capitalize on this moment.

Jade cut a look at him that would have sent a lesser man withering. "No."

"Why not?"

"Because it is not something that *can* be taught. The skill takes practice to perfect, but you either can or you cannot." That's the way it always was with Jade. Things either were or they weren't, yes or no, black or white, no in-between.

"How does it work? Is it related to a Witch's ability to sense medicinal properties in plants?" Sterling inquired. His orange eyes told her he was genuinely curious.

"Yes," Jade quipped. Then her face softened a hair when he resolutely accepted that answer. "As I'm sure you know, Witch magic falls into two categories: the body and the cure. Witches tend to be more gifted in one, more than the other. For instance, Kai is exclusively gifted in the body, and extremely so."

Kai was Serena's partner. His magic was powerful but abnormal, just like Serena's. Malaina shivered at the mention of his name, remembering the way his touch felt. The way his magic manipulated the body into feeling things to the extreme. Feeling things that weren't really there or happening. Something about manipulating nerve endings and hormone levels in the brain and other more complicated things Malaina didn't understand. His breath could feel electric, sending shivers over your skin, or it could feel like pin needles piercing your veins.

Great for sex. Great for torture.

Generally, he chose the former.

"On the other hand, you have Witches who only have a gift for the cure. They may not be able to sense what is wrong with a person, but they can create potions and elixirs more powerful than you can imagine, without a second thought. They can hold a plant they've never seen before and tell you its exact medicinal properties and how it will react with others on instinct alone.

"However, most Witches are a mix of the two, falling somewhere on the spectrum between one end and the other." She sucked in her cheeks, pursing her lips before continuing. "I was...am...quite gifted in both. A Witch needs a considerable amount of skill in the cure to be able to do what I just did."

They all watched her for a long time, unable to fully comprehend what she revealed about herself. Clearing her throat, she wiped her hands, uncomfortable as the center of attention. She turned her attention to Malaina, pushing the Shadow Spinner's silver hair back off her shoulders, looking Malaina over more carefully than necessary.

"I think the important question here is why they commissioned an antidote in the first place," Sterling said, trying to change the subject. "Sure, the Alman's could have guessed there was a hit on them, which already would have been a long shot, but they had no way to know it would be a poison or how the poison would work. An antidote wouldn't have stopped a Death Bringer."

"The Desrocs don't have the same level of wealth as the Almans. I'm surprised they could even afford our rates at all. Maybe they suspected a hit from one of the sloppier guilds," Malaina offered, voicing something that continued to nag at her.

"They do not use poison," Malachi stated.

Malaina's eyes met Jade's, and she could tell they were thinking the same thing.

"Then what were they trying to protect against?" She whispered, more to herself than anyone else in the room.

FIFTEEN

Malaina stretched her legs out on the long couch in the grand room, her feet in Sterling's lap at the other end. Her head lolled to the side, resting against the back as her eyes forced themselves closed.

Head tilted back, Sterling's mouth hung open, arms crossed across his chest. The Shifter wasn't even pretending to stay awake as Lybbi paced before the cold fireplace.

"They're late," she grumbled, not for the first time.

"We have hours before the stores close. It's fine." Malaina yawned, nuzzling further into the corner of the cushions. "The sun hasn't even started to set yet."

Lybbi had woken them early, bouncing when she told them she'd made plans with Ra and Layshan to head into the business district that evening. The last place she or Sterling wanted to be after what they'd witnessed, but they weren't about to tell Lybbi that or ruin the plans she was so eager for.

"It's not fine. We agreed to meet here ten minutes ago, and they are late," Lybbi snapped.

Malaina turned her face further into the soft material of the couch.

The elevator doors opened.

"Finally!"

Malaina peeked out from beneath heavy lids. Lybbi's gloved hands grabbed one of Sterling's arms and yanked him awake before running for the elevator. He ran his palms over his face and mumbled, "Your sister is exhausting."

"Before sundown, she's your sister. I don't claim her."

Grinding the heels of his hands into his eyes, the Shifter half-heartedly chuckled in response.

A pillow flew at Malaina's head, hitting her square on the ear. She sat up gaping, "Hey!"

Ra walked over and Malaina barely had time to pull her legs to her chest before he sat on them, plopping down on the couch. "Come on, sleepy heads. Time for some fun."

"You're the one who was late." Malaina rubbed the side of her face where the Kinetic had sent the pillow flying.

"Sorry, but that one was taking forever to get ready." He gave a pointed look at Layshan's perfectly fluffed and styled blonde hair, ready for a day on the town.

Layshan gave a small shrug. "Perfection can't be rushed. Don't know what to tell ya." A cocky grin spread across his lips.

Lybbi ran up behind him, standing on tiptoes to ruffle

his immaculately styled hair before sprinting off. Her satisfied giggles bubbled through the hall, bouncing off the guilders and making the stars painted above glitter.

Scowling at her, the Air Wielder shook his head, sending scattered wisps of wind everywhere. When the wind died down, his hair was flawlessly styled once again.

"Up!" Ra chirped, patting both her and Sterling's knees before jumping to his feet.

When they didn't move, invisible hands started to tip the cushioned couch forward. They both scrambled to their feet to keep from spilling onto the floor.

"Good job, let's go!" Ra bound towards the exit, where Lybbi was already waiting for them.

"Can I eat him?" Sterling grumbled under his breath.

"Go for it. With how much sugar he eats, he'll probably taste like chocolate," Layshan answered before starting toward the exit to join Lybbi and Ra.

Malaina laughed, exhausted. She slipped her arm into Sterling's and leaned heavily against him as they joined the group.

Once they found their way out, they were thrust into an entirely different world from the guild they'd just exited: the slums of the city.

Long since run down, few people still owned townhomes. The few homeowners left tried their best to keep their stoops charming, but money always needed to go towards more important things.

Food. Rent. Water. Heat.

That's why most of the townhomes were converted to multi-family homes bursting at the seams with residents. It was an attempt to keep up with the bills on the scraps nobles deemed them worthy of or what little the business owners could afford to pay.

The alleys drew Malaina's attention, though. Shadowed and dark, they drew the homeless of the city, hiding them from view. She remembered living down some of those alleys, finding friends in places she wouldn't have imagined months before.

Their little group of professional criminals strolled down those streets, cheerfully chatting. Malachi had raised them on those streets, and that's where they felt the most at home. Fond memories of practicing her climbing skills, her and Ra running up and down those alleys, warmed Malaina's chest.

They met many of the stares they drew, giving the occasional coins to those they recognized and small smiles to those they didn't.

Eventually, they made their way to the outskirts of the business district. Their first stop was a small bakery they frequented on a regular basis.

Lybbi ran through the door, the bell overhead cheerfully chiming unnecessarily. The rest of them followed suit, already discussing what they were going to order.

Almost immediately, the group quieted when they saw what the bakery held.

The cases of cakes were still there, but they weren't what any of them remembered.

The cake display on the counter had once held a new one every day. Once, it had been a multi-tiered cake, its base a deep rose, each new tier lightening to a blush, creating a gradient that reminded Malaina of the sky during an early morning sunrise. The bottommost layer had been hand-painted to resemble a garden, rays of a setting sun streaming through the bushes with cascades of flawless sugar-spun flowers on the rest of the tiers.

Now, the display was simple. Two round layers coated in an even layer of ivory frosting. No decorations or adornments to be seen. A mirror image of the rest of the desert cases.

Malaina didn't need to wonder what had happened, and from the look on Ra and Layshan's faces, neither did they. The bakery's decorators had been Shifters, able to create anything out of icing and sugar, and now they were gone, along with the rest of the city's most talented artists.

Lybbi slowed, her face falling in disappointment. Her frown deepened as she approached the glass counter, looking over the options for the day. They still had most of the usuals, but some were notably missing. Like the sugar cookies, which had always been iced in intricate designs so beautiful, they were almost too lovely to eat.

Almost.

Turning to fit through the doorway, a broad man came out from the back and pursed his lips when he saw them, recognizing the expression on Lybbi's face. His head was bald, but his bushy eyebrows and beard were the red of an oven's flame. Heavy bags hung under his eyes that hadn't been there the last time they had been to the bakery.

His shoulders drooped, scanning his display case. "Hey, guys, what can I get you?"

"Where are the sugar cookies?" Lybbi asked before

Malaina could stop her. They were all quiet as the Fire Wielder's doleful eyes watched the young girl from behind the counter.

"We have some right over here." Gesturing to the end of the counter, he attempted to sound upbeat. On one of the trays lay a batch of cookies glazed in clear icing.

Malaina opened her mouth to tell him those would be fine if only to wipe that wan look from his face, but Lybbi spoke first. "No, the *pretty* sugar cookies."

The Fire Wielders' eyes grew heavy, the bags under his eyes seeming to grow. "We…we don't have them anymore."

"Why not?" Lybbi insisted.

Malaina placed a hand on Lybbi's shoulder, trying to draw her attention elsewhere. "I'm sure they'll taste just as good," she offered.

A pout started to form on Lybbi's lips. "But those are the ones I wanted. I've been thinking about them all week."

Malaina looked around for help, and Layshan stepped forward. "Ya know, I always thought all that icing made the cookies too sweet anyway." He turned to the Fire Wielder, his usual cocky grin playing at his lips. "I'll have a croissant."

Lybbi nodded, shoulders slouching. "Yeah, that's true. I guess that's what I'll get too. Do you have any with chocolate, though?"

The baker visibly relaxed, relieved. "Yeah, kid, we do. We have chocolate and strawberry ones if you'd like."

Lybbi nodded eagerly, sugar cookies forgotten, and the rest of them ordered. A muffin for Ra, a breakfast sandwich for Sterling, and a cinnamon roll and black Witch's coffee for Malaina, who was desperate for caffeine.

Despite having Sterling and Lybbi sprawled beside her all day, sleep had evaded her. Memories of Nyda's bulging blue eyes haunted the assassin, contrasted against the memories of Nyda smiling at her sister mere hours before. In her mind, it happened over and over again. She could still feel Nyda convulsing beneath her hands.

Instead of sleeping, she tried to figure out why Nyda had been taking the antidote or how it had been made in the first place. At the time, she'd been grateful the Desrocs paid in full ahead of time, keeping her from having to collect payment after the disastrous night, but the more she thought about it, the more it felt deliberate.

Their little group of five made their way deeper into the business district, and Malaina allowed herself to really pay attention to the stores in a way she hadn't been able to when she'd followed the Alman sisters. She'd been too preoccupied to pay attention to anything else.

The conspicuous absence of Shifters was noticeable before, but now that she was truly looking around her… now it surrounded her like the bland posters hung up around town advertising the next Games.

The clothing stores no longer had window displays full of dazzling designs, trying to outdo each other at every corner, but instead held plain suits and dresses made from dull fabrics. They all appeared well-made and stitched to perfection, but there was nothing unique about the designs. Nothing exclusive from one store to the next.

Even the Kinetic shops, selling the latest inventions

from the City of Kinetics seemed drab. No longer did they carry several options with beautiful carvings and designs, but one generic one for everyone to choose from.

Many of the shops opted to change their signs, switching from colorful lettering and creative logos that pulled you into ones that appeared to come from the same average woodworker. Even some of the awnings had changed, no longer adjusting to match the latest trends and sales.

The Shifters hadn't just disappeared from the crowds, but their touch on the city vanished along with them. No one wanted to be associated with them. Businesses were changing faster than the Shifters were leaving, trying not to draw the attention of the city guard, because that would be bad for sales.

Malaina watched Sterling's face while they followed Layshan, Ra, and Lybbi. Lybbi chattered away, oblivious to the changes around her, but the tension in the group rose. They tried to ignore what was happening around them, but the changes smacked patrons in the face.

Jaw clenching, Sterling's eyes were a steely gray-blue. Having also been distracted when they followed the Alman sisters, he was only now truly seeing the damage the registration caused. As though he were trying to remember what the storefronts were like just weeks ago, his gaze went somewhere far away as they walked.

"Hey, guys!" Sterling called ahead. "Let's turn here." They all turned back to see him jerking his head to the left.

"Are we going to see Syn?" Lybbi asked, perking up.

"Yeah, are we?" Malaina whispered. They hadn't gotten word from Syn about their order of shirts for Sterling, but given what was going on, it wasn't surprising.

Giving the street around them one more glance, mustard-seed yellow started to marble those steel eyes. "I think we should." He gave Lybbi a weak smile. "He should be done by now, right?"

The young girl beamed at him. "I think we should visit him anyway."

She led the way around the corner. Syn's shop wasn't far from the main street, so it didn't take long before they were standing before his glass windows.

The displays were empty, the signs gone.

Sterling stood before the dark windows, staring, his body rigid. Malaina clutched his arm, watching his eyes flash from color to color so fast she couldn't pick one out from the rest.

Lybbi walked past them and placed a palm on the window, staring into the dark shop beyond. They couldn't see beyond the darkness, the windows reflecting the image of the street behind them, but Malaina could sense the chaos lying within those shadows.

"Maybe…" Lybbi clutched her hands to her chest, protectively stroking her gloves. "Maybe he's in the back."

"I don't think so," Malaina whispered.

Sterling's chest caved at her words, and he closed his ever-changing eyes.

"He wouldn't have left without telling anyone. He wouldn't have taken our money if he wasn't intending to deliver a product. He…" Sterling's voice caught, "He wouldn't have just left."

The Shifter approached the window, cupping his hands around his eyes, trying to see into the darkness behind the glass.

Malaina looked up and noticed Ra was gone. She whipped her head back and forth looking for him, but Layshan came to her side, hiding her frantic searching. "He'll be back."

Ra appeared further down the street, turning out of an alley and strolling towards them casually, as though it were perfectly normal for him to walk off and appear out of nowhere. His ashy brown eyes met Layshan's, and the edge of Layshan's shirt collar jerked twice.

The Air Wielder's mouth quirked to the side and he turned to the storefront. "Guess we're going in the front," he sighed.

"What?" Lybbi asked.

Ra pushed through without looking at them as if he'd never met them before. Like he owned the place. Placing his hand on the door handle, he hesitated, brows creasing with a moment's concentration. The lock clicked open, and Ra opened the door. Layshan ushered them all in, closing the door and flipping the lock back into place.

One of the first things Malachi taught every single guilder was how to pick a lock, but Malaina always envied a Kinetic's ability to do it so effortlessly.

"Would have preferred a back entrance, but no one's paying attention anyway," Layshan stated, far too calm, pushing his hands deep into his jacket pockets. "Not these days."

Sterling spun, taking in the chaos Malaina had sensed in the shadows. Bolts of fabric had been thrown across the shop, dress forms broken and in pieces, and clothing samples torn to shreds. Even the desk had been tipped over. The entire shop was in shambles.

Lybbi held a hand to her mouth, tears flowing freely down her cheeks.

Sterling's eyes were no longer spinning. They paused at a shade of gray, like storm clouds edged with blood-red rings.

He watched Ra, Layshan, and her, looking from one face to another. A fist bounced against his leg as he paced. "You guys don't look surprised."

Ra stared at the floor, kicking the toe of his boot against the tipped-over desk. "We've broken into enough businesses and houses, lately, that look this way."

Sterling's fist continued to bounce against his leg. "This…this wasn't Syn. This was someone who fought back. Syn wouldn't have fought back. He wasn't even going to charge us full price for the shirts."

Malaina bit her lip, knowing he was right. Syn never would have left without telling them or, at the very least, returning their money. And if the city guards came for him, he wouldn't have made such a scene. He would have seen it coming and accepted his reality gracefully.

No… if city guards came for him they did this themselves. They destroyed everything he had worked so hard for. Everything he had built.

Sterling burst into movement, heading straight for the door leading to the back of the shop. Malaina and Lybbi chased after him. The Shifter started rummaging through closets and drawers.

"What are you looking for?" Malaina asked, not sure what to do.

He didn't answer; he just continued ripping through the back of the shop.

"Dude, what are you doing? You're going to get us caught." Layshan hissed from over Malaina's shoulder. She shot him a look that told him to choose his next words carefully but he made an indignant face right back at her.

Sterling ignored them both. When he tore open a door leading to a staircase he didn't hesitate to plow his way to the next level. Malaina bolted after him, her shorter legs struggling to keep up. She nearly collided with his back when he suddenly stopped at the top of the stairs, causing a domino reaction behind her.

Malaina ducked around the Shifter, finding a completely untouched apartment beyond. It was exactly the kind of place she would expect Syn to live in—polished and elegant. Every piece of furniture and art had been meticulously chosen for this space, coordinated down to the last detail.

Sterling entered slowly, cautiously looking around. Expecting Syn to pop out of nowhere and yell at them for trespassing.

"Nice place," Layshan muttered, considering the space and leisurely wandering further into the living room. Sitting on the coffee table was a golden pocket watch. Examining it, Layshan ran a thumb over the surface. Deftly, the thief pocketed the watch.

Ra shook his head. "Seriously, man?"

"Not like he's going to need it."

Malaina wanted to throw something at them both, but thankfully, Sterling didn't seem aware of what was happening around him. Lybbi close on the Shifters heels, they headed for the bedroom.

"What are you looking for?" Lybbi pled. "I can help."

Sterling still didn't answer and instead threw open the doors to the carved wooden wardrobe on the wall opposite the bed. His eyes were an empty gray as he stared down, unmoving.

Malaina peered around him. The wardrobe was empty except for five white shirts crisply folded and stacked at the bottom, with a note sitting on top.

Sterling picked up the pile, opened the note, then crumpled it in a fist and let it fall to the floor before walking out of the room. Malaina picked up the note and read:

Stay human.
- Syn

CHAPTER
SIXTEEN

They stepped back into the daylight outside the shop, the world too bright. None of them spoke as they headed back for the main street, a bag filled with Sterling's shirts slung over Malaina's shoulder. They had swiped it from Syn's shop, figuring he wouldn't be needing it anytime soon.

The thundering sound of havoc started to grow the closer they got to the main street. The group picked up their speed until they were at the edge of a buzzing crowd. They skirted it until the five of them pushed through enough to see what was going on.

City guards stood in a wide circle, facing out at those watching, keeping the people back. In the center were four shifters, all on their knees, hands bound, except for one.

A wild woman fought, screaming and yelling at the guards who tried to bind her. She shared Sterling's tanned brown skin, but a vibrant pink colored the roots of her hair, fading into a sea blue at the tips.

"You can't do this!" The flailing Shifter screeched at the two guards holding her arms behind her, trying and failing to restrain her violent bucking. "This isn't legal!"

From the center of the circle, the captain of the group droned as though he had repeated the phrase several times already. "Ma'am, please cooperate." The way he stood bored and indifferent, his hands clasped behind his back while the other guards tried to contain her, made it clear he was leading this particular siege. "We are working under the direct orders of Lord Kevah, lord of the Elemen— "

Cutting off his words, the Shifter went off again. "I don't care who ordered it. This goes against the City Establishment Treaty! He can't just do anything he wants."

The captain shot a look at the sky impatiently. "Ma'am, we don't wish to cause a scene. Please cooperate."

Malaina snorted. He acted like he wasn't the one causing the scene. Sterling seethed beside her, blowing a heavy breath through his nose.

He made to push through the crowd, not caring how many people saw him. He only stopped when another voice broke through the outskirts of the throng.

"Take your hands off her!" Deep and commanding, the voice boomed through the street, echoing off the buildings.

Valis stepped forward, his chin held high. Every inch of him emanated confidence and power as he observed the guards struggling to contain the woman. The moment she heard his voice, she calmed, jerking against the guards who held her to get a better look.

From behind Malaina, Lybbi, and Ra gasped.

Layshan laughed, "No way."

The captain of the group shook his head while the other guards continued to struggle.

"Sir, I appreciate your appearance here and respect your position in this community, but we cannot disobey direct orders," the captain continued to drone as if reading from a script. As if the entire scene was a mere inconvenience in his day.

"It wasn't a question." Valis strode forward, shoulders pushed back, chest puffed out. "Take your hands off my wife."

"Once again-" The captain started to repeat before getting cut off again.

Valis brought his hands above his head, palms together, and whipped them out to the side with a force so strong it took him to his knees. A blast of air went through the crowd, sending everyone ducking and covering their faces.

Sterling's arm covered Malaina's head quicker than she could comprehend what was happening. Ra tried to take the brunt of the blow to his shoulder as Lybbi turned into him, but a counter-blast of air shielded them from the stinging lash.

Awe and adoration gleamed in Layshan's wide eyes as though he didn't realize what he had just done, his magic working on instinct alone. His blonde hair whipped back from his face, a wicked grin spreading across his lips.

The guards had been blown back, leaving a trail of plowed-over onlookers in their paths. A tornado of air encompassed the inner circle, a protective wall around the four Shifters on their knees, Valis, and his wife. Valis stood and made his way to his wife's side, helping her to her feet. He held her face in his hands, his eyes roving over her, ensuring she was all right as they spoke softly to each other.

The tornado died away as the two walked hand-in-hand to the kneeling Shifters, reaching down to undo the bindings holding their hands. The captain stood from where he had been thrown, fury beating red across his face. "Don't you dare touch them! They are the property of Lord Kevah and the City of Elementals!"

Valis's wife's almond eyes bulged, head whipping around. "Property? We are people!" She shrieked, storming towards the guard, prepared to face him head-on without a hint of doubt on her face. Ready to take him on with nothing but her anger, and anger alone.

Valis grabbed her around the waist and pulled her back, pushing her behind him as the captain stomped forward, sparks flaring at his fingertips. He spun on his heel until he faced Valis again, bringing his hands together at his chest and pushing out fury so grand the explosion made him scream.

Fire burst from his hands, hurtling towards Valis and the Shifters.

Valis didn't hesitate. He dropped and stood in the same breath, raising his hands as he did. A wall of earth sprung up from the ground, the brick that paved the street layering the outside, creating a barrier. The captain's fire exploded like his temper when it met the wall, flaring in every direction.

People screamed, a wave of heat hitting them, forcing them to step back.

The captain stomped forward, his face even redder than before. Valis barreled through his own wall like a wrecking ball, meeting the guard head-on. They stood face to face, mere inches from each other.

"Do that again," Valis dared, fingers flexing and curling by his sides, "It will be the last thing you do."

The guard held out a finger, sticking it in Valis's chest. "I have direct orders from the Lord to get this filth out of his city!" Any control the captain had had over his temper faded away in the face of an enemy he couldn't intimidate.

"Filth!" Valis's wife screeched.

Valis simply lifted and dropped his heel. A thin pillar of earth and brick flew up from the ground between him and the guard. The column hit the guard's outstretched hand, the crack of stone meeting flesh ringing throughout the street. When the pillar fell, Valis hadn't moved, but the captain now knelt in the dirt, cradling his newly limp forearm. There was an unnatural sag to his skin as if all the bones had turned to liquid.

"Don't you dare insult my lady and her people again?" A terrifying calm saturated Valis's threat, dripping from every syllable. He stared down his nose at the man on his knees before him.

"The only lady in this city," The guard screamed, tears streaming down his face, spittle flying from his lip, "Is Lady Atana! Don't you dare give your disgusting wife that title!" His words were difficult to understand as his voice rose an entire octave.

"Not anymore," Valis growled.

The bi-wielder stepped back, addressing the crowd and other guards, all hesitant to come any closer. "This is my official challenge to Lord Kevah!" His words rang out over those who had all fallen silent, drinking in his every word. "I will no longer sit back and watch him ravage this city and deface the name of the Elemental people!" Valis spun slowly, meeting every eye he could, words loud enough to reach the entire block.

Hope made Malaina's heart leap and then fall just as hard. Kevah had three elements to Valis's two. For him to stand a chance would take a miracle.

Everyone stayed silent, and had Malaina been in the challenger's shoes, she would have shrank beneath the weight of everyone's scrutiny. But Valis was used to being the center of attention, his confidence never wavering. He stood tall with the air of a man used to the pressure of grand statements and high stakes.

The silence stretched on forever while his wife finished unbinding the other Shifters. The small group stayed sitting, frozen, waiting to see how the crowd would react to Valis's challenge.

A whistle pierced the air from beside Malaina, nearly bursting her eardrum.

Ra bounced on his toes, head tipped back, continuing to let out the ear-splitting whistle.

Layshan thrust his fist into the air, cheering, letting out a prolonged "Yeah!"

Malaina found herself laughing, and Lybbi joined in, letting out a whooping yell that spread like wildfire.

Soon, the entire street cheered. Heads popped out from the top-story windows where they'd been watching. Sparks from Fire Wielders flew into the air, playful whips of wind sending everyone's hair flying in wild directions. The ground rumbled beneath her feet, and storm clouds gathered above her. Elementals of every kind appeared from nowhere to add their power to the uproar.

Sterling's arm looped around Malaina's neck, pulling her close to his side. He thrust his fist into the air, adding his own cheer to the crowd. Pride swollen chest puffing, he let his faith fill the air. For the first time in a long time, his eyes were hopeful, watching with triumph rather than staring down in the hopes of going unnoticed.

A genuine laugh shook the assassin's entire body as she cheered alongside them.

Valis stood proud at the center of the swell, grinning from ear to ear, taking in all those who stood in support of him. The Shifters got to their feet, hugging each other. One held a hand to her mouth, another to his chest, drinking in the scene around them. The crowd surged forward, and Valis became lost in the madness, thank-yous and good-lucks being yelled from all directions.

Sterling pulled Lybbi close to his other side, wrapping his arm around her shoulders. Together, they all let out cheerful whoops and hollers.

The people's support didn't automatically make Valis their new Lord. Seeing him sit in the Lord's estate would be a long road if he ever did at all. But the crowd's support meant so much more than Valis's challenge. It meant the people were on the Shifters' side. It meant things could change. Maybe people wouldn't sit back anymore and watch while Kevah and his guards took advantage of those who wouldn't fight back.

The clouds overhead continued to gather and darken until they opened up, and rain started to fall, soaking everyone to the core in seconds. No one cared, and as a city, they danced together in the rain.

THE SMALL GROUP ran back to the guild, laughing and shouting. Ra and Layshan couldn't wait to share what they'd seen. To tell everyone they had been there when Valis challenged Kevah's reign. The moment was one none of them ever wanted to forget, and they recounted every detail the entire way home, adding embellishments and practicing the way they would tell it.

Once they were home and found their way inside they split ways, Layshan and Ra already spreading the word for everyone to meet them in the dining hall, eager to share their story. Lybbi, Sterling, and Malaina opted to head to their apartment first to put on dry, clean clothes.

Bounding through the door, Lybbi excitedly told Sterling and Malaina all about what she'd seen once again, as though they hadn't been there next to her.

"And did you see the way he made that wall of air around all of them?" Throwing her arms up, she spun around, her wet braid spraying water everywhere. Sterling laughed while Malaina found towels for each of them.

Letting down her brassy brown hair from its usual rope, Lybbi took the towel and fervently rubbed it against her dripping head.

"Chill out, you'll make yourself go bald," Malaina laughed, grabbing Lybbi's still-gloved hands, now damp.

"Sorry," Lybbi giggled, going gentler on her hair. "I just can't wait to get downstairs. I don't want to miss anything."

"You're not going to miss anything. You were there, or did you forget?" Sterling shook his dripping head like a dog.

"How could I?" Lybbi rolled her eyes so hard her head rolled. "No, I don't want to miss anyone's reaction. Can you imagine the look on everyone's faces when they find out the city guard was trying to arrest Shifters?" Malaina's smile slipped as Lybbi rambled, watching Sterling out of the corner of her eye. His eyes dropped to the floor, his smile faltering.

Lost in her own world, Lybbi didn't seem to notice. "Like, seriously, did they think no one was going to do anything? I mean, you and Sterling would have stopped them." Her grin swelled until neither of them could meet her gaze. "Right?"

Malaina plastered on a fake smile and her most comforting voice. "Of course."

"You guys would have stopped it, right?" This time, Lybbi's smile deflated as her eyes searched their faces. The towel dropped to her side, her breath quickening. "Right? Sterling? You would have done something?"

He tried and failed to meet her gaze, his dark seaweed green eyes exposing the way guilt ravaged him, eating him from the inside out.

"What? What am I missing? What aren't you telling me?"

Malaina took a deep breath, then knelt before Lybbi, taking her gloved hands in her own. Syn's gloves... "It's just that...There's been a lot of...changes throughout the city since the opening Games." The Shadow Spinner tried and failed to find the right words to explain, to make Lybbi understand nothing could have been done today or the day before. She was justifying it to both herself and Lybbi, hoping to quell some of the guilt churning her stomach. "Me and Sterling...we're just two people. There isn't always something we can do. Sometimes, all we can do is hope for the best and pray to the Gods that someone who is more capable will step in. Like today, with Valis."

Lybbi cut in before she had a chance to finish. "But if he hadn't stepped in, you would have done something, right? I mean, the guards can't get away with that."

Sterling's words were unwavering. "Yes, I would have done something."

"That doesn't mean it would have been the right thing to do." Malaina glared, meeting Sterling's hard eyes.

"Why not?" Lybbi tightened her grip on Malaina's fingers.

"Because he could have gotten hurt."

"But Valis was only one person and he didn't get hurt. And Sterling is just as strong." The young girl sounded so sure of herself, so sure of Sterling and Malaina, and whom she believed them to be. Was struggling to understand how the people she understood them to be were also capable of sitting back and letting something bad happen.

If only she knew…

Sterling flinched like Lybbi had stabbed him in the chest, his shoulders slumping, caving in on himself. He turned away, unable to look at the girl that had so much faith in him.

"That's true, but Valis is an Elemental. He's not a Shifter or a…Shadow Spinner." So used to referring to herself as a Death Bringer, Malaina stumbled over her true title. The one Lybbi had no idea she claimed.

"So? So what?" Trembling, Lybbi pulled out of Malaina's hold. "So if there hadn't been so many guards, *then* you would have done something. Right? Because then you would win, right?"

Sterling's fists tightened until his knuckles turned white, and clear shame tinted his eyes and face crimson.

Lybbi finally started to put the pieces together, understanding the looks on their faces. "You…you already let something bad happen, didn't you?"

Malaina bit her lip, searching for the right words. Her heart broke at the betrayal that crossed Lybbi's too-young face.

"Well, what happened?" Moving on from hurt to anger, Lybbi's voice took on a demanding edge. She spat the words, making Malaina prickle. "Did…did they arrest someone else? Like today?"

Malaina swallowed, falling back on her heels.

The weight of the day caught up to her, and what had

been a prickle of the skin turned into an ache spreading throughout her body, her muscles heavier all of a sudden.

"And you just let it happen?" Lybbi yelled.

The blow hit Malaina like a physical thing. Pain radiated through her. Her heart stuttered in her chest, struggling to beat.

"Lybbi, we did everything we could…" Sterling tried to reach out to her but jerked away as if stung by the very air around her.

Rage painted Lybbi's features, staring him down. "No, you didn't! If you didn't do anything then you didn't do everything you could!" As her voice grew louder, Malaina's pain intensified.

Doubling over, the Shadow Spinner gasped for air, trying to draw it into her lungs to cry out. The shaking hand holding her up threatened to send her face-first onto the floor, nearly giving out.

Sterling's voice was distant to her ears. "I wanted to, I swear."

"Was it because Malaina wouldn't let you?"

Malaina clung to the ground, her shadows swirling through her fingers, scared for her. She gasped for air, struggling to fill her lungs, but they clenched tight in her chest. Sterling said her name somewhere far away, but everything was fuzzy. Her sight. Her hearing. The floor beneath her was distant, black spots dancing in her vision.

She couldn't understand the words Lybbi screamed at her. Though she caught the words "hate" and "selfish", she couldn't make herself care. All she cared about was the fading world around her as her lungs refused to take in air and her heart struggled to beat.

She caught a glimpse of Lybbi's feet storming off, a faraway slam echoing in the distance.

Almost painfully, Malaina's lungs expanded, gulping down air. Her heart sped up, catching up on all the beats it had missed. She fell to her elbows, the world returning in a rush of stark clarity. Tears streamed down her face, though she couldn't remember at what point she started crying. Sterling was by her side, an arm wrapped around her shoulders, saying her name over and over again.

Falling into the Shifter's arms, she used his chest to hold herself up while she caught her breath. She clutched at his arms, reminding herself that she was alive and he was beside her. His presence around her grounded her to the world, keeping it from spinning out from under her feet.

Lybbi had just…

But Lybbi would never…

That's how it felt to…

Malaina couldn't finish any of her thoughts. They ran through her mind faster than she could catch them.

Malachi. She needed to talk to Malachi.

A task easier said than done.

Her entire body shook as she clawed her way up Sterling until she stood on unsteady feet. He helped her up, asking what she thought she was doing, but she didn't hear him. His words were a drone in the background as she stumbled for the door. The path in front of her was all she could see as she walked on shaky legs to the elevator. When the doors opened she stepped inside, jamming her finger into the button for the grand room.

She needed to find Malachi. Now.

When the doors closed and she was alone she used her sleeve to wipe at her cheeks and nose, not caring if she was getting all gross. She ran her hands through her hair, ripping through the knots that had formed in the rain.

The rain.

Had that happened just hours ago?

Sure she couldn't rely on her own legs to hold her up, she leaned back against the wall.

When the doors opened she pushed herself off the wall, forcing herself forward. The more her vision tunneled, the more challenging each step became. She saw nothing but Malachi's office doors and focused on nothing but getting to them. She didn't see the people around her, the ones who were lagging on their way to the dining hall.

No one reached out to help her.

She didn't expect them to.

Falling against the door to Malachi's office, she used the side of her fist to pound once. The door swung open, nearly sending her to the floor.

"Oh, bless the Mother." Malaina didn't see who it was, but delicate hands grabbed her, keeping her from falling to the ground. The touch…calming. Peaceful. Then, another pair of hands found her other arm. These were bigger and more insistent.

They sat her in a chair, still shaking, but now it was from nerves, not pain. Her mind was trying to catch up to her body. None of her understood the threat was gone.

Her eyes focused on Serena, who sat in the chair across from her, their knees touching. Serena bent over her, keeping a calming hand on Malaina at all times. Malaina looked up at Malachi, at the man who had saved her, who always had the answers, and took a deep breath.

"Will you…Will…" she choked on the words, "Lybbi. She…she tried to…I don't think it was on purpose. Will you…"

Malachi nodded, resolute. "We will start training immediately."

SEVENTEEN

Back in her own bed, Malaina woke from a dreamless sleep. Her eyelids were heavy, and her magic could sense the night strengthening outside her window. An arm was slung over her middle, a hand that wasn't her own clutched to her chest. Serena's dark hand was visible through the blanket of shadows that had wrapped around them in the night. Grasping Serena's fingers, Malaina brought the mistress's palm to her lips. Serena's magic, a low, ever-present hum, brushed against her mouth.

Despite Serena pressing against her back, Malaina's bed felt…empty. She stretched her legs, her feet searching the sheets, finding nothing but the cold.

Serena's hands left hers, slipping into her silver hair. "I need to go." The Anima's voice was quiet. Gentle. A mother speaking to a broken child.

Malaina's chest caved. She didn't want to be alone.

Rolling over, she buried her face in Serena's neck, pulling her close.

"Please, stay." The meek plea made her voice crack.

Serena pressed her soft lips to Malaina's temple, "I'm sorry, but I can't. I have work to do."

"It's hard loving such an important woman."

Serena smiled. "You have my sympathies."

Even then, Malaina didn't let go. After what happened, she wasn't ready to face Lybbi, knowing the young girl may not have realized what she'd done. She didn't want to see the way Sterling looked at her. Like he knew he'd been right. That he'd seen this coming for a long time and tried to warn her. A resigned, *I told you so, but I wish I'd been wrong,* look that she couldn't stand it. Like gloating mixed with a splash of self-loathing.

Seeking comfort in Serena's presence, she pulled the mistress closer. "She starts training today."

Serena pressed her lips together into a thin, understanding line. "I know."

"I'm not ready."

"You're never going to be ready." Serena ran her fingers through Malaina's hair, sending a calm wave through her. Malaina's mind stilled in the best way, and she nearly fell back asleep, letting her thoughts drift. Her shadows ambled through the air, unencumbered by the Shadow Spinner's constant refusal to acknowledge her magic.

They brushed against hers and Serena's skin, making them shiver in unison.

"Will you come?" Malaina begged.

Serena kissed her temple again. "Absolutely not." Then

she pulled back, out of Malaina's arms and out from beneath the sheets.

With a scowl twisting the assassin's face, she flopped to the bed. She already missed Serena's touch, her presence by her side.

"Why not? I thought you were supposed to support me and all that sweet crap." She propped her chin in her hands, admiring Serena as the mistress swapped her wrinkled shirt for one of Malaina's clean ones. Neither of them changed out of their clothes after they left Malachi's office.

"I do support you." Sweet syrup dripped from Serena's words. Leaning down, she touched the tip of her nose to Malaina's. "You're doing the right thing."

Malaina reached for Serena's hand, pulling her back into the bed. "Then come, please."

"That isn't how it works, and you know it." Using a fingertip to tap the end of Malaina's nose, she earned herself another dirty look. "Early training, especially the first, is supposed to be solo for everyone's safety. You'll be lucky if Malachi makes an exception for you and Sterling." Malaina let herself fall face-first into the mattress, groaning. Serena laughed at her, removing the silk hair wrap Malaina kept on hand for their rare impromptu sleepovers. "You'll be fine, but I have to go. I'll see you later."

Following Serena's exit, the front door opened and closed, and suddenly, the apartment felt too big and empty. Devoid of life and laughter.

Slipping out of bed, Malaina changed into more comfortable clothes. It had seemed like far too much work and utterly unimportant at the time Serena had guided her back to her room. Now, she hated the way her pants cut into her waist and her shirt bunched.

On her way to the living area of the apartment, Malaina paused in her bedroom doorway, reluctant to go any further. The kitchen was spotless and empty, without a single splatter of batter anywhere.

Too quiet.

Hugging her torso tight, she tried to hold herself together sash took reluctant steps. When she started making coffee, every little clank of the cups was too loud.

While the coffee brewed, another bedroom door opened. Sterling stepped out of his seldom-used room. He pressed his lips into a thin line, eyes briefly glancing over hers as he made his way across the living room. A folder had been slipped under the front door, and he stooped over to pick it up.

"Looks like someone talked to Malachi," he said solemnly, dropping the file on the breakfast counter.

Malaina watched it slide across the counter, unable to tear her eyes away. It looked so much like one of their contract files that it made her hands shake. Lybithina Kildrae, Lybbi's full name, was scrawled across the front in Malachi's perfect script. Malaina's tongue tapped against her teeth as it silently moved through the syllables, the name too long and clunky in her mouth, too formal for someone so full of life.

When they had come to the guild Malachi had offered them the same chance he gave all the guilders: to pick a new name. Malaina had chosen a new surname for them both to share, something untainted by their father, but chose to keep their first names. At the time, they'd needed the familiarity.

Sterling stood by Malaina's side, pouring himself a cup of coffee. He studied her studying the file.

"Good plan." He leaned back next to her, sipping from the mug. "Stare at it long enough, and that Fire Wielder blood of yours might just cause it to burst into flames."

"If only," she mumbled.

"It had to happen eventually." He placed a full coffee cup in her hands, the warmth seeping through the ceramic and into her fingers. The steaming, nutty coffee burned her tongue as she absently sipped, but she never took her eyes off the file on the counter. "After yesterday…"

"I know," she whispered, not needing to hear him say it.

He side-eyed her, taking in the new dark circles beneath her eyes. "Are you okay?"

She flinched. "I'm fine."

"Seeing you like that was horrible. She nearly…"

"But I'm fine," she cut him off. Better than anyone, she understood what Lybbi had done. The memory of it made her skin crawl. The ghost of what had happened still lingered in her chest, reminding her of the way her lungs had stopped. Stopped expanding. Stopped taking in air. The way her heart fought to keep beating, on the precipice of losing. If Serena hadn't been beside her last night the nightmares would have consumed her whole.

Trying to loosen her stiff muscles, Malaina rolled her head back and forth. Even then, standing in the kitchen, her entire body ached.

Lybbi's door opened. Without a word, the young girl made her way to the kitchen.

Trying to act like it was just another morning, Malaina straightened. Like nothing was wrong.

The tension in the apartment thickened when Lybbi froze, eyeing the file on the counter.

"Is that for me?" Her eyes trace the scrawl of her rarely used name across the front.

Malaina tried and failed to smile encouragingly. Instead, her lips twisted into something like a grimace, trembling. "Yeah, it is."

"What is it?"

"Why don't you open it and see?" Her voice cracked, and she hoped Lybbi wouldn't notice.

Lybbi hesitantly reached for it, sliding the file closer. Malaina tried not to squirm at the hiss of paper against stone, too loud for her pounding head. Flipping the file open, Lybbi scanned the page once…twice… and glanced up at Malaina.

"Is this true?" Guarded, she waited for Malaina to take away whatever was inside.

Malaina swallowed. "I don't know, what does it say?"

Skeptical of Malaina's ignorance, Lybbi narrowed her eyes. "It says that Malachi is changing my lesson schedule. Instead of tutoring lessons five days a week, he wants me to take lessons three days a week and start training three days a week."

Malaina pressed her lips together to keep from letting out a squeak. Sterling hung an arm over her shoulder, pulling her close.

"When do you start?" The Shifter came off far more supportive than Malaina could ever hope to pull off.

"Immediately. I start today."

Sterling used his coffee cup to gesture at Lybbi's room and continued to tighten his hold on Malaina to keep her from protesting. "You better go get ready then."

Lybbi started, then stopped, watching them both like a Kinetic observing a malfunctioning gear. Critically. Like she was still waiting for Malaina to stop her. To tell her a mistake had been made. But when neither of them said anything Sterling jerked his head, as if to say *go before she can say no.* The young girl took off, darting for her bedroom.

When the door closed again Malaina sagged. "She didn't eat breakfast," the assassin whined.

Sterling patted her shoulder, releasing his hold on her. "You're going to be a nightmare."

"Can I take it back? I'm not ready."

He kissed the top of her head. "No." He left her standing in the kitchen, heading for his room to dress for the day.

The need to hide in her own denial blazed, and she stared at his back with the same intensity she stared at the file. It hadn't burst into flame, but maybe he would, and then she and Lybbi could run off together, living with their disillusions for the rest of their lives.

When he reached the door, he glanced over his shoulder and raised a reprimanding eyebrow as if using those animal instincts to sense exactly what she was thinking. He closed his door with the audacity of being completely intact and unburned.

On the way down to the training room, the three of them rode the elevator in heavy silence. The lower the elevator went, the bouncier Lybbi became. Her excitement turned to anxiety, too much to contain in such a small body. Lybbi had dressed in her usual attire, and Malaina had to bite her lip to keep herself from sending her younger sister back to her room to change into something more comfortable and breathable. But Lybbi hadn't asked for her opinion, so she would have to figure out her mistakes the hard way, the same way the rest of them had.

The closer they got, the denser the air seemed to become. Malaina grabbed Sterling's hand. He squeezed her fingers tight, grounding her to the earth and keeping her calm—sort of.

The elevator finally slowed, bringing them to a stop, and Lybbi's hand latched onto Malaina's. Her gloved fingers were soft and warm, and Malaina suspected that her hands were clammy beneath the supple fabric.

The doors opened to reveal an empty training room, except for Malachi rolling up the sleeves of his button-down shirt. His gray suit jacket hung on the handle of one of the weapons closets.

Unsure for the first time that morning, Lybbi hesitated. Malaina placed a hand on her shoulder and gently pushed her forward.

It took a moment for Lybbi to find her nerve again, walking into the room and turning to look around. "There's no one here."

"No," Malaina answered, "The first training session is

always alone. You don't get to join groups until Malachi says it's OK."

Lybbi picked at the seams of her gloves, cocking an eyebrow. "Why?"

"Because magic builds up when you don't use it, kid," Sterling added, looking far more relaxed than either of the sisters. "You have to make sure you can control it before you can use it around anyone else."

"Which is precisely why Malaina and Sterling should not be here," Malachi called. He eyed the three of them, a reprimanding glint there that Malaina knew far too well.

Malaina planted her feet. Ready to grab Lybbi by the shoulders and take her right back upstairs if she had to. She wasn't going to leave her there alone.

"However," he groaned, and Malaina relaxed. "Given the special circumstance at hand, I will make an exception."

But Lybbi took a step back towards the elevator. "But… I thought I was just learning to fight and climb and pick locks and stuff. I'm not supposed to use my magic."

Malaina knelt before Lybbi, and suddenly, she was back in their apartment, her lungs screaming for air, but she shook away the memory. "You won't use your magic on anyone. That's why you have to do this, to learn how to control it so you don't hurt anyone by accident."

Lybbi looked to Sterling, who was already perched on one of the observation benches, his legs stretched out in front of him, and he nodded encouragement. "You'll do fine. We'll be right here the whole time."

Lybbi bit her lip. "Ok."

Malaina stood, giving Lybbi's gloved fingers one last encouraging squeeze before heading over to the bench to join Sterling.

"But don't let Malaina get too big sister-y and protective," the young girl ordered.

Sterling laughed, wrapping an arm around Malaina and pulling her into his side. Malaina pouted at Malachi's amused snort.

Hyping herself up, Lybbi bounced a couple of times before starting towards Malachi.

She didn't make it far before he raised his voice, his order reaching every corner of the room. "Start running."

Her face scrunched on the verge of defiance. "How many laps?"

"Until I tell you to stop."

Tentative, she looked back at the two criminals sitting on the bench.

"Now, Lybbi," Malachi ordered. In the span of a heartbeat, he had transformed from a concerned and caring guardian into an unyielding authoritarian focused on one thing: perfect obedience.

Lybbi took off in a slow jog down the track encircling the training room, picking up speed when Malachi told her she was going too slow.

Malaina's knee bounced, and she resisted the urge to put her hair up just so she could tear it down again.

Sterling stroked her shoulder with his thumb. "Come on, it won't be that bad. Don't you remember your first training session?"

"Yes," she forced through clenched teeth, "It was horrible. I puked up my guts twice."

Sterling chuckled. "I don't know, mine wasn't so bad."

She scowled. "You were also older, already in shape, and had been using your magic your whole life. Yours wasn't even necessary."

"What can I say? There are perks to being this awesome."

Malaina glared at him and flicked her fingers, sending a ribbon of darkness at his face, knowing Malachi would be too preoccupied playing drill sergeant to notice. The puff of black scattered when it hit, and the Shifter swatted at it like a physical blow.

Panting caught Malaina's attention. Lybbi passed them, beads of sweat already starting to form on her forehead, threatening to drip into her eyes.

Malaina anxiously tapped her fingers against her legs. She should have made Lybbi change. Should have told her to eat breakfast.

Lybbi was clad in clothing, with a long-sleeve shirt hiked up to her chin, Syn's gloves pulled up to her elbows, and thick pants tucked into a pair of sturdy boots. The outfit was too much. She was going to overheat, puke, and pass out from exhaustion. She would…

"She's fine," Sterling cut off the Shadow Spinner's rambling thoughts.

"She should've eaten."

He shrugged. "Less to puke up."

The assassin glared at him.

Malachi stood in the center of the room, radiating a

commander's air. Hands clasped behind his back, his words were cold when he spoke. "Lybbi, I want you to listen while you jog. I do not want you to stop unless you absolutely have to, and then I want you to walk until you can jog again. Understood?" Malachi wasn't satisfied with her nod. "Verbal answers only in this room. Is that understood?" His voice boomed. Malaina flinched at the memory of hearing this side of him for the first time.

"Yes, I understand," Lybbi rasped.

"Good." He cleared his throat. "The first thing you need to understand is that this will not be an easy process. Recognize that every person you have met and will meet in this guild has been through this and succeeded. This first session will be hard, but things will only become harder.

"Magic is like a form of energy building up in the body. It needs an outlet. Otherwise, it gets pent up. Magic is not controlled by, but can be fueled by, our stress, fear, and anger. After such a long time without a proper release, it will be eager to be of use. During this first session, my goal is to overexert you so your magic will be…manageable. For most, my only goal is to make sure their magic does not become too much for their bodies to handle, but considering your specific magic, this first session will be that much more exhausting. Tired magic is controlled magic, and in your case, this could not be more important."

Eventually, Malachi let Lybbi stop running, only to push her harder and harder in one demanding way or another. One more pushup, one more sit-up, one more lap. Lift that and carry it over there, now carry it back. Drag this over there. Over and over again he pushed until sweat poured off her, her face red and splotchy. Brassy strands of hair flew free of her usual braid, only to be plastered to her face and neck.

By a quarter of the way through, Malaina was on her feet, pacing back and forth before the benches. Running her hands through her hair, she could hardly stay on the sidelines when Lybbi's knees started to buckle.

Lybbi met every demand the guild master threw at her and completed every challenge. Dejection bunched her brow after every new order Malachi barked at her. Her stubborn side wanted to fight back and refuse, but she didn't. Instead, she took deep breaths, but her seemingly aching lungs protested every time she stood up straight again.

Until she didn't…

Down on her hands and knees, Lybbi panted, sucking down air, ribs heaving. Sweat dripped from her forehead, pooling on the padded ground beneath her.

Malachi ordered one more lap around the room.

The young girl's fingers curled in frustration, as if trying to carve gouges into the floor. From where she paced, Malaina couldn't tell if those were tears welling in her eyes or if it was sweat dripping down her face.

"Up," Malachi ordered, "One more lap."

Lybbi tried to push herself up onto her feet, but her legs shook and she fell back to the ground. "I…I can't…" she gasped.

Malachi stood before her, staring down at the shaking girl.

Every day, Malaina thought Lybbi seemed a little older,

a little taller. But at that moment, she thought that her little sister had never been so small. So broken.

Malachi lifted a hand towards Malaina and curled his fingers before turning away. That was the only encouragement Malaina needed. Water in hand, she took off across the room, skidding to a stop on her knees before Lybbi, who thudded back onto her butt, her head hanging between her knees.

"You're doing great," Malaina assured her, not bothering to keep the pride from her voice. Lybbi had always been stubborn, but seeing her use it for good instead of annoyance had the older sister beaming through her worry.

Lybbi grabbed the water bottle from Malaina's hand, took a long swig, and wiped stray drops of water from her chin. "This sucks."

Malaina couldn't stop the halfhearted laugh that bubbled up. "Yeah. Yeah, it really does."

Lybbi tipped the bottle back again, drinking heavily. Malaina took the water back mid-gulp. Lybbi reached for it, a whine in her throat.

"Not too fast," Malaina scolded half-heartedly, "You'll make yourself sick."

"That's enough," Malachi admonished her.

A protest built-in Malaina's throat, but she swallowed it down. She took one more look at the sweat-drenched gangly girl pleading for more water. Stepping in, playing the guardian role, and stopping everything was tempting. To put an end to this necessary torture. But Lybbi needed this. Needed to make it through on her own.

So Malaina went back to the bench and plopped back down next to Sterling. Elbows on her knees, her hands clenched so hard her knuckles turned white. Sterling leaned in, trying to pull her into his side, but her body was so tense she didn't budge.

He ran a hand down her back instead. "You're being, as Lybbi put it, big sister-y."

"Shut up," she muttered over her fisted hands.

Malachi stood before Lybbi, observing her the way a person studied a difficult puzzle, head cocked to the side.

"Take off your gloves," the Kinetic instructed her cooly.

Lybbi sat back on her heels, studying her hands. Her expression turned to one of apprehension, as though the whole thing were a sick joke. Fear coated her shaky words. "I'm not supposed to. I'm never supposed to take them off."

The guild master crouched down until he balanced on his toes. His trainer's facade dropped for a moment, warmth entering his gray-green eyes. It was amazing how easily he could switch back and forth from hard to soft, from cold to warm.

His unflinching confidence met Lybbi's scared eyes. "I know you are not supposed to, and when you are outside this room I want you to keep them on until we agree you do not need them anymore. However, when we work together you must obey without question. When I say take off your gloves, you must trust me, and take them off. Understand?"

From the other side of the room, Lybbi's quivering whispers were almost inaudible, "What if I hurt someone?"

Malachi didn't hesitate. "I promise, this is a safe place." He pointed to the back of the room, towards the medical offices where the guild's Witches worked. "Jade is right behind that door, and she is one of the most talented Witches in this city. Possibly in all of Thaumoria. Between the two of us, we will ensure that you never hurt anyone."

She turned his words over in her mind before removing her gloves finger by finger. Malaina held her breath. For the first time in years, Lybbi's hands were completely exposed, save for a few stolen moments of freedom between switching gloves here and there. Malaina wondered if the sudden tension was a pulse of magic or her own fears pulsing in her ears, or both.

Lybbi shakily placed the gloves in Malachi's outstretched hands, careful to avoid skin-to-skin contact.

"Good." Malachi stood and backed away from her, turning cold again.

"I don't know if I can watch this," Malaina whispered for only Sterling to hear. Running her sweaty palms over her pants the urge to call her shadows weighed on her. To seek the comfort and reassurance they offered. She wished Serena were beside her, to hold her hand and assure her in that honey-sweet voice that everything would be all right.

Sterling continued to run a hand over her back, though he had become tense and stiff next to her. "He knows what he's doing."

Malachi held out a hand and flicked his fingers toward a corner of the room. A large potted plant slid out from an entire group of greenery, sliding until it sat directly between him and the terrified young girl. The plant was the same height as Lybbi once she got to her feet on wobbly legs. Its leaves were fans, its stems thick, green, and healthy.

Lybbi watched it warily, clutching her pale hands to her chest.

"I want you to touch the plant so I can observe what happens." A hint of something in Malachi's voice was different. Off. The tiniest twinge in his words revealed he may not have been completely sure about what he was doing.

Lybbi swallowed hard, never tearing her eyes from the plant. "Do I have to?"

"What did I say about questioning me?"

Lybbi pressed her lips together, fighting back a retort. She took a tentative step forward, examining the plant. Watched the way the leaves lifted and fell in the slight breeze from the overhead fans. She took a deep breath and then reached out her hand. She let a single finger hover over one of the leaves before lightly placing it on the glossy surface. All the air was sucked out of the room when tears started to stream down Lybbi's face, her heartbreak clear in her eyes.

Beneath her touch, the leaf started to wither, all the color and life being drained, radiating from the spot her finger touched. The disease spread over the fan-like leaf in seconds, turning from a once bright green to a withering gray, as if it hadn't been watered in weeks and left in harsh sunlight. The edges of the leaf curled inwards, the decay spreading down the stem and leaching into the rest of it.

They all sat in silence, watching the blight quickly devour the rest of the plant, everything shriveling into nothing. No sign of life remained. The dry, sickly brown husk hung to the floor, wilted over the edge of the pot.

The memory of air escaping her lungs, death within her grasp, weighed on Malaina.

When there was nothing left to take, even the soil seeming to have lost its vitality, Lybbi dropped her hand. She stood statue still, tears dripping down her chin, blank eyes staring through the plant. As though she could bring it back to life by means of unbridled regret alone. Regret for what she had done. For the way she was born.

The heavy weight of silence bore down on them all as they experienced a glimpse into what a true Death Bringer could do.

EIGHTEEN

Sterling didn't stalk out of Lybbi's room, in wolf form, until past sunrise. Canine or not, he looked exhausted. His head and tail hung low, his paws dragging across the carpet, eyes pale blue. He shifted back to human form before plopping onto the end of the couch. Malaina laid down, using his leg as a pillow. He pinched the bridge of his nose, rubbing at his eyes.

"Is she finally out?" Malaina asked.

"Yeah," he breathed.

Sleeping in her own room when they were all home wasn't something Lybbi did often, but when she did, she liked having someone in the room until she fell asleep, watching over her to keep her safe from the nightmares that often plagued her. Nothing made her feel safer than her own private giant wolf sprawled across her floor, watching the door.

"I knew she was the Death Bringer, and theoretically, I

understood what that meant. But seeing it like that..." Sterling trailed off, his words lost to the dark of the heavily curtained living room.

Malaina closed her eyes, fighting against the ache that threatened her sanity. Her entire life, she'd seen Lybbi's magic up close. Nine years ago had been her last kill, but it still stuck with Malaina.

Refusing to acknowledge the truth, she pushed it down. But each time she killed to protect Lybbi's identity she was reminded of what Lybbi might become.

"It's so different from what you do," he continued, "It's like you can feel the life being sucked out of the room."

Malaina didn't answer. Lost in memory, she was pulled back to a place she never let herself visit. Those six months on the streets after their father tried to burn the house down, trying to rid the world of his cursed Dark Magic daughters.

To the day she had left Lybbi behind in a crowded alley where they had been living to beg on a street corner for enough coppers to put food in Lybbi's belly. That alley had been known for attracting the homeless of the city, makeshift shelters and tents lining the walls, dirty bodies packed into the small space, cultivating the stench of waste that had nowhere to go.

Malaina had only been ten at the time and had suddenly found herself caring for a four-year-old. Caring for even herself was a foreign concept, let alone a child. The one thing she had known was that Lybbi needed three things: food, water, and somewhere to sleep. Packed in among the other homeless, she'd found them a place to sleep. Everyone had taken the two of them in, fawning over Lybbi the way everyone did, but food and money didn't materialize out of nowhere. Malaina still needed to provide, and she hadn't wanted Lybbi to be subject to the hatred begging often brought.

The young Shadow Spinner had done the only thing she could think of at the time. One of the neighbors had offered to watch Lybbi, an older man who had always been kind to them, sharing scraps and showing them the safe places to collect water. Plus, he'd had a puppy Lybbi adored, so Malaina hadn't worried.

After a long day of begging, she had received a handful of copper coins that she used to buy a few old pieces of bread from one of the bakeries and had even batted her eyes into a piece of chocolate. Pride had swelled inside her chest, excited to show Lybbi what she'd accomplished. The pittance would be a feast like they hadn't had in months, and Malaina thought maybe she could do it. Maybe she *could* take care of them.

They'd been raised in a privileged home. Sure, love hadn't been abundantly available, but she'd never once thought about where food came from. Her entire life, meals, and snacks had come from the kitchen. Now, she had to figure it all out on her own, and holding that bread and piece of chocolate in her hands gave her hope that she was learning.

Smiling at those she recognized and keeping an eye on any newcomers who might be looking to cause trouble, she made her way through the alley. The tarp door to the old man's shelter crinkled when she pushed it aside.

Entering that shelter was like walking face-first into a brick wall. The life constantly present in the alley had fallen away. Everything felt distant. The sound of all the people around them talking dulled, as though no life was capable of entering the shelter. The old man had been lying on his side on his palate bed, eyes wide, mouth hanging open, skin ashen. His chest didn't rise or fall, his eyes saw nothing. Lybbi sat cross-legged by his side, back to his stomach, the puppy limp in her arms.

Malaina had stood there in horror, not knowing what to say or do.

"What did you do?" Was all she could think to ask.

"I didn't do it, I promise," Lybbi had sworn, tears in her eyes.

Death Bringer. That's what her father had called Lybbi. What he would yell over and over again while he paced drunk around their house.

Malaina had heard the stories but she had never been able to connect those words to her little sister. To the doe-eyed little girl sitting by her side.

But the way the air in that makeshift shelter pressed heavily on Malaina's shoulders…was familiar. She'd felt it before, the day her mother had died. The day Lybbi had accidentally killed her wet nurse. Four lives. Lybbi had now taken four lives by accident.

She had done it, but it wasn't her fault—not really. She hadn't done it on purpose.

Malaina's heart thudded in her chest, the chocolate melting in her fingers, forgotten. She didn't know how to fix it. Adults were supposed to take care of these things. When her mother died, her father was the one who took care of everything. He knew what to do. Adults always knew what to do.

What Malaina knew was that they couldn't stay—not in that shelter, not in that alley, not in that part of town. No one could know what Lybbi had done.

Yanking, she pulled Lybbi to her feet. Dropping the puppy, it fell to the ground in a lifeless heap of fur and skin and bone. They had stood there, staring at it lying on the ground, nearly making Malaina sick. The puppy looked so tragic. So alone. Just hours before it had been full of vigor, rolling around and nibbling on fingers.

They needed to run, but she couldn't abandon the puppy like that.

Rushing forward, she'd picked it up. The fur had still been warm and soft beneath her fingers, decay not yet stiffening the limbs. Unable to leave it alone in the middle of the shelter, she tucked the puppy beneath one of the old man's arms, nestled against his side. The act of kindness was a little thing, and it didn't really matter in the grand scheme of things, but it had made her feel better nonetheless. At least now they would have each other until someone found their bodies. Once again, she took Lybbi's hand, and together, they fled deeper into the city.

After a long, drawn-out silence, Malaina whispered, "It's so easy to forget. Living with her every day, seeing her laugh and be so happy. Sometimes, I just…forget."

Sterling rubbed at his temple in thought. "I heard the stories growing up. I think everyone does. The stories meant to scare children into behaving and warn them against the Dark Magics. Mind Benders will bend you to their will, Shadow Spinners will hide in the dark and take you in the night." Malaina flinched. "Death Bringers will come in your window and kill you with a kiss. I remember them. You just don't expect someone so…small. So kind and happy, to be filled with magic so…"

"Dark," Malaina finished for him. They were called the Dark Magics for a reason. A reason they rarely made it to adulthood. No parent wanted a cursed child. No one wanted someone like her and Lybbi to live in their city. Like they were normal people living normal lives.

The sun rose higher over the city, blocked by the thick curtains that hung over all the apartment windows. But the Shadow Spinner sensed the way her shadows shrank away in its presence. Their absence in the world left her drained, leaving a part of her missing.

Exhausted, she was ready to sleep for days, but the thought of her big empty bed was less than appealing. Turning, she buried her face against Sterling's stomach, feeling the comfort of his presence. He stroked her silver hair, and as the world grew brighter outside their windows her muscles grew heavier, her mind slower.

Sleep was finally starting to overtake her when a knock sounded at the front door. Sterling's eyes were barely open, head resting against a fist. They sleepily looked at each other for a while, trying to confirm if they actually heard what they thought they had heard.

"You don't think…" She started.

"No way. Not right now." He stated it like a fact, but it sounded more like prayer.

After the last couple of days, after the disaster that was the Alman contract, she couldn't imagine Malachi had a job for them now.

Lying on the ground before their front door was a flier, bland apart from the standard text printed in neat lines. The words were stark against the all-but-blank paper.

Today!
Valis Urnmot challenges Lord Kevah Oseay
Location: Stadium
Time: Noon
Come witness the historical event.

The challenge was really happening. Part of her couldn't believe it. She had expected something to go wrong—for Valis to back out of his challenge or for the whole thing to be stopped before it ever began by bureaucratic twisting of the rules. Anything. Formal challenges against the Lord or Lady of the city were a fateful event, and she hadn't expected it to happen so quickly.

"What is it?" Sterling asked, still bleary-eyed on the couch.

She held up the flier. "It's Valis's challenge." That's when she noticed the writing on the back. Immediately, she recognized Ra's chicken scratch, the letters melding together as if his hand couldn't write as fast as his mind worked.

Roof?

"I don't think we're going to get much sleep today."

Sterling moaned, his head falling against the back of the couch with a *thunk*.

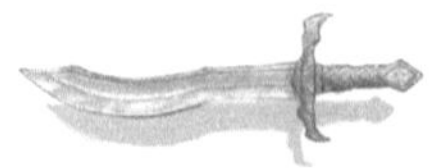

STERLING AND MALAINA had slept until they couldn't justify it anymore, stretched out in the living room, an unsaid agreement that neither of them wanted to sleep alone in their rooms. When the time had come to leave, Malaina tried to talk Lybbi into joining them, but the Death Bringer had barely looked up from beneath her covers. Still curled up in her bed, she showed no signs of wanting to leave.

Malaina's heart frayed at the pointed silence, but she didn't push it, so she left Lybbi to sleep.

Sterling and Malaina took their time making their way through the city to the stadium. The streets were eerily quiet and devoid of people. Even the ever-persistent sea birds seemed to have taken a break from harassing the streets. Storefronts were dark, and nearly every sign flipped to closed. No children played on sidewalks, no parents watched from the stoops. Even bedroom windows stayed closed rather than open to move stale air in the spring breeze.

They didn't talk as they wound through the city. The words would have been too loud, and there was nothing to say anyway.

Traditionally, challenges against the Elemental Lord were a graceful and accepted cycle of life. The next heir was often identified at a young age and raised by the current Lord or Lady's council to learn how to lead and prepare for the responsibility they were to take on when the time came.

Kevah had been identified as a tri-wielder young, and his family was given the opportunity to live on the Lord's estate while he grew up and was raised to take on the role expected of him.

Fifteen years ago, when Kevah had come of age, he formally announced his challenge at the opening night of that year's Games. It hadn't been a tense or sad event. Instead, the former Lady had gracefully accepted the challenge. A few days later, they dueled, and when it became clear Lady Aladonna had no hope of overpowering Kevah, she admitted her defeat, as expected, and the power passed from one hand to the other. That day, Lord Kevah walked away a powerful man in more ways than one.

But that had always been the plan.

Today would not be so clear-cut and cordial. An unexpected challenge didn't happen often. A person didn't declare a challenge against the Lord lightly, though technically any Elemental of age could do it, in spite of their family name or where they lived.

Kevah hadn't been challenged once since he had claimed his title. There just weren't many people capable of holding their own against a tri-wielder, let alone winning.

Getting swept up in the thrill of Valis's challenge in the street had been easy, but now reality was setting in, and the facts were Valis was a bi-wielder going up against a tri-wielder and trying to win. From what Malaina understood, he had no formal fight training. Sure, he won Games single-handedly, but Kevah had been *raised* to win this. He had been trained in one-on-one combat practically from the time he could walk and taught by the best how to wield his elements to be their deadliest. Groomed from a young age to sit in that estate and rule over the city.

Valis hadn't.

When they got closer to the stadium, the number of people on the streets grew. Entire families were out, dressed in their temple best, ready to attend a possibly historic moment.

Malaina tried not to think of the day her father had taken her to see Lord Kevah take his title. That day was one of her few positive memories of her father, and she had no interest in seeing him in any sort of favorable light.

Once the stadium was in sight, the crowd was so thick there was no way to get to the entrance. Instead, Malaina and Sterling veered to the right, finding their usual building. They climbed to the rooftop where they normally watched the Games when they couldn't score seats in the stadium. Ra and Layshan were already perched on the ledge.

"You guys made it." Ra jumped to his feet.

"Finally," Layshan muttered, flipping his hair from his eyes.

"Good call on the roof," Malaina said, "I don't think we ever could have gotten inside."

She peered over the ledge at the massive crowd outside the stadium entrance. People were funneling themselves inside, but bodies already packed the seats. Spectators were already sitting on the ground between rows, taking up space on the stairs, standing in the back, and leaning against walls. There was no way everyone outside the stadium would find space, but people would settle for merely hearing the duel—to be able to say they were there when it happened.

Around them, groups of people hoping to catch a glimpse inside the stadium topped every building that had even the slightest view and accessible roof access. Gathered families and business owners still in their smocks and uniforms paced back and forth. Everyone capable of sparing the time found a way to be present in some way.

Their usual roof was mercifully empty, save for Ra and Layshan. Malaina guessed it was because this particular building didn't have any convenient roof access and had to be scaled if one wanted what the criminals had determined years ago to be the best view.

"No Lybbi?" Ra was already turning back to the stadium.

"She had a long night and wasn't quite feeling up for it." Sterling gave Layshan one of those guy hugs that turned from a handshake into a shoulder pat. "Sorry, your biggest fan won't be here today."

Layshan rolled his eyes and ran a hand through his blonde hair. "She's a good kid."

Malaina crossed her arms, scanning the crowd below. "She has the biggest crush on you," she said off-handedly, though she watched him out of the corner of her eye.

The Air Wielder shrugged. "She's got good taste, don't know what to tell you."

Ra sneered. "I'm sure I could tell her a few stories to change her mind."

"Would you? I'd rather she focused on someone her own age. Oh, and not a professional criminal," Malaina said, only partially kidding.

Sterling's lips quirked, giving her a mocking smirk. "Well, that seems a little hypocritical."

Unable to argue the point she stuck her tongue out at him. Lybbi growing up in the guild meant she would probably follow in the footsteps of everyone around her, but Malaina had always hoped she would take another route. A safer one.

Layshan laughed, too full of himself to work up a decent blush at the mention of Lybbi's crush on him. Of course, he'd always known. At thirteen, Lybbi wasn't very subtle. And while he wasn't Malaina's favorite, she appreciated that he had never taken advantage of Lybbi's young naive feelings.

"Did you guys hear about what happened to Ani and Ermyn on their last contract?" Ra changed the subject.

"The forgers?" Sterling asked.

Ra nodded. "Yeah! So they got to the drop point for a bunch of registration cards, and it was a total setup…" He went off, ready to share the latest gossip.

Malaina only partially listened, his words working in the back of her mind while she observed the people below. How many of them were hoping for Valis to come out on top today? How many of them stood behind Kevah and his new regimes? It wasn't like the Games, where the crowd bore colors and waved flags representing who they supported.

If she'd learned anything about people in her time working for a criminal guild, it was that people weren't as upfront about their morals as they'd like to seem. Nobles who would talk a big game about hard work and outwitting their opponents in business wouldn't hesitate to kill off their competition if they thought it was the only way to get ahead. Pettiness and deceit ran deep in that city, where people like Ra and Layshan stole wealth for others, where death dirtied Sterling's and her hands over a few stolen coins.

Today wasn't a Game, and there was no clear-cut way to look out into the crowd and know who people truly rooted for in their hearts.

As the sun rose closer to its apex in the sky, closer and closer to noon, Malaina started to sweat. She'd worn a light jacket and pants tucked into a pair of boots and was starting to think she should have dressed lighter. But she'd worn the jacket for a reason. Shoving her hands deep into the jacket pockets, she relished the darkness hidden there.

Normally, she wouldn't allow herself the luxury of indulging in her magic so publicly, even if it was in the privacy of her own pockets. Losing herself in the feeling and becoming lazy would be too easy. To accidentally reach for one when she shouldn't. But today, she gave herself a free pass to play. She needed to let her magic out of its cell, even if it was bar by bar. If she didn't give in to that incessant need at least a little she didn't think she'd get through the day.

After so many years of forcing it down, of locking it away, she hardly noticed the need in her chest during her day-to-day life. The way it built up and pounded against her breastbone, beating at the bars of the cage she had forced it into years ago. That uncomfortable feeling had become a part of who she was, just like calling herself a Death Bringer.

But today…today she needed relief. So she dug her fingers deeper, closing her eyes and seeing through her fingers. A moan nearly escaped her parted lips, letting that small relief consume her. The shadows eagerly complied, weaving between her fingers. That suggestion of a caress moved along her hand. She became so lost in that little bit of magic she almost forgot the way the sun moved across the sky, growing stronger by the minute. Beating down against the top of her head and burning her scalp.

The noise of the people all around her faded into the background, a new familiar buzz taking its place. The hum of her shadows was only in her head. It wasn't real. It was a reaction to the hypnotic peace using her magic gave her.

Shadows couldn't make noise. They weren't physical things a person could feel and hear.

But still…sometimes, she thought they spoke to her, a language all their own, made just for her.

A horn blasting through the stadium wrenched her back into reality. The peal stopped her heart cold. Her eyes snapped open, and every person within earshot of the stadium stilled.

"Citizens of the great City of Elementals!" An announcer's voice rang out around the stadium. Malaina's lip curled at the greeting.

Citizens. Cities didn't have citizens. They were all people of Thaumoria.

She wondered if that was a slip on the announcer's part. Wondered if their impartial commentator actually had a favorite in this duel, and that was their way of showing it, or if it was a script they were reading from, doing their duty the way they were instructed.

"Please turn your attention to the center of the arena. Today's duel is about to begin!"

NINETEEN

They stood on the edge of the roof, none of them bothering to sit on the sweltering stone. They were all wound too tight to sit still. They needed to be on their feet, needed to be able to move.

The tunnels the leagues usually entered through rose, and the ground rumbled in response, sending waves over the moat surrounding the arena. Valis entered the arena through one, Lord Kevah the other. They were both bare-chested and bare-footed, wearing the same pants clinging close to their waists and ankles and flowing loosely about the rest of their legs. The crowd cheered as they walked towards the island in the center of the arena, both their names being screamed from every angle of the stadium.

Lord Kevah smiled and waved to his people, turning so he could address every single person in attendance. The arena was his stage, a place to perform rather than a place to fight for his right to rule. A long tail of fiery red hair fell down his back, his piercing blue-green eyes visible even from the roofs. His lean, muscular form no longer hid under loose flowing shirts and robes, he was…lankier than Malaina would have expected. Like his limbs were slightly disproportionate to the rest of him. But despite never being challenged in the fifteen years since he took the Lordship practically uncontested, he clearly still trained for duels. Ropes of muscle ran over every exposed inch of him.

Opposite him, Valis looked far more serious. His relaxed shoulders and languid stride almost hid the tension coiling through him, ready to snap at any moment. Warm brown eyes analyzed Kevah's every movement, watching for tells and weaknesses. Obviously, he spent a lot of time honing and strengthening his magic for the Games, but that didn't necessarily translate to dueling. How much did he know about physical combat and sparring?

The tunnels closed behind them, and the paths cutting through the water sunk back below the surface. There was no more turning back, no way out. This wouldn't end until one of them conceded or, more traditionally, until one of them died. Though no one had been killed during a Lordship Challenge in generations, civility took precedence over ancient tradition.

"The tradition of Lordship Challenges goes back to the core of who the Elemental people are and the blessings of our Gods and Goddesses. Long ago the people of Thaumoria lived as one, ruled by none. Until the infamous Alvar Andelit, the only Elemental to be blessed with the ability to wield all four elements attempted to take what he believed to be his God and Goddess-blessed right to rule Thaumoria. It was a time of violence and turmoil, of division between magic classes, until the people came together and stood against Andelit's conquest. As a result, the magic classes each established their own form of rule to keep control of those who may one day follow in Andelit's footsteps and signed the City Establishment Treaty."

Malaina couldn't conceal the snarl twisting her face. She wondered if anyone else felt the irony of the announcer's words.

"Today, we honor that tradition, set in place by the first Elemental Lady, Lady Kell, who earned her place by fighting her way into Lordship. Today, the blessings of the Gods and Goddesses will reign supreme, and we will see who has the right to sit at the head of our magnificent city and represent our people." The crowd cheered again, stomping their feet and shaking the ground in the wake of the simplistic history lesson. When things quieted again the announcer continued, "The rules of the challenge are simple. Once the duel begins, no one may interfere on behalf of either challenger. They must duel, relying on their own power and magic, until there is one left standing. The challengers may use any means they see fit to win, so long as they are relying on their own abilities alone. The challenge will not end until we have a winner, and that winner will take their rightful place as Elemental Lord."

A chime rang out around the arena, smashing itself against Malaina's eardrums, sending a shiver down her spine despite the heat.

And the duel began.

Immediately, Valis stomped one foot, sending a rip

through the ground. A spike of stone pierced the earth beneath Kevah.

Using the momentum of Valis's attack, Kevah glided through the air and called a thick stream of water to meet the soles of his feet. At inhuman speed, he skated along a slide of ice, glittering in the afternoon sun, guiding himself towards Valis.

In a move he'd done dozens of times in the Games, Valis shot bullets of air at Kevah to knock him off his slide.

Kevah effortlessly dodged the attacks, air missing him by a blade's width. Turning this way and that along the track, he could have been on a luxurious skating trip rather than being assaulted. The smile never left his lips, and his smug eyes stayed trained on Valis.

Another pillar of earth shot up, breaking through Kevah's ice. The force of it sent him soaring again. A massive boulder flew straight for his airborne form.

Exuding the grace and confidence of an Air Wielder, Kevah flipped mid-air, his back nearly skimming along the boulder's rough surface. His feet landed on the opposite side, and he pushed off, sending himself back and the boulder flying toward Valis.

Earth wrapped itself around the challenger's ankles, creating a pair of solid boots holding him in place so he could shield himself. The boulder smashed on impact, shattering into hundreds of smaller rocks. Spinning on his heels the boots released. Manipulating scattered currents of air, he sent rocks the size of his head flying back toward Kevah, who waited on the outskirts of the arena.

As if he were gracefully maneuvering a dance floor,

Kevah wove through the flying rocks, ducking and dodging killing blows with a wave of his hand. He stalked across the water, a predator toying with its prey.

"You don't have to do this." Kevah held his arms out to his sides, palms open. There was a hint of amusement in his voice as if he was enjoying the spectacle of everything. "This can be over now. You can go back to being the city's beloved star."

Anger flamed through Valis's bulging veins while he listened to Kevah speak. His fingers curled into fists by his sides, and the ground in the arena rumbled. Raising his fists in front of him, Valis erected two walls of earth on either side of Kevah.

A laugh echoed in the shadow of those walls, unconcerned about the potential of being crushed. Unfurling his fingers, Valis brought his hands together, and the walls closed in on the Lord.

Fists shoot out to either side of Kevah, and the rocks burst apart on contact. Still smiling, he stood untouched, earth raining around him.

"Dear Aais…" Sterling absently leaned back, putting distance between him and the sight before them. "Kevah hasn't even attacked yet. He's not even trying."

Malaina shook her head in disbelief. "I remember his duel against Lady Aladonna, and it was nothing like this. It's like he's enjoying it."

"I would give anything to have that kind of power." Unabashed awe bathed Layshan's gawking expression. Ra reached out and gave him a small smack to the back of the head. Layshan rubbed the spot and returned the favor. The thieving pair glared at each other. "What was that for?"

"You're being an ass."

"I'm being honest. I'm not saying I like the guy, but I can only dream of having that kind of power. I'm just saying it's impressive."

"Scary. The correct word is scary." Sterling couldn't tear his eyes from the arena. "Valis doesn't stand a chance."

In an attempt at comfort, Malaina placed a hand on his arm. "You don't know that. Things could change." She didn't sound convincing even to herself.

Valis erected a half-circle wall of earth around himself. It guarded his back as he turned, staying in the center of the arena. His elements were earth and air, so his go-to strategy was staying away from the water entirely. Unfortunately for the challenger, Kevah didn't need to be near the water to wield it. From half an arena away, he called forth tidal waves worth of water without strain.

Finally, Kevah attacked. Water flowed around him in masses, constantly at his beck and call, inches away. An arrogant, Mind Bender's smirk darkened his features when he grazed the nearby water with his fingers and shot a deadly spike of ice at Valis's head.

Just in time, Valis fell to a knee. The spike wedged itself deep into the wall of earth, half buried, square where the bi-wielder's head had been.

Another thrust of the Lord's hand sent another shot of water.

A fraction of a second too slow, the water struck Valis's

hand, smacking it back against the wall. The water froze solid, a cuff on sparkling ice holding his hand in place.

Stuck on his knees, he could do nothing when Kevah shot again, and Valis's other hand froze to the wall.

Malaina's hands fell limply to her sides at the sight of Valis on his knees.

It was over. It had to be.

Taking his time approaching his prisoner, Kevah prowled across the arena but still kept his distance.

Yanking on his handholds, Valis desperately fought to get free, but he couldn't get the leverage to wield anything. A deadly spike of earth thrust up until its point pressed itself against the soft underside of his chin when Kevah's heel struck the ground.

The crowd went silent. Nobody moved, watching the spectacle before with awed quiet. Those outside the stadium stilled, sensing the shift in the salty air.

"Concede," Kevah commanded.

Baring his teeth, Valis's words traveled throughout the stadium on Kinetic-enhanced sound waves. A growl ground between clenched teeth. "Never."

The ice around the challenger's hands started to glow.

A collective gasp went through the crowd as the ice confining Valis's hands melted away. Fire shot from his outward-facing palm, barreling into Kevah. The force of it threw the Lord back, having barely had a chance to shield himself from the attack.

Valis jumped to his feet and smashed his palm against Kevah's spike, pushing it back into the ground.

Sweeping relief caused an involuntary laugh to bubble

out of Malaina. She clutched Sterling's arm, fingers digging in as he stumbled back in shock.

The crowd went wild, screaming and cheering. Distantly, she heard words like "cheater" and "impossible" yelled out from the audience, but the overwhelming mayhem erupting from the stadium drowned them out.

"He…he was hiding a third element?" Ra yelled, trying to be heard over the roar around them.

"Why would someone do that?" Layshan answered with his own question.

"Does it matter?" Sterling laughed, "They're evenly matched now. Earth, fire, and air, versus earth, fire, and water."

"He has a chance," Malaina whispered, more to herself than to anyone else. Hope bloomed in her chest despite the overbearing heat of the sun.

Valis threw fireball after fireball, backed by the force of his air. They flew so fast that Kevah could only deflect them, staggering back. Every moment that the Lord struggled to come to terms with his change of circumstances was a moment Malaina savored. Every staggering step back lifted her hopes higher. She almost didn't remember to keep a container on her magic, her joy ready to send her secrets flying.

Too quick, Kevah found his bearings and spun beneath another fireball. From his open mouth came a tornado of flames that engulfed the arena. Licks of flame crawled up the edges of the arena walls, lapping at the hands of spectators along the railing, rivaling the heat of the sun above. A devastating attack that would have been overwhelming and duel-ending... if Valis wasn't a tri-wielder.

When the flames died away, both men stood on either end of the land, panting and unharmed.

The Kinetic-enhanced sound waves spread the words Kevah snarled, wavering for a moment as if even the Kinetics themselves couldn't believe the words that sent everyone into horrified silence.

"You just lost your right to concede."

For the first time during the duel, Kevah's muscles strained. Lifting his hands at his sides, two waves formed on either side of the arena, draining the water from the rest of the moat. The water rose higher and higher, building until there wasn't any water left. His arms came crashing down, and with them, the water went hurling at a devastating speed.

Wrapping his arms around himself at the last minute, a sphere of rapid air shielded Valis.

Kevah used water to pummel him, refusing to let up. From the momentary gaps in the unrelenting waves, they saw Valis losing strength. The sphere of air keeping him alive grew smaller with the heartbeat, and he fell to his knees.

Playing in the games gave Valis incredible endurance, but that involved teammates and breaks. Had he ever had to use his magic like this before? Without a moment to rest? Most people would have already drained their magic, but at least he had years of training to sustain himself for hours. But even that may not be enough against Kevah's inhuman power.

A horrifying, ear-piercing scream rang out from the crowd. With her colorful hair easily visible, Malaina spotted the source easily. Valis's wife clutched the railing separating spectators from the arena, her wordless screams echoing off of every surface.

On the Lord's balcony, Lady Atana was dressed head to toe in her usual gold attire, hair curled into an updo showing off a high-collared jacket and fitted pants, both white and embroidered in golden details. The strands glittered in the sunlight, emanating the essence of someone blessed by Elosyn to stand among the daylight. Graceful elegance radiated from her, the perfect image of what the Lady of Elementals should be. She stood at the balcony's edge, no longer seated in her usual spot, the only show of concern she made. Otherwise, she maintained a stoic facade, full of faith that Kevah would be the one to walk away.

"They may be equal when it comes to elements, but Valis's power is nothing compared to Kevah's." Layshan shook his head, running a hand through his hair.

It occurred to Malaina that she would never understand what this moment must feel like for the Air Wielder. She and Ra grew up in the City of Elementals, but Layshan was the only actual Elemental among them. Distantly, she realized how amazing the show of power they were watching was, but Layshan truly understood it. He probably had the same connection to air that she felt to her shadows, but she couldn't imagine the responsibility and force of holding an entire element in her hands.

This wasn't about a city to him, it was about who would represent him as a person.

When Kevah eased up, letting the water flow away, Valis was on his hands and knees. His fingers dug into the ground as if he was holding on for dear life. His sphere of air dissipated, leaving him soaked where he knelt.

His wife continued to scream from the sidelines, yelling his name over and over again.

Heaving, the challenger lifted the ground from where it lay, rising like a rug, and used the strength of his entire body to slam it back down. It sent a wave through the arena that left Kevah off balance.

Amassing renewed strength, Valis leaped through the air, forcing a gust of wind behind him to gain speed and distance. When he had a clear shot, he sent out sharp swipes of wind, cutting across Kevah's bare chest.

Streaks of blood welled against the Lord's earth-colored skin, but he didn't seem to notice or care. He punched the air, orange flames shooting from his knuckles.

When Valis landed he caught the shots and vigorously sent them blasting back.

One of the volleys caught Kevah's shoulder, sending him reeling back. In that momentary opening, Valis circled his arms before him. But this time, instead of conjuring a sphere of air around himself for protection, he encircled Kevah. The sphere closed in tight, giving Kevah little room to move.

"I'm done taking orders from you," Valis spat, "You do *not* represent me. You do not represent the Elemental people, you twisted, arrogant man!"

"That's the only way he's going to win," Sterling shook his head, fingers rubbing his lips as he spoke aloud to himself. "He needs to use air. It's the only advantage he has left."

Layshan laced his fingers together behind his head and stepped back. "It won't be enough."

"Why not?" Malaina asked.

Turning away, the Air Wielder refused to watch anymore. Eyes closed, head shaking, he walked away from the edge of the roof. She gave Ra a questioning glance, but he only shrugged.

Shooting out of his hands, Valis sent Kevah and his sphere cage flying. The Lord's body cracked against the far wall of the arena.

Even Kevah couldn't wield the metal that made up the walls to save himself. Only one Elemental family had that particular God's blessed gift, and they were in the City of Kinetics.

His limp body fell towards the water below, and they all held their breath, waiting for the bone-breaking snap of the collision. But that thud never came.

Kevah stopped mid-fall, hovering halfway between where he hit the wall and the moat below. Collectively, everyone turned to Valis, trying to figure out what he was doing. The crowd's confusion was mirrored on the challenger's face as he studied his own hands.

Pushing off an invisible platform, Kevah got to his feet. Shaking off the impact, he rolled up to stand tall.

A sadistic laugh twisted his features, his head lolling

back and around, stretching his neck from one side to the other. "Oh, that hurt you little shit."

Fear flooded Valis's face. With staggered steps, he started backing toward the opposite end of the arena, trying to put space between himself and the Lord.

"No…" Malaina's hand flew to her mouth, holding back a horrified gasp. Sweat dripped from her hairline, streaming down her back, and the world started to spin.

"But…that…he…" Sterling started several sentences he couldn't finish as Lord Kevah got his bearings.

Ra shuffled from foot to foot, one hand on his hips, the other waving through the air, trying to find an answer. "That's impossible. That…That would make him… That would mean he can…"

"He can wield all four elements," Malaina said the words none of them wanted to be true.

"No!" Scarlet streaked Sterling's umber brown eyes as he started to shout his denial. "No! There's only ever been one person who could do that. One. This isn't possible. The lineage was wiped out, wasn't it? Isn't that what they teach us in school?"

It was. But it didn't matter.

Sterling knew that but was grasping at anything that made what they were witnessing make sense.

Magic wasn't always hereditary. More often than not, it took on the magic of the strongest parent, but not always.

But magic had rules of its own.

She and Lybbi were proof of that. Sometimes, it seemed the Gods picked and chose at random, pairing magic with people based on nothing more than preference.

Two Water Wielding parents could theoretically give birth to an Air Wielding child. It was rare, but it happened. Two Fire Wielding parents could give birth to two Dark daughters. One man with no significant lineage to be told of could be born with the ability to wield all four elements with God-like strength.

It shouldn't happen, but it did.

It had.

"Lady Aladonna told me from a young age to keep one of my Elements hidden," Kevah explained, slowly walking down a staircase of his own hardened air. Addressing the audience, he defended his actions to his people. "She knew I would take Lordship one day, either way, and she didn't want Alvar Andelit's legacy to precede everything I did." When he stepped onto solid ground once again, he turned, addressing the stunned crowd members with arms stretched wide. "But today, I will not let that secret keep me from my rightful place."

Fear shook Valis's entire body, trying to take a defensive stance and prepare for the inevitable.

"I'm done with this," Kevah growled, unleashing a fury of attacks. He threw element after element at Valis, uncontrolled rage unleashing brutal attacks unlike anything anyone had ever seen. Every single person stared in horror. Some screamed, calling for guards to intervene, though they all knew they wouldn't.

One blood-curdling scream broke through the rest. For the rest of her life, Malaina would never stop hearing it. The scream of a dying man's wife. A wife about to watch with agonizing slowness as her husband, whom she loved more than anything, lost his life for a city he loved. She screamed and screamed. At one point, she even tried to climb over the railing, but hands held her back.

As the announcer had said, no one would interfere.

Only one person didn't look scared. Didn't scream or cry out. One person who didn't even have the decency to look surprised.

Lady Atana stood at her balcony railing, smiling down at her husband. Smiling, he launched attack after attack toward Valis, unleashing everything he had. She seemed… proud. Proud of the man who terrorized their city. Proud to be his wife. She wanted to see this. She wanted to see him stop hiding.

Valis knelt, hardly defending himself from Kevah's unrelenting attacks. Water rushed into his mouth faster than he could spit it out, choking out his words. Taking advantage of whatever small reprieves Kevah granted him, he breathed in gulps of air before that very air assaulted him as well.

Rock shot from the earth, encasing Valis's wrists and ankles, holding him in place while Kevah took his time approaching. The jovial mask Kevah loved to put on for his people faded away when he sneered down at the broken man before him.

"I…I concede," Valis sobbed, spitting blood and water.

Everyone sat silent and still watching Kevah.

Valis conceded. Kevah won. This could be over.

Kevah took Valis's throat in his hand. Releasing Valis from his earth-bound cuss, Kevah lifted him until they looked each other in the eye.

"I gave you your chance to concede," Kevah seethed, and with a twist of his fingers, water started to force its way down Valis's throat. The dying man thrashed and fought in the Lord's grip, but there was nothing he could do.

The crowd was in an uproar while, as one, they witnessed the Lord drown his challenger.

Malaina dug her fingers into Sterling's arm so hard it would leave bruises. Bile rose in her throat, and she fought back the urge to vomit. She'd seen people die. More people than she could count. She'd caused most of those deaths. But she'd never seen anything like this.

Eventually, Valis stopped moving.

Malaina wasn't sure which screams and sobs came from his wife. They all melded together. The overwhelming roar of thousands of people's anguish surrounded her. From the stadium to the crowd outside on the street to those watching from nearby buildings, cries of heart-wrenching dismay filled the air. Parents fought to cover their children's eyes, and families fled the stadium altogether. Those outside the stadium yelled for any news on what was happening inside.

Fingers uncurled from around Valis's throat, dropping his body to the ground in a heap. Those fingers rubbed together as if trying to rid themselves of the filth they'd just touched.

Kevah regarded the mass in front of him like a disgusting sack of soiled cloth rather than a corpse that had been a person moments before. Cold eyes stared, not caring that he'd publicly taken the man's life in a brutal way.

His fingers finally clean of the invisible filth, he smiled

up at his wife on the Lord's balcony, and the adoring look that passed between them felt sick and vial. As though Kevah hadn't just committed a heinous act. As though Atana hadn't witnessed the whole thing. The Lord pressed his fingers to his lips and lifted them to the sky, sending her the type of love such a monster shouldn't be capable of. When she placed a hand over her heart he turned away, addressing his people once again.

"Everyone, please, quiet." Kevah waved his hands, shushing the crowd. A parent calming a child. A teacher bringing order back to a sugar-fueled classroom.

The crowd quieted for him, more out of fear than respect.

He clasped his hands together, pleased. "Citizens of the City of Elementals, I want to thank you for attending today's duel. I am so pleased to get the opportunity to continue acting as your representative to the rest of Thaumoria." His congenial mask had returned, back turned to Valis's body as if it weren't there at all. "I have a quick announcement I would like everyone to hear before today's events conclude."

Malaina's fingers started to tremble, and her heart raced. The heat of the day and thick horror-filled sea air combined to roil her stomach.

What else could this man possibly want? The last time he made a special announcement he had effectively eliminated Shifters from the city. What else could there be?

"As many of you may remember, years ago, there had been rumors that the next Death Bringer had been born to us right here in the City of Elementals," Kevah continued.

Malaina's heart stopped beating altogether, sinking through her stomach like lead. This couldn't be happening.

Ra, Layshan, and Sterling all turned to look at her, as though Kevah had spoken directly to her.

"Today, I have the pleasure of announcing that those rumors were not only true, but the Death Bringer is still in this city!" Kevah said it the same way someone would announce a surprise present. Like he was giving positive news to the people. Like every word he spoke wasn't destroying Malaina's world. "This is an official call for the Death Bringer to be brought to me personally at the Lord's Estate. A reward will be offered to anyone who has information that aids in this call. Thank you, my people, and I hope to see you at the next Games!"

Kevah smiled broadly, waving his way back to the tunnel he had entered from.

Everything erupted into a frenzy. The stadium, the streets, and the other rooftops. Everything.

The world spun around Malaina. Sterling wrapped an arm around her for support and to keep her from falling to her knees. She didn't hear anything he or the others said. She thought she heard something about heading back home—perhaps a question from Ra, or maybe Layshan— asking what route they should take back. The Lord's words repeated over and over again in her head.

This is an official call for the Death Bringer.

The excruciating light of day bared down on her back, irritating the magic locked away behind a thick wall of metal in her chest.

This is an official call for the Death Bringer.

Salty air from the coast coated her tongue, shoving itself down her throat until it started to chock out the air.

This is an official call for the Death Bringer.

Malaina vomited up what little was in her stomach right there on the roof.

TWENTY

When they got to the alley entrance the small group of four didn't bother splitting up to find separate ways in. Instead, they all crowded into the small hall, Sterling at the back, waiting just outside the door until they could all fit through.

"You need to close the door before I can—" The Kinetic on guard started from the hiding spot.

Ra gave an inpatient huff through his nose and shoved to the front of their little group.

"Open the door, Rit," he spat, "Or I'm opening it myself."

"You're not allowed to do that," Rit whined.

Impatience winning out, Ra pounded a fist against the door, and it opened. He hooked an arm around Malaina's shoulders and pulled her through the door and into the relative safety of the guild.

Criminals of every variety were packed into every in of

the room, pushed together in small groups, talking in hushed tones. Every eye in the room went to Malaina, the soft voices going silent.

Thankfully, she'd collected herself on the way back. Otherwise, she would have wilted beneath their judging leers. Instead, she took their condemning stares in stride, showing them the hard mask they'd come to expect from her. Many refused to meet her challenge, looking away when her eyes met theirs without shame.

Some looked away with guilt, others looked away in fear. More than usual, though, met her gaze with accusing, unyielding stares. They were all thinking the same thing: they didn't want her in the guild anymore. The thought of having a Death Bringer living among them made most people uncomfortable already, but she'd always been good at her job, and they couldn't do anything about her presence.

But she'd screwed up. Screwed up so badly that it caught the attention of the Lord. In a profession where secrecy and anonymity were everything, drawing the public's eye was the greatest sin she could have committed.

Operated closer to a business than a criminal crew, Malachi's guild served as a haven for those who worked for him. It was the first place most of them truly felt safe. For some, it was the only home where they had their own bed, a stomach full of nourishing food each night, and someone to train them in not only their magic but also a profession.

Kevah's call for her endangered everything they held dear, which meant she threatened them all personally.

A heavenly voice rang out above the crowd. "I suggest you all find somewhere else to be."

Relief almost crumpled Malaina when Serena parted the people like a Water Wielder in the sea. Some guilders grumbled, but none of them argued, slinking off toward other rooms and floors. Malaina might have been a threat, but as mistress, Serena served as Malachi's third in command, which afforded her a level of respect no one would dare question.

Serena reached out and grabbed Malaina's hand, sending a wave of soothing through her.

"Thank you," Malaina whispered, pulling Serena closer.

Serena gave the assassin a weak smile in answer, and then her feline green eyes were on the thieves still standing beside Sterling. "You two may go as well."

"No way." Ra's eyes hardened as much as Ra's eyes could. "I'm not letting Malachi kick her out."

Malaina flinched. So she wasn't the only one who picked up on the room's vibe when they walked in.

"You have my word, Malaina will be fine. But Malachi asked to meet with her immediately, and you two are not invited." The silky smooth dismissal was cloying in a way that almost hid the command behind her words.

Ra's jaw twitched, trying to decide if it was worth arguing when Layshan started to guide him away. "Come on, man. She'll be fine."

Ra gave Malaina one last look over his shoulder before following Layshan to the stairs.

"Now that they're gone, tell me the truth."

Serena didn't meet her gaze, using her free hand to brush the hair back off Malaina's neck. "I think we should get you to Malachi."

An ache hit Malaina square in the chest, making her sag. Trying to find comfort, she squeezed Serena's hand in search of the mistress's soothing touch. But the Anima held back her magic, letting the assassin work through her feelings on her own.

Sterling put a hand on both their backs and started guiding them toward Malachi's office.

The doors opened in anticipation of their knock, revealing Malachi sitting behind his desk. That alone nearly made Malaina want to turn around and run.

This wasn't going to be good.

He stood when they entered, straightening his jacket. The twin chairs sat empty before his desk, waiting for her to sit and learn her fate.

Malaina reluctantly took one, Serena the other. Sterling opted to stay standing, propping himself against the back of the loveseat.

Malachi sat again, leaning back in his chair, pinching the bridge of his nose between his thumb and forefinger. Drawing out the heavy silence, the clearing of his voice pounded against Malaina's ears. They all waited, taught kinetic springs wound too tight, anxious to hear what he had to say.

"I am not going to force you out. Not yet, anyway."

Malaina released a long breath, letting her whole body slump forward and relax until her elbows rested on her knees. Sterling and Serena's relieved sighs blew away the tension hanging in the air.

Malachi held up a hand. "However," a pause, "I cannot let things continue without addressing what happened today."

Malaina nodded. "I understand."

"So what do we do?" Something edged Sterling's voice, making it razor sharp.

Malachi glanced at Sterling and then back to Malaina, leaning forward in thought. "We have a few options. I feel the safest for both Malaina and the guild would be to take her off the streets."

Malaina's back straightened. "What? No, you can't do that."

"I have already taken the liberty of rejecting all pending contracts requesting your specific services," Malachi continued, pointedly ignoring her outburst.

Malaina shot to her feet, unable to stay sitting. "Malachi, how are we supposed to pay rent without jobs? I have three people to provide for."

Malachi looked up at her from beneath heavy lids, knuckles pressing against his lips, unaffected by her sudden outburst. "I should hope you all were wise enough to save some of your earnings. Otherwise, it would be possible for Sterling to take on another partner temporarily."

Sterling exploded, talking over Malachi's words. "No. Out of the question."

Malachi's voice rose, trying to be heard. "I would not pair you with another assassin. You would simply be a guard to another guilder in need of one until I find a suitable partner."

"This is insane!" Sterling roared. "She did nothing wrong. What happened with the Alman contract—"

Malachi stood, voice rising in volume as he did. "What happened with the Alman contract was unacceptable!" The chastisement was sharp, cutting through Malaina and Sterling's outbursts. They both quieted, stunned.

Malachi closed his eyes for a moment, jaw clenching, trying to calm himself. The knuckles of his fists pressed into the top of his desk, and when he spoke once again, forced composure evened his words. "I was willing to let it pass on the condition history would not repeat itself. However, the reality is if any other person here pulled what you two did, they would have been out. I have bent the rules many times to accommodate Malaina. In part because she brings in more money than anyone else. But...I already have one person living here without working for their residence." A pointed look told Malaina he was talking about Lybbi.

When they first came to Malachi, Lybbi had been too young to work and he almost didn't let her stay. But Malaina swore to do anything to protect her sister and earn both her and Lybbi's places. Over the years, Malaina became complacent about Malachi's generosity. She'd long ago earned their places among the guilders and had taken advantage of Malachi's soft spot for the young Death Bringer. He treated her the same as any other guilder, giving her lessons and allowing her to benefit from all of the guild's perks when he had no reason to. Lybbi could have started working years ago, but Malaina had always been able to cover both their spots. But if she couldn't work…

"I cannot allow three people to live under my roof if they do not pay their dues." Malachi almost sounded resentful of that fact. As if he would change the rules if he could, but he couldn't.

Other guilders would quickly catch on that the three of them weren't paying for the apartment they were staying in. Plenty of other groups vied for it, wanting the status that came with living there. But they were the only ones who required all three rooms and were the only ones who could easily keep up with the payments. The food Malachi provided, the lessons, the training equipment, the medical care, the safety, and protection. All of it needed to come from somewhere. Needed to be paid for somehow, and that's what their rent covered. They didn't just rent the apartment, they were paying for their entire lives.

If he bent the rules and allowed the three of them to stay in the largest apartment, taking advantage of all the amenities without anything to show for it, the order of the guild would fall apart. Others would start demanding the same leniency. Their presence would cause more unrest than it already did, and he couldn't let it slide.

"We have some money saved up," Sterling answered, resigned. "We can pay for a couple of months."

Malachi tapped his knuckles against the desk, then nodded slowly. "Good." There was a long pause, his thoughts almost palpable in the thick, tense air. "I would like Lybbi to continue training. As you know, while guilders are in training, their stay is covered until I deem they are ready to start work. Which, in her case, could take quite some time. Of course, they are normally staying in the group dorms, and their stay is much cheaper; however, if you continue to pay your rent..."

The words trailed off, but Malaina understood what he was trying to say. He was finding some reason for them to stay. A way to justify his mercy.

"I understand," Malaina stared at the ground. Serena reached up and squeezed her fingers, and then she and Sterling turned to leave.

"Sterling," Malachi said, "I highly suggest reconsidering my offer."

Sterling didn't pause at Malachi's words. He stalked through the doors and into the grand room without looking back.

Malaina followed at a distance, letting herself fall back. When she reached the door she heard Serena's sweet voice float through the air. "Malachi, is this really necessary?"

Malaina stepped to the side, out of sight. Shadows twined around her fingers in her pocket, helping her focus on Malachi and Serena's voices. The small release of her magic made her mind clearer and their words crisp.

"Do you have another suggestion?" Malachi asked in return.

"What if the contracts were more selective? Let me vet them first," Serena suggested, though even she didn't seem sure. She was already overwhelmed with vetting clients for her seductors; she couldn't take on all of Malaina's clients as well.

"You and I both know what happened with the Alman

contract was no coincidence. She is gaining too much attention."

There was quiet for a while, and then, "What if she no longer posed as the Death Bringer? Lybbi is in training. Let Malaina switch professions. Let her be the Shadow Spinner she is."

Malaina held her breath, waiting for Malachi's answer. For nine years, she'd been claiming the title of Death Bringer. She hadn't considered the possibility of using her own magic instead. The very idea of not having to hide her true self made her heart soar.

"And how do you suggest we announce that to the others? That we have not one, but two Dark Magic wielders among us."

"Malaina handled being a Death Bringer at a young age. No one tried to...well..." *Kill her,* Malaina finished for her. No one tried to kill her.

Which wasn't completely true. The scars Malaina hadn't let Jade heal burned across her knuckles at the memory.

Fear of the Dark Magics ran deep within Thaumoria, so when she showed up and started telling everyone she was the Death Bringer rumored to have been born among the Elementals, she received instant scorn. The other children had forced them into the crappiest bunks in the back of the group living quarters, threw food at the back of her head from across the dining hall, and would crowd the showers until she didn't have a choice but to go through the day gross. They were aware Malachi had 'forbidden' her use of her fake magic, but she still scared them...to an extent.

Lybbi had been too young to truly understand what was happening and why people were treating them differently, but Malaina understood. Spending every moment Malachi would let her sparring, she'd thrown herself into training, practicing until she was covered in bruises and scars but could win against even the biggest kids in the guild. Over the course of two years, she'd pushed herself from scrawny and scared to lethal.

But that hadn't stopped them from coming for her that day in the showers.

"Malaina was different, stronger. Lybbi is soft. She will not be able to handle the way people will treat her when they discover what she really is."

Malaina hated it, but Malachi was right. Lybbi grew up accustomed to being adored. Running free and happy, without a care, she'd grown up safe inside the guild. She didn't have to worry about watching her back the way Malaina had, and that's exactly how the assassin wanted to keep it. That's why she took on the title of Death Bringer in the first place. There could only be one, and if it was Malaina, then Lybbi had to be something else. Something safe.

When Malaina came to the guild, she had told Malachi the truth—every single bit of it, from who their parents were, what she and Lybbi were, how they ended up on the streets, and even what happened with the old man and his puppy. Sitting in the safety of Malachi's office, everything fell out of her, the words never-ending.

When he had asked her what she wanted she had only

one request. The only thing she wanted at ten years old. The only thing she worked for every day.

"I want to keep my sister safe."

So Malachi had devised a plan.

Rumors of the Death Bringer being born had already spread around the city, so rather than shy away from them, they would lean into them. Keep the rumors spreading and growing. If she did everything he asked and suppressed her own magic deep down within herself, then she could take on the guise of someone deadlier than the Gods themselves. And what profession could be more suitable for a Death Bringer than an assassin?

It didn't matter that she hadn't fully understood what she was committing to that day in Malachi's office, because that night, she and Lybbi fell asleep in a real bed. They dreamed the night away, stomachs full and hair clean. It didn't take long for the place that saved them to become a home. Where they found Sterling and where they made friends. Where Malaina found love.

Somehow, these criminals had become their family.

And Malaina never told Lybbi.

The words had never come.

So many avoided them already because of Malaina's reputation, so she didn't worry about anyone saying anything to Lybbi about Malaina's position in the guild. Lybbi grew up believing that everyone feared Malaina's shadows, especially since Shadow Spinning was classified as Dark Magic. Lybbi thought she worked as a spy, an informant for wealthy nobles, and that's how they afforded the life they did. They didn't talk about Malaina's Shadow Spinning because they didn't want to scare people.

Eventually, the lie Malaina told to keep Lybbi innocent grew a life of its own. There came a point when it went too far, and she didn't know how to turn back or how to make it better. It all became so intertwined that she didn't even know where to start unraveling.

The air next to Malaina moved. When she opened her eyes, Sterling leaned against the wall next to her, his ears pointed and twitching like a cat's. Their eyes met, and she knew he'd overheard everything being said. His eyes were deep lead gray, almost blue. Sad and resigned, he reached out and took her hand, giving her fingers a reassuring squeeze.

They were going to lose their home, and it was all her fault. But she didn't have to drag Sterling down too. He could stay, get re-partnered, and pick a different job that wouldn't go against everything he believed in. Being her partner was never something he'd asked for. Each contract targeting a new undeserving person destroyed him little by little, the same way it did her.

But she needed to do this—she needed to kill. He didn't. He chose to stay by her side, and if she and Lybbi left, he would have the chance to start over.

He pushed away from the wall and pulled her towards the elevators. The thoughts written in his eyes were clear.

Let's go home.

He wouldn't leave her or Lybbi, no matter how much he should. Malaina didn't know why or how it happened, but from the day Sterling arrived and found his way to her side, he became a fundamental part of their family. He'd never given her the full story of why he'd come to the guild, and after so many years, it stopped feeling important. No one wanted to talk about their past and how they'd come to sit in Malachi's office that first day.

All that mattered was that he was by her side and wasn't going anywhere.

TWENTY-ONE

An unexpected voice broke the silence of the night, making Malaina lurch. "If you jump, I'll stop you before you hit the ground."

Sitting on the edge of the guild's roof, the ex-assassin's feet dangled as she took in a full view of the street below. Complete with its boarded-up windows, slumped-over drunken bodies, and those walking home from work carrying a single bag of groceries.

From this part of the city, she could just make out the ship ports. Outdated white-sailed ships sat between sleek metal designs from the City of Kinetics. At this time of night, the port was still, a stark contrast to the constant activity of the day. During daylight, produce from the farmlands was loaded onto ships, and sailors took it to ports across the island of Thaumoria, supplying food to other coastal cities.

It was a preferable sight over the opposite side of the

guild, which overlooked the stables where the guild's Anima cared for the horses who pulled the carriage. The Anima were fascinating to watch work, coaxing the horses into trots around the courtyard, speaking a language all their own, but the smell was more than a bit off-putting. The poor carriage sat mostly untouched nearby after what happened to Bren and Aneyra, only being taken out for the furthest jobs.

Weeks had passed since Malachi took her and Sterling off contracts, and she was starting to go stir-crazy. She hadn't sat in the guild for such an extended period since Malachi took her off training status and given her her first contract. Coming up to the roof had been an attempt at just breathing. Breathing in the night and fresh air. Breathing in the darkness. The apartment had started to feel too cramped despite its size, and she could only spend so many hours working out in the training room before her arms simply refused to throw another punch.

Ra walked across the roof and sat beside her on the ledge, back turned to the outside world.

"What are you doing up here?" She asked.

Leaning way too far back for her comfort, he studied the stars. "Oh, you know. Catching up on my astronomy and whatnot. Seeing what's new in the star world." A half-hearted smile formed on his face, and she snorted. Satisfied with himself for drawing a small spark of amusement out of her, he sat back up. "Nah, Sterling told me you were up here, so I thought I'd check on you."

Cowardice had her looking away, unable to hold his gaze. Sometimes, she resented the way his ashy brown eyes always seemed to be smiling, the way he could find joy in anything, if only because she wished she could be a little more like him.

"How are you doing?" He sounded far more serious than usual. She didn't like it.

"Don't you remember? I'm public enemy number one. Isn't that every criminal's dream?" Sarcasm seeped from her. The only way she was managing to keep herself sane.

The thief nodded slowly, pressing his lips into a tight line as he glanced down at his feet. "And from what I've heard, you've been handling it really well. Lybbi's practically been hiding out at our place. She told Layshan you're impossible to live with."

Malaina huffed a humorless laugh.

Lybbi had been around less and less since they'd been confined. Malaina couldn't figure out how to explain to Lybbi why they couldn't work, and Lybbi could tell something was going on that no one was telling her. At first, she'd been thrilled at the idea of Malaina and Sterling being home more until she realized that didn't mean regular trips out into the city. Until Malaina's Fire Wielder temper started biting everyone's head off.

Everything made her skin itch, pulled too tight around her muscles until she couldn't experience a second of comfort. Malachi insisted that if she stayed, and Kevah's bounty on her head was still the biggest news in the city, then she couldn't so much as leave. It wasn't clear if or when she'd be allowed to work again. Or if they would need to find a new place to live and start their lives over.

The not knowing killed her. The endless waiting.

Ra's eyes pierced her, daring her to meet his gaze. "You're going to get through this. I've never met someone so hard-headed and determined."

"Oh, don't go flattering me or anything," she answered flatly.

"Seriously. Don't you remember the day you chased me down?" His infectious smile had her returning one of her own.

Of course, she remembered. The day she chased him down for two copper coins and found so much more. The day her life changed forever.

"How could I forget? What kind of asshole pickpockets a homeless kid for a couple of coppers?" Her shoulder playfully bumped his.

Rubbing the back of his neck, he laughed sheepishly. "Oh, come on. I was eight and had just been allowed out on the streets. I went for the easiest target."

"And how did that work out for you?"

"Not for shit. Malachi was so mad he handed my ass to me in training for the next week."

A genuine smile spread across her face at the thought, no doubt it was true. Malachi always went hardest on the other Kinetics, holding them to a higher standard.

Ra reached into his pocket and dug out the two copper coins she'd passed back to him the day she and Sterling came back from their contract and Ra had been on guard duty. The copper coins danced across his knuckles.

"All over a couple of old coins. What a waste."

He offered her the coppers and she grabbed them, studying the worn insignias of the City of Elementals.

"What are you really doing up here, Ra?" She saw his smile falter out of the corner of her eye.

His lips twisted to the side. "Layshan and I got a contract—a big one. We'll be headed out tonight and thought you should know. So maybe you could talk to Lybbi, let her know she'll need to actually spend time at home for a little bit." Jealousy held tight to her stomach, refusing to let her go at the thought of him getting to leave. "You need to tell her. Tell her everything."

Malaina swallowed, her words coming out choked. "What do you mean?"

"You told me and Layshan a long time ago to never talk to her about what you do, and we've respected that. But she's asking questions we can't answer. We tell her to talk to you about it, but she says you'll 'lie like always.' I'm not saying you need to go into detail or anything, but…"

Vigorously, she shook her head. "She's not ready."

"Is it her who isn't ready, or you?" He didn't take his eyes off her as he threw out the accusation.

Her own hard gaze met his insistent one. "You sound like Sterling."

"He has a point. She's old enough."

"She's only thirteen. She's still a kid." Malaina spat, though it sounded more like a whine to her ears.

"And how old were you again when you came to the guild? When you signed on to kill people for a living?" Not wanting to admit the answer he already knew, she bit her lip in response. "How old were you when you made your *first* kill?"

The last question stung. One year younger than Lybbi

now, she'd been twelve when she made her first kill. Malachi let her train longer than he should have before he needed her to start working to cover both her and Lybbi's places. But the day needed to come eventually.

That memory was one of the many that she pushed down deep inside of herself, refusing to remember.

"It's not the same. *We* aren't the same."

Ra whistled, running a hand through his feather-soft brown hair. "Oh, I think you guys are a lot more alike than you realize."

Malaina smirked, not willing to admit he may be right.

"Look," he started. Not sure she wanted to hear what he would say next, she met his glittering brown eyes. "I've known you longer than anyone else here. Longer than Sterling or Serena. I know you want to protect Lybbi. I know you would give anything to keep her safe from the realities around her. And I know you're scared because you were so young when you had to give up your innocence, and you want to let her hold on to hers a little while longer. But she's growing up, whether you want to see it or not. So, just think about it, ok?"

She focused on the coins in her hand and nodded, unable to find the words to answer him.

He patted her on the shoulder before standing. "Good." Starting back across the roof, he walked towards the door that led down into the guild. He paused and turned, giving her a cocky smile. "Oh, and those are only a loan, by the way. To help with your rent. I expect to be paid back with interest."

She tried glaring at him but couldn't hold back a

genuine smile. He laughed at her expression and winked before ducking beneath the door and heading out for his job.

THE NEXT COUPLE of days passed in a blur. With no reason to, Malaina didn't bother to keep track of time. The strength with which she sensed her shadows became the only thing telling her the difference between day and night.

The training room became her hideaway each night, either sparring with anyone who would step into the ring or watching Lybbi's grueling sessions. Malachi continued to push her harder than he'd ever pushed Malaina, driving her strength to its edge, only to then try and drain her of her magic. A necessary evil, but still hard to watch. Lybbi needed to get her magic to a controllable level so it never came out unexpectedly again, but it never seemed too slow. It had been pent up for too long, and no matter how many times Malachi drained it, it was still beyond manageable.

Every morning, Lybbi fell into a deep sleep, drained of all her energy, even on nights she only attended lessons. She hardly spoke to Malaina, and Malaina took to sneaking out of the apartment and spending her days in Serena's bed whenever Serena wasn't working.

The two stayed awake for hours, talking about anything that came to mind while Serena's magic flowed into Malaina and played with the shadows in the corners of the room.

Malaina didn't know what time or day it was when a pounding at Serena's front door woke them from a deep sleep in the mistress's warm bed.

"How could you possibly have a client at this hour?" Malaina buried her face in Serena's neck.

"The only clients who personally come knocking at my door are guilders." Serena slid out of bed, kissing Malaina on the forehead. "Maybe it's Kai, and he can join us," she teased.

Malaina smirked and feebly tried to hit Serena with one of the many pillows on the bed. Serena giggled and stepped back, easily missing the pillow. Grabbing an emerald green robe embroidered with golden swirls hanging on the closet door, she straightened her shoulders and headed for the door. The stitching passed for nondescript swirls until you looked closer and realized they were animals of all kinds.

Malaina admired the way the Anima's body moved, sliding on the silky robe over her long limbs. She wished she'd come back to bed.

Malaina rolled over, nuzzling into one of the pillows, pulling the silken red sheets higher. The fabric flowed around her naked skin as she stretched her legs, the same way her shadows slid along her body.

She was already back on the verge of sleep when a familiar deep voice boomed from Serena's front door.

"Where is she?" Sterling asked.

Malaina groaned, pulling the sheet over her head. Maybe if she hid he wouldn't find her.

"Get up," the Shifter demanded. He was much closer now, probably standing at the end of the bed.

"No," she whined. She wished he would just leave her be.

Sterling yanked the sheet off her, leaving her bare in the middle of the mattress, and she gasped in shock at the cool air hitting her naked body. She sat up, angry, meeting his hard scarlet gaze. Having seen her naked hundreds of times in their years living and working together, he didn't even bother glancing down at the rest of her. He'd never been interested in such things anyway.

He tossed the sheet back on the bed, making sure it never hit the ground.

"Get up. Now."

"Why? What could possibly be so urgent? Is Malachi going to let us work or something?"

He placed his hands on the bed, leaning down to look her in the eye. "Layshan's downstairs. Alone."

Malaina's muscles went rigid. His words took a moment to process. For her to fully comprehend what that meant.

With a start, she scrambled out of Serena's oversized bed. It wasn't until she was halfway to the door that she realized she couldn't leave the mistress's apartment naked. Clothes covered the floor, and in her haze, she couldn't discern hers from Serena's. Then the emerald robe dangled before her, hanging from a single long finger.

Malaina grabbed it hesitantly. "Are you sure? It's your favorite."

Serena shrugged, a wicked gleam in her eyes. "I know where you live."

Malaina slid on the robe and reached out to cup Serena's face in her hands. She gave her a hasty kiss. "Thank you."

"Come on." Sterling barked from the front door.

Malaina tied the robe closed and ran for the door. Her feet caught on the hem, and she nearly tripped. Her legs were shorter than Serena's, and the robe hung a few inches too long.

Sterling met her at the elevator, already holding the door open. The moment she stepped in, he jammed his thumb into the button for the grand room. Malaina bounced on her toes, the ride taking too long.

"You might want to try spending a day in your own bed some time," Sterling said. From anyone else, the comment would have struck her as judgmental. But from Sterling…it just sounded longing and sad. This had been the most time they'd spent apart in years, despite being stuck at home together.

Leaving him alone every day when he needed her was selfish. He needed someone to lean on and talk to also. She knew he felt equally responsible for their stay-at-home orders. Always the strong one, leaning on him came so easily that she sometimes forgot he needed the support, too.

She watched her feet, bare toes pocking out from beneath the emerald silk. "You're right. I'm sorry."

He threw his head back, letting out a bark of a laugh. "Damn, I didn't know you knew those words. How did that taste on your tongue?"

She narrowed her eyes at him, biting her lip to hold back a smirk. "Like vinegar."

When the elevator stopped and the doors opened, Malaina didn't care about the stares she got, dressed in nothing but a silk robe. Recently, all conversations stopped in her presence anyway.

Together, she and Sterling went straight for Malachi's office.

Sterling pushed the doors open with one powerful heave, not bothering to knock.

Layshan sat on the loveseat before the fireplace. Only the back of his head was visible, but she didn't like the sight of his disheveled blonde hair or the way his shoulders slumped, elbows resting on his knees.

Malachi sat in his usual chair, patiently watching the Air Wielder. He gave them a quick glance when they entered and a longer once-over when he saw Malaina's outfit. A glimmer of amusement flittered across his face, the only reaction he gave. He waved his hand, and the doors shut, cutting off the rest of the guild.

Slowly, Malaina made her way around the side of the loveseat. The way Layshan was shaking, his bloodless pale skin, and the dark circles under his eyes all made her mind race through the worst possibilities. But ultimately, the thief seemed untouched. He didn't seem to notice when she gingerly sat beside him.

Malachi pressed his lips together, shook his head a little, and shrugged his shoulders. He didn't know what had happened, either.

"Layshan," she said gently, letting a hand hover over his shoulder, not sure if she should actually touch him or not.

From the corner of his eye, the thief glanced at her,

recognizing her presence but not meeting her gaze. His eyes were red and wet from tears, glassy and distant.

"Layshan, what happened? Where's Ra?"

He pressed his hands to his mouth and then ran them through his hair, sending it in all directions. "He's gone. They took him." The words shook his entire body, coming out uneven.

Her fingers curled, and she tried to keep herself from jumping to her feet and pressing him for more. "What?"

He started rocking forward and back, shaking his head as though he didn't realize he was doing it. Words rattled out of him, a broken damn that couldn't be mended. "We went in for recognizance. Something seemed off about the house. Too quiet. It was a trap. They took him." Malachi squeezed his eyes shut, leaning his head back against his chair as Layshan continued to ramble. "I left him. He told me to, but I shouldn't have. I left. We're partners. I should have stayed. I should have got him out. They have him."

"Malachi, what the hell is going on? First the Alman contract, and now this..." Sterling asked, his eyes pleading.

Malachi rubbed his forehead. "I do not know. This is… unprecedented. I have not had so many issues at once since starting these operations."

"Well, what are we going to do?"

They all looked to Malachi, who met each of their eyes, reluctant to answer. For a moment, his gaze went distant, as if reliving a long-lost memory that left him looking haunted. Falling forward in his chair, the guild master's hands went limp between his knees, staring at the floor. "Nothing."

"Nothing?" Malaina bit out.

The words came out flat, as though he read them from a page in a manual. "Everyone who signs on here is aware of the inherent risks of what we do. If I sent out a team every time someone did not return—"

Malaina cut him off. "But we know where he is. We can do something about it. We can bring him home."

Layshan shut his eyes, leaning forward, intertwining his fingers behind his head. Arrogant, confident Layshan was falling apart before her eyes, Ra was Gods knew where going through the Goddesses knew what, and Malachi… Malachi was going to do nothing.

The Kinetic ran a finger over his mouth, refusing to meet her gaze. "Malaina, I understand you have been looking for something to do, and you have not appreciated staying inside, but I have protocols. Perhaps, instead, you should distract yourself by returning my mistress's robe."

Something inside Malaina broke, and suddenly, she became nothing but empty, unending cold—cold, calculating anger.

For so much of her life, she lived by the rules and followed protocols. She'd hid in corners and effaced herself, as her father told her to, because children, especially cursed ones, should neither be seen nor heard.

She'd learned the rules of the streets. Always watch your back, never drink untreated water, and all food is fair game until it's been claimed. Trash cans are communal, but makeshift shelters are sacred.

She'd molded herself into the person Malachi decided she should be, following his protocols to the word. Stay inconspicuous but keep your ears open, always have a plan and memorize every escape route, and never become involved in outside drama so as not to call attention.

Malaina had done everything everyone asked of her, living up to and exceeding every expectation. And now... Malachi was going to do nothing. Because it broke his made-up rules.

Done.

She was done.

Done following the rules, listening to the protocols, and letting everyone else take care of things.

That word: *nothing.* It pounded in her ears, drowning out everything else.

"Screw your protocols." She stood from the loveseat and headed for the doors, the robe flowing out behind her. Sterling followed, pushing open one of the doors for her.

"Malaina, Sterling, do not dare go looking into this further."

Malachi's desperate words hardly registered from behind her as she walked away from the office, Sterling by her side. The elevator sat there, waiting for them. They walked through the door and turned to push the button.

The guild master stood in his office doorway, watching them. Fuming.

She didn't care.

Malaina held his gaze as the doors slid shut, hoping he saw the Fire Wielder's blood in her silver eyes.

"So, what's the plan?" Sterling asked.

"We need to get into their apartment and figure out who the client and the target were." Already, she was thinking through and making a mental list of everything they'd need.

The Shifter rolled his wrists, cracking his knuckles. "Lybbi will probably know how to get in."

"Don't remind me." Malaina scowled but was grateful deep down.

The moment the elevator doors opened, she beelined for her room. The assassin's hands worked from memory, grabbing her usual work clothes and pulling them on without thought. The dark material hugged her, preparing her to step into the night and disappear.

Nothing. The word pounded again.

With every knife she pocketed, she felt more like herself. Like the Death Bringer she'd become over the years. Closing her eyes, she melted into that persona, the way she did before every job. The fact that she didn't actually have Death Bringer magic didn't matter. Death followed on her heels. A loyal cohort, left behind with her every footstep as she trekked through life.

Somedays, her job was hard, but most of the time, death came easy. Even if she did choose who lived and died most of her targets would still be dead. Deemed unworthy of this life by even her incredibly low standards.

And today…today she was out for blood. In fact, she hoped there would be an excuse to cut down every person who stepped in her way. Her hands itched for something to do, ready to be coated in blood. She wanted to relish it dripping between her fingers, caked into the creases of her knuckles. Wanted to see life flicker and dissolve in some-one's eyes, painfully draining from their body.

She thumbed the blade of one of her daggers, checking its sharpness, as she walked back into the living room. Sterling was already there, dressed in Syn's clothes when a knock sounded at the door.

When they opened it Layshan stood there, disheveled and angry. He pushed his hands deeper into his jacket pockets, and bloodshot eyes darted between them.

"What are you doing here?" Malaina asked, sheathing her blade.

The thief swallowed, bouncing on his toes. "You're going after him, right?" Malaina nodded. "Good. I'm coming with you."

Sterling's brows creased. "Are you sure you're really in the right place to—"

Layshan cut him off with a sharp glare. "I'm coming. I'm bringing my partner home."

Malaina and Sterling exchanged a look and nodded resolutely. Nothing they said would change Layshan's mind. Either way, they needed his help. He knew where Ra was… or at least, where he had been. And if things were different, if Sterling were left behind, there wasn't a force in the world that would keep Malaina from leading that rescue mission.

"What's going on?"

Malaina turned to find Lybbi standing at her bedroom door.

Unyielding resolve set Malaina's shoulders. She wasn't going to hide anything anymore. She'd made her rules to keep Lybbi safe, to keep her innocent, but all it did was keep her ignorant of the world around her. "Ra didn't come home. We're going to go get him."

Lybbi hugged herself, taking in every detail of the criminals gathered before her. "You're going to stop something bad from happening?"

Sterling nodded. "Yeah, kid. We're not going to sit back and watch this time."

Lybbi digested the words, deciding whether she believed them. Her hands rubbed against her arms, the recent shadows under her eyes fading a little, pride straightening her spine. "Good luck."

TWENTY-TWO

They staked themselves out on a neighboring rooftop, waiting a few hours until the sun started to set. Layshan would have preferred to plow right in, waiting and planning be damned, but they all knew they needed the dark. They held the advantage at night. Where the three of them lived, where they thrived. Most people feared the nighttime, jumping at shadows. Jumping at the thought of her hunting them in the dark.

As they should.

It was still unclear what happened with the Alman contract, where things had gone so wrong, but Malaina was determined not to let it happen again. This time, she was going to wait for the perfect moment.

The only problem was that Layshan hadn't been lying about the eerily quiet house. There was nothing to watch, no one to see. They studied the empty townhouse from every angle they could find. There was no furniture, no people, no decorations or adornments. The building sat still and quiet, the hours passing in a slog.

Malaina hoped Layshan would get some rest while they waited, but instead, he paced—back and forth, over and over, never taking his eyes from the townhouse. The circles beneath those bloodshot eyes grew darker. With every passing moment, the look in his eye grew feral—a wildfire waiting to be unleashed, a caged animal waiting for its dinner.

Finally, the sun started to set, the long shadows lengthening around them. Malaina took advantage of the moment. She drank in the approaching darkness, letting it chase away her weariness. She let it fuel the anger that opened a dark, endless abyss at Malachi's words.

Nothing. Nothing. Nothing.

He would have done *nothing*.

The knowledge festered and grew inside her, eating her alive from a pit in her stomach until it bloomed in her chest —a raw, insatiable, icy rage.

A black raven flew overhead, calling out to her before it swooped down, dive-bombing the roof. At the last second, he pulled up, and Sterling shifted back into human form, already in mid-stride.

"It's empty like you said. I checked every window. There's no sign that anyone's inside," he reported, cracking his knuckles.

Layshan shook his head. "No. He's in that house. I know he is."

"Man, you have to tell us what happened. Otherwise, we're walking in blind."

Layshan froze, ceasing his endless pacing, still refusing to look away from the townhouse. His thumb flicked the end of his nose, clearing his throat. "We've hit this house before. A few months ago. It seemed weird to be hitting it again so soon, but the pay was right, so Malachi told us to take extra precautions before really carrying things out. We watched a day and a night, but no one entered or left, and there was no sign of anything inside. Just like now. It was just…empty.

"We thought maybe we got some bad info. That the family moved or something, I don't know. It was stupid, but we were trying to figure out what to do next. So we went in to look around and see if anything had been left behind. If nothing else, it would give us uninterrupted time to scope the place out and get a mental map for any future jobs on the house before taking the info back to the guild and searching for the family's new address."

A deep, shaking breath rattled out of him before he continued. "We checked every room, every floor. All empty. Not even a damn nail left behind. But…" For the first time in hours, he pulled his eyes from the house and looked over his shoulder at them. "You see, this house is kind of weird. It has a basement."

"Seriously?"

Basements were rare in the richer districts of the city. In the lower parts of the city, the older sectors, tunnels connected many of the warehouses and townhomes. When those areas fell into disarray, the tunnels became commonplace for people to camp out and for crime, specifically human trafficking, to take place. Many of the wealthier nobles in the city petitioned to make sure the newer, nicer districts didn't have underground levels that could result in the same thing.

Layshan nodded. "We found it on our first contract. Thought it was weird, but we didn't need to go down there for anything, so we left it be. Made note of it, but otherwise left it. But…with the house empty, it seemed like a good opportunity to see what was up with it. The first time we found it, it had been heavily locked up, but this time, they'd left it cracked. Made sense, right? Why would you need to keep something locked up when no one lived there?

"We went down, and it was so fucking deep. The stairs went on forever. We couldn't imagine why someone would need to put their basement so far underground, but we figured it had to be something good. Like a huge safe or something. We finally got down there, and…well, the stairs kind of opened up into this room. Just one big room. Dark as shit, so we looked for a light. They always have electricity in this part of the city. We found it in the middle of the room. Just one light. The whole room…covered wall to wall…"

Listening to him talk, they waited silently, not wanting to push him over the edge.

"With shelves and tables and hooks covered in tools. Knives, hammers, chisels, ropes, rocks, buckets of water, and…just so much other shit. A metal chair sat in the center of the room, a drain under it. Everything was covered in blood—dried stains in the tile grout on the floor and splatters on the tools. So much you could *smell* it."

Bile rose in the back of Malaina's throat. A torture

chamber. That's why they built it so far underground. So no one would hear the screams.

"Ra went in first and found the light. When we realized what it was…he pushed me back towards the stairs. I should have made him go first…I shouldn't have ran, but I was just so fucking scared. I didn't mean to, but I used my air to get up the stairs faster, and he fell behind." Layshan's words started to crack, the air around him swirling. Gusts lifted his hair and blew back his jacket. The more he talked, the angrier it became, whipping around him so fast she thought it would send him up into the air in his own personal tornado, but he continued on, forcing the words out. "This…this door. This metal door came down, cutting the room off from the rest of the house. I went back, but it was completely solid. Nothing to grab, no way to lift it…I couldn't do anything. Faintly, I heard him yell, pounding on the door, telling me to run. The idiot told me to do it. I know I shouldn't have listened, but I didn't know what else to do, so I…"

Malaina bit her lip, her heart breaking. She couldn't imagine being in such a position, what it would be like if she or Sterling were the ones to get separated. The guilt would have eaten her alive if she ran, even if fleeing was the only option.

In the guild, when the pairing was right, your partner became your family. For nearly everyone there, their partner was their only family. They worked together and lived together. They became best friends and probably the only person who knew everything about each other—the one person who watched their back no matter what.

Sometimes, it took a few tries to get it right.

In Malaina's case, it took six tries to get it right—and those were just the ones who made it to the first contract. Even more had failed to make it past the training ring with her. Each time, her partner would decide they couldn't handle it. Couldn't handle the pressure of working alongside a Death Bringer, of what it meant to work so closely with someone like her. They were too scared or disgusted to come close enough to even land a hit while sparring. Scared of what it would mean to touch her. Even though Malachi made it clear to the whole guild that he'd forbidden her from using her "magic" outside of work.

Then Sterling came along.

The memory of that day was one of the few she remembered clearly and relived fondly.

While they had all waited for Malachi to come down and start sparring sessions, the guilders in training had crowded the benches, leaving an arms-length empty space surrounding Malaina. When the guild master entered, though, he'd been guiding someone new, someone she hadn't seen before.

Even at eighteen, Sterling had been the largest person she'd ever seen. Well over a head taller than anyone else in the guild, muscle already padded every inch of him. His confident swagger matched her own as he scanned the room, and when mysterious purple-gray eyes landed on her for the first time, they didn't look away. Instead, they'd locked on her. Rather than being scared like all those before him, he'd been intrigued.

Immediately, her defenses went up, and she twisted her

face into her usual scowl, which made most people cower. Usually, that was all it took.

Guilders were always full of themselves, too confident for their own good…until it came to her. One dirty look was all it ever took for them to find something else to look at. But not Sterling. He saw her scowl…and smirked. The very audacity of such an expression made her rage.

"Malaina," Malachi had ordered without looking at her, "First ring."

In an attempt to wipe that smirk off his face, she gave Sterling her best feral smile, rising from her lounge on the benches, letting him know what he was in for. The whole room had gone quiet, and had they not been so scared of pissing her off, there would have been a collective oohing and awing. Their collective thoughts and unsaid whispers rang in her mind.

Malaina's getting a new partner. How long will this one last?

She hadn't cared. Only fifteen at the time, her massive ego had been stroked enough that she didn't slouch under Sterling's stare. He'd watched every movement she'd made, every step and twitch of her fingers. She'd readied herself for a one-on-one and made her way to the edge of the ring, pulling her hair into a messy ponytail.

Malachi held out a hand, calling a staff that smacked against his palm. Without getting a second for Sterling, he handed it to her. She cocked an incredulous eyebrow at him.

He can't be serious, she'd thought, *who the hell is this guy?*

Sterling had rolled his head from one side to the other, cracking his neck as he paced back and forth. She'd been entranced by his eyes, shifting from one color to another. She'd never seen anything like it before.

Malachi hadn't said anything as she took the staff and stepped barefoot into the ring, taking an offensive position. After one last appraising look at Sterling, the guild master clasped his hands behind his back and let them take each other in.

And then Sterling did something no other prospective partner had had the guts to do. The arrogant bastard actually walked to the center of the ring and held out his hand.

She stared at it warily, looking from it to his shifting eyes and haughty smirk, before deciding to take it. They shook, his massive hand engulfing hers, before backing up to their respective sides of the ring.

"Go," Malachi commanded, and before her, Sterling shifted.

It was the first time she'd ever seen anything like it, and a collective gasp went through the rest of the room. Where a mountain of a man had stood, there now crouched a pitch-black cougar. Frozen in place, she didn't know how to react. She'd never sparred against a Shifter before, they were so rare at the guild, and she had never heard of a Shifter being able to take on the form of an entire animal. In stories, sure, but in real life? Never.

How was she supposed to spar a fucking mountain cat?

After giving her a moment to gather herself, he'd pounced, and one swipe of his paw had sent her flying out of the ring.

With a *thud*, she'd skidded across the floor on her back, coming to a stop beside Malachi. He looked down at her, trying and failing to bite back an amused grin. He'd raised a pleased eyebrow as if to say: *try and scare this one off.*

She'd ground her teeth, ready to take the bait and win that challenge. She'd rolled to her feet to find Sterling already back in human form.

Then that absurd Shifter chuckled. Actually *chuckled* at her.

"Rematch," she'd barked.

That happened four years ago, and they'd been partners ever since.

The thought of him trapped in a torture chamber…she couldn't imagine.

Layshan's tornado continued to grow around him, fueled by his rage. His eyes bore into the townhouse so intensely she wondered if he was trying to blow it away.

Sterling walked over and placed a hand on Layshan's shoulder. The whirlwind became less violent but didn't still.

"It's not your fault," Sterling said, "You did the right thing, and we're going to take Ra home."

Layshan's fists clenched in his jacket pockets, but he gave a curt nod of his head and the wind died away.

"So," Malaina started, trying to change the subject, "How do we get in?"

Sterling looked back at her. "All the windows are locked."

"That can be changed." Locked windows and doors never stopped them before.

Layshan shook his head. "No, I'm going in the front. I want them to know we're coming." His voice came out steady and cold, a promise of death in those words.

Malaina knew this wasn't going to just be a rescue mission. This strike was going to be a massacre.

Thieves didn't generally have a need to kill, so Malachi never forced the issue the way he had with her. But they all knew how, and there was always a first for everything. If Layshan wanted to rampage, Malaina wasn't going to get in his way. If anything, she was ready to give him some pointers.

She walked to Layshan's side, slid a knife from her sleeve, and held it out to him—an offering and an understanding, support and encouragement.

He regarded it without a flicker of emotion before looking away. "Don't need it." He turned away from the edge of the roof, away from the townhouse. The icy determination, which could only be fueled by an incomprehensible need for revenge in his voice, sent a shiver up her spine.

Sterling blew a breath through his teeth and followed Layshan.

Malaina took one more look at the townhouse in the fading light and re-sheathed her dagger. Preparing herself, she pulled up her hood to shadow her face and lifted her face covering. No one in that house would be living long enough to register her features and use them against her, but the habit made her feel armored. Ready for what was to come.

This wasn't going to end well. The question was, who would it not end well for? Them or the people in that house?

Night descended, shrouding the world in a quiet black blanket.

The three of them stood before the front door of the townhouse, taking in the quiet stillness for a few more minutes.

Then Layshan took a hard step, shifting his weight forward, and with an outward sweep of his hands, he sent the door flying open. The force bent the hinges and nearly splintered the door on impact.

The Air Wielder straightened, lifting his chin as he smoothed his jacket and strode in, head held high with the confidence and intent of someone who owned the building. Sterling and Malaina flanked him, following him through the empty house.

The bareness of everything put Malaina on edge. Her fingers twitched for her blades, ready for something to jump out at them at any moment. From the feel of the shadows around her, though, she could tell nobody was nearby. That alone felt off, making her skin prickle.

Layshan didn't stop to contemplate where he was going. He navigated the halls until they were standing before the odd basement door standing slightly ajar, the way he'd described.

What he said about it being propped open because no one lived there made sense to her up on the roof, but now, it felt like a menacing invitation. A challenge. *Enter if you dare,* should have been painted across the front of it. The dare wasn't one she wanted to take, but nothing in Thaumoria would keep her from going beyond that door.

Sterling approached first, pulling the door open the rest

of the way without a hint of uncertainty. Turning the corner, he jumped headlong into the dark, shifting. Malaina caught a glimpse of a tail as he dove into the dark, and she knew he'd shifted into his favored massive wolf. Layshan followed on Sterling's heels, disappearing into the stairwell.

A snarl ripped through the air, emanating from the darkness, and Malaina suddenly felt right at home. Her shadows no longer warned her away but drew her into their embrace. The darkness of the stairwell shrouded her, consumed her. She felt her way through her magic, letting it dance around her where no one could see. She felt the stairs, felt where the wall met the ceiling, felt Layshan and Sterling in front of her.

Without her shadows, her descent would have been slow, feeling her way down step by step. With them, though, she could practically see the stairwell before her. They guided her, sinking into her skin like a Witch's magic and pulling her forward.

Layshan hadn't been exaggerating about how far down the stairwell went. The descent felt endless. On and on they went down the stairs until Malaina's legs started to burn.

Finally, light streamed up through the hall. Malaina sent her shadows away, leaving them behind as she stepped into the light. Her heart raced in response to the brightening stairwell.

They'd made it to the basement.

Sterling slowed, crouching low to the ground, and approached the room. His claws skimmed the seam where the stairwell met the room, and he paused. The wolf's hackles raised as he scanned the chamber.

In the center of the room sat Ra, slouched over, pinned to a metal chair by his ankles and wrists.

Malaina couldn't tell from where she stood how he was being held to the chair, but she could see the way blood dripped from his hanging head. His matted hair hid his face, but it couldn't hide his bare chest and the ways he had been carved. Dark trails of blood stained the tile floor beneath him, leading down the drain. He sat so still it was hard to tell if he was still alive. His breath was so shallow that the effort didn't even lift his shoulders… if he breathed at all.

Layshan surged, trying to pass Sterling, but Malaina put a hand on his arm, holding him back. His wild furious gaze whipped to hers, and she tried to communicate with her eyes that he needed to wait. They would never get Ra out if they got themselves killed, and going in blind could be nothing but a bad idea.

Sterling inched forward, canine eyes sweeping the room back and forth, searching for any kind of threat. Malaina took the chance to scan the room from where she stood outside the entryway. The slick metal walls were segmented at regular intervals.

The room wasn't big, but large enough that the light-bulb hanging above Ra's head left the corners dark. Other-wise, there was nowhere to hide in the empty chamber.

Sterling circled Ra, ensuring he laid eyes on every inch of the room. When his lip stopped curling and he made eye contact with Malaina, she knew the room was clear.

The instant she lifted her hand from Layshan's arm he

bolted, moving faster than should be possible. The air wafting behind him lifted the hem of her hood.

The Air Wielder dropped to his knees before Ra, skidding to a stop. He reached out, but his hands didn't make contact. His fingers hovered over Ra's skin, wanting to inspect him but not wanting to cause any more pain.

Malaina approached apprehensively and saw that Ra still breathed, but barely.

"Ra? Hey, it's me," Layshan whispered with heartbreaking gentleness.

Recognition made Ra's head bob. He tipped his head up just enough to determine if the person before him was truly Layshan or a mirage, and Malaina caught a glimpse of his face. Seeing the carnage on her friend nearly made her sick.

Both eyes were purple and swollen. Burst blood vessels made the whites around his brown irises so red it was amazing he could see at all. Half of his mouth had been sliced clear up his cheek, like a sick, twisted smirk he would never be able to shake. His shoulders were purple from being dislocated, and clean holes punctured his muscles up and down his forearms, all barely crusted over with the blood still dripping from his fingertips.

She tried to see him through her assassin's mind, cold and unfeeling. Tried not to take in any more, but every time she inadvertently scanned a new part of him she saw another thing to be horrified by. A new slice or patch of skin peeled away.

Malaina knelt next to the chair, trying to figure out how

he was being held and how to get him out. At first, she didn't understand what she was looking at.

Metal cuffs hugged his wrists and ankles, seamlessly attached to the chair itself. Maybe they had welded him into the chair, but nothing indicated that the metal had been melted and cooled. Instead, it was all one solid piece of metal—like the chair had morphed around him, swallowing him so he couldn't move.

She tried not to notice the unnatural angles his fingers were crooked at, popped at the knuckle at one angle, then popped the other way at the next.

She continued looking for any weakness, thinking maybe they could carry him and the chair out together if it came down to it. They could figure out how to free him once they were safe. But the chair melded into the ground like it had grown out of the floor in a single piece.

She swore under her breath. The butchery all seemed like massive overkill for a simple thief.

"What were you guys stealing?" She hissed at Layshan, but he ignored her. He saw nothing but Ra, no longer in the room with her but consumed by his broken partner in front of him.

Sterling continued to circle them, nose twitching as he sniffed the air. He clearly smelled something off and was trying to discern what it was.

"Lay…" Ra choked out, the syllable coming out muddy and lopsided. "I….home…" A mixture of blood and spit fell from his lips, his words incoherent.

"I'm going to get you home," Layshan assured him with

a hard edge of determination. "Nothing else bad is going to happen. I promise." He laid his hands on Ra's knees without thinking, and Ra flinched, whimpering and crying in pain.

Malaina pulled down her hood and face cover, looking to where Sterling still prowled. "We need to get him off this chair."

He ignored her, his canine gaze fixated on the middle of the back wall. She hissed at him again, and he tore his eyes away from the spot, shifting to join them in trying to free Ra.

Malaina jumped to her feet as a door slid down, blocking them off from the stairwell.

Layshan turned, his eyes going wide. "No," he breathed.

Malaina ran to the door, searching it over desperately, Sterling by her side. The Shifter slammed a fist against it, but it didn't bend under his strength. The barrier was thick, solid, and seemingly impenetrable.

Something moved behind them, and they turned to find one of the metal panes on the wall opening, the shelves sliding apart. The pane spun to reveal a small dark room beyond and two figures standing there.

Malaina's entire body went cold when she recognized one of them and instantly rethought every detail of her life.

The man stepped forward out of the dark, dressed in a pristine navy blue suit. His slicked-back black hair showed off pale white skin and brilliant blue eyes. On his daughters, Malaina thought those eyes looked like they could have been gifted by Sarhea, the Water Goddess herself, born from the moon, but on him...they felt like cool pools of death watching over her, ready to pull her under and drown her. More akin to the ocean in the midst of a storm rather than on a beautiful day.

Malak Alman.

Beside him stood a man she didn't recognize at all. Thin and wiry, he held up a hand. Spidery fingers twisting with the movement of the door. He had the complexion of an Earth Wielder but...grayer. Normally, Earth Wielders were blessed with the beautiful cool undertones of soil, but this man looked like he'd never seen the sun a day in his life. Locked in a dark room, away from joy and warmth. Maybe that's why his eyes were colorless, dull, and gray.

Where Malak smirked at them maliciously, the man beside him looked through them as if he didn't care whether they were there.

Malaina stopped herself from retreating when Malak stepped out of the darkness and into the room, picking imaginary lint off his perfectly pressed suit. His eyes locked on Malaina.

They studied each other, measuring each other up.

Layshan didn't move from where he crouched, watching both the men with unflinching hatred.

Sterling's muscles bristled, but he didn't dare shift without knowing what they were facing.

Malak Alman broke the tense silence that fell over the room, his vicious blue stare never once leaving Malaina's hard silver one. "I hoped to meet you here, Death Bringer."

TWENTY-THREE

Malaina didn't know how to answer. He was looking for *her?*

Alman stepped forward, looking down at Ra's body slumped in the chair with disdain. Disgust curled his lips.

"You have…loyal friends," he sneered, emphasizing the word *loyal* as if it left a sour taste on his tongue. A disgusting word he didn't understand and had no place in his life.

Malaina's mouth fell open, unable to comprehend what she heard. Once again, she surveyed Ra's broken body, finding something new to be horrified by.

"You did this to get to me." She wasn't quite sure which word in that sentence to emphasize. It didn't make sense.

"Yes, well, I hoped for better results. You lot are trained well, I've learned." The Water Wielder's eyes scanned Ra, but the carnage he caused didn't seem to appall him.

Instead, he came off both disappointed and disgusted at his apparent lack of results.

The assassin took an involuntary step forward, wanting to lunge at the man in blue. To use her bare hands to rip him to shreds. "Is this revenge for Nyda? He had nothing to do with that."

Alman sniffed. "Yes, I'm aware. I was simply attempting to gain information on the location of your *nest*." His daughter's name had no effect, glossing over it as though she hadn't said it at all. "My guard, the one you left alive that is, provided me with your description. However, the Lord wanted more concrete information."

Malaina felt sick. Of course, people were looking for her, trying to pin down any details that would gain Kevah's reward and favor, but this…what Alman had done to Ra? That was too far. She couldn't let anyone suffer like this for her. Her sorry excuse for a life wasn't worth *this*.

"Why him?" Malaina asked, not feeling the need to clarify who she referred to.

"I needed information, and your employer rejected my requests for you personally. I assumed an acquaintance would be the next best thing." Malak said the words so casually he could have been talking to a colleague about business plans.

Malaina stood statue still, putting the pieces together. Alman wanted her; he'd asked Malachi specifically for her, trying to lure her in. When Malachi said no, Alman contracted someone else in the guild to gain knowledge on her. The twisted scheme was genius. If you can't gain intelligence from the source itself, then go to the next best thing.

Why hadn't Malachi caught on to the obvious setup in the first place? Maybe it was hindsight, but it seemed so clear.

And he still hadn't been planning to do anything when Ra didn't return. Ice flowed through her veins, her fingers clenching into fists by her sides.

Layshan didn't glance at Alman as he talked so casually about his pathetic reasons for what he had done to Ra. Instead, the Air Wielder's stare hardened, concentrating on the rise and fall of Ra's chest, probably aiding his breathing.

She imagined what Layshan must be thinking, listening to Malak admit to why he had done this. How much Layshan must hate her. What happened to Ra, the state he was in, was her fault.

"I may have killed Nyda, but I was hired to do a job. You should be going after the person who put the target on her head." Bringing up Nyda again may not have been the best choice, but she hoped to put him on someone else's scent. Distract him, so he focused his energy on Desroc instead of them.

Alman waved his hand dismissively. "It was quite tragic, wasn't it? Her sister and Mother have been devastated." He blew out an annoyed breath, his family's grief nothing more than an inconvenience. "But what did they expect? I needed to ensure you were the real thing."

The entire room faded away, Malaina's vision tunneling to only Alman. The words he was saying. The things he was admitting to. Her jaw clenched so hard she thought her teeth might crack from the pressure.

Thankfully, Sterling spoke the words she couldn't comprehend.

"*You* bought that contract?" His rage shook the walls around them, reverberating down to her bones. "You targeted your own daughter and then made her go through that torture of the antidote. For a *test?*"

"Indirectly, yes," Alman replied evenly. "It's unimportant now, and all this talk bores me. You're here, so that's that. I'd prefer you come willingly. I quite detest blood." Abhorrence gleamed in his eyes, staring down his scrunched nose at Ra's massacred body.

Malaina was done with this conversation. Palming two of her blades, she tested the familiar weight on her fingers. The urge to send them flying was almost overwhelming. To witness them sink into the disgusting man's throat. But she needed Ra free from that damned chair. They would never get him out without help. She still wasn't even sure how they had gotten him into the thing.

"I suggest you open this door, free my friend, and you might leave alive." A lie. Alman's life would end whether he helped them or not, but maybe offering him the chance to live would make him easier to manipulate.

Alman's gaze skimmed her again, as unimpressed with her as an Anima facing a particularly sassy pup.

"Hm," he grunted. "That's unfortunate. Nonetheless, I wish to introduce you to my friend here." Fingers flicked on the Water Wielder's raised hand, calling forward the sad-looking nothing of a man whose wide, blank eyes hardly noticed his surroundings. Alman gave the man an appraising once-over, his lips twisting to the side for a beat. "Well, 'friend' may be an exaggeration. This is Cass Argis. I'm sure you recognize the name."

Malaina's heart sped up. Everyone in the City of Elementals recognized the line of Earth Wielders, known for their legendary ability to wield metal and metal alone. The gift ran in their family, and last she'd heard they were all in the City of Kinetics, aiding in invention-building and innovation projects. What was he doing here? In this horrible basement, helping such a disgusting man.

Suddenly, details started to make sense. The chair. The cuffs holding Ra seemed perfectly formed around his wrists and ankles, fused to the chair seamlessly because they were. Cass had manipulated the metal so it was built around Ra, going so far as to fuse the chair to the floor itself.

A talented Kinetic with a knack for metal may have been able to break simple welds, pulling them apart at the seams. But metal that had been melded back together so it was no longer two separate pieces but one whole piece of unbroken alloy? That was a different story. That didn't have the same weak spots. A Kinetic controlled motion, they moved things from one place to another. They couldn't control the very being of something itself the way a Wielder did. If there was nothing to pull apart, nothing to leverage, then a Kinetic was helpless.

No one but another Earth Wielder with the Argis gift would have been able to break out of that chair.

"Cass here is a logical creature, a quality I greatly admire." Alman placed a hand on Cass's shoulder, as though they were really on friendly terms. "Raised deep in the Kinetic mines, he cares very little about your fondness for this fellow here." He gestured off-handedly at Ra. "Rather, I have paid him a great deal of money to ensure you leave this room by my side."

Malaina gritted her teeth, her anger and disgust getting the better of her. She threw the knife from her hip. The blade flew true, flying for Alman's throat. She listened for the satisfying gurgle of him choking on his own blood, the blade sprouting from his neck.

But he never flinched. A cat watching an annoying fly on a lazy day, he tracked the soaring dagger.

Cass lifted a hand faster than her knife flew, never blinking. Mere inches from severing Alman's vocal cords, the knife melted as though it hit a wall of invisible fire. Alman observed the liquified blade fall to the floor in a puddle, uncaring.

At the sight of her blade turning molten on the floor, Malaina couldn't blink, couldn't breathe.

Sterling held an arm infant of her, pushing until he shielded her with his own body, the need to shift rippling his muscles.

Alman sighed. "That's a shame."

Cass lifted his other hand, long, delicate fingers pointed toward the ceiling. Those dull gray eyes remained blank, unaware as his fingers curled into the beginning of a fist. The cuffs around Ra's wrists crunched, caving in on themselves and tightening.

Ra ground out a groan of pain.

Layshan's eyes went wide and wild. "No!" His fingers clawed at the bonds, trying without hope to pull them free.

"I am not a patient man, Death Bringer." Alman's voice turned dark, a clear threat in his words. He was a man used to being listened to, used to getting his way.

"Fine!" She shrieked from behind Sterling's shoulder, wishing this would all just end. She made to push around the muscle in her way, but the Shifter didn't let her around.

Sending her stumbling into the wall, he shoved her back before lunging. Leaping through the air, he shifted back into wolf form, flattening Alman against the floor.

Malak let out an ear-splitting scream that echoed off the metal walls.

Sterling tore into his throat.

Cass scrutinized the attack, unflinching, stepping aside to avoid the spray of blood.

The screams were abruptly cut off as Alman lost his vocal cords. Sterling spat a chunk of bloody flesh from his mouth. Red dripped from his maw as he turned his attention to Cass, snarling.

Cass didn't even have the decency to express a speck of fear for his life. Instead, he tilted his head, watching Sterling stalk closer.

"Fascinating," he breathed.

"Don't!" Malaina yelled.

Sterling stopped but continued to snarl, saliva turning to foam that dripped from his bloodied canine teeth. He couldn't kill Cass, not yet. It would kill their only hope of getting out of the room. Their only hope at getting Ra home. They needed the Earth Wielder alive to free them.

"Let us go, and he'll let you live," Malaina lied, hoping the unfeeling man might have some sense of self-preservation.

He didn't move. Didn't flinch. Didn't blink. Just studied Sterling with academic-fueled curiosity. Like he wasn't used to speaking in front of others, his words were hoarse. "I am under orders."

Then his fingers closed into a fist.

The bonds became impossibly tight around Ra's wrists, and he let out a scream that split the air. Bones crunched, resisting for a heartbeat, before liquifying under the pressure of crushing metal. Flesh and blood seeped from the cuffs, nearly severing Ra's broken hands altogether.

Layshan bared his teeth, jumping to his feet. In two strides, he found himself behind Cass. He grabbed Cass by the throat and slammed the Earth Wielder against the open door with the force of a hurricane.

The metal gave way where Cass hit the wall, bending to the contours of his body just enough to save his life.

The room turned into a self-contained tornado, tools nearly whipping off the walls. Layshan's blonde hair lifted into a wild halo, but the rest of him remained terrifyingly still.

For the first time, Cass seemed to truly comprehend what was before him, staring into Layshan's wild eyes.

"You have three seconds," Layshan ground between bared teeth, almost inaudible over the whipping wind around them.

Ra continued to scream, but Cass kept his fist clenched, fear freezing every muscle in his body.

Malaina ran to Ra, trying to see if the metal loosened at all, but found them tighter than ever.

Layshan's fingers tightened. "Three…"

Cass' eyes darted around, from the still-snarling Sterling to Ra and back to Layshan. His mouth opened to speak again, but Layshan dug his fingers in, pulling Cass away from the wall just to slam him back again. The veins in Layshan's hands bulged. Blood started to well around where his manicured nails broke the skin.

"Two…" Layshan growled, the essence of walking death.

Cass relaxed his fingers, and the cuffs around Ra's wrists and ankles released themselves. Ra fell away from the chair and into Malaina's arms before he crumpled to the floor. He went unconscious, his entire body limp, dead weight. She tried not to notice how his body moved in all the wrong ways. The way his joints bent at unnatural angles.

When Layshan loosened his grip the wind started to die away, though it didn't completely calm.

"The door."

Cass swallowed, lifting a hand, palm up. The door slid open.

Malaina tried to hook Ra's arm over her shoulder and start dragging him towards the door, but she didn't know where to grab it. Nothing seemed solid or whole. She almost grabbed his wrist when her fingers met liquified flesh, and she had to hold back a gag.

Sterling shifted, coming to her aide. His jaw clenched when he effortlessly hefted Ra into his arms and started up the stairs.

Layshan released Cass, watching the Earth Wielder fall to the ground.

Cass' wide eyes beheld the Air Wielder, a mix of fear and fascination warring in his gaze.

"He said you were a thief," he whispered, voice croaking and cracking around the words.

Layshan crouched over him, a renewed fire in his eyes. "I am, but apparently, you didn't learn the thief's code. An eye for an eye. You stole my friend, so I'm stealing your life." Then the air whipped again, rushing to Layshan's raised hand from behind. He pulled his hand back, and the air started flying in the other direction, back into his face.

Frantically grasping at his throat, Cass' eyes bulged.

Malaina watched, captivated.

Layshan was robbing the breath from Cass's lungs. He never tore his eyes from Cass's as he stole the life from his body, the ultimate heist. When Cass stopped moving, Layshan stood. He didn't look sad or regretful. He didn't even give the man a second glance. The thief simply turned and headed for the entryway to the stairwell.

"Ra?"

She kept her words even like the glassy surface of the sea on a calm night, afraid that even a single ripple would cause a storm to rise. "Sterling is taking him up."

Layshan nodded, smoothing his jacket and starting up the stairs without looking back. A steady hand pushed his hair back out of his eyes. Just like that, a mask of calm fell over him, uncaring and cold once again.

Malaina gave one more glance back into the wrecked room. At the mutilated bodies. She tried to feel something for the men she was leaving behind. Tried to think of a reason she should mourn them. But all she saw was Nyda writhing in her bed, seizing while the antidote fought against the mercifully quick death Malaina tried to give her. Thought of Kaida's carefree love for life as she twirled in the dress shop and how she must have crumpled with grief over what Malaina had done. What Malak had paid her to do to his own daughter.

And for what?

Money. Favor among Lord Kevah. Power.

When she eyed those stiffening bodies, one bloody and one slumped, she felt nothing but disgust. Not at the slaughter but at the waste of life they had been. Leaving the bodies to rot, she turned away and headed up the stairs.

She was huffing for breath when she finally made it to the top of the stairs, cursing whoever built that room so deep within the ground. Sterling closed the door behind her, flipping the lock.

Good. Not only would it keep anyone from figuring out what happened for quite some time, but maybe they never would. Maybe whoever bought the house next wouldn't bother to inspect what was beyond, deeming it too much work, and Malak Alman and Cass Argis would be entombed forever in the dark.

She hoped they feared the dark, leaving their souls entrenched in terror for eternity.

Layshan knelt on the ground, Ra's head in his lap. Holding Ra close, he gently ran a hand over the Kinetic's knotted hair again and again. Malaina knelt beside them, watching as Ra's breaths came slower and slower.

"Can you do anything?" Layshan glanced at her from beneath his lashes.

Her heart broke at the perfectly logical question. As the Death Bringer, the one and only person who commanded death, shouldn't she be able to *stop* death?

If only it were possible. She didn't have the heart to tell him how misled he was.

The Shadow Spinner shook her head.

Layshan looked back down at Ra, dejected. Tears streamed down his cheeks, pulling Ra closer. He pressed a cheek to Ra's forehead, and whispered, "I'm going to take you home, ok? We're going home. Together."

Tears welled in Malaina's eyes, and everything in her gave out. Her arms shook as she leaned on them, and she remembered flashes of her life.

Ra sitting next to her on the roof, trying to help her be a better person. A better big sister.

Ra cheering at the Games, betting on the most outrageous odds just to see what he would win.

Ra sneaked sweets into the group living quarters to share with the guilders who weren't old enough to work yet.

Ra when he stepped up on her first day in group training, the only person willing to spar with her. The only person willing to spar with her for years.

Ra the day he pickpocketed her two coins.

He'd been by her side for so many years, seeing her through so many ups and downs. He'd given her everything. She owed him her entire life. She could have died on those streets. Lybbi could've died. Yet when it came down to it, Ra was willing to sacrifice his life for hers.

No, not just for her, but for everyone in the guild. Had he given away the information Malak wanted, it would have put everyone at risk. Ra gave his life for all of them, a gift none of them would ever be able to pay back.

Ra said something between weakened breaths Malaina couldn't hear. Layshan's eyes squeezed at the words, more tears falling, but his lips gave a weak smile. "You'll see her again. I promise." Layshan whispered back. The intimate moment felt wrong and intrusive to witness.

Sterling crouched beside her. "Maybe we should get to Jade."

The suggestion was empty; Jade could do nothing at this point, but it gave them a sense of familiarity—a sense of ritual. When someone in the guild was hurt, you took them to Jade. It's just what you did. She made everything better, like a mother kissing an invisible wound after her children fell.

"I can shift and carry him…" Sterling started, but Layshan shook his head and cut him off.

"No." Layshan scooped Ra into his arms and headed for the busted door. "I'm taking him home."

TWENTY-FOUR

Ra didn't make it home.

It wasn't clear at what point in the journey he stopped breathing, but she would bet that Layshan could pinpoint the very moment he didn't pull another breath. All the way home, he'd carried Ra through the backstreets, through the shadows of the night, not once slowing or complaining. At some point, his arms started trembling under the weight, but even then, he wouldn't let go. He simply stared ahead blankly, placing one foot in front of the other.

Malaina did her best to use her shadows discreetly to shield them from prying eyes, but once they made it to the lower part of town it didn't matter. There were no guards to ask questions anyway, and everyone on the streets was used to seeing death. Had become intimately familiar with it long ago. When bodies often littered the street corners, no one thought twice about one being escorted home. Many glanced up, but they all adverted their gaze quickly, a knowing shimmer in their eyes.

When they entered the grand room, gasps went out among those present, but Layshan never glanced up. His blank stare into nothing continued, tears falling, arms shaking.

Sterling broke off and headed for Malachi's office. Quickly, Malachi, Serena, and Jade stepped out.

Jade reached them first, scanning Ra for any sign of life but resigning herself when she found none. She turned her sharp gaze to Layshan, dulling the blade to the extent that Jade could. She said something and then laid a hand on the top of Ra's head, but the words didn't register in Malaina's ears. Serena reached out a hand, placing the tips of her fingers on Layshan's arm.

His eyes snapped to Serena's so abruptly that Malaina jumped, breaking his catatonic state.

To her credit, the Anima didn't flinch in response. Her soft gaze met his devastated one. Tears instantly sprung to her eyes, and Malaina knew she was taking on as much as she was giving, trying to put Layshan in a state he could handle. Easing his pain just enough.

"Layshan, hon," she whispered, meeting his eyes without hesitation, "We need you to let go."

For a moment, Layshan's fingers curled tighter, clenching Ra closer. Jade grimaced, fingers flicking unsaid words. She bit her lip and studied Ra's stiff, broken body. Serena never took her green eyes from Layshan's devastated face.

"It's okay. He's not going to hurt anymore. He's safe

now," the mistress assured him, her voice cracking. She felt everything. Her hands started to shake as she took on Layshan's suffering, letting it tear her down like it was her own.

"What's going on?" A small voice piped up over the ring of people who had gathered.

No. Malaina moved to block the view, but Lybbi had already pushed through. Lybbi stopped mid-step, falling back, a hand flying to her mouth, gasping. Malaina wound her arms around her younger sister's shoulders, pulling her back against her, trying to turn the young girl away. But Lybbi wouldn't tear her brassy eyes from the scene before them. Lybbi's free hand clutched at Malaina's arm, desperate for comfort that Malaina couldn't offer.

"Shhh." Malaina tried to soothe. "I know."

Mercifully, Lybbi stayed quiet, but Malaina could feel the way she started to tremble. No one around them spoke, letting Serena do her thing.

Serena gave Layshan a sad but encouraging smile. "You have to let go, hon."

Layshan slowly loosened his grip on Ra's body, nearly dropping him. Sterling swooped in, catching Ra, setting his jaw so he didn't react to holding the mangled corpse. Backing away slowly, he started towards the elevator, Jade ushering him away.

Layshan stared longingly at his best friend disappearing from his life. Grief and loss took him to his knees, his fingers digging into the carpet, clutching at the ground to keep the world from falling away beneath him. Serena kept a hand on his back, soothing what she could, but she was barely holding her own heart together.

Bren stepped forward, breaking away from Aneyra and the crowd. He wrapped one arm around Layshan's shoulders and hauled him to his feet. The three of them walked to Malachi's office without meeting anyone's eyes.

Malachi followed behind, looking lost and useless.

For the first time, Malaina thought Malachi looked… old. Tired. So unlike the pillar of strength and assurance, he'd always been in her life. At that moment, though, his head fell, gray-green eyes trained on the floor. When he reached his office doors he glanced back at the guilders who watched him, every eye looking to him for guidance.

He met all of their stares before he let out a heavy breath. "Just…go home." Then he turned and closed the door.

THE NEXT NIGHT, every guilder who wasn't out on a job crammed onto the roof. With vague curiosity, Malaina wondered if so many bodies on the roof were a safety issue, but staring at that box, she wasn't sure she would care if the whole thing caved in.

She stood near the front, Sterling on one side, Lybbi on the other. Before them, before the entire guild, sat that box. It was made of thin, easy-to-burn cheap wood that acted as nothing more than a barrier so they couldn't glimpse what lay inside. No one wanted to witness that again.

The crowd split, a row parting down the center, making way for Malachi, closely followed by Layshan.

Layshan's eyes were nothing but shadows, empty of any emotion. Holding his quivering chin high, he refused to meet the stares following him. He was trying to be strong, but the way his throat bobbed when he saw that box made it clear he was barely holding it together. Frozen at the edge of the crowd, he refused to get any closer.

Malachi continued forward, smoothing his usual gray suit. A single hand hovered over the wood, unsure. After a long pause, he placed his hand on the box, stroking it once. Twice. A slow, precious movement. He looked like he was trying to penetrate the wood with his eyes, to see beyond, to what lay within. He stood still another moment before he pried his eyes away and turned back to the guilders.

The guild master cleared his throat. "We all know why we are here, so I will not belabor the subject. Ra had been with this guild for over ten years." Malaina's chest tightened at Malachi's use of past tense. *Had.* Ra *had* been with the guild for over ten years. "He joined us younger than most, and from the moment of his arrival, he brought nothing but joy to those around him. I believe he was the only one who could ever make Layshan loosen up now and again." Some in the crowd gave a sad, half-hearted chuckle under their breath, but Layshan simply stared. He stared at that box. Stared at nothing. "It is not often we get the privilege of seeing off one of our own, but if anyone deserves the honor, it is Ra. He was a light in the night, and his presence will be truly missed."

Malaina wanted to be angry as Malachi spoke. He

didn't even want to go after Ra. He would have done nothing. But she couldn't bring herself to feel anything but heartache. Lybbi grabbed her hand, squeezing. Sterling pulled her close, letting her lean into his warmth and safety. But Ra's last resting place evoked nothing but deep, bottomless grief within her.

Malachi started back down the aisle, passing Layshan. He paused by Layshan's side, placing a hand on the thief's shoulder. He tried to meet Layshan's gaze to communicate something, but Layshan continued to stare ahead.

He didn't move, he didn't turn, he just stared.

A flash of hurt and pity passed through Malachi's eyes before he straightened and continued on.

Malaina stepped forward, getting her last chance to say goodbye. She dug the two copper coins out of her pocket, noting the way they gleamed in the moonlight, and placed them on the box.

One last trade. You deserve them.

Sterling and Lybbi followed, both placing a hand on the box. Two by two, each pair of guilders stepped forward. Each one placed their hand on the lid in a final farewell, some simply tapping the box, others taking their time to close their eyes and pray to whoever might listen to the prayers of a lowly criminal. None of them took her coins, though a few fingers brushed them. They didn't need a full understanding of why she left them to understand that those were Ra's now. One last haul to take with him.

A thief's final fortune.

Everyone stepped forward except for Layshan. He didn't move. Didn't budge from that spot as he beheld each guilder who sent off his partner. Some passed him, whispering condolences or placing a hand on his shoulder, but he didn't respond to any of them.

When the last guilder touched the box, Bren stepped forward. He shot a brief look to Layshan for permission, but when Layshan didn't acknowledge him he rubbed his hands together and turned towards Ra. He bent his head, lips moving in silent prayer.

Absently, Malaina pondered who he prayed to. Elosyn? To help take Ra on to the next life, maybe. The Kinetics believed in no God, but maybe he prayed to anyone who would listen, asking them to forgive Ra for how he used his magic. Whoever watched over them, she hoped they heard the prayer. Hoped they saw Ra for who he was at his core, and not for the job he took to survive.

Bren pulled his hands apart, holding them down by his sides, and then pushed them forward. He scooped his palms, pulling heat from the air, gathering it in his palms, and guiding it forward.

Ra's box went up in flames. Bren's brows creased as he continued to push, the flames growing larger and hotter.

The longer the fire burned, the emptier the roof became. Everyone lingered as long as they felt necessary, but as Ra turned to ash and the smell of burning flesh overtook the night, people needed to start getting back to their responsibilities. Eventually, only Malaina, Sterling, and Lybbi kept Layshan company. Bren stayed too, making sure the fire didn't die out too soon or grow out of control.

Flames doused Layshan in flickering light, but he hadn't

moved. He continued to stay planted in that spot, watching, hands buried in his pockets.

Malaina walked to his side, studying him out of the corner of her eye. She wasn't sure what to say to make things better. To help him come to terms with what had happened.

She kept seeing it over and over again in her mind. Fighting and failing to ignore the images of Ra in that chair, the sound of his screams, the tender moments of him using his final breaths to whisper to Layshan.

"What did he say?" She asked gently.

"Hm?" Layshan grunted, the only sign he'd heard her.

"At the house, he whispered something to you, and you said, 'You'll see her again.' What did he say?"

Layshan's blank gaze became downcast. He watched the ground instead of the flames, barely coming to. He cleared his throat. "He said…" He stumbled over the words, over the memory. "He said he missed his Mom."

"Oh," Tears sprang to her eyes once again. "I didn't know…" her words trailed off. There were so many ways to finish the sentence. *I didn't know he stayed in contact with his Mother. I didn't know he liked his Mother. I didn't know.*

Layshan shook his head. "It's not like that. His Mom… she was a maid working for one of the noble Elemental families. A Kinetic trying to find her way in a new city without family. She…well, she slept with…" Malaina nodded, understanding. She'd slept with the husband. Willingly or unwillingly, it didn't matter now. "Anyways, when he found out the baby was his, he fired her. She spent a few years job-hopping but the father made it impossible for her to find stable work. Eventually, she convinced Malachi to take Ra and practically left him on the door stoop, so to speak. Ra saw her a few times after, but after a few years, she kinda fell off the map. Turns out, Ra got her magic and his dad's power."

"So, she's still around?" If his Mother still lived in the city, looking in on her son then she deserved to know. Maybe they could find her and… Layshan shook his head.

"We tried to find her a couple of years ago. Give her some money to get back on her feet. We never found her. He maintained that she had just moved or something, but deep down, we both knew the truth."

Malaina closed her eyes, sucking on her lips to keep from letting her tears fall.

You'll see her again.

She hugged herself, trying to hold herself together.

Layshan shrugged. "We never talked about it again, but he still set a little money aside after each job. Hoping."

Neither of them spoke for a long time, standing in silence while the flames danced.

"Are you going to stay?" Malaina asked before she could think better of it.

Layshan's eyes went distant again. Sterling appeared at Layshan's other side, holding something silver in his hands. A flask. He unscrewed the top, took a shot, and handed it across to Malaina. She held her breath and took a shot herself. She grimaced at the burning trail that slid down her throat, but it started to warm her icy veins in an instant.

She handed it off to Layshan. The Air Wielder didn't seem to register what he held but tipped it back anyway, stealing a long drink. And then another. His eyes turned glassy. He used a sleeve to wipe his mouth, holding his arm to his lips as angry tears started to fill his eyes. Fingers curled around the flask, and Malaina thought he might throw it, releasing some of the anger he'd been suppressing.

Lybbi appeared before them, hugging her elbows and looking up at Layshan with round eyes. He did his best to swallow both his anger and his tears at the sight of her.

She seemed to be trying to find something to say, looking into Layshan's disheveled and devastated face.

"It's not as bad as people think," Lybbi blurted out.

Layshan just stared at her, not seeming to register what she said.

"What's not, kid?" Sterling asked when it became clear Layshan wasn't going to answer.

Lybbi swallowed, shifting from foot to foot. "Death. It's not as bad as people think. It... doesn't hurt. It's a lot harder for the people left behind."

Layshan's tears spilled over, but he kept his features steady aside from his trembling lips. He looked moments away from falling apart. From giving into the sobs he'd been fighting. Clearing his throat, he fought it all down. "How do you know?"

Lybbi shrugged, staring into his red-rimmed eyes. "You'll have to trust me."

He nodded, accepting that answer. Biting his lip the sobs finally bubbled up. Like a dam breaking they overtook him until he doubled over. They ripped through him, tearing at his chest, feasting on his entire body. The wall he built broke and he fell to his knees, his wails of heartbreak blanketing the city.

Malaina knelt beside him, pulling him close while his sobs racked through him.

They stayed with him until the sun started to peek over the horizon and the flames long since died out, having finished devouring Ra where he rested. When Bren left he'd taken Layshan, who had long since cried himself out. He offered to let Layshan crash on his and Aneyra's couch so Layshan didn't have to go home to an empty apartment. Bren mumbled something about letting Aneyra cook up a special concoction to help Layshan fall into a dreamless sleep.

Malaina, Sterling, and Lybbi didn't talk as they headed back to their apartment. There was nothing left to say.

Malaina's swollen eyes were heavy. She didn't even bother changing before falling into bed. She curled into a ball, her entire body caving in on itself.

The bed moved and dipped behind her, and a small back pressed against hers. She peaked over her shoulder and saw Lybbi lying beside her, curled up and facing away from her. A few seconds later, Sterling sprawled out across the foot of the bed, reaching out and stealing one of Malaina's pillows.

As she fell asleep, Malaina realized how grateful she was to not be alone.

TWENTY-FIVE

Malaina forced her eyes open when night started to fall again. Waking seemed impossible when she couldn't think of a reason to do it. Her eyelids weighed a thousand tons and threatened to send her right back to sleep. Rolling over she reached for Lybbi to pull her close, searching for a reminder of what was worth waking for, but she found nothing. Stretching her legs she found the end of the bed empty also. No Sterling either, then.

Shadows had settled around her in her sleep and she brushed them off. Muffled voices came from beyond her door, more than just Lybbi and Sterling's. Slipping out of bed she changed out of her clothes from yesterday, opting for something more comfortable.

Stepping through the door, she was surprised by what she found. In the kitchen stood Serena, her dark braids pulled half up into a knot, showing off her smiling face.

Bouncing beside her was Lybbi, holding a wooden spoon in front of the stove. While Lybbi cooked, Serena directed, explaining when and how much to use the spices she must have brought over.

Kai leaned against the entrance to the kitchen, a mug in hand. A mischievous smile danced on his full lips, giving contradictory advice to everything Serena said, causing nothing but trouble. Throwing dirty looks at him over her shoulder, the mistress looked a few more smart quips away from throwing a spice jar at him and sending him away from the kitchen altogether.

Sterling lounged on the couch, legs stretched out, mug in hand, unmanageable black waves pulled up into a messy bun on the back of his head. Given his appearance, it was clear that waking hadn't been a choice. A book lay open in his lap, and Malaina recognized it as one of his many academic tomes on animal anatomy and biology he had stolen from Malachi's office long ago.

Laid out on the floor before their rarely used fireplace, a pillow propped under his head, an arm thrown over his eyes, splayed Layshan. He looked like someone plucked him off Bren and Anyera's couch and placed him on the floor without ever waking him.

Tilting her head, her exhausted brain couldn't figure out what he was doing on their floor.

Sterling noticed her questioning gaze and shrugged, turning back to his book. "He was here when I got up."

"They had to work," Layshan groaned, never opening his eyes or fully stirring. He said nothing more, like that was all the explanation they needed before he went back to sleep.

Her mouth popped open to ask how he got into their apartment in the first place but closed again when she decided to just accept his presence.

On her way into the kitchen, Malaina slipped past Kai, clipping the countertop to avoid brushing against him. Nodding his good morning, he flashed her a small smile before taking a sip of his coffee. Malaina forced herself not to blush beneath his stunning purple gaze, peering over the top of his mug. Reminded herself that being stunning was part of his job description. Watching someone as if they were the only beautiful thing in a world of bland nothingness was a habit cultivated from years of practice.

Noticing the beginnings of red creeping up her neck he winked over a perfectly practiced smug smile that suggested a million dirty thoughts. She forced a lighthearted scowl in response and headed for Serena.

"Good, you're awake. Lybbi and I are making breakfast, it should be ready soon," Serena's silk-laden voice wrapped around the assassin's heart, warming her from the inside. Malaina wound her arms around Serena's waist from behind, pulling her close. Nuzzling against Serena's soft, cloud-like, oversized sweater, the mistress's signature sweet and spicy scent filled her senses. Serena laughed, sending a flutter through Malaina's chest.

A scoff that sounded almost like a gag came from the stove, and Malaina peaked over Serena's shoulder to find disgust twisting Lybbi's face. "Gross, I'm trying to cook here. Stop flirting."

A genuine smile formed on Malaina's lips, and it felt like an eternity since that had happened. Holding Serena close and being surrounded by friends made their apartment feel alive for the first time in weeks.

"You're here," Malaina whispered.

"Of course," Serena whispered back, leaning her head against Malaina's. Then, louder, she said, "Lybbi came and got us."

Malaina snorted. "Oh really?"

"Really," Kai grumbled under his breath, taking another sip of coffee.

Lybbi didn't look up from her cooking and shrugged. "We needed friends, and Sterling said it was okay."

"Ah, so this is all Sterling's fault then," Malaina teased.

Twisting, she peered around the corner at Sterling, who didn't bother glancing up from his book. Toasting his coffee mug, he gave a silent *you're welcome* salute before taking another long drink.

Malaina couldn't hold back a tired laugh at how exhausted they all looked. All of them looked like someone had dragged them right out of bed and given them just enough time to put on something appropriate. All the while Lybbi bounced around obliviously, just happy to have the company.

"So, what's for breakfast?" Malaina asked, kissing Serena on the neck before pulling away and going for her own mug.

Serena opened her mouth to answer when Lybbi shrieked, "Oh no! It's a surprise. Now go. You're distracting Serena and I need her help."

Malaina pressed her forehead into the crook between Serena's neck and shoulder one more time, running a hand over the back of her soft sweater. "Okay, okay, I'll go. It smells great, though."

The scent of mixed spices filled the apartment, making the Shadow Spinner's mouth water. The recipe had to be from the City of Anima, which meant the dish would be vegetarian. She already knew what Sterling would think, though he would never say anything for fear of breaking Lybbi's heart.

Serena, Lybbi, and Kai continued to chatter in the kitchen. Malaina slipped out, about to head for the living room when a hiss came from the front door. A blank and familiar folder slid beneath it.

She stiffened at the sight of it. That was a contract file.

She set down her mug, and hesitantly made her way over to the door, crouching to pick up the contract. Her hands shook, the file crinkling between her fingers, not sure she wanted to open it. Not sure what it meant. Was Malachi letting them work again? After what happened with Alman and Ra, she couldn't imagine how. She'd been so preoccupied with Ra, she hadn't had time to stop and think what the whole thing would mean for her place in the guild, but she'd assumed they would be out. That the failed rescue mission would be the end.

At first, the file appeared to be a normal contract,

complete with name, age, last known address, and magic class: a Shifter.

Malaina's heart raced, dreading Sterling's reaction. Malachi had never given them a Shifter target, and for good reason. They were all aware Sterling would go berserk. Possibly, this was their punishment for going after Ra, but she'd never known Malachi to be so vindictive. He believed in rules and punishment when expectations weren't met, but this?

She continued to read, wondering what could possibly be the reason for the contract, but it had been left blank. Alarm bells went off in her head. She'd never received a contract without a reason before. Malachi wouldn't allow it.

Instantly, her eyes went to the client's name, and the world around her fell away. The chatter in the kitchen became a fuzzy background noise, and the weight of her shadows outside floated away. The world around her became a void, and all she saw was that name.

"Hey!" Someone barked, making her jump, jolting her out of her own little world. Everyone was watching her, but she only found Sterling's curious orange eyes. "I just asked what we got.".

At a loss for words, she looked between him and the papers in her hands. When she didn't answer, he set aside his book and mug and walked over.

Seeing what she held, he asked, "Malachi's letting us work?"

She gave him a weak nod and reluctantly handed him the file.

He looked it over, his eyes shifting, growing darker with every new piece of information he read. Then he saw the name.

"He can't be serious," Sterling whispered.

She opened her mouth, trying to find something to say, but nothing came.

"Did you guys get a job?" Lybbi fidgeted, gripping the wooden spoon tight in her gloved hands.

Malaina started to answer, but Sterling beat her to it before storming out of the apartment. "No. We didn't."

Serena gave her a concerned look, but Malaina shook her head, at a loss for words.

Serena placed a hand on Lybbi's shoulder, and quickly the concern and curiosity on Lybbi's face eased. Serena turned Lybbi's shoulders back towards the stove. "Why don't we focus on breakfast? It should be almost done."

Malaina gave her a grateful smile before following Sterling out of the apartment at a jog.

She caught up to him but he didn't speak the entire way down to Malachi's office. He didn't pause at the office doors, just pushed through, waving the papers up in the air. "What the hell is this?"

Malachi sighed from where he leaned back against his desk. He'd clearly been waiting for them, knowing exactly what he had just sent up. A quick glance closed the doors, so no one would overhear.

"How about we all sit and discuss this?" Malachi offered, gesturing to the couches.

Sterling didn't budge. "Explain," he demanded.

Malachi met Sterling's angry stare, crossing his

arms. "The request came in earlier this morning. I considered rejecting it. However, I felt as though I could not."

"Let me do it for you, then. No."

"I do not think that is a wise decision."

"You want us to target a Shifter, as requested by Lord Kevah? Are you insane?" Sterling boomed, throwing the papers down on the chair in front of him. "How does this even happen?"

Malachi patiently watched Sterling, waiting for an opening before calmly explaining, "You know the process well enough. Clients are gained through word of mouth. They are given contacts to give their request to, which passes through a network of connections before I receive it. From my understanding, the request passed from Lord Kevah himself to one of his close advisors, who sought out one of our previous clients, and so on."

"And at no point did anyone notice how screwed up this is? He's put a bounty on Malaina's head, and now you want her to willingly perform a job for him? To kill someone whose only crime is existing?" Sterling ranted, pacing back and forth across the office.

"And how else do you suggest I handle this?" Malachi asked, a thumb and forefinger rubbing against the creases in his forehead.

"Say no!" Sterling threw his hands into the air, meeting Malachi's exasperated look with one of his own. "He's trying to draw her out, can't you see that?"

"Of course, I can. Why else would he ask to meet with her upfront?"

Sterling gripped the back of the chair he stood behind,

knuckles going white. "Malachi," Sterling pleaded, "This is suicide and you know it."

Malaina stood back while they argued, still trying to process. Kevah had found them. He might not know their exact location, but not everyone would hold out under torture the way Ra had. A picture of Ra in that metal chair clashed through her mind, bile rising up her throat.

With influence and power like Kevah's, working through Malachi's network of runners until he found someone who knew the exact location of the guild wouldn't be hard. Asking to meet her upfront was an option very few of her clients opted for. The assassin saw it for what it was: a courtesy. This was a chance for her to turn herself in. A chance to save all of them before he came looking for her himself. Not only a courtesy, but if they refused it would become a threat. He could find them if he wanted to.

Malaina placed a comforting hand on Sterling's arm. "I'll do it."

Sterling jerked back, her consent striking him like a physical thing. The red in his eyes started to bleed away into something else altogether.

"What?" He whispered.

She stared at Malachi instead, unable to stomach the way ash clouded Sterling's eyes. "I said I'd do it. I'll meet him."

Malachi nodded, absently. He understood. Saw the request for the thinly veiled threat it was.

Sterling stared down at her, betrayal written across his face. He looked at her like she was already lost. "Why?"

"Don't you get it? We don't have a choice. This isn't

about a job or about this Shifter." She gestured down to the papers scattered across the chair. "Either we take this meeting and hope he'll leave us be, or we reject him outright and he comes after the guild. No one will be safe." If they said no, if they ran, then Ra died for nothing. He endured torture for nothing. The guilt would eat her alive if she let Ra die in vain. If she let his sacrifice become worthless.

"And what happens when he finds out you aren't really the Death Bringer?"

Malaina fixed him with a hard stare, crossing her arms, unwilling to consider the possibility.

"What? We're just going to ignore this? I know you two like to pretend like all of this is real, but it's not. At some point, someone needs to say it out loud. Malaina isn't the Death Bringer. Lybbi is. So what happens when we walk in there and he wants proof, or actually does want a job performed, or something goes wrong, and he realizes what she truly is? What we've all been hiding?"

"I've been doing this for nine years," she reminded him, not backing down from the Shifter's frantic gaze. "For nine years, I've pretended to be something I'm not. For one reason and one reason alone. For Lybbi. To give her a shot at a semi-normal life, where she doesn't have to apologize for the way she was born. To keep her safe. I'm not going to throw that away because you're scared."

They stared at each other. Two unstoppable forces facing down.

"Enough, you two," Malachi said, drawing their attention back to him. "Sterling," the guild master sighed, "I understand why you are so upset, but since you have insisted, let us be honest. This guild is an illegal underground business that faces little resistance in the way of government interventions. Several people have tried to track down our exact location, however, we have built a loyal and powerful client base who keep us protected from those attempts. Turning this down, ignoring this job, would surely eliminate both our clientele and their protection."

"So you want us to sacrifice ourselves for the guild?" Sterling asked.

Malachi pressed his lips together. "No...I am only asking Malaina to."

"Excuse me?" Malaina gaped at him.

Malachi glanced between the two of them before continuing, "You are concerned for Malaina's safety, but what of Sterling's?"

"What do you mean?" Sterling asked him, prickling.

"Lord Kevah has made his feelings towards Shifters quite clear. Few can identify someone wielding Dark Magic without seeing the magic performed, making it easy for us to pass Malaina off as the Death Bringer. One look at Sterling's eyes, however, and it becomes quite clear what he is. You call this a suicide mission, and yet, you want to waltz in as if there will be no consequences?"

The realization plowed her over, making her step back just to escape reality. Sterling couldn't go. She had to do this on her own.

"I will join Malaina in the meeting. It is only right for something so important," Malachi continued.

Sterling's entire body went slack, hands hanging limply

by his side. "No." The statement sounded more like a plea. "No. Absolutely not. No." He shook his head. "I can't just sit here and hide while you throw yourself at the mercy of…that sadistic man. You saw what he did to Valis. When I took this job I didn't sign on to be an assassin, I signed on to protect you at all costs. *That's* my job. How can I do that if you go off and do this without me? How am I supposed to explain that to Lybbi if you don't come back?"

"And who will explain to Lybbi she's all alone if you do come and neither of us returns?" Malaina retorted.

Sterling looked away, rubbing his face, guilt written across his features. A war waged, between his loyalties to her and his loyalties to Lybbi.

If she went by herself, without Sterling, to meet Kevah then she knew Lybbi would be safe. There was no one she trusted more in this world to step in and continue taking care of her younger sister if she didn't come back. But if they both went and neither of them came back…who would step up then? Who would take on a thirteen-year-old girl? A girl who couldn't even control her ability to kill on demand?

Someone needed to pay the bills. Someone needed to keep a roof over her head, make sure she went to Malachi's lessons, make sure she didn't eat pancakes all day long and learn what it meant to love. To be there when her heart broke for the first time, and while she tried to figure out who she was. Someone needed to be there to guide her through life and figure out how to live outside that guild.

No one taught Malaina those things. One day she lived in a well-off neighborhood, in a townhouse that cost the price of the entire lower part of the city combined, her only worry being whether her father would notice her shadows on any particular day. Then, suddenly, she had a four-year-old to take care of. One decision, to climb out a window with Lybbi in tow and run away from their burning home, made her the closest thing to a parental figure Lybbi would ever know. No one taught Malaina how to do any of this. Every day she guessed, doing her best.

Sterling coming into their life made it all a little easier. He took some of the responsibility off her shoulders. Never once had he hesitated to play the big brother role in Lybbi's life, something Lybbi desperately needed at the time. Something she still needed.

But he also played an important role in Malaina's life. Her best friend. He was her shoulder to lean on when things became too much. The one who always protected her back, no matter what. The one person who would always choose her, over everything else, no questions asked. She wanted to do something colossally stupid? He would be right by her side. He would tell her how colossally stupid she was being, but he'd also match her stride for stride as she walked into that fire. Her safety net beneath the tightrope she walked every day, he made it safe to fall. Safe to fail. Safe to try. Without him there to catch her…

They hadn't spent a full twenty-four hours apart since the day they were partnered, and she didn't want to start now. She didn't know how she could do this without him by her side.

"What if he didn't know?" Sterling asked, pulling Malaina out of the spiral she was falling down. She wasn't sure who he was asking, her or Malachi, but his swampy eyes never left her face.

"What do you mean?" Malaina asked.

"Well, not to sound too full of myself, but the way I shift is…legendary. It's so rare that most people don't even realize it's possible outside myths. I could be in the meeting and he would never know." Sterling held up his hand, and it shifted until razor-sharp claws tipped a giant fluffy paw.

Something about the image made Malaina snort. Perhaps she was exhausted, emotionally and physically, but she couldn't hold in the pathetic laugh. "You want to be my…pet?"

Sterling shrugged, a hint of a smirk beginning to form. "Why not? We've done it before."

"Yeah, for a few minutes here and there, but never like this. Never something so…" She didn't know what word she was looking for. Something so long? Important? Permanent? If Kevah truly wanted her to work for him, and she walked into that meeting with a beloved pet by her side, he would expect the pet to be there every time. This wouldn't be a casual stroll through the business district or a meeting to intimidate a client. This could change the entire dynamic of their partnership.

The assassin held her hand up to the Shifter's raised paw, placing her palm against the pad. The ruff skin scraped her fingers, the fur silky and soft. Her stretched fingers barely reached the toe pads, let alone the claws the length of her fingers.

Malachi huffed, a single thoughtful finger running over

his lips. "You know…that may not be a bad idea. Sterling, do you still have my copy of *Apex Predators and Their Prey*?"

"Of course. I was studying it when the contract came."

"Good. We will need it." Malachi walked over to one of his walls of books, scanning until he plucked one off the shelf. He studied the cover before continuing down the wall. Occasionally he stopped, held up a hand, and another tome would fall off a shelf far out of reach and land in his waiting palm.

"What are you thinking?" Malaina asked.

"I think..." Malachi's words were slow and drawn out, a plan starting to form. "I will have you two meet me downstairs."

TWENTY-SIX

Malaina fidgeted, her fingers starting to tremble as their carriage rolled down the road, the occasional bump knocking her against the wall. The ride became smoother when they reached the well-maintained roads leading to the nicer parts of the city. In the area where they started, though, a carriage ride could lead to a concussion if the driver wasn't careful.

A single ribbon of shadow weaved between the Spinner's shaking fingers, trying to calm her buzzing mind. Normally, she wouldn't dare indulge in her magic in front of Malachi, but today, she didn't care; she needed the release. Needed to ease some of the pressure in her chest from pent-up angst.

Sterling stared at the wall as if there were a window for him to look out. Various unpleasant colors flashed in his rapidly shifting eyes, but they never settled on any single one for long. His massive form took up so much of the bench they shared that his thigh pressed against hers. The entire carriage shook as his leg bounced.

Usually, the pair opted for alternative forms of travel through the city for that very reason. Sterling was simply too big to be comfortable riding in the carriages. The weak smile he attempted didn't reach his ever-changing eyes when he glanced at her.

The small shadow weaving over her knuckles drew her attention again before his elbow nudged her side. His chin jerked towards the bench opposite them where Malachi sat.

Profuse amounts of sweat dripped from the guild master's brow as he ran a handkerchief over his face and along his neck. Malaina bit back a smile when he flinched at every noise coming from the city outside the carriage.

She cocked an eyebrow at him. "Malachi...are you doing ok over there?"

"Hm?" Jumping at the sound of her voice, he whipped his head from side to side. Seeing threats through the wooden walls around them. Malachi, the notorious guild master who never flinched in the face of murderers, thieves, or drug dealers. The man who led and trained the most skilled criminals the City of Elementals had to offer. The man who ran her ragged for hours in the sparring ring, never blinking as they all took hit after hit, was *nervous*.

"You just seem...uncomfortable," she said, not sure how to approach the subject.

"Yes, well..." He wiped at his palms. "Let us just say that the last time I took this trip, it did not end well."

Sterling and Malaina exchanged a look. "What do you mean? Have you…been to the Lord's estate before?"

Malachi cleared his throat, refusing to meet their curious looks. "It was a long time ago."

"How long?" Sterling asked, drawing out the question with caution.

The Kinetic's eyes flitted over them before going distant, lost in a dark memory. "Long before either of you were born."

The partners exchanged another look.

"Are you…scared to go back?" Malaina asked, unnerved by the very idea of Malachi fearing anything. She knew everyone was afraid of something, but in her mind, Malachi had always been ten feet tall and intimidated by nothing. He'd been the first person to look upon her magic without fear, and because of that, it was impossible for her to think of him as anything but an impenetrable pillar of strength.

But…sitting across from him in that carriage, watching the way sweat stained the collar of his shirt, it occurred to her that Malachi was just a man—a man with a past she knew nothing about. It was hard to picture him as anything but the guild master she knew him as, but there had to be a time before when he was just Malachi.

"What happened?" Sterling asked, voice quiet.

Malachi licked his lips, eyes darkening as he studied them both out of the corner of his eye. "It is unimportant now."

Malaina crossed her arms. "Oh, come on. I've known you forever. Nearly a decade, and I feel like I don't know anything about you other than the fact that you're a…" He cut her a piercing glare, changing her words from *stuck-up hard-ass* to, "A Kinetic."

"Which is significant how?"

She shrugged. "I don't know. We're heading into this meeting which very well could go horribly wrong. It just seems like the time to tell all."

He didn't answer right away. The carriage bounced when it hit a bump and Malachi swore under his breath, running a hand over his eyes.

Sighing, he sat forward and rested his elbows on his knees. "I was raised in the City of Kinetics to parents who were of significant influence. They afforded me a comfortable life, the best education, and wonderful business opportunities, one of which required me to travel to the other cities around Thaumoria. On my trip here, I was in my room getting ready for bed when a young boy slipped into my room to relieve me of some of my valuables." His voice became wistful at the memory, trailing off before he continued, "In fact…Ra reminded me of him greatly." His voice cracked around Ra's name as if he were barely holding himself together. "He looked so scared as we watched each other, him halfway in my window, me exhausted from the day. We stood like that for several minutes and I was so stunned I simply asked him what he was doing. In response, he replied, 'I'm robbing you.' I had never in my life seen a child so thin.

"I handed him the coins from my pocket and watched him float them into the air to examine them with poor control. Before that moment, I had not imagined it possible he was Kinetic, and the realization there were children living in such a way…well, that night changed the course of my entire life. I never told my parents what happened nor what I planned to do." He paused for a moment. "I hope for their sake they never found out. For all I know, they believed me to be missing."

Malaina couldn't help but ask, "When was the last time you talked to them?"

Malachi stared at his feet before picking at a speck of lint on his pants. "The day before I left."

"But what you've done, what you've built, it's amazing. You've taken people from digging through trash cans to buying themselves entire homes," Sterling said in awe. "Why wouldn't you want them to know what you've done?"

"Things are very different in the City of Kinetics," Malachi snapped. "There is no place for nuance. Things are black and white, either right or wrong, as determined by the collective. What I have done goes against everything I was raised to believe to be the common good and everything the City of Kinetics stands for. My parents…they would not have understood."

"You could have tried…" Malaina offered, but Malachi shook his head.

"Someone long ago taught me a very important lesson: intentions do not negate actions. Just because you or I may see what I have built as virtuous compared to some of the alternatives out there does not mean it truly is." Malachi's voice quieted, "What right do I have to decide what is right and wrong? What makes me any better?"

None of them spoke again for a long time.

Malaina found it odd to think of Malachi as flexible. As someone who recognized the gray areas between black and white and that the world was more complex than simple right and wrong. He always seemed so rigid to her, someone who constructed rules and stuck to them no matter what. Maybe that was a product of the way he'd been raised. Maybe it was the product of what made him who he was today…

The only other Kinetics Malaina knew had all been born in the City of Elementals, so she'd never made the connection between Malachi's upbringing and his rigid need for structure and rule-following.

She thought back to the meeting in his office, where he decided to do nothing about Ra.

I have protocols, was what Malachi told them. At the time she couldn't fathom how such a thing made sense. She couldn't understand how it was reason enough to do nothing, but now she understood. Malachi created rules because he couldn't help it; he needed rules in his life, and stepping outside of those rules was like stepping outside himself. The very life of a guildmaster stepped outside the rules he was raised on. Every day, he fought against that way of life, and he needed some sense of structure for it all to make sense. Without rules and protocols, was he even Kinetic?

Another part of Malaina wondered if those rules had stemmed from what had happened to the boy he mentioned. Wondered how many of his rules that seemed so odd to her were the result of mistakes he'd never stopped regretting.

Nothing.

Malaina considered the possibility that maybe, a long time ago, there had been a time when Malachi had wished that's what he'd done.

Eventually, the sounds of the city faded away. The carriage was passing the larger estates on the outskirts of the city.

After some time, three knocks tapped against the front wall of the carriage. Capel and Grif were sitting up front, keeping watch while they drove the carriage through the city. All of them sat up straighter within the carriage at the signal, indicating they were approaching their final destination.

Malachi adjusted his coat and cuffs, forcing himself back into the person Malaina knew him to be. "That is our queue."

Malaina looked at Sterling, taking in every detail of him, from his messy black waves pulled back from his face to the tanned skin that made him look permanently sun-soaked to his hard jaw. She didn't know how this would end, and she never wanted to forget the way he looked at that moment. He gave her a thin grin though his eyes continued to cycle.

"I've got your back," he assured her.

She nodded, trying to convince herself more than him.

Sterling stretched an arm over her shoulder, and in the

blink of an eye, he shifted. He melted into a long, sleek form, black scales glistening in the low light as Sterling became a long black python. She scooted to the center of the bench, holding her arms out to either side. He slithered along one arm and across her shoulders until his head rested against the nape of her neck. His tail coiled around her arm, squeezing enough to stay in place.

Her partner became a living, breathing shadow.

He nudged against her neck one more time before he settled, giving her one last bit of encouragement. The Shadow Spinner closed her eyes and took several deep breaths, centering herself. She needed to become the Death Bringer Malachi had molded her into.

She told herself that *she* was the deadliest person alive. *She* was in control here. Over and over again, she convinced herself of who she needed to be, reminded herself that a Shadow Spinner wasn't walking into this meeting; a Death Bringer was. She needed to be the person they expected her to be. Lord Kevah called on *her* and needed *her* services.

The control lay in her scarred hands, and no one would intimidate her.

A different person opened her eyes. The person Malachi shaped her into after so many years of training.

She was the Death Bringer, and nothing else mattered. No longer was she a helpless Shadow Spinner whose greatest strength was the ability to make a dark room wiggle.

No, she was the Death Bringer, the person people spread stories about in hushed tones. The person people feared on sight. The reason people locked their windows at night. The assassin who hid in dark corners and haunted people's nightmares.

Since the beginning of Thaumoria, people have told legends of the Death Bringer, stories passed down through generations. At some point, they may have been steeped in some sort of fact, but now they warped into something sick and twisted. Malaina spent years learning all the stories to become the sick and twisted version of herself that they all expected her to be.

Absently, she rolled her shoulders, stretching her neck from side to side. She rolled her wrists and flexed her fingers, forcing all her muscles to relax, familiarizing herself with new skin. Every shadow in the carriage went back to its home and stilled, not daring to even twitch.

They didn't belong to her anymore.

Muffled, clipped words were barked from outside and the carriage stopped. Guards started interrogating Capel and Grif. The carriage door ripped open, the cold eyes of a guard Malachi's age staring up at them.

Malaina looked down her nose at him with an equally cold glare. It was his privilege to even be acknowledged by her.

She quickly noted the small details about him—the way his hair grayed at the temples, how he clenched his square jaw, and the way his fingers twitched with the urge to use his magic.

"Are you the...one the Lord is expecting?" His hard voice refused to speak her title.

Malaina lifted the corner of her lip, allowing amusement to enter her metallic eyes at his discomfort. This man seemed like the type who presented a fearless persona but used disgust to mask the fear dancing in his eyes.

"That would be me." She smiled lazily, letting her words drip with a sickly sweet coating.

He continued to glare at her, looking her up and down, then nodded.

"Out," he barked.

Malachi moved first, stepping down and straightening his suit once again. The Death Bringer moved to the door and reached out to the guard, letting her hand hover in the air between them in an offer.

"Mind helping a lady down?" She smiled with no kindness.

The guard stared at her hand with revulsion, backing away a step when Sterling lifted his head and slithered an inch closer over her outstretched fingers. Tongue flicking the air as if he was trying to gain an idea of what the guard would taste like.

Malachi took her hand instead, feigning assistance and chivalry. When their eyes met she practically heard him scolding her. *That was unnecessary,* that look said.

She exited the carriage and stepped right into a circle of guards, all armed and watching her every movement. Behind her, a wall stretched further than she could see. It stood tall and solid, with guards posted along the top at regular intervals. The gate they passed through groaned shut.

Someone cleared their throat behind her. The same

grumpy stiff guard who opened the carriage door watched her, his hands held behind his back.

"Yes?" She asked, cocking her hip to the side.

"Weapons check," he stated matter-of-factly, "You are not permitted to bring any weapons into Lord Kevah's home."

She snorted. "You're kidding."

The guard didn't even blink in response, his eyes hard and expressionless.

A younger guard stepped forward, pulling on a pair of gloves. His hands shook as he did so and she almost sympathized with the poor guy. He must have pulled the short stick, stuck being the one forced to touch her. The trembling young man stopped two steps away, reluctant to come any closer.

"Arms out." He attempted the command but his voice shook more than his hands, undermining what little authority he may have.

She obliged, lifting her arms out with a flourish of her fingers, bare aside from Sterling's scaled body thanks to the leather vest molded to her torso. She'd taken hours that morning picking the perfect outfit that would be both intimidating and show off her new...*pet*. The Death Bringer would be hard-pressed to hide any weapons beneath the tight but flexible pants tucked into knee-high boots. That was the whole point. She wanted to show off the fact that she didn't need any weapons.

She was the weapon.

The young guard took a single step forward, eyeing her

warily. She kept her silver gaze trained on his quaking face, and when he dared to meet it his eyes darted away.

"We don't have all day," the grumpy guard snapped.

The terrified young man stood so close Malaina felt his haggard breaths. She imagined his heart racing inside his chest. His reaching hands hesitated for a moment before he placed carefully on her arm, pointedly avoiding Sterling's long body.

His face mere inches from hers, she couldn't help herself…

"Boo," she puffed, flinching forward a hair's breadth.

The minuscule movement was enough. The young guard jumped back, lost his balance, and tripped over his own feet, falling to the ground. He sat there, panting, as he'd just seen his life flash before his eyes.

Grumpy guard took a deep breath, holding back a sigh and resisting the urge to roll his eyes by staring up at the sky.

Malaina didn't lower her arms. She continued to stand perfectly still, smirking.

"Oops," she said dryly.

"I'm going to assume you weren't idiotic enough to hide anything on your person," the older guard sneered.

The fact he wasn't willing to check her himself told her all she needed to know.

Malachi stepped forward. "You will address me from here on."

"What? It can't speak for itself?"

Malachi didn't flinch. "*She* is my employee. This is my

meeting." That wasn't entirely true, but Malaina was grateful for his interference either way.

"Whatever." The guard turned to leave, but Malachi didn't move.

The Kinetic glanced at the guard's feet. Suddenly, the man's boots seemed to weigh a hundred pounds, locking him in place.

He twisted, furious red face looking back at them over a shoulder.

"I am afraid you have not introduced yourself," Malachi said calmly. With a twirl of his finger (a gesture purely for show), the guard's boots spun in the dirt, so he faced them once again.

"Captain. You two can call me Captain or Sir." He spat. A glance at Malaina. "I won't speak my name in front of *that*, and neither will any of my guards, so don't ask."

Malaina resisted the urge to roll her eyes. One of those twisted stories reared its ugly head once again. *Never gift your name to a Death Bringer, or they will speak it into the night, and your life will be forfeit.*

Instead, she gave an exaggerated curtsy and finally lowered her arms. "My pleasure, I assure you."

Captain sneered and turned again, inconspicuously testing whether or not he had control of his boots once again.

They all started down the long drive, moving as a unit. With Malachi and Malaina at the center of a circle, the Captain led the way. She stood slightly behind Malachi's shoulder, a slight sign of respect that didn't go unnoticed by the guards around them. She glimpsed through the crack between bodies, observing the grounds around them as they passed.

An orchard consisting of row after row of fruit-bearing trees, attended to by a team of Water and Earth Wielders alike, extended beyond her sight. Continuing, she spotted various Witches walking among an expansive herb garden, inspecting each plant before picking it and placing it in a basket. A line of the most beautiful and well-bred horses Malaina had ever laid eyes on were being led by a team of Animas, with no reins or ropes in sight.

The whole thing felt impossibly picturesque and pristine. Without realizing it, she'd been envisioning lines of enslaved people, impossibly thin and being forced to work the grounds of a tyrant. Instead, everyone looked like they just stepped out of the heavens above. Smiling, dressed in the best clothing, completely relaxed.

It was nearly impossible for Malaina to keep from staring at the mansion they approached. It was the largest house, if one could call it that, she had ever seen.

Pillars framed the arched double doors at the entrance. The entire building gleamed in the daylight, the white stone making the entire structure bright and clean.

It took their little group an eternity to reach the staircase leading up to the entrance, and in that time, something occurred to her. All around her, people from all the magic classes worked seamlessly, slowly moving around each other like perfectly fitted cogs in a clock.

All the magic classes, except for Shifters…

Their absence was a glaring hole around her. No one shaped the perfectly pruned shrubs and bushes into anything more than plain square. No ornamentation decorated the perfectly polished fountains. The grounds around her missed the obvious touch of an artist, of anything beautiful that would have come out of the City of Shifters.

It felt like walking through a technically perfect painting, coated with precise brush strokes and an immaculate color palette, but…it lacked spirit or any spark of life.

It felt wrong.

TWENTY-SEVEN

A pair of Kinetics stood on either side of the massive entrance to the manor. They made grand, in-sync motions to open the doors behind them. Malaina couldn't help but notice that Malachi could have done the same thing with a mere wave of his hand.

The guild master walked straight back in front of her, refusing to glance around or acknowledge a single person surrounding them. He was stoic and calm, putting on a persona, just as she did.

Inside the estate, Captain led them down a winding series of hallways, up and down staircases. Malaina did her best to keep a mental note of each turn, but after so long she couldn't tell one hallway from another. No tapestries adorned the walls, nor did any statues grace the alcoves. The Captain tried his best to confuse them by leading them through this maze, succeeding if her level of disorientation was anything to go by.

It took an eternity of lefts and rights, ups and downs, but eventually, they stopped before a pair of ornately carved wooden doors. Stopping herself from gawking at the sight before them took every bit of self-control she possessed. The doors were not only beautiful, but they were the only form of decoration in the entire mansion. Their presence was jarring, odd, and out of place.

Carved out of dark stained wood, they looked older than the city itself. Etched layers of earth spread from the bottom up, giving way to fields and rivers flowing between rolling hills. There were even snow-capped mountains in the distance. In the center stood a tree, its roots diving deep into the soil, its branches reaching for the edges of the doors, curving at the top. Clouds swirled around the expansive sky behind the branches.

Malaina could have stared at them for hours and she would still find new details hidden among the landscape, like deer drinking from one of the rivers.

Malachi didn't wait for the Kinetics standing nearby to open the doors, instead sending them open with a lazy wave of his hand. The Captain glared over his shoulder at Malachi, but the Kinetic pretended not to notice. Instead, he continued forward, not bothering to wait for the circle of guards to keep up.

Malaina kept close to Malachi's shoulder, never more than a step behind. They didn't make it far before the Captain held out a hand to stop them, their circle of guards keeping tight to their sides.

"You wait here," he ordered.

"These must be my guests!" A familiar jovial voice that haunted Malaina day and night rang through the hall.

The Captain spun, his posture going rigid. "Yes, my Lord." The Captain walked deeper into the hall and bowed from the waist. "The…they are here if you are ready to receive them."

"Of course!" Lord Kevah called. "Let them in."

The circle of guards split, making an opening for Malachi and Malaina. They entered a hall made of blinding white marble, with the exception of a stained glass wall. In each corner of the room stood a carved marble pillar so broad even Sterling's long arms wouldn't reach all the way around them.

Each pillar represented one of the elements. One appeared to be the roots of a tree twining around boulders, stacked atop each other until they reached the ceiling. Next stood a spiral of thin ribbons so lithe they shouldn't be standing at all. A funnel of waves made up the third, surging around each other in an overlapping pattern. Lastly, a column of carved flames extended from floor to ceiling.

The colors streaming from the stained glass wall, which depicted a more detailed version of the scene carved into the double doors, painted each pillar.

The almost overwhelming effect took Malaina's breath away. However, that may have been because the brightness drove out every last lurking shadow. Their absence left a hollow expanse in that cell she kept her magic locked within, the radiance of the room almost unbearable.

She wondered if these pieces of art adorning the hall were left alone because they were permanent parts of the building that couldn't easily be removed. She imagined a team of Shifters working tirelessly for weeks or months to make the room she stood in now and tried to picture what other exquisite pieces used to adorn the mansion. That single room remained, only for the Lord and Lady to disgrace it by removing any other evidence of Shifters' involvement in the making of the mansion.

Before the stained glass wall sat two seats, giving the impression of thrones. No kings or queens ruled in Thaumoria. Only those who ran the cities and represented the magic classes. But, had kings and queens been a thing, Malaina imagined this being their one and only throne room. It seemed the Lord and Lady intended to portray themselves as being just that: royalty.

Side by side they sat, Lord Kevah and Lady Atana. They made an odd but complementary pair.

Kevah, the personification of all four elements, had striking features whose range of colors rivaled those of the wall behind him.

Atana, his exact opposite, was almost monochrome in appearance. Nothing but glinting gleaming gold in contrast to his natural beauty. Lady Atana sat tall and proud, her golden hair spun up atop her head, a matching circlet sitting among the neat curls. On anyone else, a head-to-toe golden gown would have looked tacky, but its thin straps and plunging v-neckline made Atana look regal. It draped around her, a waterfall hugging her curves all the way to the floor and past her feet. She might have been a statue if not for the gleam in her eye.

Malaina couldn't unsee the proud expression on her

face as Kevah drowned his competition and wondered if Atana cared for anyone but him.

This close, all the Lord's features became even more dramatic. Freshly turned soil made up his skin while the deepest depths of the seas raged in his eyes, all sitting beneath the roaring flames of his bright hair. He looked exactly how she remembered and then some. But his long lean form caught her attention.

Before, he had always worn loose, draping robes that hid his frame. But now he wore a fitted high-collar jacket and straight pants, making his connection to the air more evident than ever. Air Wielders always seemed disproportionally long and lean, but Kevah took that to the extreme. His legs were the longest she'd ever seen, and his fingers reminded her of spiders. Looking at him now, she wondered how they all missed it.

Then again, people tended to see only what they wanted to. No one thought it possible that he could wield all four elements, so why would they be looking for the signs?

He looked exactly how the most powerful Elemental in generations should look, and yet…she still wasn't prepared for it. Malaina called on every moment of Malachi's training to keep her features calm and arrogant rather than scared and gawking.

She and Malachi stopped halfway to the Lord and Lady, their army of guards keeping close to the door.

Kevah leaned forward. His scrutinizing gaze picked her apart, leaving her feeling exposed despite the distance between them.

"Well, well, well…" he drawled, "Aren't you a peculiar-looking thing." His cold, teasing words mocked her.

She cocked her head to the side, giving him an equally appraising once-over. "I could say the same thing about you."

Malachi shot her a glare, which she caught out of the corner of her eye, but Kevah gave her a wicked grin. Pleased. Amused.

"Yes. I guess you could." Something vile danced in his eyes, making her sick. "You all may step outside," he called to the guards without ever taking his eyes from Malaina.

"But, my Lord…" The Captain stammered, but a cutting glance from Kevah silenced him. Steps shuffled, and the doors creaked closed.

Suddenly, the assassin felt trapped, roles reversed. No longer the predator, she was the prey trapped in a cage being taunted. The guards were there to protect the Lord and Lady, but they also acted as a safety net for her. Witnesses for what was about to happen, if nothing else.

Malachi took a step forward. "Lord Kevah," he said, slightly bowing his head, "We appreciate you taking the time to meet with us."

Kevah waved his hand dismissively, "Please. I've been trying to find our little Death Bringer here for quite some time now." He paused, looking her up and down again. "You are impressively difficult to find."

Malaina kept her voice cold and uncaring, holding her hands out to the side. "Well, you found me."

Kevah clapped his hands together, delighted. A child receiving a compliment. "I did, didn't I? I was hoping you'd come forward sooner, with my public invitation and all, but this is fine as well."

Maintaining her arrogant facade strained her, fighting to keep distaste from twisting her face.

Public invitation? He couldn't be talking about his announcement at the challenge where he put a bounty on her head. That bounty had thrown her life into a living nightmare, nearly costing her the life she'd worked so hard for. And yet, he talked about it as if he had invited her to tea.

Malachi cleared his throat. "From my understanding, you are interested in hiring the Death Bringer for a job."

Sterling coiled tighter around Malaina's arm when Kevah laughed, the effort throwing his head back. "Ah, yes. *That.* You see, I worried I would never find you and felt money would be an excellent motivator."

Money, she sneered internally. Yes, that's the reason she agreed to this insanity. It certainly wasn't the threat he hung over her family and friends' heads like a banner.

"I see. So…the Shifter you contracted…?" Malachi asked, unsure how to proceed.

A tickle started to build at the base of Malaina's skull and the overwhelming light of the room started to take its toll on her. As a creature of the dark, she found the presence of shadows comforting on its own. That room felt like an unnatural place for her to even be standing. Land to a fish, or night to the sun.

Kevah gave another dismissive wave. "No need to worry about that. Turns out she was in our care this entire time." He gave another wicked grin. "Our bad," he mocked, amusement glittering in his eyes. Atana smirked beside him, looking charmed by his disgusting sense of humor.

The pressure in the back of Malaina's mind started to grow, her stomach clenching. Reminded, for a moment, of the way Serena's magic caressed her mind, this felt similar but different. Darker. Harder to ignore. More persistent.

Kevah lifted his wife's hand to his lips and kissed her fingers before releasing them to stand. The glittering strands of his jacket caught the many colors streaming in behind him as he slowly descended from his dais.

Malaina's stomach roiled at the prospect of Kevah coming closer. Sterling coiled tighter around her wrist, a sudden lack of blood flow making her fingers tingle.

Kevah stopped mere feet before her, holding steepled hands before him, his fingertips tapping against each other. His smile grew, showing brilliant teeth polished to perfection. "You see, I have been searching for a long time for you, Death Bringer, and I have a proposition."

The Lord's words raked against her, the ache in her skull growing stronger. Her brain clawed at the bone, trying to find its way out. She clenched her teeth, fighting against the pain.

Why was that room so damn bright?

"A long time?" she asked, at the same time that Malachi asked, "How can we be of service?"

Kevah started circling them. Stepping around her, scanning her from head to toe.

He sighed, delighted. "Yes, quite some time. Before I ever made the public announcement, I met with many of the most influential in my city. You, my dear, have caused quite the stir among them." He wagged a scolding finger at her, though the delight never left his words. "For years, they have requested I do something about your presence here. At first, I dismissed the accusations they brought me because I knew one day I may have a use for you myself. I discovered recently what that use would be, and that is when I started my search for you." His breath brushed against her ear, her skin crawling at his presence behind her. She heard the smile on his lips and forced herself not to cringe. "You may be familiar with my dear friends, the Almans?"

Malachi tensed beside her.

She knew Alman had searched for her to please Kevah, but this seemed far more intimate—a personal relationship rather than a business one.

"Malak had assured me he would be the man for the job. He created all these elaborate rouses to find your precious guild. A theft, a kill, another theft," She almost heard Kevah roll his eyes as he stepped behind Malachi, continuing his prowl. "His information was useful. He assured me you were the real thing, that he had found the true Death Bringer. I'm sure you're aware there are imposters all over my city." She did know, though never gave them much thought. They had never been much competition for her, quickly proving themselves to be frauds, so she brushed off the stories and rumors. The real thing didn't concern themselves with posers, it would be beneath her. "Anyway, when Malak missed a crucial meeting to discuss your final whereabouts, I thought I would take matters into my own hands."

Malachi eyed her, but her mind spun faster than a Kinetic's gear… every detail came back to her: the Desroc contracts, the target on Nyda, the antidote, the guard who didn't stop her, and Ra's torture for the guild's location. So much could be traced back to this, to Kevah's search for her.

Malak had done all of it. He bought the contract against Desroc, trying to find his way into the network. He conned Desroc into getting a contract against Nyda to draw Malaina out. He commissioned an antidote to test her.

The second guard…he hadn't attacked. He just stood in the doorway, observing her…he wanted to be able to identify her. Even in the torture room under the house…they waited until she pulled down her hood and face covering before they revealed themselves because Alman knew what to look for.

Every inch of her became numb as she realized how stupid she'd been. How stupid they had all been, falling for every single move.

They were the criminals. They were supposed to be two steps ahead of everybody, but instead, they'd been played. And Ra had paid the price.

Kevah stopped before her again, watching her closely. The pressure in Malaina's mind became a hammer pounding against her skull, the entire room blinding. Sterling coiled even tighter when Kevah stepped closer. The assassin met the Lord's penetrating stare, unwilling to let him see her waver.

She was the Death Bringer, and she would not cower.

Malaina wanted the Elemental to be the one cowering under her stare, the way so many did, but instead, it pleased him even more. He wanted to see the promise of death in her eyes.

"I'm sure you are aware that I have been attempting to make my city pure." Kevah eagerly clasped his hands together. Her fists clenched involuntarily at the word *pure*, as though Shifters somehow polluted his city. "I would like your help in these endeavors. I have not been satisfied with the success of my forces, or lack thereof."

Sterling slithered along her shoulders, squirming at Kevah's words. He gave a warning *hiss* in Kevah's direction, warranting a concerned glance from the Lord.

"You want me to kill off the remaining Shifters in the city who are hiding from the city guards?" Failing to keep an incredulous tone out of her voice, Malaina hoped she pulled off an air of intrigue. Trying to comprehend everything was taking its toll. Kevah wasn't just taking Shifters prisoner or sending them to other cities. He was killing them.

Were there Shifters in his dungeons, or just bodies?

"Who better to…take care of unwelcome visitors than someone who works and lives among the most offensive of my city's citizens?" The Lord stepped even closer, his eyes seeming to stare right through her.

They were close she could discern each strand of sea green and deep cerulean in his vivid eyes, along with every speck of malice hidden among them. Sterling tensed against her, his body becoming a spring wound too tight.

Kevah once again studied Sterling as though he'd never seen a snake before.

"Is this your pet? It is very odd." Kevah tilted his head to the side. "I wasn't expecting you to bring an animal."

Malaina took an involuntary half-step back, her head pounding. Her teeth ground with the effort of not bearing them. "Yes. I bring him with me to all my jobs."

"Well, that's quite fascinating." Kevah matched the half step she took back, keeping the distance between them too close for her liking. He loomed over her, seeming to grow even taller the closer he got, and the closer he got, the worse the pain in Malaina's head became.

She breathed a sigh of relief when Malachi pushed himself between them, trying to regain control of the meeting.

"While we appreciate your reaching out, I am afraid I do not think our services are quite what you are looking for, my Lord." Malachi's tone left no room for questions or arguments. Him creating space between her and Kevah made it a little easier to breathe, but she now noticed how he was sweating, with the collar of his shirt and jacket drenched. The way the guild master clenched his jaw again and again.

When Kevah didn't answer, Malachi turned away. For just a moment, Malaina blanched at his bold defiance.

He nodded at her, prodding her to turn away with him, desperation in his eyes. So she did. A casual hand on her lower back guided her towards the exit. With every step they took, the pressure in her mind eased bit by bit, and she could almost take a full breath when Kevah spoke again.

"For the sake of your precious guild, you may wish to reconsider, Malachi Starik." Kevah's voice was low and menacing, the threat hanging around them.

Malaina could hear the horrid smile on his face.

Malachi froze. Malaina thought she could hear his heart pounding in his chest. Fear rolled off him, thicker than her shadows on a moonless night. The Kinetic was grasping at what was left of his calm and controlled facade as his fingers curled against her back.

She'd never heard Malachi's full name before. Since she'd joined the guild, no one had even asked.

Hearing Malachi's full name on Kevah's lips had rage boiling through her veins. She wanted to go back and rip it from his tongue.

Malachi turned back hesitantly, and Malaina followed his lead, unsure of what else to do. She wasn't sure Malachi had any idea what he was doing anymore, either. They'd lost every bit of control they thought they had.

Kevah took slow and deliberate steps forward, the heels of his shoes clicking against the marble. Staring back into the room, the light once again felt overbearing, and she had to restrain herself from shutting her eyes.

"As I've said," Kevah started, each word careful and drawn out, "Your guild has been running a muck around my city with very little opposition for quite some time. While most of it has been simple inconveniences, with the occasionally stolen artifact or assassination of a particularly arrogant and annoying governor's child, many of my officials have been insisting I step in. I haven't at this point because I've always seen the potential you and your charges held. You all are the best, I think that is quite apparent.

"But let me make something clear. You have been operating on borrowed potential, and should I no longer see a way to use you to my advantage, then…" the Lord paused, weighing their worth in his hands. "Well, I'm sure you can imagine what will have to be done."

There was the threat they'd been waiting for. The threat they knew was coming. The true reason for the contract.

If he had attacked the guild first, she might have gotten away, and all would have been lost. Or he might have taken her prisoner, and she might have refused to work for him. This whole thing had been a performance building to this moment, to this threat.

Sterling spun around her arm, constricting and loosening like a fist someone clenched to channel their fury. Within Malaina, her own rage won the battle against fear, pushing it aside. It was her turn to step forward, to shield Malachi and make her own threats.

"Might I remind you who exactly you're speaking to," she spat, forcing the words through clenched teeth.

Every nerve in her body screamed, the pressure in her skull growing to a peak, nearly making her cry out in pain. Instinct took over, and she needed comfort. Something in her reached for the shadows, any shadows, that may have been in the room, searching for anything. Something to bring her back to herself and ease the growing tension threatening to tear the muscles from her bones.

In the furthest corner of the room, hidden among an intricate detail of one of the pillars, she found one. It was eager and ready to answer her call, waiting for her to acknowledge it. Just knowing it was hidden there helped settle her mind and make her feel a little more in control of herself.

Then Kevah took an abrupt step back, cocking his head to the side. He looked her over again, this time with a new dissatisfaction. A slow predatory grin warped his face, taking him to an entirely new level of terrifying.

"And who exactly would that be, Shadow Spinner?"

TWENTY-EIGHT

Malaina's heart stopped.

The words repeated over and over again in her mind. *Shadow Spinner. Shadow Spinner. Shadow Spinner.*

Kevah gave her a feral smile. "Turns out you won't be of any use to me after all. I do hope the true Death Bringer is somewhere in that guild of yours."

The world came to a halting stop beneath Malaina's feet, nearly sending her veering.

Kevah turned his back on them.

Time slowed, freezing everything around her. No movement. No noise. That horrible moment stretched on forever.

Then, in the span of a heartbeat, everything burst into chaos.

As if someone tied one end of a rope around his middle and the other end anchored to his throne, an invisible force sent Kevah flying. A crack reverberated through the room when his body met his seat.

Malachi stood with arms outstretched, one holding the doors behind them closed, the other keeping Kevah pinned to his metaphorical throne.

Atana scrambled for her husband, frantic hands trying to free him before turning vicious eyes on Malachi.

Straining his voice, Malachi shouted, "Go!"

Malaina spun, hoping to find a door she hadn't noticed before or a window she could open, anything to escape through, but found nothing.

Something clamped down on the Shadow Spinner's mind, taking her to the ground. Fingers knotting in her hair, she grasped at either side of her head, crying out in pain. Bright white light surrounded her, piercing her like daggers to her brain and knives to her eyes. She squeezed them shut, trying to block it out, but it did nothing to ease the gut-wrenching pain in her skull.

She couldn't think.

Couldn't react.

A force hit her chest, knocking the air from her lungs. It sent her flying back towards the stained glass wall.

She opened her eyes in time to see the scene within the hall unfold.

Malachi's eyes were glued to her. The hand that had tied Kevah down now stretched towards Malaina, beckoning her to him. But, no…he wasn't drawing her closer; he was throwing her away. Back towards the wall of stained glass.

In the back of her mind, she knew she should do something—try to stop the inevitable or at least brace for impact, prepare herself for what was to come. But all she did was watch Malachi as the distance between them grew.

Watch as Kevah stood, raising his hands before him.

Watch as flames engulfed her guild master.

The impact of crashing through the glass sent shards of color drifting through the air. Moving so fast, so lost in the scene before her, she hardly felt the wall shatter.

Then she was falling...

She blankly stared at the quickly retreating sky, unsure what else to do. Nothing could slow her fall. Flailing helplessly, the wind whipped around her, and she waited for the impact of the earth against her back. It wasn't clear at what point she lost Sterling, no longer coiled around her arm and shoulders. For all she knew, he never left the throne room and was currently suffering the same fate Malachi did.

A large shape blotted out the sun the started spearing towards her so fast she thought it might hit her before she splattered against the ground. It banked and knocked the air from her lungs once again.

Her hands grasped at anything as she skidded across... whatever it was, trying to find something to hold onto. Something soft entangled her fingers, and she held tight with all her strength. The abrupt change in momentum nearly ripped her shoulders from their sockets, but she wasn't falling anymore.

Malaina was flying.

Feathers poked between her death grip to keep from flying off the massive eagle she held tight to. She pulled herself up, her arms protesting every moment but thankfully not giving out. When the Shadow Spinner stabilized and caught her breath once again, she oriented herself. Estates and farmlands rolled out before them, the city growing closer by the second. The Lord's estate grew smaller behind them, Malachi still locked within those walls.

"No," she breathed.

The flame danced with color, roaring beyond the hole in the stained glass wall.

"No!" she screamed, the words racking against her throat and she pounded a fist against Sterling's back. "No! Turn around! We have to go back."

He didn't acknowledge her cries or change directions. Just continued to fly away, gaining speed as he carried her further and further away from the estate. Sterling flew faster and higher until they looked down upon the city, the estate disappearing into the distance.

Angry storm clouds swirled in the distance, building on each other, growing thicker and darker. They gathered around a far corner of the city. An old part of the city. A particularly bad part of the city.

Their part of the city.

These precious few moments gave Malaina a chance to try and gather herself, to make sense of what just happened, and to try to make a plan…any plan…

There were only two things she knew for sure.

The first: Malachi was gone, and with him, the guild. Their home and everything they had worked for was over because, without Malachi, there was no home.

The second: Kevah was after Lybbi.

They needed to reach her first... taking her far from Kevah and the city—somewhere the Lord would never find her.

As the storm clouds grew closer, Malaina realized that she should be crying or yelling. That she should be feeling...something. Rage or determination or terror. Anything at all. But she felt nothing. A blank hollowness consumed her.

Protect Lybbi. The words became a mantra, the only thing keeping her focused. Keeping her calm.

The wind whipped the assassin's face as she shimmied her way up toward Sterling's neck and peered down at the streets. A mass of city guards flowed through the streets, plowing a path through any resistance. More guards than she could count occupied every street, closing in on the guild. Not only were they effectively herding everyone in the city in that direction, but they were cutting off any possible escape route.

How were there already so many of them? How could they have already made it to the guild if Kevah only just sent them off?

Because he didn't *just* send them off. This siege must have been going on for the entire time they were within the estate walls. That's why they had to walk all the way up the drive instead of being allowed to use their carriage. That's why they were led through every hallway.

Kevah had been biding time, keeping them busy while he marched his guard on the guild without them there to protect it.

He may have wanted her services, but he never

intended to let them go back home. With or without her cooperation, he always planned to destroy the guild.

Their home came into view, and already a fleet of guardsmen invaded the street, swarming the door and all the street-level exits. Three figures occupied the roof. Two of them moved in perfect synchronicity. The third stood between them, waiting. The storm clouds grew thicker and darker as the figures continued to move, the charged air making Malaina's hair stand on end.

Recognizing Layshan and Tralia was easy; moving in sync, their water and air working together to create the perfect storm above them. Years of drills and practice kept them in perfect unison.

Between them, Bren was easily identifiable. His grown-out orange hair bright against the dark storm brewing around him, it was a beacon for them to follow. He stood eerily still, his hands splayed to his sides. The expanding zealous energy around them grew, waiting for him to release it.

Sterling aimed directly for him, the building growing closer and closer. Malaina locked eyes with Bren, and she could tell he was waiting for them.

The assassin ducked her head, bracing herself against Sterling's back, clinging tight. They brushed the ledge of the roof just as a bolt of lightning struck the ground behind them, missing them by mere inches. Lightning carved a crater into the street below, thundering with a deafening crash.

Sterling shifted beneath her as they struck the rooftop,

both of them bouncing and sliding to a stop when they reached the opposite side, hitting the low wall.

Groaning, Malaina tried to push herself up onto her hands and knees. Everything in her hurt.

Sterling forced himself to his feet, staggering and steadying himself on the low wall. He shook his head, clearing it of something.

"What the hell happened in there?" He roared.

"You're asking me? Where were you during all that? Why didn't you shift?" She grabbed onto the wall, trying to stop the shaking in her legs as she pulled herself to her feet.

"I tried, but I couldn't until we left that damned room." He took a step, his feet crossing funny as he staggered.

"You're draining yourself. You need to stop."

He shook his head again. A dog shaking off a flea. An unmistakable fierceness fueled his fiery red eyes, which nearly made her take a step back. "Try and make me. I'm heading downstairs to help. Go find Lybbi."

He steadied himself long enough to take a single controlled breath and shifted again, the form taking longer than normal to fully take shape. A familiar wolf stared back at Malaina, smaller than usual. Sterling's whole body shook, and he bound for the door leading down into the guild.

Malaina started to follow him, but when she reached the door, she glanced back at Layshan, Tralia, and Bren. Sweat already rolled off Layshan and Tralia, their hair plastered to their heads, clothes dark and damp. Bren was preparing for another strike.

They fought the way Malachi had taught them. Had

taught them all when they drilled this over and over again, preparing for just this sort of attack. Malachi prepared them for everything, except his own demise.

This time, Malachi wouldn't be coming back. Wouldn't show up and tell them when to stop and head for cover or when to run and gather later.

Malaina couldn't leave them to figure it out on their own. To realize Malachi wouldn't come for them and tell them when they had finally done enough.

Bren turned on a heel at the sound of her approach, ready to strike anyone who posed a threat. When he realized it was her running up on him his expression turned from relief to concern.

Malaina wasn't where she was supposed to be. She was supposed to be heading downstairs to join the majority, preparing for whoever might break through the fortified front door no one ever used.

Layshan and Tralia stopped, too. Though the clouds above them continued to swirl, the storm had already started and was becoming unstoppable.

"What are you doing?" Bren asked her.

"You need to go. All three of you. Grab whoever you can on your way to the escape tunnels, and go. Malachi's not coming back, the guild is…" Is…is what? Dead? Over? Compromised? She didn't know exactly what, but she knew they all needed to run. This wasn't a fight they were going to win.

At first, they all looked at her as though she'd grown another head because how could Malachi not be coming back? Like the idea of such a thing was some sick joke. But when she didn't budge, when she didn't take the words back, what she had said started to sink in.

The realization hit all of them differently. Bren froze, shocked like he had never considered the possibility. That Malachi may not come back one day. She didn't blame him.

Tralia was ready to bolt and waiting for everyone else to catch up.

But Layshan… looked furious. He put a hand on Tralia's arm and pushed her towards the door.

"Go! All of you. I'll hold them off," he barked.

Malaina almost asked him how, but the gleam in his eye made her realize she didn't want to know. Grabbing Bren and Tralia by the hands, she pulled them towards the door. She pushed them both in front of her. One last time, she looked back at Layshan as he headed for the edge of the roof.

The thief stepped up onto the low wall and analyzed the guards gathered on the street. Studied the people threatening his home and his people. This city had taken everything from the Air Wielder, and nothing filled those eyes but pure fight.

Malaina turned away when he stepped over the edge, falling out of sight.

Layshan didn't intend to walk away from this fight.

Malaina darted down the stairs, Tralia and Bren long gone. It didn't take her long to find her own front door. She burst into the apartment, expecting to find Serena and Lybbi waiting right where she left them, but the apartment sat eerily quiet. All the curtains were pulled closed, shrouding the apartment in darkness. It deadened the noise coming from outside, somewhat cutting off the apartment from the chaos.

The shadows shivered at her presence, her heightened emotions stirring them, but everything was conspicuously deserted of human life.

"Lybbi?" The sound of her voice was too loud in the empty rooms.

When no response came from the darkness, terror seized her heart. What if...what if Lybbi and Serena weren't there? What if they had gone down to the dining hall, or...Gods forbid the grand room? They might be right in the thick of everything, in the middle of all the chaos on the main floor.

Malaina sprinted first to Lybbi's bedroom, then to Sterling's. She searched every corner, calling Lybbi and Serena's names. With every empty hiding spot, her sense of dread grew, becoming an ever-tightening knot inside her.

"Lybbi!" She sprinted from Sterling's room, running headlong for her own. The last safe place left.

Peeking out from behind the door was Lybbi, her brassy brown eyes round and glistening.

Malaina nearly broke down into tears at the sight of her younger sister. She reached out, grasping Lybbi's shoulders. "Oh, thank the Gods."

"What's going on?" Lybbi's voice shook, rattling her entire body.

"I'll explain later. Right now, we need to go. Where's Serena?" Serena had said she'd keep Lybbi company while she and Sterling were at the meeting, to keep Lybbi calm.

Lybbi shook her head. "She left when all the fuss started."

Malaina pressed a hand to her mouth, everything inside her breaking into shards that tore at her heart.

Of course, Serena had left. As Malachi's third her responsibility was to make sure things were held down in his absence. To keep people motivated and quell the fear thick in the air. Malaina imagined Serena, fighting fiercely, giving orders, and taking on everyone's distress, shoulders weighed down by emotions that weren't her own.

"Ok," Malaina choked, gripping Lybbi's hands, trying to convince herself to get up and move. "Ok. I need to grab a few things and then we are going to go find Serena and Sterling."

Malaina went straight for her closet, moving on muscle memory alone. She grabbed the bag she took on jobs, already filled with water and some food. Grabbed some sort of sweater off a shelf and stuffed it into the bag before heading for her dresser. Opened the top, grabbing the knives and daggers and any other weapons she kept hidden. Mechanically she grabbed everything, not fully comprehending what she was taking. She shoved things in until nothing more would fit. She secured the bag and started slipping knives into her boots.

A crash from outside shook the building. White knuckles gripped the dresser as she tried to keep on her feet, but all she could do was freeze. Her muscles locked up, refusing to move. The whole world was far away. Her life crumbled like the walls around her—the life she had worked so hard to build, the stabilization she'd fought so hard for.

Was she breathing? Malaina wasn't even sure her heart still pounded in her chest. Everything was out of her control, including herself.

Another crash outside, the sound of wood splintering, the building shaking.

Screams from outside…and close by.

Lybbi's screams.

Lybbi's cries broke Malaina from her catatonic state, forcing her into action. With a shake of her head, the assassin moved mindlessly again, slinging the strap of the bag over her head until it lay across her chest. She grabbed Lybbi's hand, pulling her to the front door, ready to find Serena and Sterling and leave this nightmare behind.

Their front door burst open. Sterling crashed through, still in wolf form. Blood dripped from his chin, but his steps were uneven and unsteady. He slowly became himself, shifting limb by limb instead of all at once in the blink of an eye. Like he was trying to remember the shape of his own body.

After all the time he spent in serpent form at Kevah's estate and everything since the Shifter was running on fumes. He wouldn't be able to stay in any form much longer if he shifted again.

A hand braced against a chair kept him on his feet. Sweat rolled down his face, mixing with the blood still dripping from his chin. His dark hair was plastered to his forehead, and he was struggling to catch his breath.

"We need to go," he panted. "Now."

"I know," Malaina answered, numb, "I just need to find Serena and…"

He shook his head. "No. She sent me up here. It's done down there, she's staying until the end."

Eyes locked, they stared each other down.

Malaina couldn't register the words he was saying. She stood motionless, frozen again, hands gripping the strap of her bag. The shadows around them swirled in an angry swarm, Malaina no longer able to hold them back.

The Spinner was out of time...she hadn't moved fast enough.

Malachi gone. Serena gone. Layshan, Ra, Tralia, Bren...all of them were gone.

Was the floor still beneath her feet? Everything was empty air around her, and she was falling. Still plummeting to her death outside the Lord's estate. She lost herself in Sterling's empty white eyes, unable to look at anything else.

Another crash outside, more screams, and then what sounded like a tornado ripping through the streets.

Lybbi gripped Malaina's arm.

Looking down at her little sister's terrified face, she swallowed everything down.

Later...she'll experience everything. Later, she'll think back to that moment and live it again and again, wondering if she could have done anything differently, drowning herself in doubts and questions. Later...but right now...

"Ok." Her voice sounded far away, empty and distant, as if it hadn't come from her at all. "Let's get down to the tunnels."

Nothing. No emotions. No pain.

She felt nothing.

Only one thing remained within her control. The same goal she'd had since she was six.

Protect Lybbi.

Sterling shook his head, his dark hair falling into his eyes. The back of his hand wiped at the sweat on his forehead. "No. We won't make it." He gathered himself enough to head for his own room. After a moment he reappeared holding his own work bag stuffed with Syn's shifting clothes and pushed it into Lybbi's hands.

"Then how…" Malaina started, but he eyed the windows. Instantly, she understood what he was thinking. "Sterling, no. Absolutely not. You can't."

He walked to the windows, tearing the curtains from their rods until they fell to the floor. He stared out into the daylight, opened the window, and panted, "I can get us far enough out." He straightened, shaking the fatigue from his shoulders.

Malaina shook her head. "No."

Another crash and she heard the front doors give way. A new type of scream came from the main level. Battle cries turned to pained shrieks of terror. The other guild members who hadn't been able to get away or stayed behind to give others time to escape…her friends. Her family.

"We don't have much of a choice." He backed into the living room, finding a straight shot from the far wall to the open window, getting as much distance between himself and them as possible. He bounced from foot to foot, shaking out his arms.

The Shifter looked at Lybbi, taking in her small shaking form and reminding himself what they were fighting for.

Then he looked at Malaina and gave his partner a weak smile, barely lifting the corners of his lips. He reached out, grasping her fingers and giving them one quick squeeze before dropping them again.

"I've got your back," he promised.

Then the Shifter took off, hurtling towards the largest window. A heartbeat behind, Malaina grabbed Lybbi's hand and drug her after him.

Sterling dove through the window head first, disappearing beneath the ledge.

"Jump!" Malaina yelled to Lybbi, not giving her another choice.

Seconds behind him, Malaina and Lybbi followed Sterling through the window, leaping into the open air.

CHAPTER

TWENTY-NINE

T he wind whipped Malaina's silver hair across her face as she fell for the second time that day. This time, though, she clutched Lybbi's hand in a death grip, refusing to let go. Lybbi screamed, but Malaina hardly heard it. She felt nothing and didn't care if Sterling caught them.

They fell endlessly, and she wondered if Sterling had enough stamina left to shift, or if they'd just keep falling until they splattered against the stones below. It was taking too long…

A strong gust of air hit their backs, slowing their fall and sending them back up into the air. Below them, Layshan stared, hands outstretched toward them.

Malaina met his eyes one last time. They exchanged a silent goodbye as the guards overtook him, and he became buried beneath the swarm.

Then they jerked to the side as they hit Sterling's feathered back.

Malaina's grip on Lybbi tightened even more, and she tried to grasp anything with her other hand to keep from sliding off. She clutched a handful of feathers and prayed to any God who would listen that they wouldn't give way when momentum swung Lybbi, testing Malaina's grip strength.

Malaina gritted her teeth, refusing to let any of her fingers relax even a little.

Eventually, Lybbi found a handhold and stopped her swing.

Once the arm Malaina held firmly grasped Sterling's back, the assassin let go and adjusted herself to be better secured.

The city started to grow smaller as Sterling flew higher, shadows streaming from his wings like ribbons. Malaina tried to dismiss them, knowing they would only draw attention, but her mind was in too many pieces and she couldn't focus long enough to disperse them.

Sterling's muscles shivered beneath her, and silently, she urged him to hold on just a little longer. He was barely staying in form, and she worried his magic would give out at any moment.

They flew with the coast to their backs, further into the heart of Thaumoria. As they flew away from the sea, the city started to fade into farmland.

Malaina had never been to the farms that were the City of Elementals' main export. She knew they were expansive, but even from their distance in the sky, the farmland stretched on forever.

Over the side of Sterling's back, she watched them soar further. The edge of the city just faded out of sight when they started to descend.

The almost unnoticeable change started slow, but then their descent turned into a plunge. Sterling shuddered beneath them and they fell faster and faster. Malaina dug her fingers into his back to keep from flying off, their flight turning into a plummet.

"Sterling?" Lybbi cried, tears streaming down her face.

Malaina wished she had something to say, but there was nothing. No words came.

They were going to die.

Malaina tried to brace herself for the inevitable. With tens of feet left Sterling pulled up, slowing their momentum. But he couldn't hold out any longer.

With about twenty feet to go, he shifted, the feathers beneath Malaina's hands gone. He twisted in the air, pulling Lybbi to his chest and taking the full of their combined impact with the ground to his back.

Malaina bounced, her shoulder colliding with the earth, skidding through the crops that they destroyed. Rocks ripped through her skin, and her bag flew out to the side before slamming against her again.

When she finally stopped she gasped, taking in shallow breaths. She didn't move, didn't open her eyes. Just laid there.

Pure madness whirled around her mind, slowly settling and unraveling inside her. The longer she lay there, the slower her heart became, but her breathing didn't come any easier.

Noises rattled around her, but she couldn't tell if they were from animals or humans. The sounds weren't coherent to her mottled brain. Cotton balls stuffed her head, making everything soft and fuzzy, and language was no longer distinguishable.

Malaina tried to think of everything Jade taught her about injuries and the body.

Adrenaline. Her body was running on adrenaline right now; no matter how much pain she was in, it was only about to get worse. So Malaina forced her eyes open and immediately regretted it. The world spun before her, sky blinding. *Probably a concussion.*

She squeezed her eyes shut again and did a mental examination of herself, working from the top down. Her head spun, but aside from the rocks digging into her skull from lying on the ground, there were no sharp pains per se.

That was good.

With a gentle tongue, she examined her teeth. Nothing was missing or loose, but blood filled her mouth, and the movement wasn't pleasant. She had bitten a chunk out of her tongue at some point.

Malaina continued down her body, flexing this muscle and that, curling and uncurling her fingers and toes one by one. Slowly, she tried to take deeper and deeper breaths until, finally, she couldn't stand the pain. Probably some broken ribs.

Gently, she rolled herself from her side to her back. The shoulder she landed on ached, and when she tried to move it, a sharp pain shot through her. She gritted her teeth against the scream she wanted to let out, and instead, it came out as a strangled groan.

The assassin let her breathing settle again before her good arm reached over, prodding against the skin. Even the softest touch hurt and her fingers came away covered in blood.

The sounds in the background started to clear, her mind slowing as she came to her senses.

Cries. Cries from…Lybbi. Her little sister cried Sterling's name again and again.

Then… "Malaina?"

Lybbi was crying for her.

I need to move. I need to get up.

Malaina took one more breath, as deep as she dared, gritted her teeth, and rolled onto her good side. Even that movement was difficult. She used her good arm to push herself up onto all…three. Three, because no way would her bad shoulder take any weight, letting everything fall onto her good forearm instead.

She clutched at the dirt, everything continuing to spin, and nausea rolled through her. Her silver hair fell in dirty curtains, thankfully blocking out her view of the world and some of the blinding light. The shadows around her made anxious twists, hiding in the curtain of her hair, helping block the light.

"Malaina!" Lybbi screamed again. She sounded scared and desperate. Panicked. But not too far away.

Malaina glanced up around her, just enough to figure out what kind of field they landed in. It looked like…corn, probably. Still green and young, it was tall and thick enough to block her view of where Lybbi and Sterling landed.

Lybbi yelled her name again. Malaina swallowed, blood and dirt coating her mouth. She gagged but kept herself from vomiting.

"I'm...I'm over here," she called back, but it came out choked, the words grating against her tongue

Malaina looked around and found her bag. She reached for it, falling face-first into the soil. With an iron grip on the strap, she clung to it as though it would give her salvation from her pain.

"He won't wake up! Malaina, he won't wake up!" Lybbi screamed.

Pain lanced through Malaina's chest at the words, her first thought being: *he's dead. Sterling is dead.*

Of course, he was. He took the full force of his and Lybbi's fall straight to the back. He probably broke his neck or snapped his spine. All to keep Lybbi safe...

Malaina relived those moments in the air, watching Sterling twist and pull Lybbi to his chest just before taking the full force of the earth.

No. No...he couldn't be dead. Malaina wouldn't let herself believe it until she pressed her fingers to his neck, her head to his chest, and knew for a fact that his heart didn't beat. He couldn't be dead because she needed him to live. She needed him with her.

What she needed was to get up. She needed to get to them.

Stand, that's all she had to do.

Easier said than done.

She rocked on her knees back and forth, warming up her muscles and trying to gain momentum to move.

1…2…2 1/2…

"Malaina!"

3…and she forced one foot beneath her. Her ribs screamed in protest, but she pushed against that foot. Her leg wobbled as she forced herself to stand.

Black spots swam in and out of her vision, the world blurring at the edges. The strap of her bag was still clutched in her hand. It bounced against her leg, the bottom dragging against the ground.

Malaina's breaths were shallow, and she wondered if the swirls in her visions were her shadows or the result of the concussion she was confident she had.

"I can do this…" she breathed. "Lybbi?"

"We're over here!" Lybbi's desperate plea reached her, coming from behind her.

Malaina turned and stared at the thick wall of stalks standing between her and her family. There had to be a better way to go about it, but she couldn't think of one, so she started forward. She plowed through the stalks, tripping on every root and rock and even her own feet. The razor-sharp leaves scraped against her skin and grabbed at her bag, but she hardly felt them. They were a prick compared to the rest of the pain shooting through her.

After what seemed like miles, the wall of stalks abruptly ended. A line of them lay flat against the ground.

Malaina stumbled over them, unable to lift her feet over the broken stalks sprawled across the ground, sending her back into the dirt. Her good arm caught her, her bag snagging as it dragged across broken crops.

"Oh, my Gods…"

Malaina tried to catch her breath and force herself to her feet again when a clatter of footsteps headed for her, leaves and stalks crunching underfoot.

Lybbi's glove-clad hands grabbed at her good arm. She pushed a shoulder under Malaina's arm, helping her to her feet. Malaina groaned, but with her sister's help, she stood easier.

With extra care, Lybbi led Malaina to a massive lump lying in a crater. Malaina was so focused on each and every step she took that it wasn't until she was at the crater's edge that she realized the massive dark lump was an unmoving Sterling.

Unconscious, not dead.

Despite Lybbi's support, Malaina fell at Sterling's side. He was lying on his side, the earth mounded up behind his back, keeping him upright. She dragged herself to him, leaving her bag behind, wanting nothing more than to make sure he was alive. Breath didn't seem to move his chest, but that might be because the world was one giant blur.

She *could* see his large form growing darker. At first, she wondered if he was shifting again, then realized her shadows were coating his body, worrying over him. She ran a hand over his face as gently as she could manage, which was not at all.

The Shifter's skin was warm beneath her touch. That

was a good sign, but his skin was also pale compared to its normal warm brown.

Malaina felt along his jaw, fingers searching along his thick neck for the spot she knew would give her a pulse. She pressed her fingers hard, laying her forehead against his cheek. Her adrenaline was starting to ebb, and all she felt was exhaustion and pain. She couldn't even hold her head up anymore.

Malaina held her breath, focusing on the sensation beneath her fingertips. Searching…waiting…there!

A sigh of relief. A half-manic laugh.

Sterling was alive. She wasn't sure how or for how much longer, but her stubborn Shifter was alive.

Lybbi dropped to her knees at the crown of Sterling's head, looking unsure if she should interpret Malaina's nonsensical laughing.

Malaina smiled to the best of her abilities. "He's alive. He has a heartbeat."

With a final breath of relief, Malaina sat back on her haunches, leaning against Sterling's large form. She let her head loll to the side, resting on his arm.

She wasn't sure how much damage had been done, and she didn't know how she was going to fix Sterling or herself. She didn't know what they would do next or where they would go. All Malaina knew was at that moment both she and Sterling were alive. Lybbi was alive. That's all that mattered.

The assassin closed her eyes, letting the world go black, and focused everything she had on simply breathing.

Her knees knocked against her leg. Gloved hands

landed on either side of her face, but she couldn't be bothered to open her eyes.

Sterling's alive. Lybbi's alive. That was all that
mattered.

"Malaina? No, don't fall asleep! I don't know what to
do!" Something in the back of Malaina's mind recognized
the sound of tears in Lybbi's voice, but tears meant she was
alive, and that was really all Malaina cared about.

Malaina reached around her, feeling with her good
hand until a hand appeared in hers. She squeezed Lybbi's
fingers weakly and laughed again. "I'm so tired. Just…just
touch anyone who comes by." A bubble of laughter rose in
her at her own absurd joke.

"But Malaina…"

She was sure that wasn't the end of the sentence, but
Malaina didn't hear the rest. She was overcome by exhaustion, and Lybbi's voice faded into the distance.

ACKNOWLEDGMENTS

Over three years ago, I created the fantasy world I'd always wanted to read about. One where everyone had magic, and the magic was more than just one thing. I wanted a world of diversity that would be fun to write about, and somewhere a reader could call home, with more than just witches or elementals. However, after many hours of research and brainstorming, I realized I didn't have a story for this fantastic world I had created.

Thaumoria sat untouched and untold for a long time before one day, I sat down and wrote almost ten thousand words without even trying. I quickly realized I had characters inside me fighting for their story to be told. After eleven drafts, countless rewrites, edits, sleepless nights, and pep talks from my husband, The Death Bringer was complete.

I truly hope you found this story unlike any other, with unforgettable characters and magic around every corner.

First, I need to thank my husband. When I say that this book and series and my future as an author wouldn't exist without him, I am vastly underselling just how big of a role he played. His support is the reason The Death Bringer exists at all. He has read every draft and every rewrite and helped me edit several sections without complaint. He was my first fan, the first to fall in love with these characters, and sometimes I think he's even more invested in the story than I am.

Next, to my cover designers, who put up with my vague ideas and general lack of direction and created a series of covers that I can't believe I get to call my own.

To my editor, Ayesha. Finding a new editor just in time for my debut novel was something I was genuinely dreading, and you made it so much easier. I'm so glad I trusted you with my story.

To my betas, who truly are my lifeline some days. You all have been my cheerleaders, and I am incredibly proud to call you all my friends. There are days when I don't know how I would get through this process without you. You've helped bring my stories to life; I am eternally grateful for that.

To my family, for giving my stories a chance and never once deterring me from pursuing this dream. Even my non-reader family has been purchasing my books and supporting my dream, which is more than I could have ever asked for.

Lastly, but certainly not least, to my readers.

I have gotten to know so many of you during this journey, and it has been an absolutely amazing experience. The book community has been more than welcoming of me and my world; the community we have been building together is every author's dream. I've seen readers become friends in my comment sections and share theories on their own posts.

It truly warms my heart to see so many people loving my books as much as I do.

Until next time…

Forever grateful,

A.M. Eno

About the Author

Originally from Howell, Michigan, A.M. Eno travels full-time with her husband and cat. In 2017, she earned her Bachelor of Science from Black Hills State University, majoring in Psychology and a minor in Sociology. As a life-long avid reader, she hopes to create worlds and characters that invite readers to fall in love and feel at home. She strives to write high fantasy series that are a safe space for people of all backgrounds.

www.authorameno.com